Also by Rose Tremain and published by Sceptre

The Colonel's Daughter and Other Stories
The Cupboard
The Garden of the Villa Mollini
Letter to Sister Benedicta
Sacred Country
Sadler's Birthday
The Swimming Pool Season

Rose Tremain

Rose Tremain is the author of six novels: SADLER'S BIRTHDAY, LETTER TO SISTER BENEDICTA, THE CUPBOARD, THE SWIMMING POOL SEASON, RESTORATION, which won the *Sunday Express* Book of the Year Award in 1989 and was shortlisted for the Booker Prize, and SACRED COUNTRY, which won the 1993 James Tait Black Memorial Prize. She has also written three volumes of short stories: THE COLONEL'S DAUGHTER, which won the Dylan Thomas Short Story Award in 1984, THE GARDEN OF THE VILLA MOLLINI, and EVANGELISTA'S FAN. She has written numerous plays for radio and television, including TEMPORARY SHELTER, winner of a Giles Cooper Award. Rose Tremain lives in Norfolk and London with the biographer, Richard Holmes.

∫

SCEPTRE

Restoration

ROSE TREMAIN

SCEPTRE

Tremain, Rose *1943–*
Restoration
I. Title
823.914[F]

ISBN 0 340 63980 6

Printed and bound in Great Britain by
Cox and Wyman Ltd, Reading

Hodder and Stoughton
A Division of Hodder Headline PLC
338 Euston Road
London NW1 3BH

For Penelope Hoare

CONTENTS

PART ONE

ONE

THE FIVE BEGINNINGS

I am, I discover, a very untidy man.

Look at me. Without my periwig, I am an affront to neatness. My hair (what is left of it) is the colour of sand and wiry as hogs' bristles; my ears are of uneven size; my forehead is splattered with freckles; my nose, which of course my wig can't conceal, however low I wear it, is unceremoniously flat, as if I had been hit at birth.

Was I hit at birth? I do not believe so, as my parents were gentle and kindly people, but I will never know now. They died in a fire in 1662. My father had a nose like a Roman emperor. This straight, fierce nose would neaten up my face, but alas, I don't possess it. Perhaps I am not my father's child? I am erratic, immoderate, greedy, boastful and sad. Perhaps I am the son of Amos Treefeller, the old man who made head-moulds for my father's millinery work? Like him, I am fond of the feel of objects made of polished wood. My telescope, for instance. For I admit, I find greater order restored to my brain from the placing of my hands round this instrument of science than from what its lenses reveal to my eye. The stars are too numerous and too distant to restore to me anything but a terror at my own insignificance.

I don't know whether you can imagine me yet. I am thirty-seven years old as this year, 1664, moves towards its end. My stomach is large and also freckled, although it has seldom been exposed to the sun. It looks as if a flight of minute moths had landed on it in the night. I am not tall, but this is the age of the

high heel. I strive to be particular about my clothes, but am
terribly in the habit of dropping morsels of dinner on them. My
eyes are blue and limpid. In childhood, I was considered angelic
and was frequently buttoned inside a suit of blue moiré, thus
seeming to my mother a little world entire: sea and sand in my
colours, and the lightness of air in my baby voice. She went to
her fiery death still believing that I was a person of honour. In
the scented gloom of Amos Treefeller's back room (the place of
all our private conversations), she would take my hand and
whisper her hopes for my splendid future. What she couldn't
see, and what I had not the heart to point out, was that we no
longer live in an honourable age. What has dawned instead is
the Age of Possibility. And it is only the elderly (as my mother
was) and the truculently myopic (as my friend, Pearce, is) who
haven't noticed this and are not preparing to take full advantage
of it. Pearce, I am ashamed to admit, fails to understand, let
alone laugh at, the jokes from Court I feel obliged to relay to
him on his occasional visits to me from his damp Fenland house.
The excuse he makes is that he's a Quaker. This, in turn, makes
me laugh.

So, to me again – whither my thoughts are extremely fond of
returning.

My name is Robert Merivel, and, although I'm dissatisfied
with other of my appendages (viz. my flat nose), I am exceedingly
happy with my name, because to its Frenchness I owe a great
deal of my fortune. Since the return of the King, French things
are in fashion: heels, mirrors, sedan-chairs, silver toothbrushes,
fans and fricassées. And names. In the hope of some preferment,
a near neighbour of mine in Norfolk, James Gourlay (an ugly,
rather disgusting person, as it happens), has inserted a "de"
into his otherwise Scottish-sounding name. So far, the only
reward to come to the pompous de Gourlay is that a French wit
at my dinner table dubbed him "Monsieur Dégeulasse". We
giggled a great deal at this and some new scarlet breeches of
mine were stained with the mouthful of raisin pudding I was
forced to spit out in my attack of mirth.

So this is how you might imagine me: at table, rustling with
laughter in a gaudy suit, my migrant hair flattened by a luxuriant

wig, my freckles powdered, my eyes twinkling in the candlelight, my pudding being ejected from my mouth by that force within me which snorts at sobriety and is so greedy for foolishness. Do not flatter yourself that I am elegant or worthy in any way, but yet I am, at this moment that you glimpse me, a rather popular man. I am also in the middle of a story which might have a variety of endings, some of them not entirely to my liking. The messy constellations I see through my telescope give me no clue to my destiny. There is, in other words, a great deal about the world and my role in it which, despite all my early learning, I utterly fail to understand.

There was a beginning to the story, or possibly a variety of beginnings. These are they:

1. In 1636, when I was nine years old, I carried out my first anatomical dissection. My instruments were: a kitchen knife, two mustard spoons made of bone, four millinery pins and a measuring rod. The cadaver was a starling.

I performed this feat of exploration in our coal cellar, into which, through the coal hole, came a crepuscular light, augmented a little by the two candles I placed on my dissecting tray.

As I cut into the thorax, a well of excitement began to fill and glimmer within me. It rose as I worked until, with the body of the starling opened and displayed before me, I had, I suddenly recognised, caught a glimpse of my own future.

2. At Caius College, Cambridge, in 1647, I met my poor friend, Pearce.

His room was below mine on the cold stairway. We were both by then students of anatomy and, though our natures are so antipathetic, our rejection of Galenic theory, coupled with our desire to discover the precise function of each part of the body in relation to the whole, formed a bond between us.

One evening, Pearce came up to my room in a state of hilarious perturbation. His face, habitually grey-toned and flaky, was rubicund and damp, his stern green eyes suddenly afflicted with a louche brightness. "Merivel, Merivel," he babbled, "come down to my room. A person is standing in it who has a visible heart!"

"Have you been drinking, Pearce?" I asked. "Have you broken your vow of No Sack?"

"No!" exploded Pearce. "Now come down and you will see for yourself this extraordinary phenomenon. And, for a shilling, the person says he will permit us to touch it."

"Touch his heart?"

"Yes."

"It's not a cadaver then, if its mind is on money?"

"Now come, Merivel, before he flees into the night and is lost to our research for all eternity."

(Pearce, I report in parentheses, has this flowery, sometimes melodramatic way of speaking that is interestingly at odds with the clipped, odourless and self-denying man he is. I often feel that no anatomical experiment would be capable of discovering the function of these ornate sentences in relation to the whole, soberly-dressed person, unless it is a universal but contradictory fact about Quakers that, whereas their gait, habit and ritual are monotonous and plain, their heads are secretly filled with a rapturous and fandangling speech.)

We descended to Pearce's room, where a fire was burning in the small grate. In front of the fire stood a man of perhaps forty years. I bade him good evening, but he only nodded at me.

"Shall I unbutton?" he asked Pearce.

"Yes!" said Pearce, his voice choking with anticipation. "Unbutton, Sir!"

I watched as the man took off his coat and lace collar and began loosening his shirt. He let the shirt fall to the floor. Bound to his chest, and covering his heart, was a steel plate. Pearce, at this moment, took a handkerchief from his sleeve and mopped his moist brow. The man removed the plate, under which was a wad of linen, a little stained with pus.

Carefully, he unbound the linen and revealed to us a large hole in his breast, about the size of a Pippin apple, in the depths of which, as I leaned forward to look more closely at it, I saw a pink and moist fleshy substance, moving all the time with a regular pulse.

"See?" exclaimed Pearce, the heat of whose excited body seemed to fill the room with a tropical dampness. "See it retract and thrust out again? We are witnessing a living, beating heart!"

The man smiled and nodded. "Yes," he said. "A fracture of my ribs, occasioned by a fall from my horse two years ago, was brought to a terrible suppuration, voiding such a quantity of putrefaction that my doctors feared it would never heal. It did, however. You can see the sconce of the old ulcer at the edge of the hole here. But its ravages were so deep as to expose the organ beneath."

I was dumbfounded. To observe, in a living being, standing nonchalantly by a fire, as if about to welcome friends for a few rounds of Bezique, the systole and diastole of his heart affected me profoundly. I began to understand why Pearce was in such a lather of excitement. But then – and this is why I set down the incident as a possible beginning to the story now unfolding round me – Pearce produced a shilling from the greasy leather purse in which he kept his pitiful worldly income and gave it to the stranger, and the man took it and said: "You may touch it if you wish."

I let Pearce go first. I saw his thin, white hand creep forwards and tremblingly enter the thoracic cavity. The man remained still and smiling. He didn't flinch. "You may," he said to Pearce, "put your hand around the heart and exert gentle pressure."

Pearce's thin mouth dropped open. Then he swallowed and withdrew his hand. "I cannot do that, Sir," he stammered.

"Then perhaps your friend will?" said the man.

I rolled back the lace at my wrist. Now, my own hand was shaking. I remembered that, just prior to Pearce's appearance in my room, I had cast two pieces of coal onto my fire and hadn't washed my hands since, but only wiped them carelessly on the seat of my breeches. I examined my palm for coal dust. It was faintly smudged with grey. I licked it and rubbed it again on my velvet buttocks. The open-hearted man watched me with an utter lack of concern. At my elbow, Pearce, in his vaporous dampness, was breathing irritatingly through his mouth.

My hand entered the cavity. I opened my fingers and, with the same care I had applied, as a boy, to the stealing of eggs from birds' nests, took hold of the heart. Still, the man showed no sign of pain. Fractionally, I tightened my grip. The beat remained strong and regular. I was about to withdraw my hand when the stranger said: "Are you touching the organ, Sir?"

"Yes," I said, "don't you feel the pressure of my fingers?"

"No. I feel nothing at all."

Pearce's breathing, at my side, was rasping, like that of a hounded rodent. A pearl of sweat teetered on the tip of his pink nose. And my own mind was now forced to contemplate an astounding phenomenon: I am encircling a human heart, a living human heart with my hand. I am now, in fact, squeezing it with controlled but not negligible force. And the man suffers no pain whatsoever.

Ergo, the organ we call the heart and which is defined, in our human consciousness, as the seat – or even deified as the throne – of all powerful emotion, from unbearable sorrow to ecstatic love, is in itself utterly without feeling.

I withdrew my hand. I felt as full of trouble as my poor Quaker friend, to whom I would have turned for a tot of brandy, except that I knew he never had any. So while our visitor calmly strapped on his linen pad and his steel plate and stooped to pick up his shirt, Pearce and I sat down on his extremely hard settle and were, for a good few minutes, devoid of words.

From that day, I was unable to have the same reverence for my own heart as other men have for theirs.

3. My father was appointed glovemaker to the restored King in January 1661.

I was by then at the Royal College of Physicians, after four years at Padua, studying under the great anatomist, Fabricius. I was at work on a paper entitled "The Footsteps of Disease: a Discussion of the Importance of the Seats of Tumours and Other Malign Diversities in the Recognition and Treatment of Illness". But I was becoming lazy. Several mornings a week, I would sleep late at my lodgings, instead of attending, as I was pledged to do, the Poor Sick of St Thomas's. Several afternoons, I would walk in Hyde Park, with the purpose only of snaffling and leading to what I call the Act of Oblivion some plump whore – when I should have been at lectures.

The truth is that, when the King returned, it was as if self-discipline and drudgery had exploded in a clap of laughter. I became much too excited by and greedy for life to spend much of it at work. Women were cheaper than claret, so I drank women. My thirst for them was, for a time, unquenchable. I tumbled them riotously. Two at a time, I longed to take them, immodestly, like the wild hogs whose hair my own spare locks resemble. In public places even: in the night alleyways, in a hackney coach, on a river barge, in the Pit of the Duke's Playhouse. I dreamed of them. Until the day I went to Whitehall. And after that day – so extraordinary and unforgettable was the impression it made upon me – I started to dream about the King.

Admiration for craft and skill is, I now understand, at the root of the generous but stubborn nature of King Charles II. He took my father into his service because he recognised in him the dedicated, skilled and single-minded craftsman. Such people delight him because they inhabit an orderly, meticulously defined world and never aspire to cross over into any other. The haberdasher, my father, never considered for one moment becoming, say, a gardener, a gunsmith or a money-lender. He laid out a precise territory with his skill and kept within it. And King Charles, while trying on a pair of my father's exquisitely moulded kid gloves, revealed to him that this was how he hoped the English people would behave during his reign, "each," he said, "in his appointed station, profession, calling or trade. And all contented in them, so there is no jostling and bobbing about and no one getting above himself. In this way, we shall have peace, and I will be able to rule."

I don't know how my father answered him, but I do know that it was on this occasion that the King promised, "at some future time, when you are bringing me gloves", to show my father the collection of clocks and watches he kept in his private Study.

No doubt my father bowed humbly. Very few people ever enter the King's Study. The only key is kept by his personal servant, Chiffinch. And it was at this moment – on his knees, perhaps? – that my father spoke up for me and asked the King whether he could bring his only son, from the Royal College of Physicians, to make his acquaintance, "in case His Majesty should ever have need of an additional physician in his household . . . a physician for the People of the Bedchamber, perhaps, or even for the scullery boys . . ."

"By all means," it seems the King replied, "and we will show him the clocks, too. As an anatomist, I expect he will be interested in their mechanical complexity."

So, on a November afternoon, with a chill wind blowing him forward up Ludgate Hill, my father arrived at my lodgings. I was, as had become my habit on a Tuesday, engaged in the Act of Oblivion with the wife of a ferryman called Rosie Pierpoint. Her laugh was as rich and juicy as that part of her anatomy she coyly referred to as her Thing. Encircled both by the Thing and the laughter, I was giggling ecstatically and bumping so energetically towards my brief Paradise, that I didn't see or hear my father as he entered my room. I must have been a risible sight: my breeches and stockings still tangled round my ankles, the sandy hogs' hair that sprouts in the crease of my bottom unflatteringly visible, Mrs Pierpoint's legs flailing either side of my back, like a circus tumbler's. I blush to remember that my own father saw me like this and, when he was consumed by fire a year later, I had, in the midst of great sorrow, the cheering thought that at least this memory burned with his poor brain.

An hour later, my father and I were at Whitehall. I had put on the cleanest coat I could find. I had washed all trace of Rosie Pierpoint's rouge from my face. My hair lay concealed and tamed under my wig. I had polished my shoes with a little furniture oil. I was excited, eager and full of admiration for the attention my father appeared to be getting from the King. But then, as we walked down the Stone Gallery towards the Royal apartments, I felt myself suddenly hesitate, gasping for breath. The public wandered freely here and all the people we passed looked at ease. But, to me, it was as if the presence of the King had altered the air.

"Come on," said my father. "Thanks to your acrobatics, we're already late."

The doors to the Royal apartments were guarded, but were opened to my father's nod. He held, over his arm, a silk pouch containing two pairs of satin gloves. We entered a Drawing Room. A fire was roaring under a vast marble mantel. After the chill of the gallery, I would have moved towards it, except that by now I felt almost too weak to move at all and wondered whether I was going to inconvenience my father (who had had enough embarrassment for one day) by falling down in a faint.

Moments passed, as if in a distorted, dreamlike time. A servant came out of the King's bedchamber and asked us to go in. I felt us glide, like skaters, across thirty feet of Persian carpet, stumble through the great gilded doors and fall flat on our faces at the feet of a pair of the longest, most elegant legs I had ever seen.

I realised, after a moment, that we were not prostrate, but only kneeling. Somehow, we the skaters hadn't fallen. This in itself seemed to be a miracle, because everything around me – the canopied bed, the candle sconces, even the brocaded walls themselves – appeared to be moving, coming in and out of focus, first clear, then dim.

Then a voice spoke: "Merivel. And who is this?"

These days, enmeshed as I am in the tangle of the story, the voice returns to me frequently: *Merivel. And who is this?* First my name. Then a denial of all knowledge of me. *Merivel. And who is this?* And the memory is so fitting. I am not now the Merivel I was that day. On that November afternoon, I was shown a roomful of clocks, chiming and ticking in disunion. I was offered a sweetmeat, but could not swallow it. I was asked questions, but could not answer them. A dog snuffled at my foot and the touch of its nose felt repellent, like the touch of a reptile.

After an interminable time (and I do not know to this day how that time was filled up) I was out in the gallery again with my father, who began to shout at me for being a dumbcluck and a fool.

I walked alone back to Ludgate and climbed wearily to my room. There, in my shabby loft, the enormity of what had happened became suddenly and terrifyingly visible to me, as if a nest of maggots had all at once broken out of the wall. I had been within a glove's length of obtaining power, and I had not taken it. It had been there for me, and now it had gone for ever.

I began, like a pig in pain, to howl.

4. It is not clear what started the fire in my father's workshop in the New Year of 1662. It was of course crammed with wooden boxes and shelves holding the flammable materials of his trade: felt, buckram, goatskin, fur, lace, feathers, ribbons and bales of satin, camlet and silk. A small blaze begun by an upturned oil lamp or candle would have had ample substance on which to feed.

All that is known is that the fire began in the late evening, engulfed the workroom and spread ravenously upwards to my parents' apartments, where, it seems, they were at supper. Their servant, Latimer, managed to open a small skylight onto the roof, to scramble up and endeavour to haul his elderly master and mistress to safety. My mother had a hold of Latimer's hand when she suddenly fell back, retching and choking on the smoke. My father tried to lift her up again towards Latimer, but she was unconscious in his arms.

"Fetch a rope!" my father screamed, perhaps, but his instructions were muffled by the dinner napkin he had tied round his nose and mouth and Latimer could not make out what he was saying. He stared helplessly in, while all the time the smoke became thicker and darker and to belch out in his face while he clung precariously to the leads of the roof. He told me, in the bitter chill of the following morning: "I watched them die, Mr Robert. I would have given all my life's wages to save them, but I could not."

The burial was well attended. Lady Newcastle, for whom my father had made moleskin eye patches, arrived in a black coach with her horses decked with black plumes. The King sent two Gentlemen of the Bedchamber. Amos Treefeller, now in his dotage, hired a sedan-chair to carry him to the graveside, where he began to blub. The January wind carried the prayers up and away into silence.

The following day, I was summoned back to Whitehall.

The death of my kindly parents, as well as slaking for the time being my thirst for women, set moving in my anatomist's brain an acute awareness of the speed at which the body can succumb to death. I am not squeamish. At Padua, short of cadavers in the summer months, Fabricius once conducted an anatomy lesson on the body of a pauper that had been floating in the river for three days. The German students, notorious for their interruptions and disorderly behaviour, now took to vomiting and swearing all round me. I stayed perfectly well and calm and took notes as Fabricius worked. However, after my mother and father perished, I looked at my own body, of which I had never been at all proud, with a new distaste, with a new antipathy and with a new fear. And it was this fear which, in the contradictory workings of the world, brought me to the honour about to be conferred on me. Fear of death, you see, had lessened, if not obliterated, my fear of power. So when summoned to Whitehall, I was no longer overcome by the scent of majesty and thus no longer idiotic and dumb. My poor father would have been very pleased, in fact, by the way in which I was able to conduct myself.

The King received me in his Drawing Room. He talked at length and most flatteringly about my father's skill. He repeated his theory that no man should get above himself, but know his own talents and his own degree. I nodded and bowed. Then he said: "Out of my affection and admiration for your late father I have summoned you, Merivel."

"Yes, Sire," I said. "Thank you."

"But I have a task for you, a task in which you must succeed, because my heart will suffer very much if you fail."

"Did you know, Your Majesty," I ventured, "that the human heart – the organ itself, that is – has no feeling?"

He looked at me with sorrow. "Ah, Merivel," he said, "where have you learned that?"

"I have seen it, Sir."

"Seen it? But what we see is but a fraction of what it is. You, as a physician, must no doubt have understood that. Look at my hand, for instance. Wearing a glove made by your late father.

What we *see* is the excellent glove, a little rucked on my fourth finger by the large sapphire ring I am fond of wearing. Whereas, underneath the glove is the hand itself, capable of a thousand movements, *en l'air* like a dancer, supplicant like a beggar, fisted like a ruffian, in prayer like a bishop . . . but then again of what fantastic complexity is the arrangement of bones in the hand . . ."

He went on to describe, with some degree of accuracy, the skeletal structure of the human hand. By the time he had finished, I thought it prudent not to return to the subject of the heart, but to allow him to come at last to his reasons for calling me to the palace.

"One of my dogs appears to be dying," he said. "The veterinary surgeon has bled him repeatedly, shaved the hair off his back in order to cup him, has tried without success lesions, emetics and purges, but the little creature doesn't rally. If you can cure him, Merivel, I will offer you a place here as a Court Physician."

I knelt. Aghast, I noticed there was a stain of boiled egg on the thigh of my breeches. "Thank you, Sir," I stammered.

"I will have you taken to the dog immediately, Merivel. Food and drink and night linen will be brought to you and any surgical instruments you may need made available to you. You will stay until the dog dies or recovers. Call for any medicines you deem suitable."

"Yes, Sir."

"The dog's name is Bibillou. He also answers to Bibi and Lou-Lou."

"Lou-Lou, Your Majesty?"

"Yes. Your own name, by the way, has a very pleasing cadence."

"Thank you, Sir."

"Merivel. Very pretty, to my ear."

I left the royal presence and followed two servants down acres (or should I say *hectares*, in that the King appears committed to distributing French names everywhere?) of corridor. I was shown into a pleasant bedroom, with a view of the river and the crowded wharves. A fire had been lit. In front of the fire, in a little basket, a brown and white Spaniel was lying. Its body was pitifully thin and its breath rasping. On a table near the window, a decanter of claret, a goblet and a dish of Portuguese figs had been placed. Laid over the bed was a fine linen nightshirt and a matching nightcap, which, once the servants had left me alone with the dog, I immediately put on, suffering as I was that day from a scabrous itching under my wig. I also removed my shoes and coat and poured myself a glass of claret.

I felt extraordinarily tired. I had slept badly since the fire, but it was more a total exhaustion of the mind, rather than of the body, that I felt. I was glad to be alone. I took the claret over to the bed and half reclined on it, sipping the wine greedily, like a Roman senator. Once or twice, I glanced in the direction of the dog. It twitched and whimpered in its dreams. "Lou-Lou," I called softly, but it didn't stir. Presently, I told myself, I will get up and examine the dog and see what can be done. Meanwhile, I went on drinking the claret, which was some of the finest I'd ever tasted, and soon began to feel a delicious ease, like velvet, caressing my mind. Once, experiencing a sudden hunger, I forced myself to get up and eat a couple of figs, but my body felt as heavy and unsteady as a barrel of eels in a swell, and I stumbled back to the bed, where I passed out in a stupor of claret and delayed grief for my parents' dying.

I slept, it seems, for seven hours. When I awoke, it was dark, but my room had been lit with candles and a supper of roast partridges and boiled salad placed on the claret table. Had the servants tried to wake me? If so, they would have had to report to the King that Physician Merivel lay in a drunken sleep, with his nightcap fallen over his eyes. I groaned. For the second time, I had been near to preferment, and yet again I had let it elude me.

I got up, my legs still unsteady. I knelt down by the fire, which still burned well, with fresh logs laid on it by the invisible servants. I stroked the head of poor Lou-Lou. To my surprise, he opened a watery brown eye and looked at me. I bent and listened to his breathing. The rasp in it had lessened. I looked in his mouth. His tongue was swollen and his muzzle dry. I

fetched water from my washstand and spooned a little into his
mouth. He lapped it with all the eagerness a sick Spaniel can
muster. It is as if, I said to myself, the purging and vomiting
he's been forced to endure has drained his body of its vital
moisture. And with this realisation, I suddenly saw that my
hopes of curing the dog were probably greater now than they
had been when I had arrived eight hours before. My own neglect
of him could, indeed, be the key to his recovery. For while I'd
slept, he'd been left alone, possibly for the first time in several
days and nights, and nature had had a chance to work quietly
within him.

"*Studenti!*" Fabricius would thunder, his voice echoing like
the word of God round the tiers of his primitive anatomy theatre.
"*Non dimenticare la natura!* Do not forget nature! For nature
is a better doctor than any of you – particularly you Germans,
who are so noisy – are ever likely to be!"

I watched over Lou-Lou for the next seventeen hours. I sent
for alcohol to dress the boils and lesions made by the cuppings,
but otherwise I didn't touch him, only gave him water, and when
his fever lessened, fed him morsels of partridge mashed in my
own mouth. By the following night, when a meal of guinea fowl,
cream and radishes was brought to me, I was confident that he
wouldn't die. And I was right. Four days later, I carried him to
the King's bedchamber and set him on the Royal lap, where he
stood entranced and wagged his tail.

5. The fifth beginning is the strangest, the most unlooked for
and the most momentous. Without it, the story in which I find
myself would not have happened as it has.

I can tell it with reasonable brevity. (I am, unlike Pearce,
usually able to come swiftly to the *point* of a story, whereas his
tales are so larded with lugubrious metaphysical observations
that his audience is prone to lose the thread of the thing almost
before he's begun.) Here it is then:

I abandoned my studies at the Royal College and my lodgings
at Ludgate. I was allotted two pleasant rooms inside the Palace,
which lacked only, alas, a view of the river, which was of great
fascination to me, in all its hubbub, vagabondage and changing

light. My duties were defined as follows: "The daily Care and Comfort of the eighteen Royal Dogs, with, as required, the right to perform operations upon them, prescribe Remedy for Disease and do all in my power to ensure the Continuity of their Life." The stipend paid to me was one hundred livres per annum, and this, added to the two hundred and thirty-seven livres left to me and mercifully found unharmed in my parents' damp cellar, was quite enough to keep me in good claret, high-heeled shoes, silk coats, Brussels lace and well-made wigs for the foreseeable future. Astonishing good fortune had, in short, fallen on me ("All undeserving you are, Merivel," noted Pearce, who was struggling on, trying to cure the paupers of St Barts and – ghastly enterprise – the lunatics of Bedlam).

I celebrated by visiting Mrs Pierpoint, getting drunk with her at the Leg Tavern and tumbling her in a muddy ditch on Hampstead Fields. Afterwards, she had the temerity to ask me whether, now that I was in the King's employ, I could get some position at Court for the uncouth Mr Pierpoint, who is a mere bargeman, and I learned at once a lesson I never let myself forget: that power and success carry in their train a clamouring queue of greasers and supplicants, the noise and sight of which haunt my private pleasures and my dreams, but from whom multifarious and handsome bribes may very often be had.

A year passed most profitably and pleasurably. My nature, I quickly understood, was in every particular well suited to life at Court. My fondness for gossip and laughter, my brimming appetites, my tendency to sartorial chaos and my trick of farting at will made me one of the most popular men at Whitehall. Few games of Cribbage or Rummy were started without me, few musical evenings or *soirées dansantes* were given to which I was not invited. Women found me hilarious and in magnificent numbers allowed me to tickle not only their humours but their charming and irresistible centres of pleasure, and I seldom slept alone. And – most fortunate of all – the King showed towards me from the start a most flattering affection, stemming, he told me, not only from my curing of Lou-Lou, but from my ability to amuse him. I was, I suppose, his Fool. When I made him hold his sides with laughter, he would beckon me to him, take hold of my squashed nose with his elegant hand and draw me towards him in order to smack an affectionate kiss on my mouth.

After a while, I realised that he actively sought my company and this realisation was to me a most astounding thing. He would show me his gardens and his orchards and his tennis court, and began coaching me at tennis, at which I proved more adept and nimble than I expected. He gave me presents: a handsome French clock from the collection I'd seen that first afflicting day, a set of voluminous striped table napkins, large enough to cover my whole suiting while I ate, lending me the risible appearance of a man in a tent and thus causing mirth at the dinner table, and a dog of my own, a sweet Spaniel bitch he insisted I christen Minette, after his own adored sister.

Impossible to say I wasn't happy. My half-finished knowledge of medicine was adequate to keep the dogs well, particularly dogs fed on milk and beef and bedded in warm rooms. And as to comfort, diversion and women, I had all any man could ask. I was growing fat and a trifle indolent, but then so were many at Court, not possessed of King Charles's great energy and curiosity. When Pearce visited me, he grew white and rigid at the sight of so much profane luxury. "This age suffers from a woeful moral blindness," he said stonily.

And then . . .

On an April morning, the King sent for me.

"Merivel," he said, "I want you to get married."

"*Married*, Sir?"

"Yes."

"Marriage, Sire, is not, has never been, on my mind . . ."

"I know. I'm not asking you to want it. I'm asking you to *do* it, as a favour to me."

"But – "

"Have I not done very many favours to you, Merivel?"

"Yes, Sir."

"*Voilà!* You owe me at least this one. And there will be compensations. I propose to give you the Garter, so that your bride will have a title, albeit a modest one. And small but agreeable estates in Norfolk I have confiscated from a recalcitrant Anti-Monarchist. So arise, Sir Robert, and go to your duty without hesitation or barter."

I knelt. We were in the Royal Bedchamber and from the adjoining study came the disunified tick-tocking and pinging of the clocks, which perfectly mirrored, at that moment, my own confused thoughts.

"Well?" said the King.

I looked up. The Royal visage was smiling at me benignly. The Royal fingers caressed the dark brown moustache.

"Who . . .?" I stammered.

The King leaned back in his chair and crossed his legs. "Ah yes. The bride. It is, of course, Celia Clemence."

The knee on which my weight was balanced trembled and then tottered beneath me. I fell sideways into the carpet. I heard the King chuckle.

"It means, of course, that you – and possibly she – will have to spend some time in Norfolk, thus depriving me of your respective companies now and then. But this is a sacrifice I am prepared to make."

I endeavoured to right myself, but my left knee had gone suddenly numb and wouldn't support me, so I had no alternative but to lie in a kind of foetal heap by the Royal footstool.

"I don't," said the King, "need to explain myself further, do I, Merivel?"

"Well, Sir . . ."

"I do? I'm surprised at you. I thought you were one of the most knowledgeable people at Court."

"No, it is merely that this is . . . this matter is . . . somewhat difficult for me to grasp."

"I can't for the life of me see why. It is childishly simple, Merivel. The frequent presence of Celia Clemence in my bed has become a necessity in my life. I am, as everyone knows, utterly beguiled by her. Likewise, my *grand amour*, Barbara Castlemaine, is absolutely essential to my continuing health and well-being. In short, I love and need both mistresses, but I have no wish to continue to endure Lady Castlemaine's tantrums on the subject of Miss Clemence. They make me edgy and give me indigestion. So she must be married at once – the better that I may come by her again secretly, without Castlemaine's knowledge. But to whom must I marry her? Not, I think, to a powerful aristocrat, who will soon irritate me profoundly by starting to consider his own position and honour. No. What I am looking for in Celia's husband is a man who will enjoy and profit from his estates and title, and who will be kindly and amusing company to his bride on the rare occasions he is with her, but who is far too enamoured of women in general to make the mistake of loving any particular one. And in you, Merivel, I have surely made the perfect choice. Have I not? You also, as I am fond of observing, have a pleasingly fashionable name. To ask Celia to become – in name alone, of course – Lady Merivel, is something I feel I can undertake with equanimity."

So that was it, uttered: the fifth beginning.

The dogs were to be taken from my care and in their place was to be put the youngest of the King's mistresses. The practical matter which most absorbed me, as I left the King's presence, was that I could not remember how far from and in what relation to (viz. north-east or directly north of) London lay the county of Norfolk.

TWO

WEDDING GAMES

On her wedding eve, my future bride was to be locked, as custom dictates, with her bridesmaids inside her father's house. In the morning, I would ride to her door (from the rather lowly inn I would be forced to occupy on the night of the sixth of June), with all the village running and shrieking before me, got up in homespun garters, love-knots, ribbons and general fooleries, playing flutes and viols and banging tambourines. I was looking forward to these proceedings. You do not need reminding that I am a glutton for foolishness, and this rowdy pageant was, in prospect, greatly to my taste.

I was also looking forward to putting on my wedding clothes, chosen by the King and made by his personal tailor: an admirable white silk shirt, a sash of purple, breeches striped white and gold, white stockings, purple shoes, gold-buckled, a black brocaded coat and a purple and black hat with white plumes of such magnificence that, from a distance, I appeared to be wearing a three-masted barque upon my head.

I had, of course, invited Pearce to the wedding, but he had declined my invitation, much to my chagrin. I would have liked Pearce to see me in my garb. I can only conclude that he refused, not from envy or mean-mindedness, but that he feared the sight of me might cause his circulation to cease, thus cruelly sundering him from his mentor, the late William Harvey, the first man to understand that blood moved in a circular motion, outwards from the heart and to it again via the pulmonary veins. "Not a day passes," Pearce once said to me, "when I do not *feel* WH within me." (Pearce is much given to metaphysical utterances of this kind, but my affection for him makes me charitable towards them.)

To my bride's father, Sir Joshua Clemence, I had had to go, in mid-April, to beg his daughter's hand. The King, it seems, went before, to vouch for me as a man of honour, talent and wealth, owner of the country estate of Bidnold in Norfolk and desirous only of making his daughter contented and comfortable in all things, for as long as I should live.

So it was that Sir Joshua Clemence received me with great affability, pouring sack for me, averting his eye only fractionally when I spilt a little of it on the watersilk arm of my chair, and assuring me that the King's word was all he needed to deliver his pretty daughter into my hands. What I do not know is whether, at the time of the wedding, Sir Joshua already knew that Celia was the King's mistress. I suspect that he did and was flattered by the knowledge. For the King moves like God in our world, like Faith itself. He is a fount of beauty and power, of which we all yearn, in our overheated hearts, to feel some cooling touch. Sir Joshua struck me as an intelligent and in all respects noble person, yet even he, when he heard that the King was to be a guest at the wedding, couldn't conceal the hectic spots of joy that broke out on his cheeks. He told me that his greatest love was music, in particular the playing of the viola da gamba. "Now," he said rapturously, "I will play at my daughter's wedding and at the same time achieve my life-long dream, that the King, restored to his throne, would one day listen to my music."

With Celia, I had, prior to the wedding, half a dozen meetings, all presided over by the King, with whom my bride (as was generally gossiped round London) appeared so deeply in love that her hazel eyes hardly ever strayed from his face. I had a sense, at these meetings, of my own superfluity, but was too enthralled by the maps of Norfolk the King produced, on which to show me Bidnold Manor and its lands, to let this feeling discomfort me.

The glimpses I allowed myself of my bride confirmed her to

be a pretty, small-featured woman of about twenty. Her skin
was pale and absolutely without blemish. Her hands were tiny.
Her hair was a weak brown, swept up from her face by ribbons
and allowed to tumble to her shoulders in ringlets. Her breasts,
I perceived, were meagre and her feet narrow. Her countenance, like her father's, was admirably serene. Though able to
confirm that she was a quiet beauty, I was relieved to find that
she was a woman not at all to my taste. She was too refined,
her back held at too straight an angle, her curves too modest.
Compared, say, to Rosie Pierpoint (despite the women available
to me at Court, I had found it impossible to break off my riotous
relationship with this naughty drab), Celia was as the mouse to
the kittyhawk. In my amours, I crave the tearing beak and the
cruel claw. I like a fight, a drubbing. The passivity I saw in Celia
rendered her, in my darker imagination, useless.

What, then, of my wedding night? Well, I shall tell you in
time, for no man in England can have had one so strange. But
first, I must relate how I went with the King and Celia to Bidnold.

It was a Jacobean manor, moated and bordered by a substantial
park, in which red deer harmoniously browse. Its interior was
plain and dingy, reflecting the Puritanical tastes of the unfortunate John Loseley Esquire, its previous incumbent. Though
struck by its drabness, I rejoiced in it. For from these plain
rooms, I decided at once, I would fashion interiors that reflected,
in their crimsons and vermillions, in their ochres and golds, in
their abundance of colour and light, my own excessive and
uncontainable nature. I would transform the place. I would open
it up and let it explode with diversity, in the same way as the
glorious complexity of the starling's anatomy had exploded to
my eye in the shaft of light from the coal hole.

On my first visit, I bounded from room to room, leaving the
King and Celia decorously perched on a Tudor settle, becoming,
as my vision of the place began to catch fire, so boiling and
flushed that I threw off my coat and unwound my sash and flung
them down. My house! I had imagined passing my whole life in
cramped apartments. Now, I had thirty rooms in which to spread
myself. In one almost circular room in the West Tower, I let
out an involuntary yelp of delirium, so perfect did the space

seem – for what, I didn't know or care, I merely sensed in
prospect the degree of perfection to which, in my mind, this
space would one day arrive. It was as if, in the body of Bidnold,
I had come at last to what Harvey called "the divine banquet of
the brain". And the banquet was mine! I sat down and took off
my wig and scratched my hog's hair and wept for joy.

Arrangements for the wedding went ahead, then, with all
parties content with the arithmetic. That Celia and I had scarcely
said a word to each other, and that she eyed me with some
distaste did not appear to matter at all. The lengths to which
the King had gone in order to hold onto her, in the face of Lady
Castlemaine's jealousy, no doubt convinced her that his love for
her was considerable. And he reassured her, as he had me:
"There will be no physical union between you. When I am not
with Celia, you will give her brotherly companionship and she
will order your house."

"I prefer to order my own house, Sir."

"As you will. A hostess can be invaluable, however, if you
want to entertain at Bidnold, which I suppose you do?"

"Definitely, Sir. I am already dreaming of entertainments."

"Good. I like you, Merivel. You are utterly of our times."

So, in a mood of feverish excitement, occasioned by my
constant visits to plasterers, wall painters, upholsterers, silversmiths, tapestry-makers and glass cutters, my wedding day,
the seventh of June 1664, approached.

How shall I describe my wedding? It was like a tolerably good
play, a play of which, long after the thing is over, certain lines,
certain scenes, certain arrangements of people and costume and
light return vividly to your mind, while the rest remains dark.

The lowly inn returns to me. I see its sawdusted, spittle-
stained floor, as I cross its threshold in my purple, white and
gold attire to follow the rag-bag cavalcade to Celia's house.

I am hoisted onto a grey horse with bells on its bridle. I have
been deeply affected by the sight of myself in my outrageous
clothes and my spirit is shouting: Forward! Onward! Go! The
crowd is drunk already and full of lechery and screeching, gallants
and peasants messed together, waving gloves and ribbons. I

couldn't ask for more delirious company, and, above it, smiling and nodding on my plumes, is the midsummer sun.

Up the hill we go, children running before, a fiddler skipping at my side, his head and hair like a turnip, his tune like a maypole dance. This *is* a pageant, a play, I tell myself, as I sit on my festooned horse. I am the Player Groom; Celia a Dumb-Show Bride. And yet I am, as we set out, ecstatically happy. I want to embrace somebody – God? the King? my dead mother? – for the gift of this ornamented morning. So what I do, as the house comes into view, is lean down and gather into my feverish arms a dimpled village girl and kiss her and the men whistle and the women clap their hands and the turnip fiddle player shows the black creases of his smile.

The next thing I vividly remember is Joshua Clemence's music. We have returned from church, man and wife. Celia wears my ring on her little white hand. I have placed, as required, a chaste kiss on her narrow mouth. I have given her my arm to lead her out into the sunlight and up the lane to Sir Joshua's house. The feast set before us surpasses in splendour anything I've seen placed on a table, and I attack the food and wine with my usual relish. The King, seated next to my bride, giggles at me and makes an elaborate show of swaddling me in a table napkin. For the second time that day, I am glad Pearce isn't here after all. His abstemious nature would shudder at the number and diversity of the dishes prepared for us. With a quick sweep of my eye, I see fricassées, steamed bass and poached salmon, roast snipe, peacock, teal, mallard and quail, game pies and carbonados, tarts of marrowbone, neats' tongues, venison pasties, baked guinea fowl, compound salads, dishes of cream, quinces, comfits and marzipans, preserves, cheeses and fruits. There are sparkling French wines and strong Alicantes and of course the Sack Posset which will be consumed before Celia and I are flung, in a rumple of ribbons, to bed.

After an hour or so of gorging and toasting ourselves, and with a not unpleasing feeling of sleepiness beginning to quieten the excitement within me, I see Sir Joshua rise, take up his viola, and stand alone before us in front of a little spindly music stand. The King endeavours to procure quiet in the room, but the gallants at the end of the table haven't noticed Sir Joshua and continue with great rudeness to belch and giggle. One of them, I notice with amusement, is vomiting into his hat. Sir Joshua ignores them. He takes up his instrument and, without speech or introduction, begins to play.

I am expecting some sprightly dance, so that we can, if the mood takes us, remove ourselves from the table and break into a little canter. But it is music of the utmost seriousness and melancholy that Sir Joshua has chosen, Dowland's *Lachrimae*, if my musical knowledge has not misinformed me, and within a moment or two, I find myself overtaken by an unquenchable urge to weep. I stare at Sir Joshua's face, looking down towards his viola, and, layer by layer, in my anatomist's sadness, I peel back skin and muscle and nerve and tendon, until I can see only the white bone of his skull, the empty sockets of the eyes . . .

I look away. I bury my face in my table napkin. I don't want my make-believe wife to see me crying. I pretend I am choking. I rise from the table and fumble my way out of the room. Tears are pouring from my eyes and I am sobbing like a sick mule. I blunder into the sunshine and throw myself onto the lawn, where I lie down and weep for a full ten minutes.

When I sit up at last and blow my nose on the sodden napkin, I become aware that a man is sitting silently no more than a few feet from me. I wipe my eyes and look at him. It is Pearce.

"What are you blubbing for, Merivel?" says Pearce.

"I have no idea."

"So," says Pearce, with his habitual gravitas, "you are married."

"Yes. What do you think of my wedding garb?"

Pearce stares at me intently, noting, I presume, the priceless-ness of my buckles, the faintly royal air the colour purple lends to the whole ensemble. Luckily, I am no longer wearing the three-masted barque, for I feel suddenly glad that Pearce is there, and wouldn't want, at this moment, to cause any malfunction of his blood vessels.

"It is terrible!" he says after a while. "I expect it is that which has so unmanned you."

I smile and he smiles, and I reach out a hot hand to him, which he takes and encircles with his glacial fingers.

Pearce and I take a turn round the rose garden. Two gardeners observe us with stony faces. "I am the groom," I want to say, "you must rejoice with me," but then I remember the confusions inherent in these words, so I say simply to Pearce: "If they want to be glum, it doesn't matter one whit to me."

Almost as soon as we have returned to the feast and I have settled Pearce at the table, persuading him to take a few hesitant nibbles at a duck thigh and a sip of Alicante, the King rises and calls for the Sack Posset. So the moment approaches! I watch my wife look anxiously at her Royal Liege. He smiles at her the dazzling Stuart smile, in which half the men and most of the women of our country claim to spy proof of his divinity. Then we all get to our feet and, even before the toast is ended, I feel myself being surrounded by my Court friends, who have begun braying and whooping and banging the table, setting the remains of the fricassées and pies juddering about and bottles of wine tumbling. Then I am hustled, half pushed, half lifted, out of the room and into a long corridor. I hear Celia and her bridesmaids making a giggling progress behind us. Though I am half enjoying this charade, I look forward to returning to the table and drinking more wine and then losing myself in dancing and debauch. But I go on, herded up two flights of stairs, and into a magnificent bedchamber where, with shrieks of gaiety, my clothes are unceremoniously untied and unbuttoned and torn from me, leaving me naked but for my wig, my stockings and my garters. With a cackle of ribald laughter, a purple ribbon is tied around my prick. I admit that this amuses me very much. I push my friends away, so that I can walk to a mirror and there I am revealed: the Paper Bridegroom. My eyes are red and puffy from my attack of weeping, my moth-covered stomach distended from the quantity of mallard and carbonado I have packed into it, my wig awry, my stockings sagging and covered in grass stains and dribbles of red wine, and my cock tied with a bow like a jaunty gift.

But I have no time to dwell on this arresting image of myself.

A nightshirt is bundled over my head and I am led out along the passage to another bedchamber, at the door of which most of the wedding guests are clamouring. When they see me, a cheer goes up, and then a relentless chant begins, as I am pushed forward into the bedroom:

> "*Mer-i-vel*
> *Bed her well!*"

> "*Bed her well*
> *Mer-i-vel!*"

I enter the room. Celia is sitting up in the high bed. As I am hurled towards her, she averts her eyes, but the guests press in on us, so that we're forced close together, and I am aware, now, of the need to act my part. I put my arms round Celia and kiss her shoulder. Her body is taut and rigid, but she forces herself to laugh, and the company pounce on us, pulling the ribbons from Celia's hair, the love-knots from her wrists and the stockings and garters from my legs. With a final braying, the bed curtains are drawn around us and, though the chant of "Mer-i-vel, Bed her well" can still be heard, it begins to grow fainter as the guests move out of the room and make their way back to the feasting tables, where musicians have now begun to play a sprightly polka.

I release Celia from my token embrace and she looks relieved. Absurdly, I find myself wondering whether Pearce has eaten all, or only part, of the duck thigh. I begin to giggle. I know what is going to happen now. The King has planned it with his usual attention to detail, and I find it hilarious. "Well, Lady Merivel," I begin to say to Celia, but she's in no mood for even a short conversation with me. Already, she's out of bed and opening the door of the adjoining closet to let in the King who, like us, is now attired in a nightshirt. He is smiling mischievously as he takes Celia by the arm.

"Well done, Merivel," he says, "good performance."

I get out of the bed and the King and my wife get into it.

I go into the closet where, laid out for me, as arranged, is a clean suit of clothes (scarlet and grey, this time), a white wig, a false moustache and a mask. I close the door on myself and start to take off my nightshirt, when I realise for the first time the one flaw in the plan. In order to return to the party – which of course it is agreed I should do – my only route is back through the bedchamber, in which, by the time I've struggled into the new clothes, the King and Celia will be engaged in some nuptial tumblings. I am not, as I've told you, squeamish, but I really have no desire to bear witness to these, nor to interrupt them. I can only hope that they will remember to draw the bed curtains and that I will be able to creep out of the room without being mistaken for a spy or a voyeur.

I dress as speedily as I can. As a famed lover, the King I imagine will not go to the act in a hasty way, but precede it with well-placed kisses and caresses and teasing words. Thus, I have a little time. I put on the mask. It squashes my flat nose even flatter and the eye-holes are so small that I feel like a horse in blinkers. The thought of keeping this thing on for the remainder of the night is exceedingly irksome but, if I want to go down and enjoy myself without revealing my identity, I have no alternative.

I am ready now. The red and grey suit is very nice, but I think with a moment's regret of the lost gold striped breeches and the outrageous coat. They expressed the essence of Merivel with such perfection and finesse. As a memento of this extraordinary day, I have at least kept the purple ribbon tied round my prick.

I open the door of the closet and this is what I see: the King, completely naked, kneeling by the bed, his arms encircling Celia's spread thighs and his glossy head buried in her little bush. I stand rooted to the expensive carpet. My face, under the mask, becomes boiling red. I close my eyes. I cannot move. I retreat back into the closet and close the door.

Back inside the small room, I feel lonely and suffocated. Surely, the reward for what I've done today cannot be to condemn me to a night on the floor of a closet? I will wait, I decide, till the King and Celia have got to the "divine banquet" (*pace*, Harvey) of the thing and pray that it will be done inside the curtains, or at least that it will be noisy enough to conceal from them my hurrying footsteps.

Meanwhile, what shall I do? I decide to think about my future. I cannot see it at all clearly. I take off the mask. What I believe I can see now is that I'm weary of medicine. All my anatomical studies seem to have brought me to a great sadness. When a man plays a viola da gamba, I want to share in his joy, not see his skull. For where will such visions end? What if, on an August evening, I am on the river with Rosie Pierpoint and I suddenly see, not the red of her lips nor the pink of her thighs, but the white of the maggots in her bones? Such a perpetual and visible awareness of mortality would, I am certain, bring me to despair in a very short time. And what would become of me then? Even my rooms at Bidnold wouldn't be able to comfort me. I'd go mad and be locked up in Bedlam, only to be visited by poor Pearce, who would shake his head and say he could do nothing for me.

I must avoid, then, coming to despair and madness. I must try to forget anatomy. Forget it utterly. I must whisper over it words of oblivion. I must forget the starling. I must forget Fabricius and the drowned pauper. I must forget the interior of the human temple altogether. Instead, I will do decorative things. I will buy more furniture and pictures and drapes. I will paint pictures, even, for like my father, I am a good draughtsman and I am not afraid of trying my hand at oils. So this will be it: forgetfulness of the cavity, the cavern, the cave, the ghastly deep. My life will move in reverse order: I have endured the night; now, with my mind on superficial things, will come the morning. I am, after all, a citizen of a New Age.

Some minutes have passed while I have conversed with myself about my future. I replace the mask over my eyes and nose and listen. I can hear laughter – Celia's and the King's – a hopeful signal that they're rowing noisily together to heaven.

I open the door and find, to my intense relief, that the bed curtains have been drawn. I duck down nevertheless and crawl on my hands and knees to the door, which squeaks loudly when I open it, but then closes on me with hardly a sound.

*   *   *

A while later, I am in the park of Sir Joshua's house. Some hours have passed, in which I have jigged and polka'd and drunk and flirted and generally flung myself about in such an untrammelled way that I am now exceedingly dizzy. It is cool outside, because the sun has gone down and I am tottering towards a little shadowy copse in which, I have convinced myself, Pearce is hiding.

I stop to piss. I take down my breeches and see the ribbon on my cock. The ribbon slides off and falls to the ground and I moan gently to myself as I piss onto it.

I pull up my breeches. Ahead of me, just at the edge of the wood, someone is moving. It must be Pearce, to whom I will now confess that I am abandoning medicine altogether. "I cannot go on," I will say.

But it isn't Pearce. For now, the person has put on – I would recognise this confection anywhere, even in the coming crepuscule – the three-masted barque! Even to tease me, Pearce would be unable to bring himself to place such a thing on his head.

I hear laughter. It is high and cackling. And there, suddenly, in front of me, laughing up into my face, is the plump village girl I kissed that morning on my way to my wedding.

"Bridegroom," she giggles, "Sir Master Bridegroom!"

I reach up a hand to my face and realise with terror that my mask is no longer there.

"Come inny, Bridegroom!" cackles the girl. "Come to Bridey!"

She is drunker than I am. The hat falls over her eyes and she hiccups. I reach up swiftly under her skirt and cup and squeeze the flesh of her buttocks in my hands and in this way propel her forwards into the woods. As I pitch her down and feel myself stagger and fall onto her, it's as if the night descends on us like an executioner's blade, leaving our severed bodies to wriggle in the darkness.

THREE

MY NEW VOCATION

The most beautiful room at Bidnold (aside from the little circular space in the West Turret which, for the time being, I kept empty, my imagination not yet having discovered the most satisfactory way to reveal its perfection) was the Withdrawing Room. As one who had spent the greatest part of his life in meagre apartments, I could not prevent a foolish grin from breaking out over my face every time I remembered that I was now the owner of a room so designated. The title, "Withdrawing Room", entranced me. For it inevitably implies that one is living a busy and pleasurable life on its periphery, from which one occasionally "withdraws" in order to sip a little brandy by its excellent fire, or to indulge in sweet and silly talk with the likes of my handsome neighbour, Lady Bathurst, on its scarlet and gold sofas. Thus, with my usual excess of enthusiasm, I set about making certain that my life at Bidnold was full of diverting activity, from which I could "withdraw" from time to time.

I equipped myself with a Music Room (I had not, at that time, yet learned to play the oboe), a Billiard Room (I had not, then, ever held a billiard cue in my hands), a Card Room (I was already fond of Rummy and Bezique), a Studio (in which I would begin my new vocation as a painter), a Study (in case Pearce should visit me and find himself discomforted by the oriental brilliance of my Withdrawing Room), a Morning Room (facing east, where I would sit between nine and ten to do my household accounts) and of course a most sumptuous Dining Room (the abundance

of its table such that one would need to "withdraw" a little
after dinner to let the digestive system work in comfort and
tranquillity).

My stipend from the King as Celia's husband was two thousand
livres per annum – riches I could not, a year before, have
dreamed of. This money enabled me to buy a great quantity of
Chinese furniture for my Withdrawing Room, to hang the walls
with ruched vermilion taffeta and Peking scrolls, to upholster
my chairs in scarlet and carmine and gold and to lay upon the
floor a carpet from Chengchow so elaborate in design it had
been a thousand days upon the loom.

I was exceedingly pleased with these decorations. As I poured
beer for my exhausted upholsterers, I congratulated myself that
I had got the rampant tones of red, pink and gold so absolutely
right that I must quickly hit upon some ingenious idea for
ensuring that the guests, in whose company I would withdraw
into this room, would not sully it with drabness. It came to me
speedily: I would order to be made a dazzling collection of scarlet
sashes, bilberry shawls, ruby slippers, pink bonnets and yellow
plumes, with which to adorn my *invitées*, thus affording my eye
considerable delight and my spirit a great deal of mirth.

Celia, as you will have understood by now, had no part in the
designing of my house. Though it was thought that, when
expedient, she would spend some time at Bidnold, the King
preferred her to be nearer to him and had thus installed the new
Lady Merivel in a pretty house at Kew, a short journey by water
from Whitehall. It was gossiped, I learned from my Court
friends, that on summer evenings, when his desire for my wife
overcame his *passion journalière* for Barbara Castlemaine, he
would skull himself alone and in disguise to Kew, thus putting
himself grievously at risk from the vagabonds of the water.
Unlike myself, so prone to cowardice with regard to my own
mortality, the King appears to be a man without fear. I had
become by this time, I feel obliged to admit to you, extremely
fond of the King, and experienced some pain in the realisation
that, now I had served his purpose and been rewarded with
lands and a title, he could, if he chose, forget about me utterly.
I thought with fondness of the smacking kisses he had once

slapped on his Fool's lips, and earnestly hoped it would not be so.

Let me relate to you my first attempts at becoming an artist.

Thirty canvases, fourteen brushes, fifty-eight boxes of pigment and an easel were sent to me from Pelissier and Drew in London. My tailor made for me a floppy hat in the manner of the great Rembrandt, and a hessian smock, in which garment, I admit, I looked more like a swine feeder than a Renaissance Man.

The mixing of pigments was an activity to which I responded with great eagerness. If I have a visionary side, it is visions of colour and light that I see. Thus, I longed to dispense with drawing and dabble pure colour onto the virgin canvases. I was aware, however, than an artist must have a subject and the only subjects I could execute well with my charcoal were parts of the human anatomy – the very thing I has sworn to consign to oblivion, but found myself unable to forget.

My first picture, then, was of a man's thigh and buttocks. The background, I had decided, would be ochre, suggesting a pastoral scene, in which the severed half of my man was striding through a field of corn. (I made a rather feeble attempt at drawing some stooks in the distance and a few single ears of wheat close to.)

The musculature of the buttocks and thigh was, I think, reasonably well and accurately drawn but, such was its detail, that when I came at last, in a state of trembling excitement, to apply oil paint to it, I was all too aware that I had no idea whatsoever how to render shadow and light (and thus the third dimension) in this medium and, although I worked at it for hours and long into the night, my picture was an utter failure, resembling in the end a garish still-life of a plate of bacon and scrambled egg. I took off my floppy hat and smock and withdrew, this time to my bed, where I was forced to gnaw upon my sheet to stop myself shedding tears of frustration and rage.

The next day, a brilliant idea came to me. If I could execute parts of the body quite competently, it would surely be within my power to draw a body in its entirety, particularly with the help of a model.

After breakfast, I called for my horse, Danseuse (another gift from the King), and rode up the hill to the village of Bidnold and knocked on the door of the Jovial Rushcutters, a nice little inn I was in the habit of visiting from time to time, when in need of rough conversation and the smell of beer, tobacco and spittle.

The barmaid of the Jovial Rushcutters was one Meg Storey who, in her manner and in the teasing fullness of her breasts, slightly resembled Rosie Pierpoint, and to whom, in conse-quence, I was involuntarily drawn. I now managed to flatter Meg Storey sufficiently – with praise and promise of silver – for her to agree to coming to my Studio to pose for me. Not, I assured her, naked, but prettily draped with scarves and sashes and wearing quite possibly a posy of geraniums in her hair, thus giving me access to my reds, which I had used to baleful excess in the man's thigh, but without which I could not imagine any picture of mine succeeding.

She arrived on a rather chilly September morning. At the sight of me in my smock and hat, she let out a hoot of derisive laughter. I was further discomforted by her complaints, as she took off her cloak, about the cold and sunless nature of my Studio.

"It faces, as it must, north," I said, beginning to sharpen my piece of charcoal. "Artists must work in a northerly light."

"Why?" asked Meg Storey.

I looked up. I did not wish to admit to this saucy tavern jade that I had not the least idea. "Because," I snapped, "a north light is cruel."

After a great deal of shivering and protesting, Meg Storey agreed to remove everything but her drawers, sat down on a tall chair and allowed me to drape a magenta scarf around her neck to fall flatteringly over one of her large, bright-nippled breasts. I stood back. Her hair was sand-coloured, not unlike my own, but a deal finer and silkier. She looked exceedingly pretty. I felt my enthusiasm for my picture grow. Now I under-stand, I told myself, what the Flemish masters felt as they prepared to render their voluptuous Dianas, their fleshy shepherdesses . . .

I began to sketch in Meg Storey's neck, shoulder and right

breast. At her waist, the drawers began, but I ignored them. In my knowledge of the form of the female leg, of the degree of fatty tissue in the upper thigh, I was able to depict what was, in fact, invisible to me. I was now excited by my work to such a degree that I felt my loins grow hard and had to force out of my mind, as I drew her hand, a sudden image of it flaying my bottom with its little pearly nails. Luckily, the size of the canvas and the voluminous nature of my smock prevented Meg Storey from witnessing any arousal in me, and for two hours or more she sat obediently still, despite the cold.

At mid-day, she had to leave to serve dinner at the Jovial Rushcutters. I pressed a florin into her palm and asked her to return the following morning. I made no attempt to touch her, though the urge in me to do so was very strong. Art, I told myself, must be put before beastliness.

But I couldn't stay away from my picture. Even on my return from an excellent supper with my neighbour, Lady Bathurst, at a very late hour, I went at once to my Studio and lit several lamps and stared at my drawing of Meg Storey and felt myself greatly pleased by it. It was a relief to see, reasonably well drawn, an entire body and not bits and pieces of it. Art, I thought picturesquely (and with a metaphysicality worthy of Pearce), will make me whole, where before I was but half made up.

The next morning dawned sunny, thus slightly altering the light in my studio. I had spent a peevish night trying to decide which pigments to use and in what quantities in order to achieve the exact colour of Meg Storey's neck, her hair, her heel, her nipples. I longed with such envious longing to put onto my canvas something that was more than a mere portrait of Meg Storey. I wanted to capture in colour her very *essence*, so that anyone seeing my picture would be able to "see" her, exactly as she is, both beautiful and vulgar, and these two opposing conditions conflicting in her with such subtlety that one's perception of her is a constantly changing thing. But how was I to do it?

I stood at my easel exhausted and downhearted. How can you capture in a medium which is static that which is constantly moving and altering? I began, without confidence, to mix my pigments. Meg's nose, I noticed, was red ("From the cold I caught, sitting here, Sir Robert"), so I thought I would start with that and work outwards. At once, I could see, I had made a bad decision. You do not, if you are striving for the essence of something, begin with a small detail. I darted to the nipple and painted that. Now, my canvas had two lifeless red spots upon it. Quickly, I mixed some umbers, vermilions and browns and began to colour Meg's hair. Again, there was no light upon it or life within it, and I began to understand now that I simply did not have the technique to paint a tolerably pretty picture of Meg, let alone a portrait that would reveal her essential nature and being.

I put down my brush. I picked up Meg's shawl and put it round her and told her sadly that I would pay her to return at some future date, when I had taken some lessons in becoming an artist.

I believe I might have succumbed, after this first ignominious flop in my chosen field, to a bout of sadness, had it not been for the kind attentions of my neighbour, Lady Bathurst.

Let me describe the Bathursts to you.

Bathurst is a hunting man. He is past his seventieth year and his memory parted from him in his sixty-eighth, when his horse threw him in the field and trod on his ear, through which orifice his mind dribbled away. He wears aged green clothes which are seldom cleaned, and so carry with them the stench of saddle soap, tobacco and boiled pudding. Of his wife's name, which is Violet, he has lost all remembrance and has been heard to enquire at the dinner table: "Who is that woman? Do I know her?" But if you imagine him confined to bed, or even to his room, you would be wrong. Every morning, he is hoisted onto his horse and with his greyhounds and terriers rampages about his fields and forests running to their death hares, foxes, badgers and even stags. The walls of his great hall are hung with game-keepers' poles, hunting whips, the skins of foxes, badgers and marten cats and the heads of deer, its floor strewn with marrow bones for his dogs, which are kennelled there and do their business all over the parquet.

I am fond of Bathurst. His claret is excellent and his table manners worse than mine. His conversation is pure drivel, but spoken with a perpetual passion, emphasised by his constant farting and thumping of the table. Though his memory has left him, his spirit has not. His friends, he tells me, have deserted him; he does not know who they were or why they have gone, but he senses a void, a vacancy, where once there was conversation and laughter, and seems delighted that I should be there to fill it up a little. Confusingly, he appears always to remember my name, or rather his own Anglicised version of it: Merryvale. "Welcome, Merryvale!" he thunders, across the braying and barking of the dogs. "Welcome and Good Cheer and Devil take the Laggards and the Hindmosts!"

If I were, like Pearce, prone to Godliness and guilt, I might find myself a little discomforted by the fact that, attached as I am to Bathurst, I am deceiving him. For I am embarked, I will now admit, on a most agreeable *affaire de coeur* with his wife, my Lady Bathurst, or, as I call her in the intimacy of her chamber, Violet.

Violet is some thirty years younger than her husband and a most handsome person, very witty and smart. She called on me not long after I took up residence at Bidnold Manor, and, on that very first meeting, related to me the lamentable state of Bathurst's mind, putting particular emphasis on his forgetfulness of her existence, thus bringing into my head at once the idea that there could be something between us. For a man who has forgotten that he has a wife cannot care a great deal about which bed she chooses to inhabit, or with whom. Our amours are not of the tearing and clawing kind, but agreeably hot for all that and tolerably frequent, Violet being at that age when she sees her beauty starting to vanish and so wants to make hay while the sun still shines, albeit less radiantly than in her youth, in which, by her own account, an abundance of hay was made and time seemed forever halted at summer.

Thus it was to Violet Bathurst, lying in my arms under the silver and turquoise canopy of my bed, that I confessed my misery at my failure with art. "Without this," I said, "and abandoned as I seem to be by the King, I am a man without a direction and I very much fear that I will lose myself in drunkenness and excesses of all kinds."

Violet looked at me sharply. She was already a little jealous of my young wife and had made me swear on a copy of Thomas à Kempis that I had no carnal knowledge of Celia. The thought that I would fall into excessive behaviour clearly alarmed her a great deal.

"You must not worry, Merivel," she said, leaning on a white elbow and caressing the moths of my stomach with an elegant finger. "I will organise some painting lessons. I know a talented young man, very eager to make the acquaintance of gentry, who will be only too keen to oblige. I commissioned a portrait of Bathurst from him, and, considering that Bathurst is not able to sit still for a second, the finished work was admirable. His name is Elias Finn – a Puritan, one rather suspects, but so keen for advancement and success that he cuts his coat according to the times. He is desperate, of course, to get to Court, and perhaps, if he proves a good teacher, you might be able to set him on the road?"

"You forget, Violet," I said miserably, "that it is now three months since I had a word from the King."

"Is it? Then perhaps you should go to London?"

"I have no position at Court any more."

"But surely, His Majesty would be overjoyed to see you?"

"That I cannot know."

"He used to give you kisses, Merivel."

I smiled. "You and I both know, Violet," I said, "that kisses are as fleeting as pear blossom."

The entry of Elias Finn into my life was, I suspect, of some importance.

He describes himself as a portraitist, but leads, I discover, an almost mendicant life in the shires of England, going on foot from one great house to another, begging to paint its inhabitants. He is young, but his face is gaunt and grey and his wrists as thin as a cuttlefish. He has a shifting, uneasy glance. His lips, however, are sweetly curvaceous and feminine, giving evidence of some sensitivity. His voice is honeyed and polite. He is a paradox. On our first meeting, I didn't know what to make of him at all.

I led him to my Studio and showed him my bacon and egg man and my unfinished portrait of Meg Storey. He stared at them in alarm, as if they frightened him, which indeed they probably did, so far do they seem from anything one could possibly admire.

"Why do you wish to paint, Sir?" he said after a while.

"Well . . ." I began, "as a kind of act of forgetting. My studies have been in anatomy and disease, but I wish, for reasons of my own, not to continue with medical work."

"So you would be an artist instead?"

"Yes."

"Why, pray?"

"Because . . . because I must do something! I have a very immoderate nature, Mr Finn. Look at me! Look at my house! Since the Restoration, I have become inflamed, full of riot! We're in a New Age and I am its perfect man, but I must channel myself into some endeavour, or be lost to idleness and despair. So please help me."

He returned to my pictures. "To judge from these," he said, "you draw tolerably well, but have no sense of colour."

No sense of colour! I was dumbfounded. "Colour," I began to say, "is what excites me more than anything on earth. I was married in purple and gold! At the King's coronation, I fainted almost at the sight of his crimson barge . . ." But then I stopped myself. "You are right, of course," I said. "I have a great love for colour, but a love for something is never enough. What I utterly lack is the skill to turn love into art."

We began my painting lessons there and then. Finn had brought with him some of his own work, portraits mostly of fashionable women, which had presumably not been liked, in that they were still in his possession. I thought them admirable. "If, in time, I can execute one painting as good as any of these," I said, "I will be a happy man."

He smiled pityingly. He began to discuss his technique with regard to background, which, he said, should always be classical

– a Palladian garden with broken columns, a naval battle, or a merry hunting scene.

"You mean," I asked, "that instead of drawing a window behind Meg Storey, I should have put in ships, or horsemen?"

"Yes," said Finn. "Naturally."

I couldn't recall that Holbein's famous portraits had classical backgrounds, but I didn't mention this, because I knew I would be very grateful to Finn if he could teach me how to paint Doric columns or a battleship in full sail.

"The background," he continued, "must flatter. More, it must lend permanence to the life of the sitter, no matter how brief his actual existence may turn out to be."

For these considerations, I had of course taken no previous thought, but I could see some truth in what he was saying, and so our first morning passed in discussion of how a picture must be composed so that no part of it is "dead", so that, wherever the eye wanders, there is interest, whether it is in the detail on the hilt of a sword or a minutely rendered rowing boat on a distant Arcadian shore. We furthermore approached the question of distance and perspective: how hills, for instance, which are further away will seem paler and less well defined than those which are near, and how the sitter's nearness and vigour will be emphasised if he or she inhabits a pool of light.

"When you are next at Whitehall," Finn concluded, "go and look at the Raphaels and the Titians the King reputedly has in his apartments and you will see some of the finest examples of everything I've talked about."

So, Violet Bathurst had already informed Finn of my acquaintance with the King. I merely nodded. It was much too early for me to decide whether Finn was worthy of any favours, but I detected that his longing to go to Court was even greater than my longing to learn to paint and decided at once that I might be able to use this finely balanced inequality to some advantage.

Towards the beginning of November, by which time, under Finn's tuition, I had painted a moderately bad picture of my Spaniel, Minette, asleep by an imaginary waterfall, my little dog became ill.

A rampaging fear gripped my heart. I loved Minette. Her presence was a constant reminder to me that I had been – and still hoped to be again – the King's friend and Fool, and I was certain that her dying would be a terrible portent of derelictions yet to come.

Very reluctantly, I got out my surgical instruments and my remedies, ointments and powders, but, having set them out next to Minette on the Dining Room table, found that I was at a loss to know what to do; in my desire to forget my former profession, I had succeeded in burying knowledge that was vital to me now.

I thought of Lou-Lou and Fabricius's dictates about nature. Would I be able to cure Minette by a similar attack of idleness? I did not think so. She was vomiting almost constantly, poor thing, and on her belly was a large dribbling sore.

I diluted a little laudanum with milk and spooned this down her throat, and after some minutes she entered a quiet sleep. I examined the sore. It was a foul and stinking thing. I imagined its poison entering her blood vessels and thus being carried to her heart. If only it had been a boil I could lance, but it was not, it was an open wound which, because it was on her belly, I had neglected to notice for several days, or even weeks.

I cleaned the thing as best I could with some warm water, moistened some linen with alcohol and laid this upon it. Minette whimpered in her sleep and then her body was suddenly wracked with terrible convulsions. Foam-flecked spittle appeared at the corners of her mouth. I held onto her and waited for the convulsions to subside. At my elbow, my servant, Will Gates, was sweating and pale.

"It's no good," I said to Will. "I don't trust my own knowledge. Where can I find Doctor Murdoch at this hour?"

"Doctor Murdoch is a quack, Sir, a regular empiric."

"Never mind. He's our best hope. Where is he to be found?"

"In one place and only one."

"Well?"

"At the Rushcutters, Sir."

Why did I not send Will to the inn? I did not send him because I thought a fast canter on Danseuse in the crisp November evening would help to rid me of some of the fear and anxiety by which I felt myself gripped. Shouting to my groom to saddle the horse, I carried Minette to my bedroom, laid her on my bed and told Will not to leave her side, on pain of immediate dismissal.

"What will I do if she rack and rigor again, Sir?"

"Hold her," I said, "try to hold her still."

I mounted Danseuse and was away through the park, sending the deer scurrying from our pathway. I pressed her to a fast gallop and, as I filled and refilled my lungs with the rich air, began to feel my terror depart a little.

I was sweating by the time I tied Danseuse to her post outside the Jovial Rushcutters and my face was aflame. I walked in, blowing like a whale. I cast around for the unmistakable sight of Doctor Murdoch, with his stooped shoulders and long clammy hands, but I couldn't see him. "Doctor Murdoch?" I asked one of the hobnailed peasants with his nose in his ale. "Was he here this evening? Does anyone know where he might be found?"

Through the malodorous crowd of pigmen, game-keepers and fowl-breeders came Meg Storey. In the dim candlelight of the tavern, her hair looked fiery. The dress and apron she wore were lilac. She bobbed a cheeky curtsey to me, then took my hand and led me without a word to the cool, dark stillroom where the barrels of beer were stacked and there reached up and placed a soft kiss upon my mouth. "That is to tell you," she said, and I caught the sour scent of beer on her breath, "I am sorry for what happened to your new vocation."

I let out a yelp of laughter, and, all hot and in a lather of body and brain, gathered Meg Storey into my arms. "Nature . . ." I murmured between kisses and caresses. "Let nature work upon Minette and upon me . . ." And in moments I had abandoned my poor dog to her fate and lay tumbling with Meg on the earthen floor.

An hour later, Doctor Murdoch came into the tavern, but so confused and excited was I by my amours with Meg Storey, that I no longer thought to find him there, but spent the rest of the night riding hither and thither in search of him, until Danseuse would gallop no more and we walked wearily home.

Will Gates was asleep on the floor of my bedchamber. Laid

out on my bed, under a striped cloth I recognised as one of the large table napkins given to me by the King, was the dead body of Minette.

I knelt down and tried to think of a prayer, but found that, along with my all too insubstantial knowledge of disease, I had consigned to oblivion any number of the ancient words of God.

FOUR

AN INDIAN NIGHTINGALE

The morning after the death of Minette, Finn arrived to give me a painting lesson. Wearily, I put on my floppy hat and my smock. A chill rain, now driving against the panes of my studio window, had saturated Finn's rather threadbare outer garments and given him the look of a destitute. We were, in short, a miserable pair. And it occurred to me that, although the spur to creative endeavour may very often be melancholy, it relies in its execution on its opposing element, choleric fire, of which, that morning, I felt not the smallest flame.

"Go home," I said to Finn, unwisely as it turned out, for Finn at that time had none to go to, but had spent the previous night in one of Lord Bathurst's cowsheds. And so wet and woebegone did the poor artist feel, that he was emboldened to broach with me, not for the first nor the last time, the great subject of my influence with the King and the chance of my obtaining for him some position, however meagre – a fresco assistant, a designer of playing cards – at Court.

Now, the loss of Minette had not only saddened me, but had also made me afraid. My own deliberate act of forgetfulness had allowed her to die; King Charles, in his turn, I now saw, had consigned his onetime Fool to oblivion. I had my house and my title as recompense, but I was forgotten. Cleverer, wittier, less ignoble people had replaced me. I had served my purpose and was now cast from favour. Sick at heart as I was, however, I had no intention of revealing to Finn (himself so full of *hauteur* in his disdain of my painting talent) that I no longer had any influence at Whitehall.

"Finn," I said, whipping off my floppy hat and throwing it down on the stack of virgin canvases, "it is pointless to raise this matter with me, when it is manifestly clear that you have utterly failed to comprehend the way in which such transactions are carried out."

"What can you mean?" asked Finn, shifting his feet uncomfortably, so that I heard the squelch of his shoes.

"What I mean, Finn," I said acidly, "is that we live in commercial times. Take it or leave it, this is the world we inhabit. And he who takes no account of this is likely to die poor and unknown."

Finn's pretty mouth dropped open, giving him a childlike, idiotic look. "If I were rich," he said piteously, "I would of course give you gold to mention my talent to His Majesty, but, as you see, I barely make a living, and if I am to sacrifice the little you pay me for painting lessons . . ."

"*How* you set about the task of persuading me to use my influence in London is of no interest to me," I snapped. "I merely remind you that, although an Age of Philanthropy may one day catch our commercial English hearts unaware, the time is not now. And he who is not of the time risks the scorn of his peers and the grave of a pauper. Go home, or rather go back to Lord Bathurst's cowshed, or wherever you plan to lay your innocent head tonight, and think about what I have said."

I watched him walk out into the rain. Tall and thin, his retreating figure reminded me, as it never previously had, of my father, and I experienced a moment of regret, like a sudden wounding in my belly. I felt most extraordinarily alone. I would have mounted Danseuse and begun a mad-cap journey to London there and then, had I not promised the King to stay away from Court – "and neither at Celia's house at Kew, not in the corridors of Whitehall to show your face, Merivel" – unless invited there by him alone.

I sat down before my empty easel. I took off my wig and ran my hands furiously through my hog bristles. When I contemplated all that I had been given, I knew I had no right to feel that I had been betrayed, and yet I did. It had never occurred to me, you see, when I woke from my wedding night, alone and sickly in a dank forest, to see in the distance the King's coach moving off down Sir Joshua's drive, that I would never set eyes on him again. My future, I had believed, was now tied irrevocably to his. And without my foolishness to divert him from the cares of State, he would, I had convinced myself, surely grow grave and sorrowful and start to feel some need of me. But Minette's death now revealed to me that I had been wrong. It was now almost winter. In five months, despite frequent visits from some of the Court gallants, fond of the Norfolk air and games of croquet on my lawn with their pretty mistresses, I had had from the King no word, message or token of any kind. "Never fear," the Court wags had told me, "he will send for you, Merivel, when he's in the mood for farting!" And they had doubled up with laughter over their croquet mallets. I had, of course, joined in the general mirth. I was loved by these men for my willingness to ridicule myself. But I was not, as you can imagine, in the least comforted by their words.

I left my Studio and went to my Morning Room, where I sat down at my bureau and prepared to write the King a letter:

My Most Gracious Sovereign, I began, and the image I had, as I wrote these words, of the King as a moving, shimmering body of celestial light was overwhelming.

Your loyal Fool, Merivel, salutes you, I continued, *and prays this letter finds Your Majesty in excellent health and spirits, but – God forgive me – the latter yet not so entirely excellent that you would not, as the rememberance of my antics and my untidy person comes now to your mind, believe yourself contented by some small dose of my company. Let me hasten to say that, were you, Sir, for however brief a time and in whatever role your whim or disposition might dictate, desirous of seeing me, you have only to send word and the speed of my journey to London would be scarcely less than those swift-travelling thoughts which bring me so frequently, in my presumptuous mind, to Your Majesty's side.*

Honesty now forces me to relate a great sorrow that has befallen me here, in the midst of all my luxury and brocaded living, namely

*the death of my dog, your Minette, who was the small creature I
most loved in all your Kingdom. I beg my Sovereign to believe I
did all within my power towards the saving of her and to know
that she was never in her short life, no, not for one day nor one
hour, neglected by*

> *Her Master, Your Servant,*
> *R. Merivel*

I read through my letter, without permitting the truth-telling
inhabitant of my mind to comment upon the words written by
the liar who also lodges there, preferring as I do that these two
remain distant but courteous neighbours. I sealed it and gave it
to Will Gates with instructions that it be sent post-haste to
London.

Writing it had eased my mind sufficiently for me to call for
my coach and make the short journey through the continuing
downpour to the Bathursts, having first powdered my armpits,
put on a yellow coat and done what I could to make my person
agreeable, in case I chanced on Violet alone and was able to
bury my sorrows in her velvet bosom. Alas, I was not so lucky.
Bathurst's memory, so frequently a vessel given up for lost, had
that morning bobbed briefly but jauntily to the surface, during
which time it recognised Violet as the very woman he had long
ago bedded in a frenzy of torn love-knots and snatched garters.
He was, as her servant announced my arrival, in the act of
tearing a marten cat's head and a couple of badgers' pelts off
the wall and laying these trophies at his wife's feet.

The following Friday, Finn did not appear for my painting lesson.

It was an exceedingly splendid autumn morning, burnished by
the sun, but my mind wouldn't rid itself of the sodden and
bedraggled figure, with my father's long but awkward stride, I
had sent off into the rain. Had the poor man died of damp and
cold? Or had my Court-wisdom shocked him into abandoning
the gentry and their corrupt ways – to paint pictures of the likes
of Meg Storey, perhaps, in return for a pint of ale, or a quick
favour on the stillroom floor?

The day was altogether too fair to waste on worry or remorse.

Finn's fate was not mine to control. I put on my floppy hat and my smock and, with Will's help, carried my easel and my painting equipment to a far corner of my south lawn, from which I had a most magnificent perspective of the park – the purple and gold beeches, the russet elms, the fiery chestnuts and the soft sweep of brown beneath them that was the line of grazing deer.

I stared at this scene. I knew that to render the foliage of a tree in all its complexity was beyond my skills as a draughtsman, let alone as a painter in oils. What I could try to capture, however, were the colours. Thus, without sketching anything in charcoal on my canvas, I began furiously to mix my pigments and to lay the paint on in bold sweeps and flourishes, colour upon colour, a scrabble of white for a cloud, wavering lines of green and yellow for the rich grass, cascades of oranges, reds and golds for the chestnuts, a deep mass of purple and brown and black for the further beeches. I worked like a furnace-feeder, like a glass-blower, puffing and straining. My temperature rose and my heartbeat quickened. I was ablaze with my painting. I knew that it was as wild, as undisciplined, as excessive as my own character, but it perfectly expressed, all unskilled as it was, my *response* to that autumn day, and thus, to me, had a satisfactory logic to it. Furthermore, when it was at last finished and I stepped back from it a few paces and looked at it through half closed eyes, it did resemble to some degree the scene before me. It was, perhaps, as if a child had painted it. It was crude. The colours were too bright and too many. And yet it didn't lie (not even as much, Finn, I wanted to say, as your beautifully painted Greek columns or shepherdesses' picnics). It was, in some essential way, what I had seen. I walked round to the back of the canvas and scribbled a title on it in French: *Le Matin de Merivel, l'automne.*

It was then, as I looked up, that I saw Finn, dressed I noticed rather gayly in Lincoln Green, striding towards me across the lawn. I was glad he hadn't starved to death, even more glad when I read from the knowing half smile on his face that he had heeded my words and brought me some little inducement to carry out the favours of which he believed me capable. For I am extremely fond of receiving presents. Possessing, as I do now,

an abundance of useless knick-knacks and *objets d'art*, has not
diminished my enthusiasm for accepting more, and the gift, say,
of a fine pewter tippling jug or even the head of a marten cat
from old Bathurst can cause me an entire day's good spirits.

"Finn!" I called warmly. "You are not starving in some hovel
like Poor Tom, as I imagined you to be!"

"What?" said Finn, checked in his stride.

"Oh, never mind my follies," I laughed. "Come and look at
my painting."

Finn approached. The sun had now moved and was falling
smack across my picture, causing the colours to seem even
more gaudy than they actually were. The artist stared at my
work. Across his face began to spread a look of recoil, as if,
upon the clean waistcoat of this Robin Hood, his Maid Marian
had thrown up her pudding. I saw him struggling with words,
but they seemed to choke him and he turned away.

"Well?" I said.

"It is," said Finn, "an excrescence."

"Yes," I commented, "probably that is the right word for it."

"In the time of Cromwell, you would . . ."

"What, Finn?"

"No. I do not mean that. But really, you cannot . . ."

"What?"

"You must not show this picture to anyone. You must, I think,
burn it."

"It offends you, I see."

"It breaks . . ."

"What does it break?"

"All the laws, all the procedures and disciplines I have been
at such pains to try to teach you."

"Yes. You're undoubtedly right. It is a grievous mistake. And
yet to me, you see, it's a rather memorable rendering of all that
I *feel* about the colours of my park. Which only illustrates, does
it not, that feeling, however passionate a spur it may be to the
poor dabbling painter, is, without technique, an impotent and
ridiculous thing, like a eunuch in love, one might fancifully
suggest."

I laughed, but Finn did not even smile. I felt light-hearted, despite his loathing of my work, and sorry for him that his spirit seemed so grave.

"Well," I said, "let's forget the picture. I shall put it on the fire presently. Will you take a glass of wine, Finn, to restore your lightness of heart?"

Poor Robin agreed and we returned to the house, where I ordered some cool white wine to be brought from my cellar to the Morning Room.

Finn gulped his drink like a parched traveller. His hand shook. Almost before he had sat down, he leapt to his feet again and announced to me that he had taken good heed of my advice on how to get on in what he called "this heartless age" and had therefore spent a great deal of money and time preparing a gift for me, in the hopes that now, at last, I would speak of his talents to the King.

"Excellent, Finn!" I said. "You're learning fast. Would that you could say the same of my painting, what?"

A little nervous smile crossed his angelic mouth. Then he darted out and returned a few seconds later, carrying in his arms a large cylindrical object covered in a pretty embroidered cloth, which he laid carefully at my feet.

"What is it, Finn?" I asked, fearing suddenly that he had brought me the kind of truncated piece of Corinthian column he was so fond of dotting about in his own pictures. But he wouldn't answer, only looked from me to the object and back to me again, like a timorous fieldmouse looking for danger as it spies some spilt grains of wheat.

I removed the cloth. Before me stood a birdcage of great delicacy, painted a deep Prussian blue and gilded with gold leaf. Inside it, on a swing perch, was a bird, which at first I took to be a stuffed thing, so still and staring did it remain. Then it turned its yellow eye on me and opened its beak and let out a sweet trill. "My word, Finn," I said, "it's alive!"

Finn nodded. "It's an Indian Nightingale," he announced proudly. "It has travelled the seas."

I will at once confess that I was delighted with this gift. Seldom, I thought, can more pains have been taken over a bribe. The cage was an object of wistful beauty, like something from a departed time. The bird inside was ordinary in its appearance, with a sleek blue-black body and an orange beak. Its song, however, was a pure and brilliant sound, a sound I seemed to have heard in my mind, but could not recall in nature.

"They say," said Finn, "that it may be taught other notes, even tunes, if you play a wind instrument to it, particularly the oboe."

"How astonishing," I said. "Why particularly the oboe?"

"The oboe, I believe, is within its register."

"Ah."

"But you do not play?"

"No. But I will learn. I could, I think, acquire a strong appetite for music."

Across Finn's countenance darted a momentary flicker of fear. I knew what he was thinking and his little discomfort amused me, but I chose not to comment upon it and we sat for a few moments in silence, both staring at the Indian Nightingale.

"So," said Finn at last. "When you are next at Court . . ."

"Your gift is very fine. Thank you."

"When you are next with the King . . ."

"Hush, Finn," I said, "for I am quite unable to raise your hopes over your own matter. The King at the moment is very burdened down with affairs of State and I must bide my time until the more frivolous side of his nature turns again to me."

"I understand."

"Timing is all. And it may be that we must wait out the winter."

"The winter?" said Finn with dismay. "But I will starve, Sir Robert. I will die of cold and chilblains."

"You must believe me," I said, "no one thirsts for the return of His Majesty's gaiety and laughter more than I. But until such time, I can promise you that he will take no more painters, oboists, tennis coaches or other riff-raff into his service . . ."

By my inadvertent inclusion of the word "riff-raff", Finn looked utterly downcast. I was about to explain that, as the son of a glovemaker, failed anatomist and failed physician, I included myself in that category of people. We are all, I nearly said, so much chaff, so many airy feathers, blown by wind, burned and suffocated by fire, but I refrained, preferring to conceal from Finn, in case he might one day teach me how to paint something of worth, my modest lineage, my failures in medicine and my deterministic pessimism which could so cruelly cross the grain of his own faith. I contented myself with slapping Finn's green-hosed knee and saying boisterously: "Don't sulk, old Finn. No one could say for certain that you won't be in Whitehall by Christmas."

After several weeks had passed and I had no word from the King, I began to recognise that, while my letter to him had momentarily relieved my anxiety, the sending of it had now thrown me into a worse distress than ever. For before I had sent it I had been able to convince myself that the King's thoughts might turn to me again at any moment, that his mind had, in fact, mislaid me for a while, but that he would rediscover me during, perhaps, a game of ninepins or in the course of some immodest banquet. Now, on the other hand, I could only interpret his silence as a deliberate act of forgetting. Not even the death of Minette had moved him sufficiently to write to me. This in itself was proof enough that he no longer regarded me with any of his former affection and that I was, from his radiant inner circle, now cast into outer darkness.

The profundity and Stygian gloom of this darkness oppressed me most fearfully during the hours of the actual night, so that I began to keep a candle by my bed, or, better than this, to flee my house entirely and spend my nights in Meg Storey's garret in the roof of the Jovial Rushcutters, keeping sleep at bay with ale and rowdy couplings and foolish stories about my travels in the Land of the River Mar, a country of my imaginings, located in Meg's ignorant head as "just above Africa" and about which I invented the most absorbing lies. "The preferred element of the natives of the River Mar," I told her, "is water. And this is how they sleep, with their bodies immersed in the river. And all along the banks of the Mar, hanging from the mangrove trees, are loops made out of hide, to hold the sleeping heads out of the water, so that they do not drown." Meg would sigh with wonder at such unimaginable things and threaten to drift to sleep, lulled by my voice, while outside I would hear poor Danseuse paw the frosty ground and whinny with cold.

Though the solace afforded me by Meg Storey's plump and energetic body was considerable, I felt urgently in need of some spiritual comfort, and began, at about this time, to send out messages to God. I imagined these feeble communications as minute blips of light, little wriggling glow-worms which, unless God had a telescope pointed directly at them, he would be unlikely to notice. The days when God and I engaged in daily conversation had long since passed away. They passed away at the time of the fire, which, as surely as it consumed the bodies of my poor parents, together with the ribbons and feathers that were the stuff of their innocent trade, had also burned up what remained of my faith. I had found, since my rejection of Galen's theory of divine perfection, that anatomy had begun to lead me away from God. My comparative study of the *uterus bovinae* and the *uterus humani* had shown me that the generative process of the cow is so similar to that of the woman as to make me wonder whether there is not some essential thread connecting us to the animal kingdom and thus toppling us from the pillars of divinity upon which, not merely kings and rulers have set themselves, but upon which the vilest rogue and murderer believes himself to stand. These heretical thoughts I had kept to myself of course, but when I saw how swiftly, how cruelly my good parents died, how, without the least sign of God's lamentation, their lungs burst and their flesh burnt up like meat, I felt compelled to cease my own conversing with an omnipotent and benevolent God. For surely, He is neither? If He is benevolent, why did He send such terrible destruction on such honest and hard-working people? And if He is omnipotent, why did He not prevent it? "Ah," Pearce, would say, "but suffering redeems, Merivel. In their agony, the sins of your parents passed from them." "They had no sins, Pearce," I reply. "They attended two sermons on a Sunday. They said their prayers morning and night, kneeling by the bed from which neither of them ever strayed. But look at me! I am boiling with lust, immoderate in my consumption of wine, irreverent in my speech and a self-deceiver. Why did the fire not consume me? Why is suffering so arbitrary? No, Pearce, it will not do. If God exists, He is surely cruel. He is the old and terrible God of Moses, the God of Abraham. But the most logical conclusion is that He does not exist at all."

It is interesting to note the ease with which I had let my faith fall from me. Any love I had hitherto felt for God, I had given to the King, who had reciprocated (not as God had done, by speaking through the mouths of fat bishops and having frequent recourse to long periods of enigmatic silence) by laughing at my jokes and giving me royal kisses far sweeter to me than any embrace I'd had from any woman. It was the absence of these tender expressions of friendship and affection that had plunged me into such despair and sent me scrabbling about in the darkness once more, in search of my lost Redeemer, however cruel He might turn out to be.

This search of mine, these glow-worm prayers I sent out into the starry sky above Meg Storey's roof, if they failed to bring God back to comfort me, did, after a few weeks, send me my old friend, Pearce, who arrived at Bidnold on a mule. Strapped to the mule's back, were Pearce's pitiful worldly possessions (referred to by me, rather wittily, I think, as his "burning coals", in reference to a mad Quaker at Westminster who had wandered about calling the fops to repentance with a dish of the said coals balanced on his head). What Pearce owned, in fact, was the following: three Bibles, one copy of his beloved Harvey's *De Generatione Animalium*, various other anatomical tracts, including works by Vesalius and da Vinci and Needham's *Disquisitio Anatomica De Formato Foetu*, some quill pens, a black coat and hat, two pairs of black breeches, some torn shirts and stockings, a box of rusty surgical instruments, a single pewter mug and plate and a china soup ladle made in Lancashire. This ladle was the only legacy of his mother, who had died in poverty to send Pearce to Cambridge. Sometimes, in the melancholy moods that so frequently afflict him, Pearce would hold the ladle close to his body and let his long fingers caress its cold surface, in the manner of a lute player plucking a living tune from its dead, hollowed wood.

I was glad, I will admit, to see Pearce. When Will Gates

informed me that a man with a long neck and dressed in black was coming up the drive on a mule, I knew it could be none other than my old friend and former fellow-student and I ran out to greet him.

It was drizzling slightly and both Pearce and the mule appeared wet and muddy.

"We have come from the Fens," he announced in his voice of doom.

"From the Fens, Pearce?" I said. "What were you doing there?"

"I am a Fenlander now, Merivel," he said. "My work and life are there."

"I notice that you put them in that order, Pearce: work first, life second."

"Naturally. Except that the two are inseparable."

"Well, I do not work at all, except a little painting."

"Painting? How peculiar."

"You've left the Royal College, then?"

"Yes. I work only with the insane. Take the mule, will you, and see she's fed? We're both very weak."

Pearce then dismounted, staggered a pace or two and fell to his knees. I shouted for Will Gates, who came running like a bullet, and together he and I helped Pearce into the house. I asked the groom to rescue the "burning coals" quickly, before the mule died and rolled over on the soup ladle.

We put Pearce to bed in the least colourful of my rooms, the Olive Room, a north-facing bedchamber, in which I had left intact some dark panelling and had curtained the bed in a sombre green, only enlivened by a little crimson fringe. Here, after drinking some venison broth and enquiring whether his books could be sent up to him, he fell into a sleep that lasted thirty-seven hours. During most of this time, I stayed at his bedside, checking his pulse now and then, listening to his breathing, dozing a little and sipping claret and staring at his elongated grey face, which I found at once so irritating and yet so inexpressibly dear to me.

When he woke up at last, I was anxious to tell him of the despair into which I had fallen and to see whether he could suggest any remedy. But he had, it turned out, made the arduous journey on the mule from the Fens for one reason only: to reveal to me that he had found, in his work with the mad people of what he called the New Bedlam, located somewhere between Waterbeach and Whittlesea, a deep and profound sense of peace, and to try to persuade me to leave my life of "vanity and show" to join him in his labours.

"I sense," he said, staring at my freckled, ruddy and bewigged visage, "that you're not at ease, Merivel. The light has gone out of your eyes. Luxury is suffocating your vital flame."

I looked down. Though I had a terrible urge to confess to Pearce, amid childlike tears, that it was not luxury that had robbed me of my happiness, but the King's abandonment of me, and that I was indeed a desperate man, though not at all for the reasons he surmised, I refrained from doing so, knowing that it would only lead Pearce into more flowery discussion of how the insane are the innocent of the earth, and how, only by succouring them "like little children" can we be saved.

"Thank you, Pearce, for your concern," I said, "but you are completely wrong. If my eyes appear a little lacklustre, it's merely because I have watched at your bedside for a great quantity of time with hardly any sleep. As to my vital flame, it is burning very brightly."

"I know you, Merivel. When you stood in my room in Caius and put your hand on that man's heart, then it was burning!"

"Indeed! And if you had seen me in the park the other day with my oil paints – "

"You hope to find salvation in art?"

"I'm not speaking necessarily of salvation . . ."

"But I am, Merivel. For is not death the supreme moment of mortal existence, the hour in which we reap what we have sown?"

"You choose to see it like that, Pearce."

"No. I do not choose. The Lord tells me it is so. And what are you sowing, Merivel, here in your palace?"

"It's merely a manor, Pearce."

"No! It's a palace! And full of iniquity, if these scarlet tassels are anything to go by."

"They're nothing to go by."

"Answer me, Merivel. What are you *sowing*?"

Again, I looked down. The agricultural metaphors with which
the Bible is strewn have always struck me as simplistic and
crude, but I particularly did not like Pearce's repeated emphasis
on the word "sowing", for it somehow evoked in my mind my
letter to the King, which had been intended as a seed in the
forgetful Royal brain, but which had indubitably fallen upon stony
ground.

I looked up at Pearce, white and gaunt on his white pillow.

"Colour," I said. "Colour and light. I am sowing these."

"What pagan, freakish piffle you do spout, Merivel!"

"No," I said. "Have a little faith, Pearce. Through colour and
light, I hope to arrive at art. Through art, I hope to arrive at
compassion. And through compassion, though the journey may
be a deal more terrible than the one you've just undertaken –
your mule is dead by the way – I hope to arrive at enlightenment."

"Enlightenment," said Pearce with a sniff, "is not enough."

"Perhaps. But sufficient to be going on with."

Before Pearce could comment upon this, I plucked his ladle
off a walnut escritoire, where a servant had placed it, and handed
it to him.

"Here is your ladle," I said. "Play upon it quietly, until you
feel restored enough to venture downstairs, where I have
something of great beauty to show you."

"What is it?" asked Pearce, suspiciously.

"An Indian Nightingale," I replied. And before Pearce could
make some disdainful comment about my bird, I left his room.

I will now tell you that it had become my daily habit to sing a
little to my Indian Nightingale. I have no voice at all, and so flat
do the notes come out that Minette, in her brief life, used to
howl and whimper the moment I opened my mouth, as if I were
a desert dog from the Land of Mar. But, my lack of talent
notwithstanding, I love singing. I hear the right notes in my
head. The fact that I can seldom attain them distresses my
listeners, but doesn't seem to upset me in the least. I am, in

this respect, like a man trying to fling his body over a five-barred gate and, no matter how spirited his run or ready his heart, finding himself at each attempt still on the wrong side of it and yet nonetheless filled with joy at his efforts. Finn had told me to play the oboe to the bird, and I had sent to London for one of these instruments but, in the meantime, I sang to it, rather quietly so as not to affront it, and it regarded me watchfully, moving its tail up and down and letting fall onto the painted base of the cage tiny filaments of shit.

When at last Pearce rose from his bed and arrived in my Withdrawing Room dressed in his greasy black clothes, he found me singing to my nightingale. Shading his eyes from the brilliance of the furnishings, he approached the cage and stood blinking at it like a lizard. I ceased my singing and the bird at once let out a melodious trill.

"I recognise that," said Pearce.

"What is it?" I asked excitedly. "Something by Purcell?"

"No," said Pearce, and turned upon me a pitying, reptilian look. "That is the warble of a common blackbird."

"Don't be foolish, Pearce," I said at once, meanwhile recognising that my heart, all unfeeling as I know it to be, had started to beat erratically. "The bird was a gift to me. That creature has travelled the oceans."

"When? Who brought it?"

"I have no idea. An ornithologist, no doubt. It has been round Cape Horn. So let us have no more talk of blackbirds!"

Pearce shrugged and turned away from the cage, as if it was of no further interest to him whatsoever. "You've been duped, Merivel," was all he said.

"Very well," I said. "We will go out into the garden and find a blackbird and listen to its feeble song, and you will see that you're wrong."

"As you wish," said Pearce, "but I would remind you that it is winter and birds do not sing a great deal at this time of year."

"Further proof, then, that this is not an English bird. You just heard its lovely trill."

"No doubt it mistook its surroundings for a flower bed."

I smiled at Pearce. The insult he'd intended to my gaudy room in fact pleased me a great deal, and I mention to you, in passing, that Pearce's criticisms of me do not inevitably have the humbling effect upon me that they so strenuously desire.

Pearce and I then put on our cloaks (his so exceedingly threadbare that an irritating shiver of pity ran through me) and went out into the December morning, filigree'd with frost, sparkling and silent in the dry, icy air.

We stood still and listened. Some way off in the park, rooks were circling and cawing above the beech trees, but there was scarcely another sound at all. "Let's walk down the drive a little," I suggested, and we set off at the slow pace always adopted by Pearce, who, if God himself were suddenly to appear before him with open arms, would, I believe, forbear to run, but approach his Maker with his habitual measured and ungainly step.

After we had gone a very little way, a sound I had not expected at all began to clatter and jingle in the frosty quiet. It was the sound of a coach and four. I caught my breath. Without any doubt, it would be Violet Bathurst riding over for a little mulled claret and an hour in my bed, and here was I listening out for blackbirds with the one friend whose mind would be tormented by her arrival. I knew, if I wished to keep Pearce at Bidnold, I would have to send Violet away, however beguiling the thought of her company might be.

We stepped to one side as the coach came on, but as it rounded the curve in the drive, I saw immediately that the beautiful greys which pulled it were not Violet's horses. I was expecting no other guests and couldn't imagine who could be coming to my house at such a gallop.

I put out an arm and the coachman (recognising me by my fine clothes as the master of Bidnold) attempted to slow the horses. But their canter had been so brisk that they and the coach had gone past me before they could be pulled up, and all I had was a fleeting glimpse of a woman's face at the carriage window, shrouded in what appeared to be a black veil.

The coach had now arrived in front of the main doorway. With Pearce trailing me, like the ghost of the exiled John Loseley, I started to run towards the house, unfortunately slipping in my haste on an icy patch of the driveway, falling down in a most humiliating fashion, tearing my peach-coloured stockings and grazing my right hand.

I got up and stumbled on. "Ho there!" I called. "Hello!" But when I arrived, puffing and flushed, at my doorway, I saw that the occupant of the coach had already gone inside the house and that some large boxes and trunks were now being carried in by my footmen.

Noticing with great vexation that my hand was bleeding, I walked into my hallway. After the bright, cold sunlight, it appeared very dark, and indeed I could at first see no one at all. Then I looked up. Standing on the oak stairs was the woman in the black veil. Her stance was strangely familiar to me and, even as she reached up and flung back the veil, I knew whose face I was about to see. It was the face of my wife.

We stood staring at each other. Her stare – notwithstanding my crimson cheeks and my wig fallen over my eyebrows – was far more terrible than mine. She seemed to have aged almost out of time. Her small face, dimpled and pretty in my memory, looked grey and gaunt and her eyes were swollen and red, as if she had been crying day and night since the beginning of winter. I moved forward a pace. I wanted, in my pity for her, to say her name, but realised, even as I opened my mouth, that I couldn't remember what it was.

FIVE

TWO WORMS

During my fanciful and hectic redecorations at Bidnold, I had allowed myself to ignore the possibility that Celia Clemence would one day take up habitation under its roof.

Thus, although the house contained eleven bedchambers, none, in my mind, had been furnished for the woman Violet Bathurst jealously referred to as "Lady Merivel, Your Bride", but whose continuing existence was invariably absent from my mind. "Listen, Violet," I was in the habit of saying on the occasion of my Lady B's envious outbursts. "I am no more conscious of Celia as my lawful wife than Bathurst is of you as his. Rest assured that I never think of her."

Usually, Violet's jealousy would be assuaged by this statement, but one evening, even as I knelt over her and gently eased my tumescent member along the soft furrow between her breasts, she suddenly reached up and pushed me sideways, so that I would have fallen onto the floor had my right leg not been tangled in the sheet. "Your analogy with Bathurst," she said crossly "is misleading and, if deliberately so, then you are a cruel and cynical man. For as you well know, Merivel, Bathurst has moments of remembering and at such times becomes importunate. On Wednesday night, for instance, lucidity returned to him in the middle of supper and he began crawling towards me on his hands and knees under the Dining Room table, the while unbuttoning himself. If I had not quickly reminded him that his brace of woodcock – his favourite game – were getting cold on his plate, I simply do not know what might have happened. And so it may be with you, Merivel. That which you swear you have forgotten, you will one day come grovelling towards."

"Violet," I said, recovering my kneeling position (only disconcerted very mildly by the similarity of my stance to Bathurst's under the table), "grovelling is a thing I have done but once in my life, when I inadvertently fell over at the King's feet. The notion that I will ever, as long as I am of sound mind, grovel to Celia is a pure fiction, not to be entertained for one second more!"

I put my mouth upon Violet's at this moment, thus preventing further speech, and the evening proceeded very pleasantly, Violet's sudden attack of jealousy having roused her to a wild and shameless abandon.

But even as I saw her into her coach, I found myself remembering Celia and wondering where, in the unlikely event of her unexpected arrival at Bidnold, I would lodge her. Had I not, on my strange wedding night, witnessed the immodest thrusting of her loins towards the King's mouth and heard through the closet door a wailing of pleasure worthy of an African wildcat, I would have believed Celia to be an entirely chaste and modest person, a person of sober taste and small appetite, finding comfort and contentment in a bedchamber hung, say, with pale apricot moiré and ornamented by sombre prints of rivers and cathedrals. As it was, by the time I had ceased waving to Violet's gloved hand disappearing into the night, I had already decided that what I called the Marigold Room would be the one I would offer to Celia. Late as the hour was, I had my servants go up and light candles in the Marigold Room, so that I could take a look at it. I would have given the thing no thought at all but for Violet. For this one brief night, she had awoken in me a minute flicker of excitement at the idea of my wife's arrival. The next morning, however, Celia was once more consigned to that part of my brain I imagine to be like a coiled fistula, filled not with putrescent matter, but with utter darkness and into which so much of what I have once known is carefully crammed.

*　　*　　*

Now, here I am, in my torn stockings and with my bleeding hand, staring at my poor wife as she turns to me on the stairway and I read in her face some terrible calamity. "My dear!" I burst out, whipping from my pocket a plum-coloured silk handkerchief and fumblingly binding my hand with it. "Welcome to Bidnold! If you had given me a little warning, I would have made everything ready for you."

"I need no welcome," says Celia, and her voice is reedy, like the voice of an old dying crone. "The servants will show me to my room."

"Yes," I stammer, "or I will show you. It's to be the Marigold Room . . ."

My hand is bound now, but as I take hold of the banister rail and prepare to mount the stairs towards her, I see her recoil from me, as from some rearing viper. "Stay away!" she whispers, seemingly faint with revulsion. "Please stay away."

I stop at once and smile at her kindly. "Celia," I say, remembering her name at last, "you need have no fear of me whatsoever. I will never ask anything of you. All I wanted was to show you to your room, the colours and furnishings of which I hope may be of some comfort to you in whatever misfortune – "

"The servants will show me. Where is my woman, Sophia?"

"What?" I say.

"Where is my woman? Where is Sophia?"

"I have no idea. Did you bring her with you? She's your maid?"

"Yes. Call her please, Merivel."

I turn and look towards the front door. Two grooms are stumbling through it with a leather trunk, filled no doubt with ermine-trimmed bonnets and newt-skin shoes bought for his Dear One by my sometime master, the King. My mind is travelling in sudden sorrow towards a certain set of striped dinner napkins, now unused but kept folded in linen in an oaken chest, when I suddenly see Pearce, panting and wheezing like his late mule, arrive in my hall.

"Ah, Pearce." I say quickly. "Have you caught sight of a woman named Sophia?"

Pearce is blinking. His huge eyes, his prehensile nose and his long neck make him, on the instant, resemble a species of nocturnal tree-climbing animals I have seen described as mar-supials (a strange word).

"No," says Pearce. "What is occurring, Merivel? I scent some misfortune."

"Yes," I say, "misfortune there does seem to be. But for now we must find my wife's woman . . ."

"Your *wife* is come?"

"Yes. Here she is. Go out to her carriage please, Pearce, and tell her maid that her mistress calls."

Pearce is wiping his eyes on his threadbare cloak, the better to believe that the ghostly woman in black is indeed Celia Clemence, last glimpsed by him laughing merrily at her wedding. I am about to urge him outside once more when a buxom, ugly, dark-haired woman of perhaps thirty-five appears, carrying two or three dresses in her arms.

"Sophia," Celia calls hoarsely, "come up."

Sophia looks from Pearce to me, seems immediately affronted by the sight of us both and so goes swiftly up the stairs to where her mistress is reaching out her hand.

At my side, emerged from I know not where, I now find Will Gates.

"Will," I say with great urgency, "please conduct my wife and her woman to the Marigold Room."

"The Marigold Room, Sir?" whispers Will. "Might I suggest another?"

"No, you might not," I snap.

Will glares at me but nonetheless, like the matchless servant that he is, goes nimbly up the stairs past the two women and with his habitual unflowery courtesy leads them onwards and up. The grooms follow with the heavy trunks and boxes.

I did not see Celia again that day.

After supper, which I took alone with Pearce, I enquired of my cook whether orders had come down for food. I was told that some *bouillon* and a plum tartlet had been sent up.

"Was it eaten?" I asked.

"Either that," said my wall-eyed chef, Cattlebury, "or the dog had it."

"Dog?"

"Aye, Sir."

"What dog, Cattlebury?"

"Mr Gates, Sir, says they brought in a dog, a small Spaniel like the one as died on you, Sir Robert."

Ah, was my melancholy thought as I left the kitchen, the King is too cunning for us all! To those he knows he must one day abandon, he gives this sweet, living gift, just to be certain that our love for him remains with us (as if he could doubt that it would!) in case he may, at some future time, have need of us again. Poor Celia!

As I returned to my Study, where I had left Pearce reading some forgotten Latin text from my Padua days, I resolved that I must try, as soon as she would let me, to offer words of understanding and comfort, and in so doing perhaps find a little relief from my own despair. For there was no doubt in my mind now: the King had sent her away. She had played her part, just as I had once played mine, and now he had cast us off. I imagine him at dinner, his arm draped elegantly round Lady Castlemaine's white shoulders, the candlelight lending a seductive gloss to the little moustache he keeps so fastidiously trimmed. He leans towards Castlemaine, nibbles the emerald dangling from her ear. "What do you know of Norfolk, Barbara?" he whispers.

"Very little," she replies, "except that it is far from London!"

"Precisely!" smiles the King, "and therefore useful to me. It is there, you see, that I *envoie* all those I have begun to find tedious."

"Well," I said to Pearce, as I sat down in the Study, "I believe I know now for certain what has happened. What I greatly fear, however, is that Celia will believe her life is over. I really do not think she will ever be consoled."

Pearce (as is one of his irritating habits, detested by me since our student days) did not so much as glance up from his book when I finished speaking, but simply read on, as if I had not even entered the room. I waited. Sometimes I find Pearce so

deeply annoying that, were I the King, I would have bouts of
wanting to send him to Norfolk.

"Pearce," I said, "did you hear what I said?"

"No," said Pearce. "I didn't. I imagine it was some observation
on your wife's plight."

"Yes, it was."

"Well, I have nothing to add. Fools such as you have become
and courtesans such as she, once the whiplash of mirth or
passion has died, invariably feel the scourge of the whip itself."

I sighed. I opened my mouth to discourage Pearce from
further muddled metaphorical utterances of this kind when he
lifted the little book he'd been reading and brandished it in my
face.

"*This* is interesting!" he announced. "On the Cartesian question of spontaneous generation: 'For if generation of the lower
forms is not spontaneous, then *vermiculus unde venit*? Whence
the maggot?' "

I got up. "I'm sorry, Pearce," I said, my voice brittle and
cold, "but I do not feel able, after the troubles of this day, to
enter upon a discussion of maggots. I shall go and play my oboe
until bedtime."

With that I strode out and went to my Music Room. I shall
spare you an account of my struggles with my instrument that
evening and the quantity of anxious spittle with which reed after
reed was saturated. I shall report only that I wrestled with
simple scales for an hour or more, after which time my grazed
hand was giving me so much pain that I lay down on the floor of
the Music Room and put it between my thighs, with my knees
drawn up to my stomach, and in this childlike posture fell into a
troubled sleep.

When I awoke, very stiff and cold, with my hand swollen and
set into a premature *rigor mortis*, I saw from the grey light at
the window that the winter dawn was breaking over Norfolk,
County of Exiles. Despite my numbness and pain, I found myself,
on the instant of waking, filled with purpose and resolve. I must
go immediately to Celia. I must make her understand that,
stranger to her though I am, disagreeable though she may find
my physical self, I am occasionally a person of generous mind

and that – forswearing any hope of recompense or reward – I am content to be her protector and treat her with respect and kindness for as long as she remains at Bidnold.

I went up to my own chamber, where I changed my clothes and wig. None of the servants was yet stirring. By the handsome timepiece given to me by the King, I saw that it was a little before six. The embers of a fire were still glowing in my grate and I tried to warm my dead hand somewhat before setting out along the chilly corridors to the Marigold Room.

I stopped in front of Celia's door. I could hear a tiny, piteous sound, which I first took to be weeping, but then recognised all too foolishly well as the whimpering of a Spaniel. Minette, Minette, I thought. I grieve for you. You are buried in the park and the deer chomp the grass above you . . . But this was quite the wrong moment for self-pity, so I knocked with a firm and authorative hand (my left hand, the other one being now afflicted with a sudden intolerable pricking and tingling) and waited.

After a moment or two, an unfamiliar foreign-sounding voice, the voice of Sophia no doubt, called angrily: "Who is there?"

"Sir Robert," I replied, "I want to speak to Lady Merivel, please."

The dog was now scrabbling at the door. I believe the maid pushed it away roughly before she said: "My mistress is sleeping. Go, please, away."

"No." I said. "I will not go away. Please wake my wife. I have much that is important to say to her."

"No!" hissed Sophia. "My Lady is sleeping!"

"She may sleep later. I must speak to her now."

I was about to add that at this precise moment I was feeling a great deal of compassion for Celia but that such is the nature of mood and emotion that I could not guarantee, if forced to return at another time, to find within me the same degree of kindness, when the door was opened. The maid stood there in her nightgown and lace cap. I saw now that her skin was sallow and her upper lip uncommonly hairy. I decided she must be one of the large retinue of Portuguese women who had been shipped to England with Catherine of Braganza, many of whom had found themselves forced to serve outside their beloved Queen's

household and who, by the Whitehall gallants, were known
scathingly as "the Farthingales" after the peculiar hooped skirts
beneath which they concealed their stocky legs.

This Sophia gave me a look of the utmost loathing as I went
past her into the room. I shall be rid of you, Farthingale, I said
to her in my mind, for I am master here.

I must relate, however, that in the scene which followed (I
deliberately refer to it as a "scene", for the albeit unoriginal
notion that my life since my wedding has become something of
a farce does very often strike me as apt) I demonstrated all too
lamentably my lack of masterliness and found myself most
horribly insulted and abused. This is what happened:

I found Celia, not in bed as Farthingale had pretended, but
sitting on the orange and green cushions of the window seat,
fully dressed in her black garb, staring out at the dismal dawn.

I asked her if she had slept well and she replied that she had
not slept at all so hideous did she find the room, so vulgar, so
gaudy and tasteless. She could not, she said, imagine anyone –
except probably myself – being capable of finding any rest within
it.

Reminding myself that I should not become angry, I assured
her calmly that she was free to select another room whenever
she wished. I then asked her if I might sit down. She answered
that she would prefer me to remain standing.

By this time disconcerted by Celia's hostility, of which I truly
believed myself undeserving, I nevertheless began upon what I
had come to say. I told Celia that I of all people, who had briefly
known some affection from the King, understood exceedingly
well the quality, the measure of her sadness. I began to speak
of the terrible degree to which my being and my spirit, once
calm and content in its serving of God and the Trinity, was now
possessed by the King. I went so far as to say that I believed
there was no man or woman in the Kingdom (be they as pious
as my dead parents, be they Puritan or Quaker, be they lord or
lunatic) utterly free from and untouched by any longing to see
their own putrid lives lit up by his radiance. "Inevitably then," I
went on, "you and I, Celia, who have known something of the
man's love . . ."

"Love?" shrieked Celia. "What presumption, Merivel! What self-deception! How can you dare to speak of what the King felt for you as love! Not for one second, not for one mote of time did King Charles love you, Merivel. I advise you never again to use the word!"

"My only intention . . ." I began, but Celia, now standing and fixing upon my face her fearful eyes, refused to let me speak. She jabbed a small white finger towards my scarlet waistcoat as she yelled: "The truth is that the King, in his love for *me*, in his passion for *me*, made use of you. He used you, Merivel. He looked around for the stupidest man he could find, the densest, the most foolish, the one who would accept whatever he did like a dog and cause him no trouble – and he found you! I begged him, don't marry me to that idiot, I begged him on my knees, but all he did was laugh. 'Who can I ask,' he said, 'to be paid cuckold *except* an idiot?' Do you understand, Merivel? Dense as you are, do you comprehend what I'm saying?"

Well, I'm afraid I cannot go on with the scene. It is very painful, is it not? Of course I "comprehended", as she put it. I comprehended all too chillingly and although, in her rage and despair, she flung yet more insults at me, while the odious fat Farthingale looked on and smirked, I simply am not able to set them down.

I made no further attempt to offer my friendship to Celia, let alone enquire how the King's rejection of her had come about, but quietly withdrew from the room, shutting the door behind me before Farthingale could slam it in my face.

My first thought was: to whom, after this terrible revelation, shall I turn for comfort? To Pearce? To Will Gates? To Violet Bathurst? To Meg Storey? To my lost wench, Rosie Pierpoint? I felt a most terrible need of some kindly human company. But the hour was still early, my house dark, and I imagined them all sleeping: Pearce on his back with his white hands folded upon his ladle; Will Gates on his truckle bed dreaming of village girls; Violet enclosed by sumptuous brocade, safely absent from old Bathurst's brain; Meg in her attic, fallen asleep in her drawers and with beer upon her breath; sweet Rosie in Pierpoint's bed, stirring now to the murmur of the waking river . . . and I let them be.

I walked away from the Marigold Room to the west wing of the house and climbed the cold stone stairway to the circular room in the turret, whose discovery had given me so much joy. The room was still empty, still untouched. I went to each of the windows and looked out. A small slit of red in the sky hinted at sunrise. A white mist lay on the park, shrouding the deer.

I sat down under one of the windows. It will never be used now, this seemingly perfect room, I thought. At least, not by me. For it is surely the place which, though it aspires to do so, my mind can neither order nor understand. It is beyond my limit. I am earthbound, gross, ignorant. I will never reach to here.

It was of course Pearce to whom I eventually confided what had been said by Celia in the Marigold Room.

I had agreed to go with him upon a strange errand: to dig up a small quantity of earth from the village graveyard, from which Pearce intended to extract the saltpetre. He is suffering, among other afflictions, from a bladder stone and hopes to dissolve it in time by swallowing regular doses of this foul substance.

For the purposes of gathering the earth, he had taken with us a small spade and a leather bag. With some chivalry (Pearce still being weak from his arduous journey across the Fens) I offered to carry the spade and Pearce hung the bag about his long neck, thus giving himself more than ever the air of a mendicant.

We walked slowly down the drive and out onto the little road that leads to the village. Once we had gathered the earth, it was my intention to offer Pearce some refreshment at the Jovial Rushcutters, over which I could tell him what had been said to me. I found, however, that so slow was the pace of Pearce's walk that I was forced to prattle to keep myself from getting cold and thus had come out with my sad story long before we had reached the village, finishing it by hurling the spade away from me in a violent gesture of anguish.

Pearce looked at me. In his large eyes, I did detect a small glimmer of pity, but for some time, during which I retrieved the spade, he walked on in silence. I was just beginning to wonder whether I should embark on my tale again, this time making certain every few sentences that he was listening to me, when Pearce cleared his throat and said:

"It is my belief, all unfashionable as I know it to be, that all things, including lunacy, may be susceptible to cure."

"What?" I said.

"It has been believed since the beginning of time, that the mad are possessed of Devils and are thus filled with evil. This evil, it is universally agreed, must be beaten out of them by extreme chastisement, torture and all other conceivable kinds of cruelty . . ."

"Pearce," I said, "happy as I am to discuss your work at the New Bedlam at some later time I would ask you now to give your attention to my state of mind and – "

"I am giving my attention to your state of mind, Merivel. If you could, for once, listen to what I have to say instead of disregarding me, you will see that I have some helpful ideas on the subject."

We walked on. A pale sun now emerged from behind a bank of cloud and glimmered eerily upon us.

"Let me describe to you," Pearce went on, "a woman who was brought to me at the Whittlesea Hospital – for such is the name we have given to our Bedlam. This woman had been found half drowned in a ditch after wandering the shire for month upon month, year upon year, begging and shouting obscene words, mortifying her body, particularly her breasts and her arms with sharp hawthorn twigs. Her chief delight, in her poor suffering mind, was to defile. She kept her own excrement in a pouch, with which to smear the hands and fine clothes of those who gave her alms; with the same substance she daubed tombstones and churches. When we took her in, so terrible was her rage that, though I do not like to see this done, we were forced to chain her limbs to the wall. And for several weeks, she fought night and day with her chains, so that her wrists and ankles became running sores, no matter how carefully we bound them with cloth. Do you begin to form a picture of this woman, Merivel?"

"Yes, thank you, Pearce," I said.

"Very well. Let me recount to you then the morning upon which I went to this woman and found her quiet at last. She was sitting hunched in the corner, her limbs folded up and still. As I entered, she lifted her arm and pointed to two large turds she had recently voided onto the floor. I did not particularly wish to look at them, but her pointing was very insistent and the change in her demeanour so considerable that I did what she asked. And when I approached, I saw that writhing in and out of the greenish stools were two great worms, each several inches long, very white and loathsome. And then I looked again at the woman and she was weeping. And I unchained her and we took her away and washed her and put her in a clean bed. And from that day she was calm and talked with us of her home when she was a child and of the baby she had in her sister's care and we knew that she was cured. The worms had poisoned her blood and this poisoned blood had entered her brain. She was not wicked, Merivel. She was ill. Mercifully for her, her body at last discharged from itself the source of her illness."

"I am glad for her," I said flatly.

"And so to you, my dear friend. Now I shall tell you what I perceive has happened. You are possessed by one thought: you wish the King to draw you back to him and to love you. In the absence of this love, you are literally mad with grief. And in time this madness will work horribly in you, so that you will become, like the woman I've just spoken of, a defiler. True, you may not daub others with excrement, but you will daub them with hate. Unless you can come to see your ache for the King's favours as a morbid affliction of which you must rid yourself or die."

Pearce stopped on the road and reached out and placed his bony hands on my shoulders. I opened my mouth to speak, but he went on:

"What happened this morning, those harsh words that were spoken, I can only see as beneficial, Merivel. Do not stop me, but listen! In this knowledge, the knowledge that the King has never loved you, only used you, as I long suspected, lies the only hope of your cure. For this knowledge must be the beneficial evacuation of nature, the rank and putrefied stool which, foul as it is, carries out and away the far fouler source of poison and decay – the great worm of hope."

I stared at Pearce. I was unable to speak, so filled was I suddenly with belief in the rightness of what he had said. I could only nod my head and keep nodding it up and down, as if I were a stupid jester trying to jingle the bells on his hat.

SIX

THE KING'S DROPS

Some days passed, during which I felt a welcome calm settle upon my spirits.

When Pearce informed me he must return to Whittlesea, I thanked him – with precisely the kind of sentimental profusion he so scorns in me – for saving me, before it was too late, from becoming a veritable lunatic and earnestly begged him to visit me again at Bidnold as soon as his work permitted. He replied that he would pray for me and urged me meanwhile to return to my medical books, "in order," as he put it "to replace the world of acquisition with the world of knowledge". I had not the heart to tell him that I did not feel capable of doing this. "What I *can* promise you Pearce," I said, "is that my foolish expectation with regard to all matters Royal is dead. I do not expect, as long as I live, to see the King again. Where my future lies, I cannot tell. In my painting, perhaps?"

I report here that Pearce's opinion of my pictures was very little higher than Finn's, but he made no comment upon this last statement, only busied himself with gathering up his "burning coals" and placing them into a little tragic pile. In a sudden excess of affection for him, I offered to give him my horse, Danseuse, for his journey, but he refused, informing me that the mare was too strong and high-spirited for him and requesting me modestly to purchase a new mule for him.

One of my grooms was duly sent on this errand and returned

with a speckled, ungainly creature, "somewhat prone to bite, Sir Robert, but stout-hearted, Sir, for the long trek".

I did not tell Pearce about the biting and the mule was straight away saddled up. Pearce mounted and without further word to me, trotted off down the drive. Just as he reached the first bend, I saw the animal throw its head round and attempt to snap at Pearce's foot. Pearce answered this insult with a kick to the mule's flank and man and beast shot off at gallop, leaving behind them a small plume of dust, at which I stared until it settled.

Feeling chilly and in need of some refreshment, I asked Will to bring a jug of mulled wine to my Withdrawing Room, where I intended to pass an hour or two alone in thought. Somewhat to my consternation, I found Celia there, staring at my bird.

"Ah," I said, "I will not disturb you," beginning to turn and go from the room.

"What is the bird?" enquired Celia.

I hesitated. The notion that Celia, like Pearce, would slander the poor thing depressed me exceedingly.

"It was a gift to me," I said hesitantly. "I am told it is an Indian Nightingale."

"It is most beautiful," said Celia. "Only it does not sing."

Celia turned her face towards me then and I saw that it had regained some measure of its youthfulness and repose. It struck me, as it had never struck me hitherto, that she was indeed a very pretty woman.

"Well," I said. "It *does* sing. But it has to be encouraged. I could, if you wish, fetch my oboe and play a few notes to it and you might hear its very melodious trill."

"Pray, do." said Celia.

I shall now tell you that, in the preceding days, during which I had begun to regain some solace of mind, I had spent many hours alone in my Music Room doing battle with my instrument, as a result of which I was now able to play a little song upon it, entitled *Swans Do All A-Swimming Go*.

It was this then, after I had offered Celia a glass of mulled wine and she had, to my astonishment, accepted it, which I attempted to play for her and the bird. Like all beginners, I made a false start or two, but eventually succeeded in playing the piece quite jauntily. When I had finished, Celia, who had been watching me, turned away and put a hand up to her mouth, as if to hide a smile. I was not the least offended, because my efforts with these wretched *Swans* amused me greatly and, as I laid the oboe down, I burst out laughing. Celia now could no longer contain her mirth, and for a full minute we stood side by side and laughed and the bird opened its marigold beak and poured out at us a crystalline trill.

A most pleasant hour then ensued. Uninterrupted by the odious Farthingale, Celia and I drank the spiced wine and, with great dignity and courage, she asked me to forgive her for the insults of the morning in the Marigold Room. "The truth is," she said, "I believe we live in an age where many are made fools and many are deceived. I, in my faith in the King's love, am very probably as foolish as you. And yet I am convinced he will call me back to him."

"Celia," I began, "is it not better not to hope . . .?"

"I have no choice," she said, "I must hope or die. For to no other thing on earth do I give any value whatsoever. There *is* no other thing for me but this."

"Then with all my heart I shall pray that King Charles will send for you. But meanwhile – "

"Meanwhile, Merivel, accept my gratitude for this lodging. I shall spend much of my days alone, but I trust the times when we meet may be as cordial as this."

"Amen," I said.

"Merely, Merivel, do not expect me to be merry."

"I shall not."

"And I would ask you, now that Sophia and I are comfortable in the Rose Room, to let this be my *private* habitation. Never, if you will, come near it."

"Naturally, I would not . . ."

"Then we shall endure," she said "until a better time arrives."

She stood up to leave then. Emboldened by her honesty and courtesy, I asked her whether she would sup with me that evening. She hesitated only momentarily before replying that she would.

So overjoyed by this was I, that I descended at once to the kitchen. To Cattlebury's creative hands, I consigned a menu of eel tart, pigeon breasts stewed with madeira and Spanish plums, roasted quail with a salad of fennel, followed by egg pudding and boiled apples. Farthingale, I commanded, was to be served her supper upstairs.

She came flying down to Bidnold in her coach and the snorting and whinnying of her horses was to be heard far and wide. She entered my house in all her most magnificent finery with her head held high and proud, my Lady Bathurst with a great anger and lust upon her!

She demanded to see me. She was told I was at supper with my wife. She pushed past the servants and swept into the Dining Room, where Celia and I were at work upon the eel tart. She stared at us. She wore on her head a most admirable velvet cap, from which protruded upright two pheasant tails, a most peculiar but arresting fashion. I gazed at her.

She did not have to speak for me to understand the crime of which I stood accused. Since the arrival of Pearce, I had not once been to visit her or sent word to her. By now, the news that my wife had come would have reached her and she would have wrongly supposed this to be the cause of my neglect.

I must now tell you that Violet Bathurst's language, learnt I suspect from Bathurst and the hunting field, can turn at times most deliciously vulgar and I saw, even as Violet opened her mouth, that this would be one such time. Anxious that Celia be spared accusations that would distress her, I stood up, bowed and apologised to my wife, caught Violet by her angry wrist and pulled her peremptorily from the room.

Letting her fury rain down upon my head, I led her quickly to my Withdrawing Room, where I slammed my door behind us, took the wild struggling creature in my arms and kissed her with considerable force. Her body was hot and trembling and her rage seemed to have perfumed her skin with a scent so magnificently irresistible that in a matter of moments I had torn the pheasant tails from her head, lain her down upon the carpet from Chengchow, unbuttoned my breeches and entered her with more passion and haste than I had felt for any woman since my lost afternoons of Rosie Pierpoint. With each push of my loins, Violet swore at me, thus further exciting both herself and me, so that shrieking and foul-mouthing each other, we arrived together at our little moment of ecstasy and clung to each other, swooning and gasping as it passed.

We stood up at last. Violet had ceased her shrieking. I kissed her shoulder, swearing on the life of my sweet mother that I was not, nor would ever be, in the habit of touching my wife and promised to visit her the following evening and spend the night in her bed. At which time, I told her, I would explain my absence, which had been caused only by a visit from my friend Pearce, with whom I had had such grave discourse that all thoughts of pleasure had been dislodged from my mind.

I fastened the pheasant tail hat to her lovely head. She placed a very tender kiss on my flat nose and obediently left. I waited until I heard her coach clatter off into the night, and then returned to the Dining Room. The eel tart had been removed and the pigeons served. Celia sat upright and still, sipping her wine.

"I must apologise," I said, "for the unforeseeable interruption. Pray do begin upon your pigeons."

"Thank you," said Celia. "Your cook, at least, is exceedingly good. Tell me, Merivel, do you have mistresses?"

"Naturally," I replied, "I am a man of my time."

"And is that woman one of them?"

"She is. Her name is Lady Bathurst."

"And do you love her?"

"Ah," I said, "that word that finds itself so frequently upon our lips!"

"Well?"

"No, Celia. I do not love her. Now pray tell me how you find Cattlebury's madeira sauce?"

Celia replied that it was excellent. My unexpected exertions with Violet had given me a ravening hunger and I set upon several pigeons with somewhat unseemly attack. I was wiping my mouth in preparation for the quail when I heard the unmistakable sound of a horse cantering swiftly up the drive. Moments later, just as the quail were being put before us, the Dining

Room door was flung open once more and Will Gates came rushing in.

"A letter, Sir!" he said excitedly. "Come this very moment from London."

"Very well, Will. There's no need for such haste. Give it to me."

He put the letter into my hands. He looked at it and I looked at it. We both knew, by the unmistakable seal upon it, that what had arrived on this extraordinary night was a letter from the King.

It is in my possession still, this letter.

This is what it says.

Merivel,
To our deal Fool, we send greetings.

Pray be good enough to visit us in our Physic Garden at eight o'clock before noon tomorrow, Friday December the tenth in this the fourth year of our Reign, 1664.

This command comes from Your Only Sovereign and Loyal Servant of God,

Charles Rex

I rode through the night, taking Danseuse as far as Newmarket, changing horses there and again at Royston. Will Gates begged me to let him accompany me, fearful, I believe, that in my passion to reach London I would go flying into a ditch, there to die unmourned. But I refused. "The stars," I said, (succumbing, I know not why, to a fleeting attack of Pearceian romanticism), "will be my companions, and the very darkness itself!"

I had anticipated and indeed so it proved, that my spirit on this journey would be hurtling ahead of my body, causing me to shout at it in order to rein it in. It did not worry me if some poor cottar woke under his low eave to hear me singing or shrieking in the December night, but I preferred to undertake this noisy adventure alone, leaving Will to keep an eye on Farthingale lest, in my absence, she got intolerably above herself and began setting fire to my paintings, baiting my bird, playing my oboe, or I know not what.

As I set off, Celia was weeping. No doubt it pained her, nay, frightened her beyond measure that it was to me and not to her that the summons had come. She would, she said piteously, send some message with me, some plea, but knew not how to shape the words. And I could not linger for an instant, not even to finish my supper or powder my wig. "If I do not throw myself into the saddle at once," I told Celia, "I shall not reach London by morning, and you know as well as I that if I am not there at the hour appointed, His Majesty will not wait for me. As sternly as he commands loyalty from his subjects does he command punctuality. A betrayal of time he regards as a betrayal of faith. The first object that he ever showed me, Celia, was a clock."

And so I galloped away. Into my pockets I had thrust four or five quail to sustain me through the twelve hours of travel and at the moment of my departure, Will came running with a flask of Alicante, which I strapped to my saddle. "Farewell!" I shouted, but did not look behind. The road ahead mesmerised my being.

I entered London at seven o'clock. Over the river, unglimpsed by me for so long, rose the sluggish sun and mist streamed up off the water. I heard the swearing of the bargemen and the shouting of the lightermen, the cry of gulls and the ruffle of pigeons, and though my thighs ached and my rump was sore, I knew that my spirit was still strong.

See me, then, arrive at last at Whitehall. I have stopped at an inn to relieve myself and to drink some water, suffering suddenly from a terrible thirst. I have had the serving girl brush my breeches and wash my boots. I have shaken the dust from my wig and soaped my face and hands. I feel extraordinarily hot and as I enter the Physic Garden, I wonder if I am about to vaporise and disappear, leaving behind nothing more than a greasy puddle. Once again, as on that first most terrible visit, I feel that the near presence of the King has altered the air. "Lord God," I say, sending out one of my little bleeps of prayer, "help me to breathe."

I walk on between the neat hedges of box, smelling those herbs that outlast the winter, bay, rosemary, sage, lemon balm, thyme, and there, in the very middle of the garden, setting his watch by the sundial, I see him, the man who, if a hole were made in my breast such as the one I saw at Cambridge, I would beg to reach in and take hold of my heart.

I approach and remove my hat. I go down on my knees. I am choked and unable to speak. To my shame, I feel my eyes fill with tears. "Sir . . ." I manage to whisper.

"Ah. Merivel. Is it you?"

I raise my head. I do not want the King to see that I am crying, yet I know that in this instant he will see far more than this, that in my face he will be able to discern, with terrible precision, the degree of suffering which his neglect of me has caused.

"It is me. It is I, in fact, Sire . . ." I stammer.

He walks elegantly to where I'm kneeling, the harsh cinders of the path seeming to make wounds on my skin. He reaches out and touches my chin with his glove.

"And how is your game of tennis coming along?" he asks.

I feel, to my intense agony, a fat tear slide down my chin and moisten his glove.

"It would be coming along well, Sir, I'm sure," I say stupidly, "except that I do not have a tennis court at Bidnold."

"No tennis court? That is why you are getting fat, then, Merivel."

"No doubt it is. That and a greed of which I do not seem able to rid myself . . ."

It is at this moment that I realise that the pocket of my coat is terribly stained by the remnants of the quail, which I have forgotten to remove. I cover the pocket quickly with the plumes of my hat. The King laughs. To my intense delight, I feel his hand leave my chin and his long fingers travel upwards over my mouth, take hold of my flat nose and give it a vigorous tweak.

"Get up then," he says, "and come with us, Merivel. There is much to discuss."

He leads me, not to his State Rooms, but to his laboratory which, during my time at Whitehall, was a place that fascinated me and in which the King's restless mind was forever at work on new experiments, the most engrossing of which was the fixing of mercury. The smell in the place reminded me of the smell of Fabricius's own room at Padua where, on his night table, he was

fond of dissecting lizards. It had about it something of the smell of
the sewer or the tomb and yet my brain was invariably excited by
it. I suppose that, before I turned away from anatomy, I recognised it was the odour that accompanied discovery.

As we enter the laboratory, the King casts off his coat and
throws it down. His chemist is not at work yet so we are alone
in the room. I gather up his coat and hold it in my arms while
he strides along the tables looking and probing and sniffing. So
engrossed does he seem for a moment with the experiments in
progress, that I wonder if he has forgotten me. But after a few
moments he stops and picks up a phial of ruby-coloured liquid
and holds it to the light.

"Regard this," he says. "A purgative recently patented by
me."

"Excellent, Your Majesty," I say.

"Excellent it is. But it is no mere tedious physic, Merivel. It
has a property I did not foresee and which is both informative
and amusing. We call it the King's Drops. Presently, I shall put
some into a sip of wine for you. And we shall see what follows."

I say nothing. The King perches on a stool very near me and
stares up into my face.

"Time has altered you, Merivel," he says. "Some vital part
of you appears to be asleep."

I do not know what to say to this either.

"I see this same look in very many of my people, as if they
merely prefer to *be* and no longer to think. Put down my coat,
Merivel."

I lay the heavy brocaded coat aside, catching a fleeting whiff
of the sweet perfume with which even the King's gloves and
handkerchiefs are scented.

"Mercifully for England – perhaps mercifully for you, my dear
Fool – something has arrived on our shores which may rouse
us all from sleep."

"What may that be, Sir?"

"Plague, Merivel. Pestilence. At Deptford four people have
died. And it will spread. Some of us will be spared and some
will die. But all of us will awake."

"I heard no rumour of plague, Sir."

"No. But then you are at Bidnold. You are asleep in Norfolk. You are dreaming, Merivel!"

I am about to reply that indeed I have been dreaming of former times and wishing them with me again, when the King takes from his pocket a lace handkerchief and proceeds, with some tenderness, to wipe the moisture from my boiling face.

"Now," he says, having cleaned me up, "we must speak about Mistress Clemence, your wife. For this reason I have summoned you, Merivel. From my knowledge of your character – and I hope I am not mistaken in this – I believe you to be, like your father before you, a man who clearly understands and accepts the station to which chance and favour, no less than his own deserving, have brought him and does not diminish himself by lusting after what he cannot have. Much has been given to you, Merivel, has it not?"

"Yes, Your Majesty."

"And you do not, even indolent as I fear you have become, drive your brain to despair by wishing for more, *n'est-ce pas*?"

"No . . ."

"Or do you? Is it a Dukedom you want of me now?"

"No, no. On my honour."

"Good. Look at that toad, by the way, the thing in the bell jar. Will you help me to dissect it later?"

I look to where the King is pointing and I see an awesomely large bull toad, stiffened and bloated by death.

"If you wish me to, Sir," I say.

"Yes, I wish you to. Now, listen well, Robert. When I married Celia to you, it was to hide her, so to speak, from the very intelligent gaze of Lady Castlemaine, the better to find her again myself and sport with her unobserved."

"This I know, my Liege."

"Very well. You may imagine then my dismay, my fury nay, when I hear from the lips of your wife the command to end my liaison with Castlemaine, likewise to terminate my amours with certain actresses from the Playhouse, and keep her as my only woman, outside the bed of my good Queen. Naturally, I did not answer her one single word, for no subject on earth may command me thus. I merely gave instructions that she was to vacate her house at Kew and all her possessions save her dresses and jewellery and ride at once to you, where she must remain until the folly of her importunate conduct burns shame into her skull!"

The King gets up off his stool and begins once again to walk up and down, poking and prying at his chemical compounds. I see his cheek twitching, a tick of nature caused only and always by anger. I remain silent, only nodding. After a moment or two, the King picks up a large pestle and, using this for emphasis, continues thus:

"Yet, alas, Merivel, I miss her! Though I would whip the silly girl, the grosser part of me is uncommonly sensible to her absence. What a plight! My reason tells me to abandon her for ever, but this, the Royal tool, is waving about in search of her. And life is brief, Merivel. We should go to pleasure, as to all things, with energy and will, a gift you once had even to excess, if I recall."

"And still would, Sir, if my mind – "

"Then go to this one task with a will for me. Impress upon Celia the folly of her demands. Remind her of my fondness for order and rank and my loathing for those who get above themselves. Teach her to be content with what she has, for what she has is much, and bid her never to hope for more. Tell her then to come to me in humility and she may have it all again, her house, her servants, her money and the King in her bed from time to time."

Disliking my role as messenger, I am about to say to the King that I have had very little in the way of conversation with Celia and fear that her dislike of me may hamper my attempts to pass on his wisdom, when the King grabs my hand and declares: "Enough of that. I leave it in your hands. Now come, Merivel, I shall now pour you a cup of wine and, into the wine, we shall put one or two of my Drops!"

His anger has vanished as swiftly as it came on. He chuckles as he pours and measures. I watch his hands, then his smile, which is so beloved to me. I have a sudden belief that whatever is in this cordial, the King intends me no harm.

I drink down the draught. The King is amused and delighted and slaps his thigh.

"Good!" he says. "Now we shall start work upon the toad."

It would be vain to remind King Charles, I decide, that very many months have passed since I held a scalpel or a cannula in my hands and that, by an act of will, I have consigned my dissecting skills to oblivion. I sense also, that he is eager to anatomise the toad himself, demonstrating to me the deftness of his long fingers, the neatness and care of his work. So I say nothing, as the toad is taken out of the bell jar and laid upon the tray and His Majesty rolls up his sleeves. I merely watch and, as I do so, I find myself unaccountably invaded by an intense happiness, such as I have not known since the far-off days of Rosie Pierpoint, of tennis lessons, of games of Rummy, of the gift of dinner napkins.

The King cuts, flays and pins the whitish skin of the toad's belly.

"The gut," he says as he makes his first incision in the flesh, "has a jewelled sheen to it, as we shall see . . ."

Careful as he is, the intestines spill out, so that their precise arrangement is lost to us. Across time, the voice of Fabricius snarls in my ear, "Do not tangle with the bowel, Merivel! You are not a Laocöon!"

"Ah!" says the King. "See the colour?"

I am staring at the toad's intestines and I am aware that the soft coils have a silvery patina. But I am a little distracted, for the word "colour" has reminded me suddenly of my attempts at painting and the frenzy of mind that seems to accompany them, and without really intending to, I begin to tell the King of my desire to paint, to capture the essence of people and nature, "before they dissolve or change, you see, Sir, for everything on earth, or so it seems to me, is in a state of perpetual motion, even inanimate objects, for the light upon them changes, or the eye with which we beheld them yesterday is today re-shaping what it sees . . ."

I babble on. The King does not speak, but works methodically, unhurriedly at his dissection until all – heart and lungs and spleen and windpipe and sperm sacs – is laid out before us. I speak about my painting of my park and Finn's loathing of it. I try to describe the painting but hear myself, as if my voice is no longer mine, as if it belonged to Pearce's worm-filled lunatic, describe instead the feelings that drove me to painting: my terrible fear that the King had abandoned me, no longer loved me or found any need of my company. "I was your Fool," I hear myself wailing, "and however serious may be the business of government, do not tell me that the King has no need of laughter!"

I am crying again. Tears are coursing down my face and onto the toad on the tray, over which, finding myself now tired to my very marrow, my body has slumped.

I see the King's hands put down his instruments. He picks up a cloth and wipes blood and viscera off his fingers. And then I lose him. I do not know what happened except that I hear myself talking on and on, to the King I believe, who is no longer near me but in the shadowy laboratory somewhere, moving up and down as he always does, restless and tall and never still . . . but he is not there. I am alone in the place. He has gone out into the sunlight and I am lying down in the dark, under the oak work bench. I am getting into my grave.

I am woken by an elderly man, wearing the garb of an apothecary. I am parched. The old man understands this and gives me cool, sweet-tasting water in a beaker.

Food is brought to me. I am seated at a little table. I eat some bread. A liveried servant hands me a letter.

I am in the Physic Garden. The sky above me is bright. I break the seal of my letter.

Poor Merivel, (says the letter) *I did not warn you, the King's Drops alchemise secrets into words. And yet you have told me nothing. For everything you revealed, I saw in your face. Beware, however, that love does not turn into need. And so Godspeed with your mission to Celia. I would have her think upon our displeasure for the duration of two months, after which time, she may, if in humble spirit, return to Kew, where we shall come to her.*
                    Signed, Charles Rex

I look over to the sundial. What I wish to say to the King is, "Let me make my entrance again. Let me arrive again, knowing what I know about the Drops." But of course he is no longer there.

SEVEN

WATER

I did not linger at Whitehall.

Though greeted warmly by a posse of gallants in whose chambers I once played at cards, forfeits and music-making, I found I was in no mood for their company. My head ached intolerably and the thoughts fashioned by my brain seemed to have the quality of dreams. I had a terrible longing to lie down, not necessarily to sleep, but simply to rest my brain. Fain would I have gone to that first chamber of mine, where I had performed my cure-of-neglect upon Lou-Lou, and put on a clean nightcap and lain upon the soft pillows and listened to the great orchestra of the river.

Dinnertime found me at the Leg Tavern where I drank a good quantity of ale to slake the thirst that still burned in my stomach, and then slept an hour on one of its hard settles. I was hungry when I woke and was served a most peculiar meal, a turnover of starlings and a pig's trotter pickled in olives. "Starlings," said the pretty wench who served me, "having blackish flesh and strong-tasting, cure all men of mopish humours," and it is true that, when I had eaten, I felt my thoughts to be more sensible. Either the starlings had worked some humoural change upon me, or merely the potent effect of the King's Drops was now at last abating.

When I emerged from the Leg, I found the street burnished with most beautiful winter sunlight. I am very susceptible to weather. In a Norfolk wind, I sometimes feel my sanity flying away. My good spirits replenished, then, by the starling turnover and the afternoon sun, I decided to make my way to the house of Rosie Pierpoint. To supplement Pierpoint's meagre wage as a bargeman, Rosie had set herself up, in 1661, as a laundress, and it was among her crimping irons and her vats of starch and her great coal-burning stove that I hoped to find her. If I could not persuade her to let me touch her Thing, I would content myself with watching the sunset from her window while she washed my shirt and removed the quail stains from my coat pocket.

She was at home and hard at work. So great was the heat in the workroom, she was stripped down to her bodice and her soft arms were moist and pink – a pink so very pretty that I would dearly love to arrive at the precise colour on my palette. Even as I approached Rosie and she rested her flat iron on the stove top and we embraced each other with a good deal of joy, I remembered seeing, in some great painting, a cherub the colour of Rosie's arms and fell to wondering how, in his winged existence, the little fellow had got so hot.

What followed was most sweet and delectable, reminding me that there is scarcely any more agreeable thing on earth than the meeting of parted lovers. To the ease of mind engendered by this Act of Forgetting is added the balm of pleasant memory. As the brain banishes its ever-present consciousness of death, so the body finds itself enraptured by rediscovery. It is not, I think, fanciful to say that such meetings are both Acts of Oblivion and Acts of Remembrance.

I stayed with Rosie until the sun went down. We lay on a rumpled pile of soiled sheets, shirts, petticoats, lace collars and table cloths and on this dirty linen made a very fine feast of each other, a feast of which, if I live to be an old man, I may well, in my clean and lonely bed, find myself dreaming.

We got up at last and Rosie lit two rushlights and by the light of these would work on at her ironing table till Pierpoint came home and they had their supper of whelks and oysters and bread and ale.

And I made my way to Hydes Wharf at Southwark where I hired a tilt-boat and asked the tilt-man, who had a foxy and mischievous face, to paddle me to Kew.

"Kew is a fairish way," this tilt-man said, "and it will be black pitch night 'fore we get to there, Sir."

"I know," I replied, "but my day and the best part of last night both put me into a lather of heat and I have a great mind to feel the cool of the river."

"How shall we keep the channel, Sir, in the dark, and not stray onto shallows or be splintered to pieces by a lighter or a barge?"

"There is a three-quarter moon," I pointed out, "and no cloud. We shall see our way tolerably well."

"We shall be as cold as corpses by the time we get there!"

It was plain to me by now that Fox (as I christened the tilt-man) had no desire to take me on this journey, but, remembering that in this new age most things can be had by bribery, I offered to double his fare from two shillings to four. I settled myself comfortably under the little canopy, and we embarked on the evening tide.

Why did I wish to go to Kew? Now that the effects of the Drops had worn off entirely and I was once again capable of rational thought, I knew that I must give some attention to what the King had told me concerning Celia. For reasons which I could not completely comprehend, I felt exceedingly uncomfortable with the message I was instructed to convey. Something within me wished, for the first time in my life, to disobey the King. Why? I really did not know. Far from purging me of all hope, the event of the morning had proved to me that the King's affection for me still endured. What he had said of Celia, however, his hand gesturing with the pestle, seemed designed to convey to me that, beyond mere lust, he had no feelings for my wife at all, and that his restless spirit would very soon tire of her. In going to Kew, then, in hoping to see (all shuttered and dark as I knew it would be) the house he had given her, I believe I had it in mind to try to measure his love for her and, according to how the scales tilted, decide upon the message I would take home to Bidnold. The notion that one is able to guage the quality of one person's love for another by a moonlit glimpse of a house got from a tilt-boat is, I freely admit, preposterous. And yet there is no other explanation for the journey my heart was suddenly so determined upon. Did the King love Celia, or did he not? In the company of Fox and with a light breeze ruffling my jabot and cooling my overheated face, I believed myself to be gliding towards my answer.

Fox, once settled to the task, rowed strongly and well. Binding some threadbare cloth about his neck to protect his scrawny gizzard from the coming night, he pushed me onwards, past the Temple and its arched gate, then on past the crammed acre of Whitehall where in almost every room and chamber lights appeared to be burning and my ears caught for one fleeting moment the sound of an oboe.

By Whitehall and beyond, the river, even at this evening hour, was still noisy, the quantity of small boats making the water slap against the landing steps and the gruff shouts of "Next oars!" from the bargemen putting me in mind of the barkings of a drill sergeant trying to marshal into some semblance of a line a disorderly platoon of fops.

Past Westminster, as the Thames took a southerly turn, it quietened and on our left side I saw begin the dark mass of Vauxhall Woods, where, as an angelic child in my little moiré suit, my parents liked to take me on picnics and rambles. "If you are quiet, Robert," I remember my father whispering, "we shall presently come upon a family of badgers." But I fear that I was never quiet enough, for I do not recall ever seeing a badger in my life until one was brought to the dissecting laboratory at Caius and I saw at last the clownish markings of the animal, by which my father had been so touched.

"Tell me," I said to Fox, "are there still badgers in these woods?"

"Yes, Sir," answered Fox, "I heard tell you can see them there. If you are quiet."

I said nothing to this but, as we glided on towards Chelsea, I fell to wondering why I am so attached to noise. Even discordant noise (my own singing and my first disasters with *Swans Do All A-Swimming Go*) and noise that lacks meaning (the mad discourse of old Bathurst) creates in me a most definite gladness of heart and though, as a student of medicine, I knew silence to be essential to study, there were many days and nights where

I suffered within it. When I die, I would like to be laid to rest by a skipping troupe of Morris dancers.

The moon was up now and fattish and by its light we rounded the bend to Chiswick Meadows. Not far from Kew, I turned to Fox and enquired of this old river-rat: "They say the King keeps a mistress at Kew and is sometimes seen by you watermen skulling upriver to visit her. Is there any truth in this story?"

Fox spat into the water.

"I saw him once," he said.

"Can you be certain that it was he?"

"Certain."

"How might you be able to tell?"

Fox spat again. Perhaps he was a Puritan and a Commonwealth man?

"It were morning," he continued, "before dawn even come and nothing much moving on the river. I, Sir, I were taking cherries from Surrey to vendors at Blackfriars. Half light it were. Four o'clock in summer. And I saw this thin skiff coming on with a man very tall in it and his cloak cast aside and in this fine golden coat, and I says out loud, 'That's one man in the Kingdom and one only!'"

"Did you wait and watch? Did you see where he tied up?"

"More than that, Sir. I sold him some cherries."

"You did? So you saw his face close to, and it was he?"

"He all right. Gave me a penny for the fruit from a little jewelled purse."

"And you saw him land?"

"Yes."

"Could you show me the place?"

"Not in this dark, Sir."

I cleared my throat. "My excellent man," I said. "As I predicted, it is not dark at all, with that large moon up."

"Darkish, Sir."

"Nevertheless, please try, if you will, to remember the place and point it out to me."

We glided on. My face, that had burned for so many hours, was cool now and my hands were beginning to feel a trifle numb. Cold as I was, I felt inside me the heat of trepidation and anxiety.

At any moment, I would see Celia's house. And then, as we turned and headed back against the wind and the tide, I would have to make up my mind . . .

I instructed Fox to steer the boat towards the north bank and to slow it. I offered to take the oars while he concentrated upon his task of remembering, but he would not entrust me (quite reasonably) with so precious a piece of his livelihood, informing me instead that he could row from here to Spitalfields blindfolded, and in so doing utterly negating his badinage about lost channels and collisions with lighters with which he had wheedled from me two poxy shillings. Dependent upon him as I was, however, I could not afford to show any anger. We crept forward in silence, turning once and retracing our route along some thirty or forty yards of bank and then going on further till at last Fox spied, in the cold, glimmering light, a small wooden jetty with steps leading up to it from the water.

"There's the place," he said, "that's she."

"Ah," I said, "but there's no house."

Fox shrugged. "It's there," he said.

I had him tie up to the jetty. With some difficulty, I clambered out of the small boat (now earning its name by tilting riotously the moment I stood up) and made my way along the landing stage. A pretty iron gate guarded a narrow path running between squat bushes I took to be hazels and hawthorns. At this moment, the moon disappeared behind a cloud, plunging me suddenly into blackness. I stood still, waiting for the moon to reappear. Though behind me I could still hear the slapping of the water, I had the illusion, for a moment or two, of having lost my way.

I walked cautiously on, aware of the night around me, some scuffling animal in the dead leaves, a night bird putting forth a little stuttering cry.

And then I heard music.

Moments later, as the clouds once again uncovered the moon, I found myself in a small knot garden and before me stood the house. It was not grand or large. Its principal rooms seemed, from the size of the windows, to be modest. It is, I thought on the instant, the kind of small house I would give my daughter, were I to have one. But I could not dwell long in my mind on its size, because it was clear to me now that one of the rooms, from which came the sound of a harpsichord and a flute, was full of people. Lamps and candelabra had been lit. On the window seat, a man lolled with his arm round some pretty wench's neck. A musical supper appeared to be in full swing. As I stood and breathed and tried to warm my hands by rubbing them together, I heard a sudden flight of laughter.

All the way back to Lambeth (where I intended to lodge for the night at an inn called the Old House) I pestered Fox, telling him he must have been mistaken. "Either," I said, "it was not the King whom you saw or else he did not tie up at that jetty." But his rodent features were hard and set, as was his mind, he informed me. He vividly recalled the ease and grace with which the King tied up his skiff and climbed out of it ("as if he had been a very waterman, Sir") and he insisted that there was no similar small jetty for another half mile upstream or more.

At the Old House I dined well and fell into conversation about the art of marble cutting with a likeable fellow from the Navy Office who recounted to me that the marble-cutter's life hangs in its entirety upon patience, for though the mass of stone that confronts him may be as large as a four-poster, he can, with his little tool, cut a mere four inches a day.

Pondering such steadfastness and perseverance and wondering if I would ever be capable of it in regard to my painting, I all of a sudden remembered, with a surge of bile to my stomach, my pledge to Violet Bathurst to spend this very night in her bed.

I had a dream of a drowned body. I was at Granchester Meadows with Pearce and a group of medical students and we sat on the banks of the weedy Cam and we saw this lumpen corpse come floating towards us. We had but one thought: we must retrieve the body for our anatomical studies. We took off our coats and lay on our stomachs and reached out and took hold of the swollen limbs. And then I perceived that the body was Celia's. Her hair streamed among the waterweed and her mouth was blueish and open, like the mouth of a fish. I was about to cry out to my

fellow students to let go of her arms and legs when I woke. I
was shivering and my throat was sore and my nose full of mucus
and my thirst had returned.

I lit a candle and stumbled to the wash-stand in the unfamiliar
room in the Old House and gulped some water and then got into
the bed and tried to warm myself, but the dream of drowned
Celia frightened me so much that I was afraid to sleep again in
case it returned to me, as dreams are in the terrible habit of
doing.

"God is the engineer of all dreaming," Pearce once announced
to me. "He fills the sleeping mind with all we have neglected."
"Tosh, Pearce!" I said at the time. "For the great part of my
dreams are about food. My nights are pleasantly filled with rabbit
fricassées, venison pasties and chocolate syllabubs, none of
which I have in the least neglected." If I remember rightly,
Pearce then made some acidic rejoinder about God giving me a
vision of my own gluttony, which I utterly ignored, but now the
idea that this dream of drowning had been "sent" to me seemed
entirely plausible. For, so confused and dismayed had I been by
the sight of Celia's house filled with people and music (indeed
as if the poor girl was dead and all memory of her drowned) that
I had "neglected" to decide what I was going to tell her and in
my conversation about the marble cutter had managed to put all
thought of her from my mind.

So I lay and shivered and nursed the ague that had come upon
me so suddenly and tried to weigh the whole matter in my mind
without consideration for myself and in a detached and proper
manner, as if Celia were my patient and I not I, but some
wise Fabricius, some unparalleled physician utterly un-prone to
error.

By the time dawn broke and I permitted my snivelling self an
hour of soothing sleep, I had come to the following decisions:

I would return to Celia and inform her that the King appeared
to have forgotten her, that it was rumoured some new mistress
had taken up residence at Kew, that he had expressed very
forcefully to me his displeasure about her importunate behaviour
but had not given me to believe that he would ever summon her
back. I would then counsel her – exactly as Pearce had counselled

me – about the folly of hope. "If," I would say to her "you permit yourself to hope, you will come to insanity, Celia, and then I cannot tell what will become of you. Perchance you may come to poor Ophelia's end, drowned in a stream." I would explain to her that I had at last understood of what element the King was fashioned: "He is mercury," I would say. "He is of that same metal he spends hour after hour in his laboratory trying to extract from his flasks of cinnabar, but which is ever elusive and restless and cannot be fixed and held. And how will it profit any man or woman to love mercury?"

What I could not foresee was how I was to find any remedy for Celia's grief. I knew myself inadequate to the task. I was not Fabricius. I was not even Pearce. I had no wisdom.

This ague of mine, got not doubt from the extremes of heat and cold through which not only my body but my mind had passed in the preceding night and day, forced me to remain in my truckle bed at the Old House for an entire week.

When my fever worsened and I began to detect in my groin and in my neck some slight swelling, terror filled my heart. Plague was coming and where might it arrive more swiftly than to the malodorous Lambeth marshes? For more than fifty hours I imagined myself dying. I wept and cried out. I beseeched my poor burned mother to intercede with God for me, knowing my own prayers to be unheard. "Dear parents," I heard myself say in my delirium, "make God the gift of a hat. He is fond of plumes. Give Him a fine hat in exchange for my life!" I ranted and blubbed. My cowardice was as infinite as a well sunk from Norfolk to Chengchow.

Then on the third day, my fever lessened and my swellings began to go down. To the poor serving woman who brought me broth, I declared that I had been resurrected, which statement she read as an out-and-out blasphemy and quickly made the sign of the cross upon her bosom.

Still somewhat weak from my illness I took a stage coach to Newmarket, where I spent the night. At dawn the following morning, I was reunited with Danseuse and gratified by the little whinny of delight with which the mare greeted me. I am most fond of animals. I enjoy about them, in equal measure, that which is graceful and that which is gross. And they do not scheme. No man, woman or child exists in this boisterous Kingdom who is not full of plotting, yet the animals and the birds have not one good ploy between them. It is for this reason above all others, I suspect, that the King is so attached to his dogs.

Danseuse galloped home like a chariot horse, her spirits far out-distancing mine on this return journey. Though I clung to the reins and pressed my knees ardently to her sides, she unseated me near Flixton and as I lay winded in a ditch I suddenly perceived, not far from me, an old wrinkled woman lifting her hessian skirts and pissing onto the brambles. It amused me and I would have bid her good-day, except that I had no breath within me.

I struggled upright at last and remounted Danseuse, who was foraging for grass in the frosty lane. I tried to persuade her to trot sedately for a while, but she would not and we arrived at last at Bidnold in an unseemly sweat.

My clothes being frankly filthy and full of stench, I was in no mind to talk to Celia until I had soaked for some hours in a hot bath and put on clean linen. I called at once for Will (who reminds me sometimes of a small, nimble animal in his unquestioning loyalty to me) and within a short time I lay at my ease in a tub, regarding the moths on my stomach, while Will poured more and more hot water round me and I told him of my stay at the Old House and how Death had come into the room and laid an icy hand on me and caused me to snivel like a baby.

"If plague does come to Norfolk," I said to Will, "I shall try to show courage, but I am bitterly afraid it will be the false courage of a desperate man and not the true bravery of one whose mind and spirit are at peace."

Will shook his head, about to flatter me, no doubt, with his erroneous belief that when the hour approached I would conduct myself like a Parfit Gentil Knight, but before he could speak we heard suddenly the most lovely sound of a viola da gamba, coming, it seemed, from beneath us in my Music Room.

I sat up, causing a small tidal wave to splash over the rim of the tub. "Will," I said, "who is playing?"

"Ah," said Will, "I was about to inform you, Sir Robert: your wife's father is come."

"Sir Joshua?"

"Yes, Sir."

"Sir Joshua has come to Bidnold. But why, Will?"

"I do not really know, Sir, except or unless it be to take your wife home."

"Take her *home*?"

"Yes."

"You heard that mentioned?"

"Yes, I did, Sir. That as soon as you were returned, they would leave."

The music continued. I began vigorously to soap my body. I heard myself say to Will very tetchily that I would not permit Sir Joshua to take my wife away, that the King had commanded that she reside with me and that, besides, I had much to discuss with her.

Will gaped at me, being surprised, I dare say, at my apparent strength of feeling upon a subject to which he believed me to be utterly indifferent.

EIGHT

A GIFT OF INSTRUMENTS

Bathed and scented, with a clean wig concealing my hog's bristles and a blue silk coat upon my back, I descended my stairs. As I did so, the sound of the viola ceased and I became aware – as so often in the wake of pleasant music – of the degree to which my mind is lightened by it, as if it gave to the dark mass of my brain a momentary sheen such as I had perceived upon the viscera of the King's toad.

A moment later, Sir Joshua recommenced his playing. This time, it was a song I had heard long ago at Cambridge, entitled *I Lay Me Down in a Wood of Elm*, a most sweet tune but with the scansion a little strained, there not being a great abundance of words that rhyme with "elm". I stood in my hallway and listened as an exquisitely high and beautiful voice began to sing. It was Celia's voice, which I had never until this moment heard, but which I now knew to be a soprano of astonishing purity. A cold shiver of delight ran through me. More than her white skin, more than her languid, silky hair, more than her small mouth or her firm breasts, it was surely this *voice* of hers which had so charmed and seduced the King. Compared to it, her person was nothing, pretty enough, womanly enough, but giving no hint that concealed within it lay a matchless sound. I sat down on a tapestry-covered stool and fell to considering the probability that every one of us conceals some secret talent, though what mine may be I was not yet able to determine. Pearce's, despite his harsh criticisms of the world and most things within it, was a talent for kindness. Violet's, I was tempted to suggest, was anger, for I knew of no other person in whom rage was more delicious or becoming. And the King's? Well, he was a person of a thousand talents, but whether there was yet one more that he kept secret from us all, only time will reveal.

The song continued. "Celia, Celia," I wanted to ask, "why did no one tell me how exquisitely you sing?" And a vision of myself, suddenly skilled upon my oboe, playing enraptured while my wife sang, momentarily filled my mind. How different, how ordered and knowable life would be, if it could be arranged around a simple duet! As it was, I knew that the moment I entered the Music Room Celia would stop singing. I could play no part whatsoever in her music and by tonight she would be gone to her parents' house and Bidnold would be utterly silent, except for the occasional trilling of my Indian Nightingale. I took out of my pocket an emerald-coloured handkerchief and blew my nose, still intermittently blocked with mucus. I felt myself once again excluded from something to which I desired to contribute – however negligible my contribution might be. There is, I said to myself, as I stowed away my handkerchief, a degree of sadness in this observation.

I stood up. As soon as Celia knew of my return, she would press me for news of her situation and the moment was approaching when I would have to say what I had planned, thus smothering in her heart the small ember of hope which Pearce had led me to recognise as so fearful a thing. But as I walked towards the Music Room, I knew that I had faltered: I could not utter the words I had decided upon. For I knew beyond question that if I said them Celia's indifference towards me would turn again to loathing. As Cleopatra whipped the bearers of bad tidings, so Celia would flay me with her scorn and hatred. I, who was nothing to her, would become less than nothing. She would leave my house for ever and the whole magnificent story that the King had set in train would have reached an ending, long before its proper course had been run. And besides . . . ah, dangerous consideration! . . . I did not want to relinquish Celia's voice. So there you have it. At whatever cost to Celia's sanity and mine, I had become determined to keep her with me under my roof, at least for the two months decreed by the King.

So it was then that I entered the room and the music ceased abruptly, as I predicted it would, and Celia turned upon me a gaze full of astonishment and hope and Sir Joshua put down his instrument and held out his hand most cordially to me. I bowed to them both. "I am returned, as you can see," I said superfluously, and then began to compliment them upon their musical talents. Celia was not, of course, in the least interested in my opinion of her singing, but urged me to tell her at once what message I had brought from London. I remained calm in the face of her anxiety and impatience. I offered her my arm.

"If," I said, "you would do me the honour of taking a turn with me in the garden, I will inform you of all that has passed."

Celia cast a look of anguish at her father, but he nodded and so without more ado she laid her white hand on my sleeve and we walked to the hall, where I imperiously summoned Farthingale to go running for a cloak for her mistress.

The day was cold and the sun already a little low in the sky. The shadows cast by Celia and me were long, thus elongating me a great deal, so that had you but glimpsed us on the flat stones, you would have mistaken us for a very elegant couple.

After some moments, during which I rehearsed in my mind what I was about to say, I conveyed to Celia the following fiction, which I had invented on the spot, but by which I found myself to be agreeably impressed. "The King," I said, "would give no promise whatsoever with regard to you. He asks, simply, that you remain here – here at Bidnold and nowhere else – until what he termed 'an awareness of the changeful nature of all things' has grown upon you."

Celia stared at me, utterly disbelieving. "'The changeful nature of all things'? And why would he have me learn that, pray?"

"I cannot say, Celia," I replied. "All His Majesty would say was that he wished you to learn it, but believed it would take time, it being the case that the more youthful a person is, the harder it may be for such understanding to take root."

"And yet," retorted Celia, "has he not, in his cruel repudiation of me, made certain that I have had such an awareness harshly thrust upon me?"

"Indeed," I ventured, "but he is a great deal wiser than you or I, Celia, wise enough to know that, though there is always some learning in times of misfortune or loss, it is only through quiet reflection after the event has passed that we can put such learning to good use."

"But how long is such 'quiet reflection' to last? Am I to grow old in 'quiet reflection' and see my beauty vanish and all that once pleased him come to decay?"

"No. I'm sure he does not intend that."

"Then will it be weeks, months . . . ?"

"He would not tell me, Celia."

"Why? *Why* would he not tell you?"

"Because he cannot say. He has put the matter into your hands and into mine."

"Into yours?"

"Yes. For I am to be the one to tell him – in his own words – 'When she has fitted her mind with wisdom and put from her all illusion.'"

"So!" and at this moment Celia pulled her hand roughly from my arm, "*You* are to be Judge! The King sends his Fool to decide on a matter of learning! May he forgive me, Merivel, but this does not strike me as just."

"No. Undoubtedly not. And yet I perceive a kind of justice in it. For I am not, as some other protector might be, enamoured of my role, in that I do not consider myself to be worthy of it. Thus, it is in my interest that you embark upon this journey of learning as quickly as possible, Celia, so that I may return to my life of foolishness, you to your house in Kew and the King to your bed."

"But how am I to come by this wisdom? By what means am I to 'embark'?"

"I do not know. Unless through your one peerless gift – through your singing."

"Through my singing?"

"Yes."

"How so?"

"I do not know. I can only guess that this must be your route. In my mediocre way, I am arriving at some understanding of myself and the world through my efforts at painting and I venture to suggest that if you sing, say, of love or betrayal, or I know not what, you will learn not only something of these things, but also of the infinite ways by which men and women deceive themselves and the ruses they employ to make themselves master of another's destiny. And so your journey will already have begun . . .'

Celia did not look at all cheered by my suggestion. She drew her cloak around her and shook her head and her eyes filled with tears.

"If he had asked of me any practical thing, I would have done it," she said, "but how can I obey a command I do not fully understand? How will I ever obey it?"

"I do not know," I said for the third or fourth time. "I am certain, however, that you shall find a way, through music. And I will do all I can to help you."

That evening, Celia and Farthingale not deigning to stir from the Rose Room, I dined alone with Sir Joshua Clemence, a man who continues to treat me with great civility and for whom I have infinite respect. To my delight, he told me that the decorations at Bidnold amused him and that, though he did not find them restful, they indicated to him that I possessed "a most boisterous originality of mind and this in an age of slavish imitation and apishness".

He then, over a most flavoursome carbonado of pig produced by Cattlebury, broached the subject of his daughter, informing me (as if I did not know it already) that, having given her heart to the King, it was impossible for her to care at all for anyone or anything else on earth. "Even her mother and myself," he said, "though she is loyal and kindly to us, if the King demanded of her that she sacrifice us to get his love, I do believe she would do it."

"Sir Joshua – " I began.

"I do not exaggerate, Merivel," he said. "For this is the nature of obsession: it is like a fathomless well, into which even those persons or things previously held dear may one day be thrown."

"So what is to become of Celia, if the King does not call her back?"

"He *must* call her back! She has told me what has been said to you. And so the matter rests in your hands, Merivel. If I read the thing rightly, she has been too importunate with the King. You must help her to see the folly of this. Cynicism is the only form of armour in this age and even my sweet daughter must learn to put it on. She must learn that what she hopes for will never happen."

"What does she hope for?"

"I cannot say, Merivel. I am too ashamed to say."

I did not pester Sir Joshua on this matter and we ate the carbonado in silence for some minutes, during which I was forced to spit out a piece of gristle Cattlebury had inadvertently left in the stew. At length Sir Joshua said:

"You are quite right in believing that she may find some solace – and perchance wisdom – through her singing. While discarding much else, her love for song has remained with her, mainly because it seems it was her voice which first captured the King's heart."

"I know . . ." I began, "or rather, I did not know . . . but can imagine . . ."

"Yes. So by all means encourage her to sing. You play an instrument, I presume."

"Well, the oboe, Sir Joshua, but – "

"Good. She is most fond of the oboe."

"But will you not remain here at Bidnold? Will you not stay with us and accompany Celia on your viola?"

"How courteous of you. But no, I cannot, for my wife is not well and has need of me. I would dearly have loved to take Celia home, but I understand the King wishes her to remain with you."

"So he instructed me."

"Then she must stay. We are now near to Christmas. Pray do all you can Merivel to get her back to Kew before the spring comes."

That night, as I climbed into my soft bed, which I had not seen for more than a week, I expected to be punished for my lies in my dreams. But I was not. All I remember is a most agreeable dream of Meg Storey. I painted her portrait. In the picture, she was wearing a dress of hessian, such as I had seen upon the old woman pissing in the ditch, but her face above it appeared most beautiful and full of joy.

Here I am then, in my crimson suit, as I described myself at the beginning of this tale. You have all too clear a picture of me now, have you not? And, as you see, I am hedged about with events. I am, precisely as I suggested, in the middle of a story, but who can say yet – not you, not I – how it will end? It is too soon, even, to say how one would wish it to end. The delight or disappointment lies in all the surprises yet to come.

I am striving, since the arrival of Celia, to put some control upon my appetites, so that she may like me more, or at least despise me less. I have tempered my greed. I have made no visits to the Jovial Rushcutters. I have cut down on my consumption of wine and sack. I have restrained my farts. But tonight, alas, I am acting like a very fool and débauché. I am at the Bathursts and a great party is in progress in the hall. The Duke and Duchess of Winchelsea are here and assorted other witty aristocrats. We have drunk a great quantity of champagne, and now we are all screaming and braying with mirth, for old Bathurst, who disappeared suddenly half an hour ago, has just ridden into the hall on his vast stallion which, afrighted no doubt by the sight of us, has arched its tail and farted and then through a quivering black anus has let fall onto the parquet a most glistening quantity of shit. Winchelsea is laughing so hard, his face is puce and his eyes bulging, and when I glance up at Violet (who holds her liquor like a Wapping bargeman) I see that she, too, is convulsed behind her fan.

I sway to my feet. "A pox on wisdom!" I shout. "Let us all play at mares and stallions!"

"Olé!" cries Winchelsea and stamps his feet like a dancer of the Flamenco (feet that are perpetually kept, I must add, in

extraordinarily high-heeled shoes, Winchelsea not being as tall
as he would wish) and at once the whole company falls to clapping
their hands and stamping, all that is except an obese elderly man
opposite me who has turned to Lady Winchelsea and with his
fat hands removed her left breast from her dress and is holding
it, as if it were an object of immense weight and value – a ninepin
made of solid gold, say.

I lean over to get Lady Winchelsea's attention.

"My Lady," I say, "your neighbour has appropriated something of yours!"

She looks down. She sees her white bosom cupped in her
neighbour's florid hands. She gives me a smile of haughty disdain.
"Yes," she says, "naturally, he has."

I then feel myself punched hard in the small of the back by a
man I knew at Court, an effeminate cavalier by the name of Sir
Rupert Pinworth. "Legends!" he says. "Did you not know they
were legends, Merivel?"

"What are legends, pray?" I ask.

"Frances Winchelsea's bosoms. Are they not, Frances?"

Lady Winchelsea grins at Pinworth. Her neighbour has now
placed his quivering lips around her nipple. Taking no more heed
of this than if he had offered her a bowl of radishes, she nods
and leans back in her chair and extracts from her bodice her
other breast, upon which there is a most fetching brown mole.

The company has not ceased its stamping and clapping, but
now most have turned their gaze upon Frances Winchelsea
and are applauding her bosoms. I look at Winchelsea. Though
somewhat discomforted by the fact that Bathurst's stallion is
backing into his chair, he, too, is applauding. And I suddenly feel
most exceedingly stupid. Everyone at the table but me appears
to take it quite for granted that Frances Winchelsea's breasts
will be displayed and admired in the course of any evening where
she is present. I realise all at once how my long sojourn in
Norfolk has severed me from the sources of gossip and "legend".
I no longer know what is being done or said in high society. My
face is burning. I cannot describe to you how foolish I feel. I
hide my embarrassment by burying my face in my glass and
quaffing yet more champagne.

When I look up again, I see that Lady Winchelsea's breasts have been put away, but that her elderly neighbour is still leaning towards her, his mouth a-dribble. To cheer myself up, I have a wager with Pinworth that the old man's hand is upon his prick. I hear myself bet twenty shillings and sixpence. Pinworth guffaws very prettily, showing his elegant teeth. He pushes back his chair and scrambles under the table. He re-emerges quickly, his face aflame.

"Not merely upon it, Merivel!" he declares. "But entirely around it. He has taken the ancient thing out!"

"Then you owe me money, Pinworth!"

He giggles. He informs me he has no money whatsoever, but lives entirely off the favours his beauty can command. "Do not underestimate beauty," he declares. "It is the hardest currency to be had." He is lying about the twenty shillings and sixpence but, before I can upbraid him, he fixes me with his languid brown eyes and says: "I hear your wife is very beautiful."

I look quickly at Violet, to see if the word "wife" (the mention of which causes her such a deal of anger) has reached her ears, but she is not at her place. She has risen and is attempting to restrain Bathurst's stallion, the eyes of which are wild and white and which looks as if it will rear or bolt any minute.

Knowing that it is only the quantity of wine I have drunk which prevents me from feeling apprehensive about a sudden death by trampling, I return my attention to Pinworth. "Yes," I say, "Celia is a most pretty woman."

"But," says Pinworth, "I also hear she won't let you lay a finger upon her!"

It is at this moment that Violet succeeds in leading the horse out, Bathurst being now so drunk, he is a slack heap upon it, and so, for some new distraction, the guests now cease their clapping and stamping and turn their attention to me and my role as cuckold which, it seems, is known throughout the land and appears to be a subject that is aired as frequently as Lady Winchelsea's nipples.

I am bombarded by questions. Even Lady Winchelsea's elderly neighbour takes his eyes from her long enough to enquire of me: "How does it strike you, being locked out of the bedroom?"

I am about to reply that I give the matter no thought whatsoever, but it seems that I'm not allowed to speak, but only to be the butt of jokes and questions. As is my way, I smile good-naturedly. When I am told that I would be a good subject for a play, *Sir Willingly Deceived*, I slap my crimson thigh and guffaw in agreement. "I would be flattered to be portrayed in a play!" I hear myself declare, but in truth, drunk as I am and eager as I was this night to engage in exorbitant revelling, I feel my good humour being suddenly pricked, as if by a brittle shard of ice. And I know only I feel this. Still grinning, I look from one face to another. What I see behind the smiles and what I hear in the laughter is pity.

Later that night, while the servants toil to set to rights the hall, most horribly awash with spilt wine, vomit and flux from the horse, I am half carried to Violet's satin bed. Excited by the success of her party, she is hot and amorous. Her hands explore me. I feel her breasts touch the moths. I look down at her arched back, the strength of which I have often found strangely arousing, but feel most peculiarly numb, as if my whole body had been enfeebled by a kind of paralysis.

"Violet," I whisper, "I have drunk too much, I must sleep."

"No, you must not," says Violet, "not yet."

And she falls to work upon me with great zest. After a deal of time, I am hard enough to take somewhat feeble possession of her, but alas, my heart is not in it and I am immediately limp again, thus rousing Violet to terrible anger. "What is the matter with you, Merivel?" she demands to know. "What in the world is wrong with you?"

"I am not myself, Violet," I mumble.

"That is evident. But why, pray?"

"The wine . . ."

"Nonsense, Robert. You and I have been drunk many times."

"It must be the wine . . ."

But even as Violet goes to work on me once more, I know that it is not only the champagne I have drunk that has made me such a poor lover. Something else has afflicted me. Partly, it is the realisation that I am, at dinners and soirées in London and elsewhere, an object of pity. I believe, however, I could endure this with fortitude and good humour had the thought not entered my mind that, in my relationship with Celia, I now had cause to pity myself. Poor Merivel, goes my little lament, he has married the woman with the most beautiful voice in England and she cannot bear him to come near her! She is in his house and yet, as long as he lives, he will never touch her, never place a kiss upon her hair, even, or feel the touch of her white hand on his flat and ugly face . . .

"That's somewhat better," I hear Violet say, as she pauses in her whore's antics.

Alas, alas, my heart is saying, how excellent a thing it might be if, in my journeying from bed to bed, from Meg to Violet to Rosie Pierpoint, I could pause at the door of the Rose Room. I knock courteously upon it and the door is opened and she draws me inside, my wife, and I sit and caress her feet while she sings to me and then, not with my normal haste and flurry, but with a calm dignity, I stand up and kiss her mouth and she puts her arms round my neck, and up and down the corridors of the great houses there is no mockery or pity, for at last I am standing where the King stood, loving the woman he loved but to whom he married me . . .

I make love to Violet. She caterwauls like an Infidel, but I am silent, thinking my new thoughts.

I was not fully recovered from Violet's party for two days, at which time Farthingale reminded me curtly that it was Christmas Eve.

I try, in my life, not to think very frequently about my mother, finding myself distressed not only by my memory of her death but more horribly so by my memory of her hopes for me, by her belief that one day she would be proud of me. But at Christmas, it is difficult to prevent my thoughts from returning to her, and they did so again as the year of 1665 approached.

She would, on the birthday of Christ, allow herself what she called "an extra helping of prayer". At the time of the Civil War, she would pray for peace. Always, she asked God to spare me and my father. But at Christmas, she talked to God as if He were Clerk of the Acts in the Office of Public Works. She prayed for cleaner air in London. She prayed that our chimneys would not fall over in the January winds; she prayed that our neighbour, Mister Simkins, would attend to his cesspit, so that it would cease its overflow into ours. She prayed that Amos Treefeller would not slip and drown "going down the public steps to the river at Blackfriars, which are much neglected and covered in slime, Lord". And she prayed, of course, that plague would not come.

As a child, she allowed me to ask God to grant me things for which my heart longed. I would reply that my heart longed for a pair of skates made of bone or for a kitten from Siam. And we would sit by the fire, the two of us, praying. And then we would eat a lardy cake, which my mother had baked herself, and ever since that time the taste of lardy cake has had about it the taste of prayer.

On Christmas Day, then, kept inside the house by rain falling hour after hour from a black sky, I sat alone in my Withdrawing Room, thinking about my mother and trying to compose a plea to God, assisted by morsels of an excellent lardy cake which I had ordered Cattlebury to bake.

After an hour or more, I found I had consumed the entire cake and still had not been able to formulate my prayer. In truth, I did not know what I was asking for, or rather I knew and yet knew not. In a kind of desperation, I abandoned all idea of talking to God, but knelt down by the fire with my head stuffed into a chair (as if resting upon my mother's lap) and spoke mumblingly to her. "Guide me, my sweet departed mother," I said, "for the idea of reciprocity has entered my mind. It is creating there a yearning no longer to be Merivel, the Fool, but to be . . ." (here, I had to pause and shovel the last crumbs of the lardy cake into my mouth) ". . . to be Merivel, the proper man."

It was, as you see, not much of a prayer at all, but it was the best I could manage, at least for the time being. I got up off my knees and was about to go and sing a little to my bird, which, if my eyes are not deceiving me, is becoming somewhat thin and bedraggled in this English winter (further proof that it is of Indian origin and thus pining for the heat of the Ganges delta) when

Will Gates entered the room, carrying in his hands a most exquisitely worked leather box.

"Something come for you, Sir," said Will. "From London and the King."

Will amuses me with his Norfolk way with language. I took the thing from him and set it on a walnut card table. The box was tooled in gold and hinged with brass. I lifted the lid. Set out on a velvet cushion was a set of silver-plated surgical instruments.

Will gasped. "What are they, Sir?" he asked.

"Was there a letter with them? No card?"

"No, Sir. Nothing. Only the box. Tell me what they are, Sir Robert."

"They are surgical tools, Will," I said, "used in dissection and cuttings. With these you might remove a stone from a man's bladder, let blood from the *vena saphena*, lance an apostem, or sew together the two sides of an open wound."

"God save us!" said Will.

"Indeed," I replied. "Indeed . . ."

And then I took them up, one by one, the hook, the probe, the cannula, the perforator, the hammer, the osteoclast, the dipyrene, the spathomele and, last of all, the scalpel. I turned each one round in my hands and looked at it. I had never seen a set of instruments so perfectly crafted. I am willing to believe that neither Harvey nor Fabricius ever possessed any as fine. There was no doubt in my mind that they had come from the King. It was not necessary for him to send any message with them. They themselves were the message. Returning the scalpel to its velvet cushion, I saw, however, that its silver handle had been engraved with the date, December 1664. I turned it and found on the other side a marking of four words.

I held the thing up and saw, written on the handle of this sharpest and most terrible of blades, this terse exhortation: *Merivel, Do Not Sleep.*

NINE

THE OVERSEER

With January came the kind of ferocious winds my mother had mentioned in her prayers for the chimneys. Norfolk people call these gales "The Russian Wind", for this is where they come from, it seems, down from some petrified icy mountain range (the name of which I do not believe I have ever known) and across the northerly oceans to howl round our houses for days and nights together, like the howling of bears and wolves.

Though not as susceptible to cold as, say, Pearce (who can catch any ague from a mere draught) I nevertheless began to notice a most miserable ache in my bones, relief from which could only be had by sitting in a hot bath and having Will rub my backbone with a sponge.

I thus fell to wondering how the men and women of All the Russias survived the dead chill of the winter. I endeavoured to picture in my mind a people I knew nothing of. And this is how they appeared to me: their faces were rubicund and fleshy, all bearing a strong resemblance to the landlord of the Jovial Rushcutters. And their bodies – even the bodies of the women – were fantastically draped about with furs of every kind, furs not fashioned into coats or cloaks but simply hanging and dangling here and there, so that they looked like paupers in tatters, but were inside this assortment of animal skins most comfortable and cheerful.

Now, in my occasional visits to Meg, I let go my stories about the Land of Mar and began a sequence of inventions I entitled

Merivel's True Tales of Russia, which succeeded most well with her sweet gullible mind. But more than this, I began to imagine how much more contented all of us at Bidnold would be if we were warm and so placed an order for a large assortment of furs with an ancient London furrier by the name of Jacob Trench. I requested that Trench sew a motley of skins together into simple tabards "to be placed over the head and hang upon the shoulders, thus leaving the wearer's arms free for such tasks as his station in life dictates, but keeping his trunk warm".

Trench being old and meticulous and used to making ermine cloaks and the like, fussed me with tedious letters, requesting that I stipulate precisely what furs were to be used and in what quantities and what colour and quality of silk and satin I required for the linings and furthermore suggesting that I come to London with my staff for individual fittings.

Though I felt most vexed by the delay, I could not behave discourteously to Trench, he being such a trusted friend of my father's. I decided therefore to simplify the operation. I instructed Trench to use only badger skins and to line the tabards not with silk or satin but with a sturdy wool cloth, "such as may be worn even by my groom and my scullery boy". The cost of the tabards was going to be considerable, but so vivid had my imaginary Russians become that I had convinced myself that I at least could not survive the winter without this peculiar garment of fur. The idea, furthermore, that we could wait out the spring dressed as badgers delighted me considerably. No more would I be told I must be quiet to chance upon a badger in the woods of Vauxhall; I would *become* a badger.

Meanwhile, we waited. Ice formed in the well and the ravaging frost made cracks in the roof tiles. A chimney pot came hurtling down and decapitated a guinea fowl. "How slowly, how slowly time passes," said Celia, warming her hands by the fire. "How shall I endure it?"

There was indeed a kind of sameness to each day. In the mornings, I would persuade Celia to come to my Music Room and sing. My oboe practice had increased tenfold. I would rise at dawn, in the freezing dark and take up my instrument and struggle with scales and arpeggios until the sun crept into the sky but, despite this, I was unable to accompany Celia with any grace at all and, whenever I attempted to do so, she would cease her singing almost at once and pray me not to bother. Thus, there was not, of course, the duet that I had fancifully imagined, but only Celia's voice, singing alone, singing of lost love, while I sat on a chair and stared at her white throat and wondered if time or chance or "the changeful nature of all things" would ever allow me to put my lips tenderly upon it.

At noon, I would dine with Celia, but these meals were becoming irksome to me, owing to the constant presence of Farthingale who was growing more odious and ugly as the days passed, but from whom Celia would seldom permit herself to be parted.

In the afternoons on fine days, I would ride in my park, urging Danseuse to her splendid gallop. Celia's little dog, Isabelle, whom she could not be bothered to exercise, ran snapping at our heels for some of the way and when we outran her would turn and trot home to her mistress who sat dreaming by the fire in her room, reading the poetry of Dryden or doing her eternal *petit point*.

There was no doubt, Celia was languishing. She was polite to me because she believed the King had made me her overseer. Upon my report of her depended her return to London – or so she understood it to be. But I knew what I was to her: I was a penance she had to endure. I was as irritating to her as my oboe playing, as ugly and discordant. The idea that she could ever love or respect me, I now saw was utterly preposterous. I was on the point of abandoning my ploy to keep her at Bidnold beyond the King's stated time when a most strange incident occurred.

I had spent an evening in my Studio, trying to draw in charcoal the Russians of my unreliable imagination, abandoning my hopeless smudges and scribbles at last towards midnight. I undressed and put on my warmest nightshirt and a nightcap with a little lining of rabbitskin, got into my turquoise bed and fell at once into a heavy sleep.

I woke in some confusion. A hand was pressing my shoulder

and a voice was urging me to wake up. I opened my eyes and saw Celia, wrapped in a cloak, bending over me. She was holding a lighted candle and her long hair fell loose about her face, like a curtain.

"Merivel," she said in a whisper of great urgency, "come down. Your bird is dying."

"My nightingale?"

"Yes. You are a physician. It will die if something is not done."

I did not know what time it could be, for I had forgotten to wind my timepiece (if I had been the King, I would have had a diversity of clocks to choose from). I knew only that it was the very middle of the night and so cold that I could see my breath by the light of the candle.

Having given her message, Celia fled from my room, taking the candle with her so that I was left in utter darkness. As I struggled to light a lamp, find my wig and my stockings and wrench a blanket from the bed in which to wrap myself, I wondered why in the world Celia had been looking at my bird at this peculiar hour – she who, with the griping Farthingale habitually retired to her room no later than nine o'clock. I was more puzzled by this than filled with worry for my bird, until that is I reached my Withdrawing Room at last and saw the poor thing.

Celia had placed the cage on the carpet in front of a fire upon which new logs had been laid. I knelt down.

"Look," said Celia. "It has fallen over."

It was lying on the floor of the cage, its legs in the air, one wing feebly flapping.

"What is to be done, Merivel?"

I looked up at Celia. I had detected in her voice a note of great sadness, of despair even. I was so utterly astonished that she should appear to care so much for something that, I, too, cared about that I was speechless, thus causing her to say once more:

"Merivel, what is to be done?"

I looked again at the nightingale. Its marigold eye, usually such a bright thing, appeared clouded, almost as if a membrane obscured it, but though I diligently searched what remained of

my medical mind, I could not recollect what this might signify.
I rubbed my eyes. Starved of sleep, wearied by drawings of
Russians, I could discover no sensible path to follow.

"I do not know what is to be done, Celia," I said.

"You mean you do not care if the creature dies?"

"On the contrary! I am most attached to it."

"Then try something! Get out your instruments and your
remedies!"

I cannot. I cannot. So I wished to say. And yet I understood
that I must be seen to do something, that whereas Celia considered me to be inadequate at every human activity from
oboe playing to discussions of Dryden's rhyming couplets, from
painting to powdering my wig, she wrongly believed that in
this one area – medicine – I possessed considerable skill. If,
therefore, I could save the bird, I would no doubt earn a little
respect from her.

Noting somewhat wryly that this was the second time that
some part of my future appeared to depend upon my saving the
life of a dumb creature, I took my candle and went to my closet.
I returned with a strong physic, a senna and rhubarb preparation
dubbed among apothecaries *Pill Fortis*, some clean linen bandages and the set of surgical instruments so recently sent to me
by the King.

"Very well," I said to Celia. "I am going to purge the bird.
When I have administered the physic, I shall perform a phlebotomy on the upper leg."

Celia did not flinch. "How may I help you?" she enquired.

"Well . . . if you would hold it in your hands, stroking its head
so that it is not afraid, while I attempt to get the medicine down
its throat . . ."

"Yes," she said. "But shall we not bring a table near to the
fire and work upon it?"

"A good idea. And I will lay linen on it."

We thus, in this strange dead of night, prepared the walnut
card table as an operating tray and Celia gently lifted the bird
from the cage and laid it down. We worked by the light of three
candles and, as I saw my poor bird placed before me, I was
reminded for a few shadowy seconds of the body of the starling

in the coal cellar. How much easier is dissection, I reflected, than cure.

Celia sat opposite me. A stranger entering the room would have assumed we were at cards or dice, except that I was bizarrely clothed in a blanket and Celia in her winter cloak.

"Now," I said, "if you would hold the bird as still as you can. I am going to open its beak and hold it thus with the spatula and with my dropping-glass here dribble some *Fortis* down its gullet."

The nightingale kicked its legs, but once within Celia's hands did not struggle, only regarded us with its sad clouded eye. It swallowed the physic and we would have to wait upon its passage through the body.

"Very well," I said. "Now I shall do the phlebotomy. The sight of a little blood will not upset you, I hope?"

"No," said Celia. "I am only concerned for the bird, for if it should die, I cannot but feel some misfortune may follow."

"Why so?"

"Because it was a gift to you, was it not?"

"Yes."

"And from the King. And if what the King has given away should come to harm, then I fear for you – and for me."

I was, as you may imagine, about to inform Celia that the bird had been a present – nay, a bribe – from that *soi-disant* portraitist, Elias Finn, and had nothing to do with the King whatsoever, but then I decided not to. For, unhappy as I was to see my Indian Nightingale so ill, I also recognised that I had begun to enjoy the little escapade and did not wish Celia to desert me in the middle of it.

I began without more ado on the blood-letting, finding at last a faint pulse on the feathered thigh and making a small incision with the scalpel inscribed *Merivel, Do Not Sleep*. Dark veinous blood spurted out onto the linen. Never having thought to perform a phlebotomy on a bird, I had no idea what quantity to let out before staunching the flow. After some few minutes of seepage, however, Celia looked at me piteously. Some blood had fallen onto her hands, and it was my anxiety to wipe this away as quickly as possible that made me reach for a bandage and begin to bind the wound. Its leg wrapped, the nightingale did look most exceedingly tragic. Celia picked it up and held it close to her face, trying to feel its heartbeat. Then I folded more linen and laid this on the floor of the cage and she put the bird in and I began to clean my instruments with a little spirit and put them away.

"We have done all we can," I told Celia. "By morning, when the purge has worked, we shall see if it appears a little stronger."

"Will you let more blood tomorrow?"

"Possibly. Although I really don't know what quantity of blood is in it."

Celia stood up. "Why are you no longer a physician, Merivel?" she said.

I shall spare you the little discourse that followed, in which I attempted to explain to Celia my vision of her father's skull when he played at our wedding and the despair into which my knowledge of bone and sinew had been ready to let me fall. I knew as I spoke that Celia did not believe me. She accused me of not knowing where my own salvation lay and called me cowardly. Greatly vexed, I was about to retire once more to my bed and was picking up my instrument box, when Celia reached out and touched my hand.

"Pray don't go, Merivel. Forgive me if I spoke of matters that do not regard me."

I did not know what to reply. To Pearce I would have delivered myself of some insult to George Fox or to the soup ladle but, angry as I was, I did not wish to wound Celia. I suggested at last that we retire to our rooms but Celia, it seemed, intended to stay and watch over the bird and wished me to stay with her.

I felt mightily tired. The very act of picking up the scalpel had affected me. I wanted to lie down and dream I was a Russian in a coat of weasel-skin, carefree in the snow. But what could I do? On this peculiar January night, my wife wished to be with me – for the first time since she'd come to Bidnold. I could not refuse her.

I decided at once that we must have food to sustain us through our vigil. I hadn't the heart to wake Cattlebury, so carrying a candle and holding my blanket close about me, I walked the cold corridors to the kitchen and returned with a tray of meats: a cold game pie, a cold roasted guinea fowl and some charred pork sausages – and a flagon of sack.

The card table, so lately an operating theatre, now became a dining trestle. We ate with our fingers and drank the sack from the stone bottle, and the food and the fire banished the ache in my backbone and turned Celia's nose unflatteringly red.

After we had eaten, Celia sang. The song was a lullaby and most beautiful and, when she had finished it, she whispered to me her secret hope, that the King would give her a child. It was upon this subject that she had been attempting to write to the King when she had heard the small noise made by the nightingale falling from its perch. Interpreting this as a sign that what she was doing was dangerous, she had immediately cast her letter into the fire and come running to wake me. I did not know what comment to make upon this secret hope of hers, finding myself most afrighted by it. So I laid my head among the fowl bones and went immediately to sleep and when I woke I heard Celia crying.

I sat up. I saw a grey light at the window, heralding sunrise. The fire was low. Celia was no longer at the table, but kneeling by the bird's cage. "It is dead, Merivel," she said. "It is quite dead."

I knelt. The bird lay in a pool of greenish slime, its terminal evacuation caused by the *Fortis*. From the rigor of its body, I recognised at once that it was indeed dead, but in truth I gave this very little attention, for, weeping as she was, Celia had let herself fall forwards and reach out to me for comfort. So it was that I found myself holding her, kneeling, in my arms for three or four minutes together. Though I would dearly loved to have kissed and caressed her, I did not allow myself to do this, but only to hold her head against mine and stroke her hair.

Two days later, after we had buried the Indian Nightingale near the grave of my dog, Minette, in the park, snow began to fall. Through this snow, on a fat grey horse a man came riding to my door. His name was Sir Nicholas Hogg. He informed me that he was a Justice of the Peace for the Parish of Hautbois-le-

Fallows cum Bidnold and that at a recent Quarter Session of the Justices I had – as Squire of the Manor of Bidnold – been appointed an Overseer of the Poor.

I invited Justice Hogg into my study. My garb that day was muted, Celia having insisted that I go into *demi-deuil* for the wretched nightingale, and Hogg, it seems, took me for a serious man.

I enquired of him what my duties as Overseer might be and he replied that they would be light, "Norfolk being not at this time disfigured by a great quantity of poor", but that I should bear in mind at all times that paupers were divisible into three categories.

"Three categories?" I asked. "And all fit conveniently into one of the three?"

"They do. For you have in this land your Impotent Poor, your Able Poor and your Idle Poor."

"Ah," I said.

"But it is expected of the Overseers that they will avoid errors in their categorisation, for errors will invariably bring a man before the Justices and thus consume their precious time. So let me warn you that the commonest area of error is in the distinguishing between your Impotent Pauper and your Idle Pauper, for a great many of the Idle will counterfeit Impotence and thus a great quantity of those appearing to the unpractised eye Impotent will in fact be found to be Idle. I trust you understand me?"

"I believe I do."

"This, then, is your most important task: correct categorisation. If, for example, you come upon a person begging by the wayside, how may you be able to distinguish whether the said person is of the Idle variety or the Impotent variety?"

I thought for a moment about this. I was briefly tempted to make some flippant rejoinder to the effect that there were many at Court who would infinitely prefer to be thought Idle (which indeed they were) than to be thought Impotent (which some of them were but went through elaborate performances to conceal). But I truly wished to take my new responsibilities seriously, so I replied at last that I would first cast my eye over the person's person, to ascertain in what condition his body stood, whether mutilated, diseased or wounded, and that I would enquire of him what circumstances of personal misfortune had reduced him to begging by the road.

But Sir Nicholas Hogg shook his head.

"No, no," he said. "An unreliable method. No, no, no. There is but one question to ask him. You must enquire whether or not he has a Licence to Beg. And when he shows you his Licence, you must make sure that it is a True Licence and not a Counterfeit."

"Ah," I said, "and if he has no Licence at all?"

"Then, you have your answer. He is not Impotent, he is Idle. It is really a most simple matter!"

"And how are the Licences obtained, Sir Nicholas?"

"Application is made to us, the Justices. And each individual case is put before us at the Quarter Sessions."

"And what of the man who falls upon hard times, is hurt, say, in a brawl or falls from a tree while picking plums and his spine is crushed, and he can no longer work, and yet finds on the almanac that the next Quarter Session is many weeks off. How is he to live in the meantime, except by begging?"

"This is a hypothetical case, Sir Robert, and I know of no such precedent. At all events, he must not beg. He must find other means."

"Yet I do not know what those means might be."

"Very well. One such means is that he could come to you."

"And what must I do?"

"It is the occasional duty of the Overseer to dispense small sums, on a sixpenny or ninepenny scale, in charity, or, if preferred, dispense gifts in kind, such as a thin hen or a pigsfoot, as and where they think fit. It is for this reason only men of substance are elected to the position of Overseer, so that their own livelihood is not one whit inconvenienced."

Sir Nicholas began lighting up a very foul pipe at this juncture, thus giving me a little time to formulate other questions concerning the condition of the workhouse at Norwich, and the type of work done there, this place being the principal refuge for what Hogg dubbed the Able Poor of the county. I was told that it was a very excellent type of workhouse and that the men, women and children housed there were most merry, seated at their spinning wheels and looms "and thus receiving charity not only for their arms and fingers, which are at work, but also for their undeserving legs, which are idle".

Hogg wiped some black morsels of tobacco from his fleshy lip before he added: "Unfortunately the sick-house there has, mistakenly in my opinion, been converted to an ale house, but I am informed the few sick are cared for in an adequate shed."

I enquired whether, as an Overseer in a small parish, it would be necessary for me to visit the workhouse at Norwich, but Sir Nicholas replied that my authority extended only as far as the boundary of Hautbois-le-Fallows cum Bidnold with the neighbouring parishes of Coote-by-Leyland and Rumworth St James, an authority I shared, he told me lastly, with none other than Lord Bathurst, described as "an excellent Overseer, most generous with rabbits". The notion that Bathurst could be relied upon to tell whether a poor man was Impotent or Idle I found somewhat disconcerting and was about to make some observations on the muddled state of Bathurst's mind since his accident in the field, when Sir Nicholas walked to my study window, looked out at the snow falling very thickly now and declared that he must depart at once or risk to find the highway obliterated and all routes to what he called his "Seat at Hautbois" impassible.

I confess I was relieved to bid adieu to him and his odious pipe, yet after he had gone found myself to be in a state of some perturbation with regard to my new responsibility, having no clear picture of what I was supposed to *do* as an Overseer of the Poor. Was it to be expected that I should ride about the villages on Danseuse trawling for the Idle and sending them packing to the looms, succouring the Impotent with sixpences and chicken legs? I was not in the habit of going very frequently to Bidnold village, except to visit Meg at the Rushcutters and thus could not assess what quantity of destitute people might now be turning to me for succour. Had the snow not been falling, I would have mounted my horse there and then and carried out a quick reconnaissance, but, like Justice Hogg, I did not wish to be lost in the white wastes and so decided instead to note down all that I knew about the Poor which, alas, did not seem a great deal. I took up a quill and wrote as follows:

1. They are numerous.

2. They appear more numerous in the capital, where they throng the wharves and lie down to sleep on the steps of alehouses.

3. They are much prone to sickness, as witnessed by me during my brief time at St Thomas's hospital.

4. Madness appears present in the eyes of many of them and I suspect that Pearce's Bedlam is choking with them.

5. They are regarded by the likes of the Winchelseas as a race apart, a quite other species of man. It is, however, from the bodies of Paupers that anatomists draw their knowledge and it is nowhere suggested that the liver, say, of a Peer will be any different in its shape, function, composition or texture than that of a Hovel-dweller (unless the organ of the Peer be enlarged by the quantity of claret that has passed through it).

6. Jesus was most fond of them.

7. There is an interesting dichotomy between His belief in their nobility and the Nobility's belief in their inherent wickedness. (And this in a supposedly pious country.)

8. I have not, in all my thirty-seven years, given a great deal of thought to them – until this day, the thirteenth of January 1665.

9. How does the King regard them? In his credo that all should be content with their lot and not get above themselves, what does he say of the Pauper?

10. I have heard that in Bidnold there is a tongueless man,

sound of limb but speechless, who begs alms from all who pass him. Is this man Impotent or Idle? Has he a Licence? If he has no Licence, what am I to do with him?

I paused. I could now see from my albeit puny notes that the whole question of the Poor was a mighty complex one – one to which I had never expected to address myself. I put down my pen with a sigh. To whom should I look for guidance on a subject about which I seemed to know so very little and upon which my thinking was most horribly muddled? The answer was, of course, Pearce. So it was with another sigh that I took up my quill once more and prepared to write to Pearce, thereby to solicit a return letter full of criticism and scorn. The task wearied me even before I had begun it – but a sweet sound interrupted me: Celia was singing. I left my Study at once and went to the Music Room, where I sat in silence on a small, spindly chair and let my wife's voice drive from my mind all contemplation of the homeless and the needy.

TEN

FINN IN A PERIWIG

That same night, I had a dream of some consequence: I was standing on the leads of my house and staring at the winter stars, not through my telescope, which was nowhere to be seen, but with my own inadequate eyes. After some hours of astral contemplation (or so it seemed in the dream) I felt a most terrible hurt in my eyes and a wetness on my face, as of tears. With my coatsleeve, I brushed the tears away, but on glancing at my sleeve saw a red stain upon it and knew that my eyes were bleeding. I was about to descend, to put some sad bandage upon my face, when I saw the King, seated some distance from me upon a low chimney stack and regarding me most gravely.

"Though you bleed, Merivel," he said, "you have not understood the First Rule of the Cosmos."

I was about to enquire of him what this "first rule" might be when I woke and found that my cheeks were wet. Mercifully, they were wet with tears and not with blood, but I was nevertheless most vexed to discover myself blubbing in my sleep and lay for some time in a great perplexity, wondering whence the dream had come and what it signified. For whom, or for what was I crying? For the Indian Nightingale? For the Poor, whose sufferings were now to become visible to my mind? For my own ignorance? For my failure to intuit what the First Rule of the Cosmos might be?

I rose and washed my face, shivering somewhat but aware of a drip-dripping outside my window, suggesting to me that the snows were melting. I then returned to my bed and resumed my thinking.

Near morning, I had decided that, setting aside my hopeless lamentation for my days as the King's Fool, the thing which was causing me most hurt was my failure to play any role in Celia's music-making save that of listener. I longed – feverishly, I now saw – to be her accompanist, her consort, and yet so ashamed was I of the sounds I made upon my oboe that I had almost ceased my practice, lest Celia should hear me at it. How, then, was I to achieve the thing I hoped for? In my mind, I related my problem to the King and waited patiently for his response. I believe I dozed a little on this instant, for I saw very clearly the King take up from his lap a glove made by my late father and put it on, thus concealing several priceless diamond and emerald rings on his fingers. *"Voilà!"* he said. "You must learn in secret."

How this was to be done I was not able to tell and in the day that then dawned I was not at liberty to ponder, for no sooner had I finished my solitary breakfast than Will Gates informed me that Finn had arrived and awaited me in my Studio.

I had not sent for him. Since Celia's arrival, my new vocation as a painter had not been pursued as vigorously as before. My struggles with my oboe had all but replaced my experiments with colour and light. As I made my way to my Studio, however, it came into my mind that I would like to attempt a painting of my imaginary Russians in their snowbound wastes. Bits of snow still lay upon the park, so I should begin immediately upon the landscape (mostly white with a heavy sky of slate grey) and come later to a rendition of the people, using as my models Cattlebury and Will Gates, dressed in the fur tabards I still awaited from London. Thus, Finn's arrival was most timely. He would help me to plan the picture, showing me how the figures might be grouped and where, in the uniform white, to suggest light and shadow. To any pretentious request of his for a background of broken statuary I would peremptorily retort: There *is* no broken statuary in my vision of Russia; the frost has made it all crumble to shards.

I opened the Studio door. The light in the room seemed more than ever northerly and cold, but Finn within it was dressed not in his outlaw's ragged green but in a garb of lustrous crimsons and golds, with handsome buckled boots on his feet and – strangest of all, so that I scarcely recognised the face beneath it – a blond periwig on his head.

"My dear Finn!" I exclaimed.

The artist smiled and I noticed that a blush crept to his cheeks, which still appeared somewhat gaunt and underfed.

"Good morning to you, Sir Robert," he said. "Your eye has discerned an alteration in my appearance, I see."

"There is not an eye in Norfolk could fail to discern it, Finn," I replied. "And from it I deduce some measure of prosperity."

"Well," said Finn, "I have not yet got the place at Court on which my heart is set, but I believe I am almost there, for I have been given a commission by the King."

"Ah. So you have had an audience with His Majesty at last?"

"Yes. It was brief, I confess, but nevertheless an audience."

"Bravo, Finn!"

"After many days and nights of haunting the corridors of Whitehall and being advised at last that I should put on new clothes if I hoped to be summoned in to the presence."

"Hence this most excellent attire?"

"Yes. And it cost me all the money I had in the world, save the coach fare from London to Norfolk. So you see before you a Pauper. I have nothing in the world, Sir Robert, not one penny."

"I see. So you have come to resume your role as tutor, or am I to commit you to the workhouse?"

Finn, not knowing of my discourse with Justice Hogg, was of course unable to understand my little jest and thus did not smile, but continued with gravitas.

"One painting," he said, "one portrait lies between me and a position at Court."

"Ah," I said, "and what painting may that be?"

For answer, Finn put one of his thin hands into a braided pocket and took out a scrap of parchment much creased and thumbed, like a love letter kept day and night about a man's person. He handed it to me and bid me read. I saw at once the King's elegant hand, and this is what was written:

This paper sets forth and commands to be executed by one, Elias Finn, painter, the following commission: a noble and beautiful portrait of Celia Clemence, Lady Merivel, of Bidnold Manor in the County of Norfolk. This portrait to be delivered, complete and finished in every detail, no later than the twelfth day of February 1665. This portrait not to exceed twenty-five inches carrés, *that it may comfortably be hung in our closet. This portrait, if found to be well-executed and pretty, to earn for the artist the sum of seven* livres. *This portrait, if found to be most excellent and true to nature, to earn for the artist promise of a small place at Court.*
                              Signed,
                              Charles R.

I looked up at Finn, who now had an insufferable grin upon his face. I handed him his paper, feeling myself invaded as I did so by a most unruly anger. Gone instantly was my little excitement for my painting of Russians. Now, I would be forced – in order not to displease the King – to give food and lodging to this impoverished artist while he spent hours in Celia's company, embellishing her with silly fans and draperies and daubing in some puffing cherub above her head, receiving for his pains both Celia's admiration and a position at Whitehall, while I struggled on alone with my oboe, exiled still from Court and possessing no power to make my wife regard me with anything but disdain, save only in moments of distress such as the night of my bird's unfortunate demise. Any sympathy I had once felt for Finn had now departed from me utterly. I both despised and envied him and knew only too well what a burden his presence in my house was going to be to me. It is fortunate, however, that at such moments of sudden anger (infrequent in my nature) I seem not to be without some cleverness and cunning. Adeptly concealing my rage, I shook my head gravely and said:

"Alas, Finn, you must not depend upon this for your future."

"Why so?" said Finn, staring anxiously at his paper.

"Why? Because such commissions are numerous. I wager the King puts out no less than two or three *per diem*. And already portraits of my wife have been done, but none have been paid for and the poor artists are, as far as I know, still wandering the land like the Idle Poor or decaying in their rags on the steps to the King's barge."

I was earnestly hoping that these words would cast Finn into the Nordic gloom that fits his features so well but, much to my irritation, he smiled condescendingly at me.

"This one will be paid for," he said, "because I will make a portrait too beautiful to be resisted. I have heard your wife is a pretty woman and I will improve, even, on what nature has created."

"By surrounding her with flowers and harps and foolish garlands, I suppose? But these will not improve your chances."

"No. Not by embellishment, but by succeeding at what you attempted, Sir Robert, and failed to achieve: the capturing of her *essence*. I will capture it and the face will be a magnet, drawing all eyes and hearts towards it."

"I wish you luck," I said acidly. "But let me warn you: much of what the King commences he does not finish. The clamour about him is so noisy, so colossal, he cannot for long remain attentive to any one thing. So beware, Finn. You may arrive with your picture and he will not even set eyes upon it."

"But I have my paper . . ."

"Paper! Do you not know the First Rule of the Cosmos, Finn?"

"What 'First Rule'?"

"That all matter is born of fire and will one day again be consumed by it."

Having delivered myself of this piece of questionable wisdom and before Finn could deny its relevance to the piece of parchment in his hands, I quickly changed the subject.

"Concerning your lodging here," I said, "I suppose the King gave you money for this?"

"No, Sir Robert. As I told you, I have not one farthing . . ."

"I am to feed you and house you as a favour?"

"As a favour to His Majesty."

"For which I shall be rewarded how?"

"He did not say. But I am a person of modest appetite . . ."

"Not so, judging from your clothes."

"That is mere outward show . . ."

"As much as life proves to be. But God sees into your heart, Finn, and would He wish you to be a parasite?"

"I am no parasite. I work hard for the meagre living I make."

"And will do so here. In return for your board, you will concentrate such talent as you have upon *my* work. I wish to begin some new pictures. You will help me with questions of perspective and light."

"But what of the portrait?"

"My wife is most busy with her music and her attempts to comprehend the works of Dryden. She will not spare you more than an hour a day."

Finn began to protest and, seeing his dismay, I felt my anger abate somewhat. To Meg, when I next saw her, I would tell the story of a poor mendicant who is given a little plot of ground and sees an end to his poverty if he can but till the earth and sow some seed before the beginning of spring. He goes begging for tools – for a plough and a mule and a hoe. He returns with these, but he is too late. He did not *see* the spring come and yet, when he gets back, it is already there. He had forgotten with what stealth change occurs and time passes.

I found myself in the attic room at the Jovial Rushcutters sooner than I had intended: I lay there that very night.

The day of Finn's arrival passed most disagreeably and I was in such a lather of fury by suppertime that all I could think of was escaping from the house, so I shouted for my horse to be saddled and rode through the slush to the village. On my way, I chanced upon two poor people collecting sticks, of which I shall write more presently.

What so vexed me was Celia's treatment of Finn. Hearing from his thin lips that the King had commissioned him to paint her portrait, her eyes grew bright with joy. She summoned Farthingale and told her the merry tiding (the two of them reading into it excessive hopes for their imminent return to Kew) and they then began to fawn upon the artist, requesting to see his work and professing to find it most marvellous and brilliant and I know not what, and then bringing forth dresses and sashes and headdresses for him to choose from for the picture, the while utterly ignoring me and behaving as if I was of no account in the matter, which, alas, is true.

I observed Celia closely. Her beautiful smile, which I had seen so often given to the King, but scarcely ever to me, was almost constantly upon her lips, thus rendering her most infinitely pretty and sweet. Hers is the kind of sweetness which, once glimpsed, makes my heart tender – as if towards a child – and my manhood cruel – wanting to possess and abuse that very same childlike thing. I saw that Finn was utterly captivated by her. I saw also that Celia knew him to be captivated and did not mind, indeed allowed herself to flirt a little with him. And this last observation created in me a bitter yearning. Why – when she was my wife – could she not behave so charmingly to me?

I sat and watched her until I could endure it no longer, then went to the Music Room and played some foul blasts upon my oboe and kicked over my music stand, then threw the instrument down and went calling for my groom. On my way to the stables, I met Cattlebury who informed me that he had come by two dozen thrushes for supper. I told him curtly that I was not hungry but that he should serve up the wretched birds in a pie "for my wife and her new friend, Mr Finn". By the time they sat down to table (Celia's smile rendered all the more irresistible by the soft candlelight, no doubt) I had already consumed several flagons of ale and was conversing with a roofing man upon the abundance of rats to be found in thatch. "What if they are plague rats?" I asked. "Then death will come by the roof." And the old man nodded. "Widow Cartwright says the plague will come to Norfolk. Round and about springtime."

I went to Meg's bed very late and categorically drunk, after pissing in her fireplace and dousing what small warmth there was in the garrett. Once I held her in my arms, I went to sleep instantly, with my ugly head on her breasts.

When I woke, burdened as I knew I would be with an aching head and the smell of my own foul breath, I found myself alone, it being one of Meg's duties to rise early and sweep the floor of the tavern and air the place before the arrival of the first peasant for his cup of small beer. Ill as I knew myself to be, I rose immediately and went to the low window and looked out for, to

my great chagrin, I now remembered that Danseuse had not
been stabled the previous night and had spent it tied to a post
under the cold stars. In what condition of cold and suffering I
would find her, I did not know.

I could see almost nothing from the small window, except that
a beastly drizzle was falling, dense like a mist. It is on such
inhospitable mornings that the memory of midsummer causes
my brain sudden suffering. My Merivel ancestors, haberdashers
of Poitou, never endured an English winter. It is their blood,
undoubtedly, that has made mine so susceptible to weather.

Meg found me kneeling at the window, and apparently thought
I was at prayer, for she said, with a peevish coldness: "Prayer
will not save you, Sir Robert."

"I am not praying, Meg," I said, "but scanning the environs
in search of my horse."

"Your horse is in the stables," she said curtly, set down a pot
of coffee and a dish of apple fritters on a table, and went
out, each one of her words and gestures conveying intense
displeasure. I remained kneeling, like a penitent. My life is a
very muddled occurrence, I remarked to myself.

Finding no forgiveness or yielding in Meg that morning, I had
no choice but to set off for home, a little restored by the coffee
and fritters and mighty glad that my horse had not perished by
my neglect, but my spirits at one with the weather. The thought
of returning to be met by Finn in his ludicrous wig was so
distasteful to me that I considered riding directly to Bathurst
Hall, but found that the memory of Violet's party and the
jokes about my ignominious role as cuckold still pained me.
Furthermore, I felt no desire whatsoever for Violet, her demeanour and her coarse language now striking me as intolerably
vulgar. I could do little, therefore, but return home, planning as
I rode to soothe my body with soap and hot water and then to
persuade Celia to sing for me alone, contriving some laborious
task (such as the stretching of canvases) for Finn and banishing
Farthingale to her room.

It was at this moment that I found myself at the place where
I had seen the poor people grovelling for kindling. I reined in
Danseuse and sat looking about me. There was no stirring

anywhere, only the silent rain and the dripping of the trees.

I dismounted and tied the mare to a spindly ash. On the right of the lane was a small wood, to the left common land where the cottars of Bidnold grazed their sheep and goats. I had some vague notion of searching for the two Paupers, not with the intention of asking anything from them or indeed endeavouring to place them with one of Justice Hogg's three categories, but merely of regarding them face to face and seeing what state of misery or despair I could determine in them. In the near darkness, one of them holding a small lantern on a pole, they had struck me as people in terrible need, their faces cadaverous, their eyes fearful. In their masses, I beheld, unmoved, such poor folk in London, yet the sight of these two, a man and his wife in rags, had troubled me sufficiently to send me wandering into the wood in search of the hovel in which I supposed them to live.

I found nothing. Indeed the air in the wood was so still, it was difficult to imagine it disturbed by any living breath. After tearing my stockings on some briars, I abandoned my search and returned to my horse. As I re-mounted, I told myself that, were I in a condition of wretchedness, I would not seek out the Overseers in their wigs and wanton finery, but rather be at pains to conceal myself from them by whatever means I could devise.

At Bidnold, just as I feared, I found Finn at work upon the infernal portrait.

Celia, in a dress of cream-coloured satin, had been seated upon an ottoman (removed without my permission from the Withdrawing Room and placed near the Studio window). She held a lute in her lap and by her side sat her trembling Spaniel, Isabelle.

"Finn," I said, "you have positioned my wife in a draught. See how the dog is shivering."

To my delight, the artist looked momentarily dismayed, but Celia, without moving one half inch from her pose, informed me brusquely that she was not in the least cold.

"Ah," I said, "but you will surely catch an ague if you sit long there. I suggest we adjourn to the Music Room, where a fire has been lit."

"What time is it?" said Celia.

"I beg your pardon?"

"What hour is it?"

"I have no idea. I could, if you wish, consult the handsome timepiece given to me by – "

"I believe my guest will arrive at mid-day."

"Your guest? What guest, pray?"

"Am I not allowed guests, Merivel?"

"Naturally. I only wished to enquire – "

"He is my music teacher. At my father's request, he has agreed to make the journey from London."

"Ah."

"Thus my days will not be as tedious as they were. I will have the pleasure of sitting for a fine artist and the pleasure of singing for an inspiring Musikmeister."

"I'm sorry you have found the days 'tedious'."

"It's not your fault, Merivel. I don't belong in such a life."

"Happily," interrupted Finn, "you will soon be back at Court."

"Yes," said Celia. "Once the portrait is done, you will have to let me go, Merivel. Though it has been difficult for me to practise my singing without an accompanist, that is now remedied, thanks to my father. I am thus doing as you suggested, trying to come to a clearer understanding of my destiny through song. Thus, you must report that I have done all that the King requested."

"We shall see, Celia . . ."

"No. We shall not see. If you will not make a good report of me to the King, I shall return to London nevertheless. For the portrait changes all."

"How does it 'change all'?"

"You are obtuse, Merivel. Would the King commission a portrait of a woman he did not intend to see again?"

"Very possibly," I replied. "In remembrance of former times, now departed – as a mere *souvenir*."

Celia shook her head and glared at me coldly.

"No," she said, "I know the King. He would not do this."

I was on the very verge of revealing to Celia what I had seen that strange night upon the river, the lights in her house, the revellers at the window. But I hesitated. Not only was I unwilling to hurt Celia so cruelly, but the night in question had taken on the colours and insubstantial quality of a dream in my mind, so that I could not now swear I had seen what I thought I had seen or merely dreamed it because I wanted it to be so. Likewise, on that early morning of the death of the Indian Nightingale, had Celia clung to me as she cried? Had she let me stroke her hair? Since then, she had been colder with me than before and I now foresaw a time when, surrounded by an entourage of Finn and the music master, she would forget me entirely.

I sighed and left the Studio, aware as I did so that there had been a strange sweetish smell in the room, most cloying and odious, which I knew must come from the powder adhering to Finn's wig.

Tired to my marrow, I feel. So tired, I feel the pain of exhaustion in my anus. But here I am at supper, attired in blue with a yellow bow on my lace collar, eating venison with Celia and her Musikmeister, whose name is Herr Hümmel. His family is from Hanover and he dresses like a Puritan and complains of chilblains on his feet. "Musikmeister Hümmel is a person of great refinement," Celia has informed me, but his refinement appears least in evidence at the table for a very slight paralysis of the lower lip has occasioned a tendency to dribble. I try to guess the man's age and deem it to be about fifty. His English is excellent, heavily accented but quite without fault. I find his presence moderately agreeable.

We are drinking a good claret. The pains of exhaustion fade somewhat. I am conversing with Herr Hümmel on the subject of madrigal harmonies (about which I know very little but he a great deal, thus sparing me the effort of talking) when I suddenly remember my dream of the King on my roof and how, when asked how I was ever to master the art of oboe playing, he had advised me to "learn in secret". I interrupt Musikmeister Hümmel to propose a toast to the King. We raise our glasses and I drink with great relish, aware that, though the arrival of

Finn is most irritating to me, the arrival of Herr Hümmel may prove most fortunate. For around his temporary habitation in my house I am now constructing a plan.

I glance at Celia. Warmed by the wine, she is smiling, but not at me, of course. I lower my gaze and for a few brief seconds allow myself to watch the rise and fall of her breasts.

ELEVEN

THE UNKNOWN KNOWN

My birthday is approaching. I was born under the constellation of Aquarius, the eleventh sign of the Zodiac, the sign of the water-butler, that humble but indispensable slave who fetches from wells and rivers the element so vital to the structure of human tissue. I imagine this Aquarius as an old, stooped man, his spine warped by the weight of a wooden yoke from which hang a pair of brimming pails. On he staggers, day after day, year after year, with his precious burden, but his strength is waning, he totters and stumbles and, as he moves through time, more and more water is spilled, thereby engendering in the bellies of the ancient gods an irritation stronger even than thirst. They long to give the slave's skinny buttocks a vengeful kick. They would, if they dared, send a rod of lightning to pierce his ragged neck. And yet they must not. Hopeless as he is, they cannot do without him.

Despite my birth date, the twenty-seventh of January, I have never, I think, held any notion of my own indispensability. As a child my mother looked at me lovingly and would no doubt have wept a while had I been eaten by a badger in the woods of Vauxhall. But this is all. She would not have died without my hand to hold. As a student of medicine, I prayed that my knowledge and skills might one day lie between a man and his death, but I cannot recall now that they ever did. In my brief delirious sojourn at Whitehall, I verily believed I was *becoming* indispensable to the King, but time has shown me that here I

deceived myself utterly. More recently I have longed for Celia
to esteem and value me and hold my life to be of prime importance, but much of the time she behaves towards me as if I were
not there. Since the arrival of Finn with his commission for the
portrait, she no longer regards me as her overseer. With her
picture done, the King will, as she suspects, call her back and
that will be the end of it. The duet of my imaginings will never
be played. And yet I go on trying to please her. Her voice still
moves me more than I can express. When seated near her,
before the fire in the Withdrawing Room or at the supper table,
I long to reach out and touch her. When she returns to Kew, I
know that I shall mourn her loss. I may even write foolish letters
to her, saying what I do not dare to say to her face. For I am a
paradoxical thing: a dispensable Aquarius. I lie foolishly sprawled
in the gutter of the *via della vita*. My pails, brimming not with
water but with my own appetites and vain pleas, have toppled
me; I have not been kicked.

I am to become thirty-eight years old. I shall note the arrival,
duration and waning of this day in the following manner. I shall
sleep late, hoping to dream of tennis (a sport which used to
make me strangely happy). I shall pass some hours of the
morning with Musikmeister Hümmel, pursuing my secret plan,
the unfortunate venue of which appears to be the summer-house.
In the afternoon, I shall paint Russians. In the evening I shall
devise some merriment, pay some musicians, invite Mister
James de Gourlay ("Monsieur Dégeulasse", with whom, in that
society mocks him for his pretensions, I now feel some kindred
affection) and his wife and daughters to supper and to dancing.
I will give Celia a good quantity of champagne in the hope that
it will make her kind.

As the day approaches, the weather has turned very pretty,
the fine frost of the mornings cut like diamonds by an unclouded
sun. It is most pleasant to walk in my park with the Musikmeister
and hear him agree to collude with my plan, which is that during
the time when Celia is sitting for the portrait we shall retire
together to some place where we shall not be overheard (I
suggested the cellars, but Hümmel is mortally afraid to set eyes
on a rat there, so we have agreed upon the summer-house) and

he will teach me, in secret, to master my instrument. I have impressed upon him that there is not much time, that before this spring comes I expect my wife to have returned to London. "But it is my dearest wish," I told him, "before I lose her and do not set eyes upon her again for months, or even years, to play for one of her songs – and just the one will satisfy me – a perfect accompaniment. If you will help me to do that, Herr Hümmel, you will have my lasting gratitude."

The Musikmeister looked me up and down, as if expecting to find somewhere on my unpromising person some infinitesimal piece of evidence of musicality. Finding none, he had the courtesy to smile (where the uncouth Finn would have sneered) and promised me that he would do all he could. I see now that my first opinion of him was accurate: he is an honest and agreeable man, as indeed one might expect any friend of Sir Joshua's to be. And so I fall to pondering the truth of my own words to Celia. *Does* music teach wisdom? Does it civilise the soul? If all the men and women of England were plucking at strings and lisping into reeds would the mind of the nation be quieter and more comfortable with itself?

This, then, is the night of the day of the twenty-seventh of January 1665, my thirty-eighth birthday, and I will tell you of certain disturbing things that came to pass upon it. (I note for you in parentheses how agreeable I find the phrase "came to pass" which I do not believe existed in the body of the language until King James's mighty scholars sat down and alchemised it from ancient sacred tongues and put it there.)

The day did not begin as I had imagined. I did not lie on under my turquoise canopy dreaming sportive dreams till mid-morning, but rose early to find myself wondering whether I could hope for any gifts. I am childishly excited by presents, however insignificant they may be and always feel most grateful to the giver. The notion that I might pass the day without receiving one gift whatsoever depressed me not a little. At such moments of despondency, I long not merely to *see* the King, but to *be* the King, surrounded as he is by people pressing one upon another to lay offerings at his feet.

Knowing such thoughts to be most silly, I rose and washed my eyes and face, put on a brocaded gown and descended to my kitchen, where it amuses me sometimes to concoct for myself the kind of unskilled meal that I once made upon my fire in my rooms at Ludgate. My breakfast, then, consisted of a dish of eggs coddled with cream, upon which I laid some salted anchovies – a rather excellent invention, which I ate by the kitchen range.

Will Gates found me there and informed me that a carter had arrived from London, bringing "a quantity of furs", these of course being the tabards made of badger pelts by old Trench. There were ten of them, each very adroitly sewn, with a badger's snout rearing up on either shoulder and a row of tails forming a black fringe around the hem. Having examined them (Trench, as instructed, had used a good woollen cloth for the linings), I persuaded Will to put his on. He protested at first, saying that he would not feel nimble nor ready for work in such a garment. "Will," I said, "do not be pettish. They have been designed to leave the limbs free and agile." Alas, Will did look somewhat awkward and hampered by his tabard. He is a very short, thin man and the garment appeared both too wide for him and too long, so that the badger tails trailed upon the floor and the badger snouts hung off his shoulders somewhat dejectedly. I could not suppress a little attack of mirth.

"Alas, Will," I said, "I think your particular tabard will have to be altered."

"It's not worth the expense, Sir," said Will, heaving the thing over his hard little head, "for I shall not wear it."

"You *will* wear it," I declared. "This entire household will keep these things upon them until springtime, thus preventing chills and agues and all manner of ailments."

"Forgive me, Sir Robert," said Will, "but I shall not."

"You will, Will," I said feebly, but though I am master of my house and Will is an excellent servant, I could plainly see that upon this subject there is going to be some conflict between us.

Having dressed myself and put my own tabard on, I went in search of the Musikmeister, to whom I would offer to lend one during our chilly hours in the summer-house. Though my tabard feels, I admit, somewhat heavy, it imparts to the body an immediate and agreeable warmth. Furthermore, I look outlandish in it and require only some bizarre hat or headdress of fur to resemble very nicely the Russians of my dreams. And then a teasing thought entered my mind: Would the King not be amused by such a garment? Should I dare, on this my birthday that promised to be empty of gifts, to despatch one to Whitehall? Was it possible that my imagination could be father to a new Royal fashion? How excellent it would be if, when Celia returned to Court, she found all the fops and gallants hung with badger fur and the words *"tablier Merivel"* upon all their laughing lips!

Determining to give the matter some deep thought (the King had sent me his gift of surgical instruments; would he be offended by some return gift from me?), I got my oboe and went to the room of Herr Hümmel and from there we made our way, unseen by any, to the summer-house.

The place was indeed cold and not a little triste, the windows latticed over with cobwebs and the floor strewn with downy feathers, as if a dove chick had flown into the humble habitation and exploded in mid-air. I apologised to Herr Hümmel, who had wisely put on his tabard, informing him that in summer the place was very pleasant and expressing my hope that he would return to visit me during that kinder season. He thanked me and suggested we begin upon the lesson straight away, before our fingers became too numb. He requested that I play a few scales for him, followed by "some short piece of your choice". This could only be *Swans Do All A-Swimming Go*, it being the one thing I could play from beginning to end without fault.

He listened. His face betrayed no scorn or dismay. When I had finished, he did allow himself the ghost of a sigh. "Very well," he said. "I think we must begin again. You are self-tutored, perhaps?"

"Yes, entirely."

"And, alas, the fingering is awkward, Sir Robert, and the position of the lips upon the reed too forward. You must whisper to your reed, you see. Not kiss or suck it."

"Ah."

"But you will learn quickly, I think. You have the zeal to learn."

"Yes. Zeal I have."

"So."

Here, Herr Hümmel gently took my instrument from me, blew away my spittle and raised it to his own mouth, making some strange contortions with his lips before allowing them to settle in a hesitant-seeming posture around the reed. He then bid me watch carefully the fingering he employed for the scale of C, his hands seeming hardly to move at all. I noticed that his fingers are white and slender, as if the bone had coloured the flesh, whereas mine are somewhat red and plump. Clearly, I have not been fashioned to be an oboe player. I determined, however, that this would not make me lose heart. Music – that plaintive song at my wedding – had made me turn my face from medicine. For all those lost years of work, it owed me some recompense.

This first lesson lasted for the best part of an hour, during which time our breath clouded the glass panels of the summer-house and my feet seemed clamped into iron shoes, so achingly chill did they become. Did I make a little progress? I do not really know. And so cold was I by the end of the hour that I did not care. Such is the burden of our human clay: our spirits soar to some icy heaven while our bodies creep back to the tame hearth.

My invitation to Dégeulasse and his family had been accepted with alacrity and (still giftless towards two o'clock, no one at all having made any reference to my birthday) I was comforting myself by planning my soirée when a village boy rode up my drive on a donkey bringing a message from the vicar of Bidnold, the Reverend Timothy Sackpole. I was requested to come at once to the church.

"Why?" I enquired of the boy.

"I do not know, Sir."

"How like a clergyman, not to give a reason!"

"Except that it be dire and urgent."

"That is not a reason, lad. That is a tick of the ecclesiastical mind."

As my horse was being saddled, this thought assailed me: had the conceited Sackpole somehow found out that this day saw the dawn of my thirty-ninth year? Did he foresee some divine punishment for this stumbling Aquarian if he were not brought before an altar before the sun set? Being only a little past the shortest day of the year, the sun was indeed going down already – hence the supposed urgency of the message? Though it amuses me to go now and again to hear a sermon from Sackpole, I am not seen at church as often as I should be, preferring to send my prayers to God in the quiet of my room or (as already described) in the company of a lardy cake. It was thus quite possible that this clergyman, who strikes me as a petulant person, should wish to deliver himself of some reprimand, the tone and substance of which I could already hear in my mind. He would begin by asking me to what I had given any thought on this the anniversary of my birth. I would reply that my mind had circled vainly about an empty table on which I had imagined Celia placing the gift of an embossed music case or a handsome picture frame. He would answer that such preoccupations will bar me from the Kingdom of Heaven . . .

But it was not to be thus. When I arrived at the churchyard, I saw in the light of the declining sun a small throng of people grouped about the gate and heard the sound of voices and weeping.

"Whatever is it?" I enquired of the boy on the donkey, but he did not reply; he was staring at the scene with some alarm.

I dismounted. As I did so, the Reverend Sackpole came towards me.

"Ah," I said, "what have we here, Vicar?"

"Thank you for coming, Sir Robert," Sackpole said courteously, thus putting from my mind the suspicion that he was about to lecture me upon my lack of faith. "It seems we have need of a medical man and Doctor Murdoch is not to be found."

"Sackpole," I said, "I was once a student of medicine, but my studies were never completed. I am not equipped – "

"No great skill is being asked of you. Let us step aside a little from these good people – the boy will hold your horse – and I will explain what has happened."

"Assure me first that you do not expect me to start saving lives."

"What is requested of you, Sir, is your judgement."

"My judgement? Well, let me tell you, Vicar, that that is not perhaps as sound as it once was. I am most prone to error."

"Not one of us in infallible, Sir Robert, but this may prove to be a simple matter for you. Come."

I followed Sackpole and we passed through a small door into the vestry of the church. The place was dark and smelled of hayseed. Sackpole closed the door and laid his hand upon my arm.

"There is," he now whispered, "a most horrible suspicion come among the village people: the suspicion of witchcraft."

"Witchcraft? In Bidnold?"

"Yes. I shall tell you the tale as briefly as I may. The people outside, many of them weeping, as you heard, were mourners at a burial I performed at noon. The deceased was a young girl, Sarah Hodge, not seventeen years old and died in a sudden and terrible manner."

"What manner was it?"

"I shall come there, Sir Robert. The matter before us is this: Was there some Devil's work done on Sarah Hodge – as now some of those parishioners outside maintain – or was there none at all?"

I looked at Sackpole. I saw that the clergyman was uneasy and would not hold my glance. Clearly, he was preparing himself to ask of me something mortally not to my liking, in all probability the examination of the corpse of the dead girl. I opened my mouth to pre-empt this request by telling Sackpole that the last *post mortem* examination I had witnessed had been upon a bull toad in the King's laboratory and that I was no longer able to interpret correctly the imprimatura left by death upon the human body, but Sackpole went imperiously on: "The matter is a difficult one," he said, "and . . ."

I held up my hand at this point and requested that the Vicar go no further with his tale until he had contradicted my assumption that I was being asked to make a medical judgement upon a corpse. Somewhat to my surprise, he informed me that the body of Sarah Hodge would remain undisturbed in the ground. He then, in a manner altogether nervous and afraid (somewhat confounding my view of him as a man of impenetrable conceit) told me the following story.

An old widow woman, known to all as Wise Nell, had for many years acted as midwife to the parish. She was also a healer and primitive apothecary, cultivating her own physic garden and said to have some power of healing in her hands, this power coming to her through her faith in God, or so she claimed. For some months now, Wise Nell had not been seen at church. She protested that a rheumatism in her knees prevented her from walking there. But the people of Bidnold began to notice a change in her demeanour (where, before she had been quiet and calm, she now seemed agitated) and in her hands, particularly in the feel of her hands! The skin had become hardened and calloused; the pressure of her palms now brought to the head or limbs of the sufferers a moment's icy chill. And the whispers began to be heard: Wise Nell is wise no longer, her love of God has been replaced by love of the Devil, the power in her hard, cold hands is the power of Satan . . .

"You must know," said Sackpole at this point, "what infinite terror is felt by a God-fearing people at the idea of witchcraft. And it is to the clergy that men come with all the tales of devilry, saying so-and-so is a veritable witch and such-and-such is the proof and now there must be a burning or a drowning or I know not what terrible persecution to be played out. And yet the entire matter, to my mind, is one of great difficulty and complexity for proof of innocence and proof of guilt may both be manufactured, and I have come to believe that in most of these cases only God sees to the heart of the thing. For this reason, I hoped never to hear the word 'witchcraft' uttered against any in Bidnold. And I will not deny it, I am afraid of what may follow."

Sackpole took from his sleeve a somewhat grimy handkerchief and blew his nose. Still ignorant of what my own part was to be in this story, I waited for him to prise from his nostrils two small fillets of hardened mucus, and then asked him to continue.

"Well," he said, "we come now to the matter of Sarah Hodge. She was, as I have told you, a young girl with all her life before her and yet, it seems, had fallen into a dull melancholy, occasioned, some say, by that she had cut off her hair – of a rich chestnut brown colour – to sell for a few shillings to a wig-maker. I cannot say, Sir Robert, whether a young woman might so mourn the loss of her hair that she could weep for it for two months or more, but weep she did and would not eat and grew thin and weak and declared a loathing for all things.

"Her parents are poor cottars and ignorant and had no knowledge of how to help her, but yet in the end sent her to Wise Nell, begging the old woman to do anything she could to revive in her some joy.

"I am told Sarah Hodge was three hours with Nell. She was given a potion to drink which, she was told, contained the blood of swallows, birds of summer and symbols of man's ease.

"When she came out from Nell's cottage, her cheeks were flushed, I understand, and her body most hot all over. She felt well, she said, with the blood of the birds inside her and wanted to dance. So her brothers, glad to see her happy again in spite of her shorn head, took up some tambourines and a pipe and played a tune for Sarah and she lifted up her skirts and began to hop about and kick her feet and would not stop for half an hour or more, her face growing more and more hot until the cheeks were a dark wine-red and still she danced on, tearing open her bodice and showing her breasts that were flushed like her face, on and on until suddenly she bent over and out of her mouth came a fountain of black vomit and she fell down and began to rave that she had drunk poison from a nipple in the Devil's own neck, and within some twenty minutes she was dead."

There was a hard bench in the vestry. I sat down upon it. I had not expected to be listening to talk of black vomit and Devil's nipples on my birthday.

"It now seems," Sackpole said, "that, among the other changes in the person of Wise Nell, the village folk have noticed the appearance, on her neck, of a brownish spot she claimed to be a wart, but which has grown in size, the skin around it becoming puckered and discoloured, so that it now resembles in every way a dug or teat. And you know, Sir Robert, that such an outrage to nature is commonly held to be sure and certain sign of the presence of Satan within the soul. And this is why – to calm the people's anger and gain for myself both time and knowledge in the matter – I sent for you. What I am asking of you is that you go with me to the cottage of Wise Nell and there conduct an examination of this thing upon her neck and tell me, to the best of your knowledge, which I hear from Mistress Storey and indeed from Lady Bathurst is considerable, whether it be a proper nipple or merely some other growth such as a wart or a cyst."

I paused a moment before replying. Then I said: "And if I find this thing to be what you believe it to be, what will happen to Wise Nell?"

"As I informed you, we do not expect you to be the sole arbiter in the case, but only to give one medical opinion, after which the woman will be examined by others."

"Such as Doctor Murdoch?"

"Except that he has not been seen since the death of Sarah Hodge."

"By whom, then?"

"We shall send to other villages for their medical men."

"And if they find 'proof' of the Devil?"

Sackpole drew his fingers across his lips.

"I do not favour persecutions. Yet I cannot be seen to harbour the Devil in my parish."

"She will be killed."

"Or driven away. I shall try to see to it that she is driven away."

It is now the twenty-eighth of January. A cold, sunless morning. I grew too tired last night to finish the story of what happened upon my birthday, but I shall continue here. I am older by one day and wiser, I fear, by a good deal. For I have had a glimpse into my future.

Though I would have preferred to return home to do a little painting and supervise the arrangements for my supper party,

I had no choice but to accompany the Reverend Sackpole to the low, thatched dwelling where this unfortunate Wise Nell leads a most strange crepuscular life, so dark is her house, so low its ceilings and small its windows. I am not tall, but I could barely stand up straight in her little parlour. So this, I thought, is one among many persecutions endured by the poor: they are persecuted by their own rooms.

Though Sackpole announced our arrival in a voice of good cheer (does an executioner employ such a jovial tone when he asks a condemned person to lay his head upon the block?) I could see by the glimmer of a single rushlight that Nell, seated upon a rocking chair with her arms folded round her body, was most horribly afraid of what was about to happen. Her eyes, which appeared to me vast and bulging, like the eyes of a bulldog, stared pleadingly at the Vicar and she began to mumble that she was servant to no one but God and the King and that she knew of no reason why Sarah Hodge should have died. There was a foul smell in the room, as of a rich fart. I was considering what this might be – whether the smell of swallow corpses and the like to be used in Nell's medical remedies, the smell of a poor meal of tripe left in the air too long, or the smell of fear itself which I know to be an actual phenomenon occasioned by the malfunction or over-function of certain glands.

Most profoundly did I long to be out of this hovel, but knew that I would not be allowed to leave until I had performed my examination, for at the door to Nell's cottage were pressed the parents and brothers of the dead Sarah, their mouths full of accusation and cries for justice, and accompanied by others of the village, all having an unmistakable air of poverty and wretchedness upon them and thus causing me to wonder if they – who looked to me today for a judgement – would look to me tomorrow for sixpences.

Hoping to get the matter done with as speedily as I could, I approached Nell and told her, as gently as I was able, that I accused her of nothing, but, as sometime physician at Whitehall (I did not tell her my patients had been dogs), I was there "to look at this small thing upon your neck and see what manner of fleshy matter it truly is".

Nell turned upon me, then, her dog's eyes, pulling her shawl up round her chin, as if to bandage a wound. "Succuba . . . Devil's Woman . . . what words they lay upon me! Words from the very hell of their own skulls. But God knows my heart and I have done no evil spell in all my days . . ." Nell ranted on thus, her eyes staring the while at my badger tabard, in which, slightly to my surprise, I found myself still attired. Sackpole repeatedly tried to interrupt Nell's protestations of innocence, but what I now began to perceive was that Nell was so fascinated by my furs that thoughts about them (and indeed their wearer) were distracting her so that her speech was slowing and the words of her defence gradually being forgotten and I guessed – correctly – that she would soon enough lapse into silence.

I understood then that, if I applied a small amount of cunning, I would be able to calm Nell sufficiently for me to look at her neck without having to restrain or frighten her, the idea of which repelled me. I thus whispered to Sackpole that he should withdraw a little, to observe the proceedings from a corner of the dank room, but talk no more to Nell until the examination was over.

Sensing, no doubt, that Nell was less afraid now, he did as I requested. I approached Nell and knelt down by her chair, forcing myself not to gag, for the smell from her body was indeed very odious.

Fumblingly, from her shawl, she reached out a bony hand and laid it very tenderly on the badger's snout at my left shoulder then began stroking the head. I watched her closely. Her head was nodding, as if in recognition of something. For a long while, I said nothing and did not move. Nell's hand now moved to my right shoulder and touched the badger's nose there. When I looked again at her eyes, I saw that much of the fear had left them. Now, I thought, I will move the rushlight nearer and ask her to unbind her shawl and lay her head back, so that I may see the growth. But just as I was about to reach out to move the light, Nell began to speak again. "I dreamed of this," she whispered. "A man wearing an animal. He was not my accuser, but I his."

I said nothing.

"I his," Nell repeated.

"Of what did you accuse him?" I asked quietly.

"Gone from me," she said. "Forgotten."

"But he had done some wrong?"

Nell nodded. "Some wrong. And a long fall would be the way of it."

"In your dreams, he fell?"

"Yes."

"From the Lord's grace?"

"From all grace. And into confusion."

I was silent. My hand was out, about to take hold of the rushlight and yet I could not complete this simple action, so perturbed did I now feel. I could no longer look at Nell's face. My heartbeat had quickened. My hands were clammy. I tasted bile in my mouth. If she can see into my future, I began to tell myself, then it is certain she possesses some kind of devilish power. But then I reined in my thought, knowing it to be a judgement born only of fear and reminding myself that there are many kinds and species of bewitchment in mortal existence, of which fear may be the most terrible and love the most everlasting. That she had made this pronouncement about my life troubled me awesomely, the more so because it was my birthday. Part of me wished to question Nell further, to "know the worst" as the saying has it, yet the other, cowardly, part wished to know no more whatsoever, being in no way equipped to conduct itself courageously should "the worst" turn out to be very bad indeed. The notion of a "fall into confusion" was quite frightening enough.

I heard, at this moment, a knocking on Nell's door and some shouting from the crowd, and Sackpole, whose presence in the room I had all but forgotten, whispered urgently to me that I should proceed with the examination "now, at once, Sir Robert".

Thus, with my hand still shaking, I moved the light towards Nell and asked her to show me her mark and tell me what she thought it to be. "For it is *your* mark, Nell, and you alone know when it first came there, and whether any have touched it and of what kind, if any, is the fluid or matter that comes out of it."

But Nell did not speak or move. With the light upon her face now, I could see on her cheek a number of large moles or warts, of the disfiguring kind that so distressed poor Oliver Cromwell, our sometime leader and chief of the Commonwealth. It is common medical knowledge that a body, once afflicted by these things, is very often host to terrible flowerings and crops of them, as if they grew from spores of themselves like mushrooms, and I fully expected, as Nell at last unwound her shawl, to see another such a one upon her neck.

Revealed eventually, however, the growth, seated below the ear and on the pathway of the jugular vein, did not resemble a wart. It was the size of a small coin and of a liverish brown colour, the skin being most raised towards its centre. I had seen nothing like it during all my anatomical years. Had the skin not been discoloured, I would have pronounced it to be the puckered vestigial scar of some boil or fistula, but the pigmenting of the skin was most pronounced, whereas scar tissue becomes white over time. The thing that it most brought to mind was indeed a small nipple, such as one might see upon the half-grown breasts of a child of twelve years.

Most crucial in my inspection of the thing would be my touching of it – to see what reaction this could cause in the old woman and to determine whether any issue came forth from it.

Nell stayed still, one hand always caressing my fur, but I now felt her body wracked by a violent trembling. At my back, the thumping on the door and the shouts from the village people became more impatient.

"Well?" hissed Sackpole. "What do you find?"

And I faltered.

A moment ago, I had felt disgust, then fear. I had bid myself to be calm and go about my task with the alert yet passive mind of the physician. But now as I tried to take the nipple (or whatever the thing might prove to be) between my finger and thumb and I felt the intensity of the fear in Nell's being, I was prey to a most sudden and profound feeling of sorrow and despair. For one last moment, I remained kneeling, regarding the hard, cold, knotted hand of Wise Nell on the badger snout. Then I stood up. I turned to the shadows where Sackpole waited.

"To the best of my knowledge, there is no matter out of the ordinary here," I said. "The thing is a simple cyst."

And I fled from the place, pushing my way out through the throng of people who snatched at me – with hands and words – and then breaking into a run.

I have no recollection of what I did next. Presumably, I found my horse and mounted and rode home, but I do not remember doing this. The next memory that I have is of lying in a hot bath and being stared at by Will who had noticed several welts upon the skin of my shoulders, as if something or someone had scratched me there. "Badly, Sir," he says. "Very badly."

Then I am readying myself for my soirée. My shoulders are bandaged. I feel, in my stomach and in my mind a deep unease.

I go downstairs and I hear myself tell the musicians, who have just arrived, that my party has been cancelled. I give them money and bid them go home. I then call Will and instruct him to ride to de Gourlay's house and tell the family that I am ill and that there will be no musical evening.

At this moment, Celia descends the stairs. She is wearing a dress of dove grey taffeta, its bodice laced with apricot ribbons. In her hair, newly curled into ringlets, are more ribbons of this same bewitching colour.

I cannot move. Down she comes, down towards me, and for once she is smiling and I know that this smile is for me, and I feel the beauty of it, right to my bowel. And so at last, at the end of this most troubling day on which I have been told that my life is edging towards a great fall, I admit to myself what I have known since the night of the Bathurst's party, that I have done the one thing of which the King believed me to be incapable: I have fallen in love with my wife.

TWELVE

A DROWNING

I am ashamed to set down what happened on the evening of my birthday, yet I will try to do so, in the hope that the act of writing will assuage my guilt somewhat and allow me the rest that has eluded me for two nights.

I was not hungry and the thought of the elaborate meal I had had prepared for Dégeulasse and his family disgusted me. All I wanted was to be alone with Celia.

Taking her hand (I tried to make this gesture a gentle and affectionate one, but I fear it was rough and peremptory) I said: "Celia. It is a clear night. Come with me to the roof and we shall look at the stars through my telescope and try to read our futures."

Celia protested that she would feel cold upon the roof and that our absence would be discourteous to my guests.

"There are no guests," I said. "No one is coming."

At this moment, Finn appeared in the hall, dressed in his scarlet and gold attire and his blond wig. He looked reproachfully at my hand gripping Celia's wrist. "You may take off your silly garb, Robin," I said acidly. "There is to be no evening."

(My jealousy of Finn is like a tumour on my liver. It spreads and I grow jaundiced and sick.)

So I climb up to my roof, pulling Celia after me. We step out onto the freezing leads. I stare up at the sky and there is the crowded Cosmos, infinite and beyond measure. Of all the conflicting rules that govern its existence, I am ignorant, even, of the first one, or so I discover.

Celia is shivering. I take off my coat (a black camlet thing, frogged with gold braid) and put it round her shoulders.

I put my eye to the telescope. As I scan the sky, I see, at first, only the meaningless dust of the heavens. Then I notice that the planet Jupiter, with its little girdle of moons, is very bright tonight. "Ah," I say, posing as a man who knows his way about the planets and the stars, "*voilà* Jupiter. Uncommonly bright. Excellent. A good portent. Jupiter being of course the reigning planet of all earthly Kings. So we are smiled upon from on high."

I guide Celia to the telescope. Despite the little warmth afforded by my coat, she is still trembling. I am reminded of the fear of the afternoon. The knowledge that Celia is afraid dismays me. I must soothe and quieten her. So I put my arms around her. She cannot pull away from me, for we are on the very precipice of the roof. "No, Merivel!" she cries out. But I cannot let her go. I cannot. I have not the will. I turn her towards me. She tugs her head away from me, just as Wise Nell tried to do so that I would not touch her teat. It is not my hand that reaches for Celia's neck, but my lips. On the very place where a witch may suckle her creature, I begin to kiss her. She struggles and cries out again, but I do not let go. And now I am no longer satisfied with the smooth flesh of the neck. I want her mouth. Using all my strength, I bring her head towards mine. I feel her breasts against my chest. My head is throbbing and my breath coming in short gasps. And I force upon her a lover's kiss.

Not for one moment does she yield, but struggles every instant to be free of me. I am hot now. As heated as a boy with wanting. Celia arches her back, frees her mouth from mine. In place of the lost kiss I smother her with words. I beg her to think no more about the King. "If he is not weary of you now, then in one year he will be. For have I not said it, he is mercury and cannot be held or kept. He will never give you the child you want, Celia. Never! But I could give you a child. Have my son! For I am your husband and all I ask of you is that you allow me to love you!"

And then she spat at me. She spat in my eyes, blinding me
for a brief moment – long enough for me to slacken my grip and
for her to stumble towards the window through which we had
climbed, letting my coat fall from her shoulders. When I turned,
she was clambering in and screaming, screaming for Sophia, the
odious Farthingale.

I could have followed and caught her. I could have thrown her
down on the attic floor.

I did not. I wiped her spittle from my eyes. I damned God
and damned my parents for my foul nature. I cursed a world in
which I had no one to love me but whores and courtesans. I
kicked violently at the base of the telescope, thus cruelly bruising
my toe.

Though shivering very grievously, I stayed upon the roof for
a while, as if trying to fill my being with the icy night.

I do not know what time it was when I crept back inside the
house. I closed the window. As I walked through the attic
towards the stairs, I noticed a sweet but sickly smell which I
knew to be familiar, yet I could not remember what it was.

I have slept a little. How many days have passed now since my
birthday, I do not know. I seem to have lost hold of time.

I had a diabolical dream. Finn, naked but for a green singlet,
made love to my wife up against a wall. I killed him. I shot him
in the buttocks with twenty-nine arrows.

When I woke, I remembered where it had come from, that
sweetish smell in the attic: it is the smell of Finn's wig. And so
I conclude, he is a spy. Either of his own making, or sent here
by the King. There is no doubt he saw all that passed upon the
roof, and will report it to Whitehall, thus causing me to appear,
not merely silly, but grievously misguided – an opinion of myself
I find it most easy to share.

And I enquire of this sottish Merivel: "How have you arrived
at this state of affairs? (You, who thought yourself to be utterly
indifferent to quiet Celia, liking only women of vulgar plumage.)
Is vanity the key? On your wedding night, the King lay with
your wife, while you plunged to oblivion with a village jade; have

you, since that night, aspired to replace the Monarch in Celia's heart?"

It is beyond my comprehension. Love has entered me like a disease, so stealthily I have not seen its approach nor heard its footsteps. My mind recognises the folly of it and yet I still boil and burn with it, precisely as with a fever.

To whom or what shall I turn in order to be cured? From his damp habitation, I hear Pearce make a Pearcean reply: he does not pause or hesitate before instructing, "To yourself, Merivel."

I am composing, upon paper, an apology to Celia. I have set down that "certain events occurring upon my birthday so troubled me that my brain was prey to a sudden spasm of madness, causing me thus to force myself upon you so odiously", but seem unable to proceed with my letter further than this, causing me to wonder whether the lies and fictions underlying all human discourse may be a primal cause of the impenetrable silence we hear within our own skulls.

I sit and stare at my piece of vellum. I brush my lip with my quill. My anus aches with a fidgety tiredness, likewise my right leg. My hand upon the paper is chill. I cannot lie to myself about how ill I feel. I conceive the idea that I may be dying and feel cheered by it, releasing me as it does from the burden of declaring myself to be mad. My thoughts, as you will have discerned by now, are in a boiling muddle. To add to my discomfort, I have found lice in my hogs' bristles, which vermin plague me with an unendurable itching. I have instructed Will Gates to prepare a head bath of vinegar and guaiacum, a remedy I patented myself while at Cambridge and for which my fellow students, unwashed and lousy as they were, came eventually to thank me.

Until I have finished and despatched my apology to Celia, I do not wish to be seen by her, so I do not stir from my room, eating my meals off a tray, like a convalescent. I thus have no idea what is occurring in my house – whether my servants are wearing their fur tabards as instructed, (Will Gates is not), whether the portrait is nearing its consummation (in the rendering of a Scottish glen, perhaps, bathed in sunlight behind Celia's fair head?), whether Finn has informed upon me to the King. I sense myself to be in danger, but cannot determine from whence it will come. The visage of Nell the witch returns very often to my mind. The welts on my shoulders are slow to heal.

Today, Will brings me a letter. But this is no Royal summons. It is a poor illiterate note, written by one calling himself Septimus Frame, Merchant Seaman. The handwriting is so vile and shuddering, it gives the appearance of having been written at sea in a Hebridean gale. The tidings it relates, when at last I am able to decipher it, are dramatic. This is what is says:

Most Kind and honourable Sir,
I write upon request of the widow Pierpoint, who has not the gift of any alphabet.
She begs me to inform you how that her husband, George Pierpoint, Bargeman, was drowned this Wednesday last under London Bridge while leaning from his boat to catch a haddock and falls into the boil about the stanchions and is gone down, lost.
She requires me to say to you she knows you to be a Person of Kindness. She begs you to remember that she must buy coal for her irons and her washing cauldrons or else come to a poor end which may be the Workhouse.
In sum she requests me to ask of you the gift of thirty shillings, in consideration whereof she blesses you and declares you to be a most Proper and Charitable Man.
   From A Humble Servant of the Nation,
   Septimus Frame, Merchant Seaman.

So Pierpoint is drowned! The wise river will hear no more of his knavery and cheating and foul language, but has taken him to her deep. And Rosie eats her little suppers of bread and whelks alone . . .

I feel momentarily cheered by news of this death. I imagine for a moment the jumping haddock slipping through Pierpoint's rough hands and, as he falls, his barge going away on the current. Aloud I whisper, "There was no Overseer," but cannot determine precisely what I mean by this. All I know is that I have no feeling of pity for Pierpoint: I am glad his life has ceased.

In times other than these, it would have been my first thought, upon receiving such a letter, to make my way speedily to London, to press into Rosie's hot hand the money requested and cheerfully usurp her husband's place in her bed for a number of rumpled nights. As matters stand, however, I feel too ill, contrite, confused, lovesick and afraid to stir out of the house. I am shipwrecked here with my passion. In the distance, I can easily imagine I hear guns of a great Man-of-War. I must go to work again upon my apology . . .

Now, I perceive why I cannot write it. I cannot write it because it must end with a promise I cannot make. I construct the sentence: "On my honour, I vouchsafe never again, as long as you do not wish it, to touch you or impose upon you declarations of feelings I know you to find most loathsome," but I know, even as I write, that I will not be true to this. I know that, such is my nature, it will on some future occasion explode with the very words my wife does not wish to hear. I sense the stuff of this explosion already gathering about my heart, like pus. Does an unrequited love, in time, make a corpse of the lover? Shall I see the drowned Pierpoint before I ever lie with my own wife? (How much I despise my own self-pity.)

Sweet Rosie, I write, knowing she cannot read, but desperate at last to speak my thoughts to a friend. *I shall send, with this collection of Merivel's ramblings, a Japanese purse containing thirty shillings. The purse itself has some value and is yours to keep or sell as you will.*

I am sorry for the drowning of Pierpoint. To die for a mere haddock is most lamentable.

I would journey to London to console you for the loss of a husband except that I appear to have tumbled into a very profound melancholy and unease of body and mind so that I find myself unable to move from my room. Where I stay wrapped in badgers' pelts staring at a grey and solid sky. In short, I am not Merivel, but a mopish phlegmatic and futile person I do not like at all. My old self, though most outlandish, was amusing company. This new man is loathsome. I have asked him to leave and never more

*return, but there he sits, scratching, fidgeting, blowing his nose,
sighing, yawning and doing a little paltry writing. I wish he would
get into his grave.*

*This person – whom I shall rechristen Fogg – recently had a
dream of the King, in which His Majesty asked him: What is the
First Rule of the Cosmos? Fogg, in his solitude, finds his mind
tormented by this question. It adheres to his thinking like a mussel
to rock and yet cannot be prised open. Last night, however, on
hearing of the dying of Pierpoint, it began to yield a little to his
probing. Thus, Fogg set this down as a probability; that the First
Rule of the Cosmos is the Separateness of All Things. As each
planet and star is entire of itself and not joined to any other planet
or star, so must every person upon earth remain separate and
alone, even in death. Thus in impenetrable solitude did Pierpoint
die.*

*But whereas the planets are serene in their separateness, know-
ing any collision with one another likely to destroy them and return
them to dust, Fogg remarks that he, along with very many of his
race, finds his Separateness the most entirely sad fact of his
existence and is every moment hopeful of colliding with someone
who will obscure it from his mind. Yet what he now perceives is
the folly of such a collision. Collision is fatal because it transgresses
the First Rule. In collision, Fogg is split apart. In collision, he
turns to jealous gas, to heartless dust . . .*

At this inconclusive (and somewhat incoherent) point, my
scribbles to Rosie were interrupted. Will Gates came up to my
room and informed me that Mister de Gourlay had arrived and
urgently requested to see me.

"Look at me, Will," I said. "I can see no one until I am well
again."

"He asks me to tell you that he has brought with him something
to make you well."

"Ah," I said, "the blood of swallows, perhaps."

"I beg your pardon, Sir?"

"I would prefer to remain alone, Will. I have much to think
about."

"He is very pressing, Sir."

"There's the reason he is not popular. He has not grasped that life is a quadrille, necessitating backward as well as forward *pas.*"

Upon saying this, I immediately reflected that my apology to Celia was one such backward *pas*, without which I would not be able to resume any dance whatsoever, unless perhaps a Dance of Death. Thus, while Will was further pressing Dégeulasse's suit, I quickly laid aside my letter (if such it was) to Rosie Pierpoint, took up a clean sheet of vellum and wrote the following simple message:

Fair Celia,
I am mightily sorry for my foul behaviour. I beg you to forgive me this transgression, that I may remain your friend and loyal protector.

R.M.

I then instructed Will to bring Dégeulasse to my room and, having done so, to deliver my short note to Celia.

I put on my wig. The anxiety within me had lessened by a small measure, seeming to cause a sudden drop in the temperature of my blood. Whereas I had been boiling and burning, I now felt chill. I reached for my tabard and put it on and sat with my arms tucked under its apron. What, I wished to enquire, as I waited for my guest, had happened to my painting of Russians? Was it ever begun anywhere but in my mind?

Dégeulasse's arrival interrupted me before I could find an answer to this. The sight of him relieved me of worry about my appearance. He is one of those people who is most horribly and voluptuously ugly, but whose ugliness one seems to forget the moment he leaves one's sight, only to remember it more forcibly again the next time one lays eyes upon him. (I do find myself wondering whether he appears thus to his wife and children, so that his family like him most when he is not with them.)

To compound the fleshy grossness of his features, Dégeulasse has upon his left cheek a very virulent psora he is in the habit of trying to conceal with his hand. It pains me to see him do this. There must be some remedy, I found myself thinking, but of course I had forgotten what it was. It was he, at all events, who had come to play the role of physician, not I. He appeared honestly concerned that "since the night of your intended party, it is reported you are not much yourself" and proceeded to put before me a bottle containing some green cordial. "Got from a mountebank, a regular quack!" he announced. "Not worth the threepence charged!"

"Ah," I said. "Then why do you bring it to me, Mister de Gourlay?"

"Because it is the most efficacious cure for melancholy that has ever been distilled."

"And yet you said it was not worth the small sum you expended . . ."

"So I did! And which do you believe, Sir Robert? Is it valueless or is it beyond price?"

"I believe neither . . ."

"Very wise."

"Until I have taken some . . ."

"Precisely. Thus, you have invested it with no expectation? You are neutral?"

"Yes."

"You believe in equal measure that its properties are worthless and that it may also work a wonderous cure?"

"I believe less in cure."

"Yet you admit it to be a possibility?"

"Yes."

"Excellent. And you will promise to take some before sleeping?"

"I will."

"Perfect."

De Gourlay sat down. He was beaming. I have noticed this about human beings: secret knowledge makes them smile. It is the smile of power. It is invariably irritating but, on this occasion, I found myself intrigued that Dégeulasse was playing a little game with me. I was wondering what, precisely, the game was about, when Dégeulasse gave his large belly a comradely slap and declared: "Expectation, you see! Reason's whore! And there she clings round all our necks, *n'est-ce pas*?"

"You may be right."

"I am right. Consider your soirée, so lately cancelled. I cannot describe to you with what expectation of happiness and lasting consequence my wife and daughters had invested it, I cannot describe to you!"

"I am sorry . . ."

"No, no. Do not apologise. No one had informed my wife that great and influential men from Court would be there, who would, in the space of that one evening, advance our fortunes by three thousand livres per annum. No one had promised my daughters that at your table they would meet the sons of Marquises or young nephews of Prince Rupert. And yet this is what they expected of it! And when informed the party was cancelled, do you know what they did, all three of them? They fell to weeping!"

"Well," I said, "I regret that no eminences from Court or kindred of Rupert had agreed to come to it."

"As I did not believe they would, or at least, I did and did not believe they would in precisely equal measure and so stored up for myself no hope whatsoever."

"Most wise, I would venture."

"Precisely. Now do feel at your ease to confide in me what has happened to you, if it pleases you to do so. I am a man of absolutely no wisdom at all. Then again, my mother believes me to be one of the most clever people ever to reside in Norfolk."

Dégeulasse laughed heartily. This was the first time I had heard laughter in very many days and it reverberated in the room most curiously, like an echo or like a sound coming from under water. Then it ceased and there was silence, and, in the silence, my gaze fixed upon the crusty, enflamed skin of de Gourlay's cheek, the remedy for the psora returned to me and I said: "Alas I do not *know* what has happened to me. Thus, I can confide in no one. On the other hand, I know what will cure the suppurations on your face."

"No!" said Dégeulasse quickly. "Do not say you know! Say you know and yet you do not know."

"Very well. There are two remedies. Either of these will help the infection, or neither will help it at all. The first is plantain water mixed with a little loose sugar; the second is a treacle posset. These will or will not cure you."

De Gourlay thanked me and laughed again and seemed impatient for me to join in the laughter. But I could not. Now I saw that, by believing in the cleverness and wisdom of his own game, he was in fact rendering himself rather foolish. For what was the game but another self-deception: by juggling negatives and positives he expected to be able to protect himself from pain, yet it was clear to me that he craved as much from life as any man. For what was the insertion of the "de" into his surname but a declaration of hope?

Night seemed to have come by the time de Gourlay left my room. Though I had put a taper to my fire, I felt distressingly cold. A bath, I decided, was the only thing that would warm me.

I called for Will. He informed me that he had delivered my note to Celia.

"How is my wife?" I asked him.

"Listless, Sir. Impatient for the return of Mister Finn, so that the portrait may be finished."

"Finn has left?"

"Yes, Sir. The day after your cancelled party. On Whitehall business, he boasted."

So, I was not wrong. Finn had been appointed (or had made himself) the King's spy.

As I sat in my tub (my head lolling and somewhat uncomfortable, so that it occurred to me to design a chin-strap for myself such as I had imagined for the people of the River Mar) I tried to determine what consequences this spying would have for me. Knowing the King as I did, supreme as he is in his power over every person living in his Kingdom, I was prepared to wager that he would be amused by the folly of my love for Celia. "Well, Merivel . . ." I could hear him say, "what a clumsy impersonation of Romeo you do make! Tussling with Juliet upon the balcony! In future, do try to remember which role has been given to you. You are Paris." I smiled. So perfectly could I remember the inflections of the King's voice that I could almost believe him to be present in the room, just beyond the steam rising from my bath-water.

I closed my eyes. Will was ladling hot water over my shoulders and stomach, yet I was starting to feel cold again and it was the coldness of a fever. "Bring more water, Will," I instructed, "and let it be piping hot."

"This is hot enough, Sir. You will vaporise."

"Do not argue. Go, heat more water. I am drowning in cold."

I was left alone, then, in my tub. Outside the window, I heard the shrieking of a nightjar. I thought of Nell's prediction of my fall. I thought of Pierpoint's fall from his boat. And of Rosie, alone in her laundry, waiting for thirty shillings to fall into her palm.

THIRTEEN

ROYAL TENNIS

I remember that Will half carried me, dripping and trembling from the bath. He dried me and put over my head a clean nightshirt and lay me down in my bed and I instructed him to pile furs upon me and I could smell the badger skins; they smelled of earth.

I burrowed down. I burrowed into sleep. And when I woke in the middle of the night, I knew that I was most horribly ill, with a pain in my forehead and at the base of my skull such as I had never imagined, unless it were the pain of death itself.

I vomited copiously into a basin. The sounds of my retching woke Will, who had laid himself to sleep on the floor of my bedchamber. He took the basin away and brought me water. "Sir," he said, holding the cup to my mouth, "I see some red patches or blotches upon your face."

I lay back, the pain in my head causing me to whimper like Celia's neglected Isabelle. Will held a mirror to my nose. I squinted at myself. It was an afflicting sight, one that I may long remember. I had contracted the measles.

I will not describe for you the discomfort of this illness. It will suffice to set down that I was very vexed with pain for several days, a pain relieved only by the frequent doses of laudanum which I prescribed for myself and which, in turn, sent my brain into a kind of delirium so that I no longer recognised my room, nor Will within it, but believed myself to be, variously, at

Whitehall, in my parents' workshop, in Wise Nell's stinking parlour and on a tilt boat.

When the pain at last lessened and I was able to lie still without groaning, I knew that what was now stealing upon me was a sleep so profound it was like a swaddling of death. It held me for some fifteen or sixteen hours at a time. Then I would wake and find Will or Cattlebury at my side with a little cup of broth, which I would try to sip. Then I would piss feebly into my pot and lie down again and in minutes re-enter this velvet sleep, at one moment remarking to myself that, if it resembled death, it also resembled infancy and musing foolishly on the possibility of being reborn in a more handsome and serious guise.

This, of course, did not come about. I was "reborn" two weeks later, weak as a mole and covered with scabs. I sat up and saw Will sitting in a chair, wearing his tabard. "Thank you, Will," I said. "And for caring for me so well. Without you, I would have been in a sorry mess."

"Are you better, Sir?"

"I believe I am. Though I feel somewhat puny and hollow . . ."

"Are you recovered enough for some news?"

"News?"

"Yes. About your household."

"Meaning you and Cattlebury and the other servants?"

"No, Sir. Meaning your wife and her maid and Mister Finn and the music master. They are all gone. Gone to London."

"Celia has gone?"

"Yes, Sir Robert. And taken all her dresses and fans and so forth."

"But the portrait . . ."

"Finished. And the day it was, the King sends one of the Royal coaches, and they all get into it and are gone."

I lay down again. I stared at my turquoise canopy. "That is the end of it, then," I heard myself say. "Now, she will never return. What date is it, Will?"

"February, Sir. The twenty-second day."

One week later, as I sat by my fire, staring vacantly into the flames, Will brought me a letter. It was, as I knew it would be,

from the King. Or rather, it was not *from* him but from one of
his secretaries and set out the following summons:

His Gracious Majesty, King Charles II,
Sovereign of the Realm commands:

That Sir Robert Merivel present Himself at Whitehall Palace no
more days hence than four, upon receipt of this Royal missive.

Signed: Sir J. Babbacombe. Secretary

"So," I said to Will, who had brought me the note, "Finn did his
work."

"I beg your pardon, Sir?"

"Never mind. The King calls me to London, Will. And it will
not be to praise me."

"You're too weak, yet, to go to London, Sir."

"Needs must, Will. I shall not ride, but take the coach.
Perhaps you would be good enough to accompany me?"

"Willingly, Sir Robert."

"We shall leave tomorrow morning, then. Make sure my black
and gold coat is clean and my gold breeches."

"Yes, Sir."

"And fold up the tabard I had intended my wife should wear.
We shall take it to the King as a present. Though I fear – "

"What, Sir?"

"That no offering of this kind will be enough."

I shall not dwell upon the details of our journey, except to record
that, as we came to Mile End and Will saw in the distance the
tower and turrets of London, he grew most childishly excited
thinking of the marvels he was about to witness for the first
time, he having passed all thirty-nine years of his life in Norfolk.
And when it dawned upon his Norfolk mind that he might, in all
probability, set eyes upon the King in his palace, he began to
blub, thus causing me in the space of five minutes more delight
than I had experienced in as many weeks. (I have grown, in my
time at Bidnold, most fond of Will Gates. If he is now to be
taken from me for ever, I will remember him often.)

We rested two nights on our journey, arriving at Whitehall

towards mid-morning of the third day. We travelled wearing our
tabards, but at our last lodging in Essex I dressed myself in my
black and gold suit and put powder on my face, it still appearing
rather poxy with some measle encrustations upon it. I did not
wish the King to imagine I had the King's Evil.

Taking Will with me (he most neatly attired in a beige coat
and grey leggings), I entered once again the Stone Gallery where
I had been so overwhelmed, one auspicious afternoon, by the
near-presence of Majesty that I had betrayed all my father's
hopes for my future. As on that first time, the Gallery was noisy
with people walking up and down and I knew that many of them
would be petitioners and suitors for small favours who, tonight,
would be sent away with nothing and yet tomorrow would return
and the next day and the next.

I gave my name to the guards of the Royal Apartments and
was told to wait. An hour passed, during which time I grew very
weary from standing, so that I thought, at one moment, I would
fall over. Will held onto my elbow and leaned me against a pillar.
I could see that his mouth was agape at some of the gallants and
their women who passed us. Even on my croquet lawn, he had
never seen such plumes and buckles; even at my dinner table,
no such pearly dresses. "I warrant, Sir," he whispered once,
"these folk have even more money than you."

"Yes, Will," I replied, "I warrant they do."

At length, a message was brought to me: I was to return at
one o'clock and go to the second of the King's tennis courts,
known as his Favourite Court, where His Majesty would meet
me. I looked up, in some dismay, at the messenger. I was about
to request that he inform the King of my recent illness which
had left me so feeble that I was hardly able to walk unaided in
his Gallery, let alone compete in a set of tennis, but the man
turned rudely and walked away from me, and I did not want to
make myself foolish by shouting after him. I shrugged. "All we
can do," I said to Will, "is eat a little meat and hope it may
strengthen me."

By mid-day, then, we were at the Boar Tavern in Bow Street,
where I ordered for Will a dish of oysters and some pigeon
patties and for myself a carbonado cooked with marrowbone and

stout, a most fortifying dish. We drank a little ale and Will sucked in his oysters and gobbled his patties, but I could not manage more than two mouthfuls of the carbonado, having no real appetite at all. Will duly ate it up, while I took my timepiece from my pocket and in silence watched the hand move towards the quarter hour.

"I am about to die, Will," I said suddenly. "I feel it. This afternoon I am going to die."

Will wiped his mouth with a crumpled napkin.

"Die how, Sir?"

"I do not know yet."

Well, you know me intimately by this time. You do not need reminding how painful and yet how wondrous it is for me to come into the presence of the King. I become very flushed and hectic and beside myself with joy and yet at the same time filled with a most sad longing to make time itself (upon which the King keeps such a glittering eye) move backwards, so that I can be what I once was, Merivel the Fool.

My love for Celia – love being by its nature a possessive thing – might well have diminished my desire for the company of the King, her lover, yet it did not seem to have done so, and when he stepped out into the empty cloistered court a cold sweat of adulation and fear broke out upon my brow.

The King was accompanied by two Gentlemen of the Bed-chamber, one carrying the cloth-lined shoes he likes to wear for tennis, the other two tennis racquets, the wooden handle of the King's own racquet being bound with scarlet ribbon. Though my fear made me lurk in the shadow of the side penthouse, the King saw me at once. It is often remarked by those who have known both the sunshine of the King's affection and the frost of his indifference that his mood is discernible from his very first glance, for he is not a dissembler. Even with his Parliament (towards whom some say he should show more tact) he seems to be incapable of concealing his frequent displeasure.

Leaving Will to wait outside the court, I had taken with me my gift of the fur tabard, prettily wrapped in yellow linen, and this I now held in my arms as I executed my bow, hearing as I did so my hip joints click, like the joints of an old man. I looked up. The King, who seemed to have grown taller even than he was before, regarded me from on high with a look of unyielding severity, such as those most frequently cast upon the unruly German students by Fabricius. I had anticipated displeasure but I had not fully imagined how weak it would make me feel. I felt myself tilting. I reached out and held fast to one of the columns of the penthouse. I could not allow myself to fall.

"What is the matter with you, Merivel?" said the King.

"I have been ill, Your Majesty."

"Yes. You appear ill. But this does not surprise me. When a man transgresses the proper order of things, first his mind, then his body are bound to suffer."

I did not know how to reply. I nodded merely, and held out my gift.

"What is that?" asked the King, regarding my bulky parcel with some distaste.

"A present, Sire. An invention of mine. Designed to be of comfort in winter weather."

"It is almost spring, Merivel. Or did you not notice?"

"No. I did not notice. I have been confined to my room."

"Show it to me nevertheless."

In a clumsy, fumbling manner, I unwrapped the tabard and held it up, as I have seen Farthingale hold up dresses against her own body for her mistress's approval.

"Ha!" At the sight of the sewn-together badger pelts, the King let out a sudden explosion of laughter. His two Gentlemen also began to giggle. I wished, like some intrusive street vendor, to regale the King with the virtues of the tabard – its versatility, the freedom of movement it allows the wearer, its vital warming of the blood flowing to lung and kidney – yet suddenly found that I was a little ashamed of my product, its lack of elegance being its chief and most damning fault.

"Is it intended to be *worn*?" asked the King.

"Yes, Sir. My household have, by the wearing of these, been free of ague and cold . . ."

"But you have not?"

"I had the mischance to catch a measle."

"How Merivelian! And you look poxy still."

"I know, Sire."

"You do not need furs, Merivel. And nor do I, if I can warm myself by other means. The exercising of the body will keep disease away far more efficaciously than badgers' coats. So, come. We shall play a set of tennis. You used to show more skill at this game than with the games of the heart. And may still. Unless you are altogether disintegrating."

The King turned away from me and put on his shoes. I draped the tabard, which most evidently he did not want at all, over the cloister wall of the side penthouse. The badger snouts hung mournfully down. And I thought, with some amazement, what kind of mind could invent such an odd garment? The mind of a mad person. And only a madman would think of offering a thing of such eccentricity to his King. Merivel, I told myself, as I removed my black and gold coat, you are losing hold . . .

A racquet was put into my hand. Hastily, I tried to recollect what cunning I had once employed at this fast game and recalled that my best shot had been a low sliced thing to the *dedans* wall, usually missing the *dedans*, but bouncing so low my opponent was not able to scoop it up upon the first bounce, thus provoking a "chase". If you are familiar with the game of Royal Tennis, you will know that very many points are won or lost in a "chase" and His Majesty, though hitting the ball with a deal more power than almost all his opponents, can often be beaten by shots that cut the ball and so make it die, almost upon its first bounce, and land close to the back wall. The King's strength lies in accuracy. In any set, he will win a number of points outright by shots to the winning gallery and the *dedans*. Among some players at Court he used to be known as the Bell Ringer, with reference to the little bell that jingles when a ball slaps hard into these winning spaces.

So, in the cold February light, we began to play, the King placing himself, as of right, in the service court. I noticed that the net had grown in splendour, being, in my time, a mere piece of string but now an ornate braid hung with tassels.

No sooner had one of the Gentlemen of the Bedchamber installed himself in the marker's box than the King dealt me a most brilliant service that seemed to flutter by me almost before the ball had bounced, as if we were playing not with wads of hair and cloth but with a flight of wrens.

I remembered from a previous time that, although His Majesty likes to win at tennis, he does not like to win easily. He likes a fight. He likes the other man to run and run and never give up. What I tried, then, was to put out of my mind all knowledge of my recent illness and to play as nimbly as a lizard, scuttling forward and back, chasing every shot. Unfortunately, all out of practice as I was, my play was most horribly wild and inaccurate, one of my balls flying straight at the marker's box and smiting one of the Gentlemen in the eye, another going so high that it soared up and over the penthouse roof – to bounce, perhaps, at Will Gates's feet as he sat and digested the carbonado and waited for his first glimpse of his Sovereign.

My play was, in short, very lamentable and we had concluded but three games when I found myself feeling most horribly sick, my mouth suddenly filling with bile. I dropped my racquet, so that I might kneel for a moment on the pretence of retrieving it. I took some great breaths of air. Then I heard the door to the side penthouse open and I wondered all at once whether Celia had come to preside over the contest and smile her sweet smile upon the King's certain victory.

But it was not Celia. It was a footman come with lemon juice and sugar for us. "Lemons from Portugal in February!" said the King. "Grown under glass especially for my dear Queen." So a little respite was granted to me, albeit indirectly, by that placid and good-natured woman who seemed to be so often absent from the King's thoughts. I believed her to play no part in my story at all, yet on that day she undoubtedly saved me from casting up my meagre dinner onto the stones of the tennis court.

To my immense relief, I was able to win the fourth game. I was on the service side now. From the left-hand section of it, I managed one strangely brilliant service and three sliced shots to the *tambour* which the King adroitly retrieved but then pitched the ball under the net. In the next three games, however, such strength as I had had drained from me. Sweat poured down my face, mixing with the powder with which I had hoped to cover the ravages of my measles. I could not run any more, but only stagger. Shot after shot sped past me into the *dedans* or the winning gallery. Never send to know, I thought, for whom the bell jingles. It jingles for thee, Merivel. And then I thought of Pearce, whose favourite poet John Donne is. And I asked Pearce to remember me now and give me strength to face all that was still to come.

"As I foresaw," said the King at the conclusion of the set, "you have become slow."

"I know, Sir . . ." I mumbled.

"Very slow. And the game, of course, is a fast one."

I followed the King into the garden where I had left Will and where he still stood in his grey leggings. The King walked at such a swift pace that I had to scurry to keep up with him and had no hope of getting his attention to ask him to turn upon my servant, however briefly, his majesterial glance. But I could not afford to worry too greatly about Will. I knew that my beating at tennis was but the preliminary to a more bitter scourging.

I was led into a little summer-house, not unlike the one at Bidnold where I had briefly attempted my secret oboe lessons with Herr Hümmel. The place was swept and clean, but in the fading light of the winter afternoon a somewhat chilly habitation. I put on my black and gold coat. The King blew his nose then turned his face towards me. So close was he to me that I could see clearly the fine lines that gathered at the corners of his eyes and at the edge of his lips. It seemed to me that he had aged since my last meeting with him in his laboratory and the observation distressed me, as if I had believed that in a changeful world the King alone was outside the reach of time.

"So," he said at last, "you did not play by the rules, Merivel."

"In the tennis, Sir?"

"No. Not in the tennis. With regard to your wife."

I looked down. I noticed that there was blood in my shoe, but did not know from what part of me it could possibly have come.

"I do not know what rule I have broken, Sir," I said quietly.

"I am surprised. Why were you chosen as Celia's husband, Merivel?"

"Because you knew that I would do anything you asked of me."

"That is true of very many people in our Kingdom. No, it was not for that. It was because, at one of our earliest meetings, you told me the story of the visible heart you had seen at Cambridge. You told me you *knew* that your own heart had no feeling whatsoever. And I believed you. Yet now I see that I should not have done, for it is by no means true."

There was a long silence. Silence, when one is in the presence of the King, seems a most fearful condition, and I felt hot and faint.

"Love was not asked of you, Merivel," the King said at length. "Indeed, it was the only thing forbidden you. But so soft and coddled and foolish have you become, you could not see that in the breaking of this rule you would, like old Adam, drive yourself out of Paradise."

"Out of Paradise?"

"Yes. For what is your role now? You cannot play Celia's husband any more because she refuses to set eyes on you ever again. Thus, in trying to *be* the thing you were charged with pretending to be, you have rendered yourself useless."

I looked out at the afternoon dusk that was settling upon the garden. Near a stone bench, I could make out the shadowy figure of Will, who, when darkness descended, would find himself lost.

"I had not intended . . ." I stammered, ". . . to love Celia. I loved her voice first, her music. And I do not know how this love was transformed into a love of another kind. I do not know how."

"It happened because you *allowed* it, Merivel. You became futile. You had too little work and too much dreaming time. And then you indulged your dreams. You thought you could re-cast yourself. *Voilà tout.* And now you are no more use to me.'

The King looked away from me, and for a moment I thought these words signalled my dismissal. But they did not. He had more to say to me yet.

"Happily for you, Merivel," the King continued, "I have enough affection for you to wish to make you useful again, if not to me, then to the people. I fear it will take some time, for look at you! How wretched you have become! But we must try, must we not?"

"Yes, my Liege."

"Very well. Then hear what I have in mind. I am, for the time being, content with the arrangements of my own life. Celia is returned and appears to have learnt some wisdom – perhaps from you, although I doubt that this is so and she certainly denies it. At all events, she is returned to Kew and I am happy that she should be there. But in most other matters, I am not so fortunate. I have the impression that the 'honey-moon' of my reign is over."

The King again turned a little from me, so that I saw his face in profile and was struck, not for the first time, by the length and fineness of the Stuart nose, which is so very unlike my own. I was about to suggest that the King's love affair with his people would surely last as long as he lived, but before I could speak he cut me off.

"I lack money," he said. "We are engaged in a war of trade with the Dutch, yet I lack the means to fit out our ships. This poverty is a foul humiliation, Merivel, and must be remedied. I have been too generous, too profligate with gifts of land and estates. But now comes a reckoning. Now comes a time when I must pay attention to arithmetic."

And so at last the King came to it, to what he called his "arithmetic". He was taking Bidnold from me.

He was "repossessing" it, just as he had repossessed Celia. For, like Celia, it did not belong to me. All that I owned had come to me from him and now he was taking it back. Some French nobleman would purchase it from him, house, lands, furniture and all, and the money thus acquired would be used to buy hemp and tar and sailcloth and rigging. Bidnold would thus "become useful" again. Land would be translated into ships by the King's arithmetic and those ships would be ships of war.

And what of me? How, dear Lord, was I to be made useful again? By being forced, now that I had no land, to return to the only profession that would get me a living: medicine. I was to awake at last from the sleep into which the King had seen me fall. No longer would I be able to dream away my time under the Norfolk sky for henceforth – from this very night, in fact – I would own nothing save my horse and my surgical instruments, the only things which had been "gifts of affection" and not "gifts of expediency".

Plague was coming. Plague, as I had once before been reminded, rouses men, not only from sleep, but from forgetfulness. They remember Death. I, too, would remember that Life is brief, that Death creeps over it as surely as the dusk now falling around the summer-house. And with this remembrance would come another: I would remember anatomy. "And so, Merivel, you will once more be *doing* and no longer dreaming. You will have become useful."

I believe the King smiled at me then. To him, no doubt, the taking of Bidnold from me was a clever and satisfactory plan, killing, one could suggest, two birds with one stone by rendering me "useful" once again and furnishing the King with a small amount of money. The terrible degree to which I myself felt "killed" by the severity of my punishment the King could not begin to imagine. I had known, from the moment I understood Finn's role as spy in my household, that my behaviour towards Celia might quench any affection the King still had for me, but it had never entered my mind that he would take my house from me. I had believed that Bidnold was mine for ever. I had now and then imagined myself growing old there – with Violet as my companion perhaps, if Bathurst should chance to drop dead of an epilepsy – and being buried in Bidnold churchyard. And now that I was to lose it, together with Will Gates and Cattlebury and the carpet from Chengchow and my turquoise bed and all, the profound nature of my affection revealed itself to me. I had made it mine. In every room I saw some part of my character reflected. Bidnold was Merivel anatomised. From my colourful and noisy belly you ascended to my heart which, though it craved variety also favoured concealment, and so to my brain, a small but beautiful place, occasionally filled with light and yet utterly empty. In his repossession of my house, the King was taking me from myself.

In all my dealings with my Sovereign, I had hitherto been

obedient and accepting, doing without question or barter whatever I was commanded to do. But now, as I looked at my vacant, houseless future, I felt moved to plead with the King. I knelt down on the flagstone floor of the summer-house. I put my hands together, as if in prayer.

"Sire," I said, "I beg you not to remove me from Bidnold. I am not, as you would believe, idle there. I have embarked upon a new vocation as an artist. I am learning to play the oboe, I am endeavouring to make sense of the stars and I have taken upon me a new responsibility: I am an Overseer of the Poor."

The King stood up. As always, I was moved by the beauty and elegance of the legs before which I was kneeling.

"An Overseer?' he said. "You seem fond of the term, for you used it to Celia. But an Overseer should be impartial, distanced and kind, and you were none of these to her. Will you now abuse the Poor of your parish as you abused Celia?"

"No, Sir. And I cannot say too many times how sorry I am for what I did to Celia. I *loved* her and this was my mistake. I do not love the Poor, only pity them."

"What are you doing, then, for those you pity?"

"I am learning about them, Sir, their whereabouts, their collecting of sticks and other pitiful tasks, their work at the looms in Norwich . . ."

"And how is this to help them?"

"I am not precisely 'helping' them yet, my Liege – "

"And yet, before I met you, you were. At St Thomas's, you were helping them – with the only skill you have ever possessed."

"I cannot use that skill any more, Sir. I *cannot*."

"Why?"

"I *cannot* . . ."

"Why, Merivel?"

"Because I am afraid!"

The King, who had been pacing about the summer-house, now stopped and rounded on me, holding up an admonishing finger clothed in a glove made by my late father. "Precisely!" he declared. "And do not imagine I have not known this! But this age is stern, Merivel, and those who are afraid will not survive it. Those who are weak will not survive it. You, if you remain as you are, will not survive it."

"I beg you to let me remind you, Sire, that it was you who took me from St Thomas's. You gave me the Royal dogs. You liked me for my foolishness . . ."

"*And* for your skill. For the two, then, were in you, the light and the dark, the shallow and the profound. But now your skill has fallen away and you are all one foolish mass."

So it was in vain that I pleaded. The King had made up his mind. For a moment, I considered prostrating myself before him, but I know that this King is not moved by supplication; it merely irritates him. And, as for the dispossessed, he has no sympathy for them, for he was once one of them and had to wait years for his restoration.

What could I do then but accept my fate, the while finding it unjust and cruel, with as convincing a show of bravery as I could put on?

The King now moved towards the door of the summer-house and made to leave. Before he went, he looked down upon me one last time and informed me that I could return to Bidnold for one week, "there to make preparation for your departure. The keys of the place must then be given to Sir James Babbacombe, who is to act as my agent in this matter. And so *au revoir*, Merivel. I shall not say *adieu*, for who knows whether, at some time in the future, History may not have another role for you?"

And then he was gone. And as soon as he had stepped outside the summer-house I saw servants come with lamps to light his way. They had been waiting and watching for the moment when he would walk away from me.

FOURTEEN

"NOT WITH SILVER . . ."

Some days have passed. I am at Bath. I have put up at an Inn called The Red Lion. I have come here in the hope that the sulphurous waters will wash my mind of some of its despair. My landlady is given to singing as she beats mattresses and empties pots. I catch myself listening for some ghostly accompanist.

I have not returned to Bidnold and do not intend to do so. I have sent letters to my staff apologising for my misfortune, which in turn becomes theirs. I have requested that one of my grooms saddle up Danseuse like a packhorse with a few true possessions and trot her by slow stages to London. I, who scoffed at Pearce's "burning coals" now have little more to call my own than he. Should Danseuse step with her sweet daintiness into a pothole and break her leg, I shall be forced to purchase for myself some horrible biting mule.

My dreams are inhabited by Will Gates. He is weeping. His brown squirrel's face is squashed. He resembles a baby struggling to be born. With his fists he tries to wipe away his tears. And then he gets up onto my coach, sitting beside the coachman, and is driven away.

Will Gates. I loved you most dearly, Will.

When Will had gone, I begun to walk quite fast away from Whitehall and in an easterly direction, as if vainly trying to follow the coach. The winter night had come on and the streets were black and I was soon lost. But then, hurrying on down narrow street after narrow street, I saw in front of me the great bulk of the Tower. I had had no intention of arriving there, but my distracted mind perceived it all at once as a place of refuge. To the guards I announced that I had been sent by the King, to cast my eye upon the lions and leopards that he keeps chained up there, and they let me go in.

I knew my way to the dungeon where the animals were penned. I took a torch from an iron sconce and followed my own shadow down into the damp bowels of the Tower where, even at midsummer, no light falls on the stones and where, it is said, the ghosts of the dead Kings of England find themselves paraded with hundreds of their ancient enemies, as in some circus they did not expect. And there I saw the lions, who have the names of Kings, Henry and Edward and Charles and James, pacing round, the flesh of their shanks very meagre and their great fur collars mangy. And it was at that moment and not at any moment before (neither upon leaving the King's garden, nor upon saying *adieu* to Will and my coachman) that I felt the full terror of my fall.

I stood quite still a great while. I watched the lions, but they never once regarded me, not even to growl or snarl at the torchlight. I thought: I would rather be one of you in this pen than be Merivel. I thought: You have no memory of Africa or sunlight or a Time Before. So I would rather be you.

Quite late, with the streets silent save for the shouting of a trundle of drunks, I arrived at Rosie Pierpoint's door. I knocked and heard my knock like an echo. And as I waited, I remembered the Japanese purse and the thirty shillings and the half-written letter I had never sent.

When she came to the door, she held a shawl round her and she looked afraid. Pretty Rosie. With her I had first discovered the sweetness of oblivion.

But then she grinned. "Sir Robert," she said, "where is your wig?"

I had lost it. So it seemed. I had no recollection of taking it off.

*   *   *

I woke when she rose, at the first faint tracing of daylight. And I understood this small matter: that the poor use time differently from me. They are unable to prolong day with manufactured light, the cost of candles and oil being too great.

I lay on my truckle bed and watched her. She poured cold water into a bowl and took up some rags and washed herself, her face and her breasts and her belly and her cunt and the backs of her knees. And this secret toilette in the half light moved me very much. I wished to be of use to her (having been none that night in bed), so I got up and pulled on my stockings and my shirt and went down to her laundry room and broddled the fire of her stove and tipped in fresh coal, yet performing this task lamentably, sending chunks of coal skittering onto the floor, which I was then compelled to retrieve one by one with my hands. And I remembered – from my time at Cambridge and my rooms in Ludgate – how the black dust of coal is not like a dust but like a paste, moist and sticky, and if you keep in a coal fire you must be forever washing.

The sun got up above the river, but lay flat behind a mist. Rosie made a milk porridge and I tried for her sake to eat some of this stuff, but it and the tin spoon made a grey tableau before me and I heard in my mind the sobbing and lamenting of the old Merivel for the colours and brightness of things now lost.

We had not spoken of Pierpoint, only of me and my troubles. But now, eating her porridge greedily, she began, to my astonishment, upon a little eulogy for her dead husband, telling me how strong a man he was and how indifferent to rich people and how loyal to the river and the other river men. While he lived, I wished to say to Rosie, you scarcely had a gentle word for him and lived in fear of his drunken rages and other cruelties. But I did not remark out loud upon this, only noting privately to myself that death can work most extraordinary changes to a person's reputation and all that we have wished someone to be while they lived, they become, the moment they are dead. And so I wondered, if I had been brave enough to throw myself to the lions in the tower and let them eat me for their supper, would the King's exasperation with me be turning now to fond sadness,

Celia's loathing of me to a small retrospective love? While Rosie talked of her drowned bargeman, I meditated upon this. Pierpoint had died trying to catch a haddock with his hands, or in other words *getting* food; in my imagined death, I myself would have *become* food. Is either death noble, or are both ridiculous and laughable? Could a person of Celia's refinement feel affection for a husband who has been turned first to meat and thence to dung? I did not know. My mind, though very cluttered with questions, had no answers to anything at all. Like the porridge in front of me, my intelligence seemed to be growing cold.

I could not stay with Rosie. Our old amours had been fiery. Now, they, too, were out. I think that all we felt for each other was a sad tenderness. I gave her thirty shillings (I would not lack for money for some while, if I was prudent) and she gave me a little kiss on my cheek that was still mottled by the old imprint of my measles. And we said *adieu*.

And so I am come to Bath.

The most strange thing about the pain of the individual man is that the world, knowing nothing of it, behaves as if it was not there, going shrieking on and applauding itself, making sport and promenading and telling jokes and falling down with laughter. So, as I enter the Cross Bath and immerse myself, wearing nothing but some unbleached pantaloons, I see that round and above me in the stone galleries fully-clothed people are strolling with a superior air of contentment, gossiping and giggling and fanning themselves and looking upon the bathers with an elegant nonchalance. They know nothing of what has befallen me. They could not imagine that in these waters, which smell most curiously of boiled egg, I am trying to cure myself of being Merivel.

I look round at my fellow bathers. The Cross Bath is divided: men on one side, women on the other. In my line of men, I see one elderly creature with his wig still unwisely in place on his head. If he has come for a cure for vanity, he is already inhibiting its efficacy.

Opposite me, the women appear most strange. For modesty,

they wear peculiar yellow garments made of stiff canvas which, the moment they are submerged, inflate like balloons. I cannot take my eyes from them. I imagine them so filled with air that they will begin to bob about and then come floating towards me, helpless on the bubbling current of the bath. I can even feel the press of them round me, these balloons of women, and I fashion for the King (as my mind is so much in the habit of doing) some second-rate joke that plays on the word "prick".

But then I see that not only with my joke am I in error: I have perceived the women wrongly. Their skirts and bodices are not filled up with air, but with water. They are not light, but heavy – so heavy they are tethered to their seats, as if by an anchor. If we all stayed in the Cross Bath till nightfall, the women would ever remain separate from us. Unless, of course, the King were to come down and get into the water. Then, I believe the women would break free like minnows from their birth sacs and come wiggling towards him.

I pass very long hours sitting still in the water; I try to feel the process of cleansing occurring. I force myself to visit, in my mind, all the rooms at Bidnold one by one. I stand in each doorway and watch as all my possessions are removed and then the furnishings and the carpets and the wall-hangings so that the room has no hint of my presence in it anywhere. And then I imagine the waters of Bath flowing into it and staining it a sulphurous yellow and then withdrawing like the sea on an ebb tide. And so the room is no longer a room, but only a washed and empty place.

When I can stand the stench of the waters no longer, I retire to my room in the Red Lion. The innkeeper's name is John Sweet. His wife, Mistress Sweet, sings on with no accompaniment and no listeners except herself and Merivel. She alone knows that I am sickly, for the food she sends up I cannot eat.

I dreamed, last night, a most infamous dream. I was in a high chamber at Whitehall where a clutch of gallants and their women, together with the King and his Queen, were assembled. "Why are we all come here?" I asked one I recognised as Sir Rupert Pinworth. "Why," said Sir Rupert, "for the wedding. Naturally."

At that moment, the crowd moved to make a pathway for the bride and groom. I craned my neck to see them. They walked sedately, arm in arm, to the end of the chamber where a priest stood ready to read his prayers over them. The groom wore a villainous sulphur-yellow coat and breeches, the bride a white dress, very pretty, yet stained here and there with the sulphur colour.

And then I saw their faces. The groom had the face of Barbara Castlemaine and the bride the face of Celia. And when the priest had said some prayers and they too murmured some assents, they there, in front of all the people, began to take off their clothes and throw them away impatiently. And I saw now that it was indeed the two women whom the priest had "married" and who now began to play in earnest the groom and bride, kissing each other and touching all indecently each other's parts while the King and his Queen and all of us looked on, applauding now and then, as if at a play. And Sir Rupert leaned over and whispered in my ear: "You see what marriage is become. It is become anything we make it be."

And I woke up, very hot and troubled. And, for poor comfort, put my hand upon my prick.

Knowledge that I should hope for very little from the waters of Bath stole upon me after that night. I felt, not cleansed by the place, but sickened and suffocated by it. The sight of the bodies of the men, many old and palsied, some poxy-seeming, did not help me to love the water. And I was soon weary of watching the women squatting down in their yellow balloons. They appeared to me utterly foolish and pathetic. Rosie Pierpoint has more grace than they.

So I paid John Sweet and bowed to his wife and complimented her on her singing and left, paying threepence a mile for post-horses to return me to London. And when I came there, I saw a thing to which, at Bath, I had paid no heed: the spring had come. In the garden of the Leg Tavern, there were fat buds on a chestnut tree and celandines in the grass and the air was no longer chill as it had been the night I walked to the Tower. Visiting my bookseller, I saw on his almanac that we had begun on the month of March. "Where I shall be at the month's end," I said to him, "I do not know."

I had only to wait two days at the Leg before my groom arrived with Danseuse.

Both man and horse seemed tired and somewhat stiff, but my joy at their arrival was so great I felt, for a few hours, returned to something like contentment. That night, however, I laid out on my bed all the possessions left to me in the world and when I saw what they were, I felt a sweating of fear on my neck, for I knew that no man could depend upon them for his survival. This is what I now owned:

my case of surgical instruments,
my oboe,
some sheets of music,
some paint brushes and some boxes of pigment,
several suits of gaudy silk and taffeta,
a quantity of coloured stockings and lace shirts,
three periwigs,
four pairs of gloves, made by my father,
my set of striped dinner napkins,
a quill pen, given to me by Violet Bathurst,
some nightshirts and a nightcap,
four pairs of high-heeled shoes,
two letters from the King, tied with a ribbon,
my Bible, much thumbed and annotated,
a recipe for lardy cake, splodged with Cattlebury's tears,
a single fur tabard,
two purses: one Japanese, containing thirty shillings,
                one leather, containing forty-seven sovereigns,

Thanks to my clothes, I would not yet appear poor and, unless I was robbed of the sovereigns, I would not, for some while yet, know poverty at all. And yet there it was, spread out before me, the inevitability of my eventual destitution.

Other men, contemplating such a fall from grace, have made of their low state a springboard from which to jump up and make some new beginning. But in this age, no fortunes are made except at Court. All endeavour – even the labours of a humble glovemaker like my father – is made or marred by favour or dislike at Whitehall. Even common bargemen – like the late Pierpoint – feel, in the new, bustling commercial life upon the river, the touch of the Royal hand. And Rosie at her washing cauldrons: in the jabots and cuffs and collars of Brussels lace worn by the Cavaliers she sees a way to her own prosperity. And I, if I should try some new thing, where would all strivings lead me, but back to where I once walked and waited with my father – to a place so heavy with the King's presence I could not breathe?

What, then, was left to me? If any, I told myself, has made himself immune to the Royalty in all things, from him would I learn best how to live from now on. And no sooner had I convinced myself that at last a thought that was not entirely foolish had entered my head, than I knew at once who that person was. And I said the name of my old friend out loud. "Pearce," I said, "let me come to you."

Since my last glimpse of Pearce on the speckled mule, I had not given him a great deal of thought. He does not love or condone my follies. My behaviour towards Celia would have made him weep with shame. Thus, it was not comfortable to think of him while I was at the same time giving him cause for embarrassment and grief.

Now, cast out from Celia's life, and knowing I would soon saddle Danseuse and make my way to the Fens, I was able once again to set his palid visage before my mind's eye. It is a face most dear to me, yet one which creates in me – in equal measure – feelings of sorrow, irritation and tenderness. "Tender" is a word of which Pearce makes considerable use, it being a Quaker term applied to those tolerant souls (and there are not very many of them, if Pearce is to be believed) who do not, at the sight of a Quaker, spit in his eye or demand that he take off his hat. I am "tender" then. In our past together, I occasionally stood between Pearce and his antagonists, not because I am courageous, but because Pearce has about him some innocence of a child and I do not like to see children hurt and insulted. Yet for all these acts of gallantry, Pearce is harsh with me. He once likened my life "to a poorly done sampler, Merivel. Showing a variety of stitches, yet making up a most incoherent picture." He is a man who, for all his rapturous speech, cannot bring himself to make visible the secret affections of his heart. I know that he loves me very dearly; he, I believe, does not know that he does. And yet, when I arrive at his wretched hospital, he will run (or at least increase the speed of his gait somewhat) to greet me. When he sees me, he will be glad.

There is little in our lives, since the day I went to Whitehall, to bind our friendship. And sometimes it appears to me as a ghostly thing, a thing which had its proper life in Cambridge in the years of the King's exile. These "ghosts" were to be found very often together late at night, putting coal onto small fires, eating plum cake, trying at the same time to digest Descartes' theory that the ethereal human spirit was connected to the "body machine" by the pineal gland; then giving up at last and spitting it out and giving in to laughter.

The ghost Pearce was sentimentally fond of fishing and in summer would take the ghost Merivel with him on his angling trips. "The Apostles," Pearce would say fancifully, "as the two of them sat watching for mayfly, "were fishermen. Fishing is a contemplative, devotional thing and not entirely suited to you, Merivel, who are too restless and dazzling." And it is true, Pearce was the luckier angler. The brown trout came to his hook on the evening rise. Merivel got only the muddy grayling. But the ghosts stayed on the river, content with each other, content with the sport, till the air cooled and a thin mist began to sit on the water and they became shadowy in time. I can remember that returning to my room in Caius from these fishing expeditions was like returning from another world. And the memory of them, coming sometimes to my mind when it is vexed with trouble, has always been soothing.

So, endeavouring to put from me the devastations of the recent time, consigning to darkness the smell of the King's perfume, the sound of Celia's voice, the touch of the King's hand upon my nose, the sight of my own lust on my starlit roof, I looked at my remembrance of Pearce very closely, as it might be through a microscope, allowing that which had become invisible to be seen once more in clear definition. In this way, I prepared myself for my journey.

For my decision to go to the Fens ran some way ahead of my ability to do so. In short, no sooner had I said the word "Pearce" out loud than I knew myself to be afraid. My friend's company I knew would be beneficial to me; the company of a hundred lunatics could afford me nothing but pain. Thus, I tarried at the Leg. From the ghosts by the trout stream, I begged courage.

The date of my setting forth was the tenth of March.

I passed the first night at Puckeridge and the second in Cambridge, where I took myself to Caius and stood on the dark stairway outside the room that had been mine. From inside the room came the sound of soft, serious voices. It occurred to me that none in that room, however studious they might be, could know that the organ of the heart has no feeling.

On the third day I rode on towards Willingham and I saw how the landscape became, as it were, *less* and the sky *more* and how the creatures most numerous were the birds, who had their existence in both elements. A wind got up, making Danseuse nervous, so that she became for a while a dancer indeed, shying at gusts. But the birds rode on the wind. I watched them glide and plummet on the eddies. I saw bustards, and dottrels and wild geese.

And I observed how, in this Fen land, the crust of the earth appears thin, allowing water to seep and ooze upwards so that it is possible to imagine there are fishes and not worms in the soil. And it is a landscape of thin things – feathery marsh grasses and bullrushes and bending willows – so that I smiled when I thought of Pearce within it, thin and threadbare, and I also began to sense how I, with my wide, flat face, my fleshy lip and my soft belly, was not at one with it at all.

Though the wind seemed unable to cease (as if the vast cloudy sky held the wind trapped, as under a dome) no rain at all fell on me in all my journey and for this blessing I found myself giving thanks to the silent God of the lardy cake. And so in this way let my thoughts dwell upon the very simple credo that informs Pearce's life and which makes him immune to all the spells under which I had fallen. Despite much evidence to the contrary, he and his Quaker friends believe that the Apostolic age is not over, that God and his Son have much more to say to us yet, but will not choose persons of worldly authority through whom to say it. "The Seed of Christ, Merivel," Pearce had informed me many times, "is planted not in the souls of Priests or Kings, but in the bosom of The Commonest He," thus causing whole hundreds of proud citizens to quail with fear at the idea of God's word passing through the likes of Cattlebury or the late Pierpoint and so to denounce Quakerism as an utter heresy. Strangely, the King (who does not appear to quail at anything, even death) is tolerant towards Quakers – more tolerant of their discourtesies than he has been towards mine. Were Pearce to come into the King's presence and refuse to remove his hat, I do not think he would have his house taken from him. I could imagine, even, that the brazen gesture might be rewarded with that gift I once held to be more priceless than any other, the Royal Smile.

So, with my incoherent thoughts turning always in a circular fashion back towards myself, I trotted on towards the village of Doddington, and stayed my third night in the little town called March, where I slept a most disconsolate sleep, being full of trepidation about my imminent arrival at Pearce's Hospital.

The New Bedlam, or Whittlesea Hospital, has been founded in a place with the poetic name of Earls Bride, but which I saw at once to be really no proper place at all, but a thin straggle of poor cottages, having no forge or ale house or dairy or any means that I could see of purchasing provisions. It is like a drowned place, a shipwrecked place. Those few who cling to it must endure a life of most fearful monotony, their only visitors being the birds and the buffeting wind. Upon my first sighting of Earls Bride (is there the ghost of a true bride in the name or has it corroded in the damp air, being once Bridle Way or even Bridge?) I had this most perverse thought: that the penning up of one hundred lunatics in their midst had brought some entertainment to the inhabitants of this God-forsaken place.

As we approached the Hospital, which is a cluster of barns built around a lime-washed low-roofed house such as might house a yeoman farmer, Danseuse stopped dead and, though I kicked vigorously at her flanks, she could not be persuaded forward. I dismounted and looked about me and listened. I could hear nothing except the huffing of the wind, but I note in passing that, since my meeting in the King's summer-house, my hearing seems to have suffered a most inexplicable loss, and I could tell from Danseuse's stubbornness and from the way her ears were pricked that she had heard a sound that made her uneasy.

Around the buildings has been constructed a flint and clay wall, like a bailey round a castle except that this structure was, I presumed, designed not to keep enemies out but to keep the mad folk in, lest they go roaming about in the flat land and drown. An iron gate had been let into the wall and it was towards this that I led Danseuse, having put a comforting arm round her neck.

The gate was locked. I knocked and waited and then turned and looked at desolate Earls Bride on its little causeway. It was the look of one who, suddenly feeble of spirit, wishes to turn round and retrace his steps homewards. And I know that, had Bidnold still been mine, I would have done this. I would not even have stayed to greet my old friend. I would, in short, have run away.

A tall man, large in every respect, with a great barrelled thorax and very mighty hands, opened the gate to me and stood smiling enquiringly. He had red curly hair, very thick and abundant, and a red beard, under which he made a steeple of his fingers.

"How may I help you, Friend?" he asked.

I nodded to him, the while noting a distressing shivering in the neck of my horse.

"I have come to see my friend, John Pearce and . . . well, in truth I really cannot say why else I find myself here, unless it is in the belief that I could be of some use . . ."

"Please enter. We will get oats for your horse. It is not a glad place you have come to, but a place of suffering. I expect you noticed our words from Isaiah upon the gate?"

"I saw some words, but did not read them."

"Ah. Then read before you come in."

The large man now returned his hand to the gate and pushed it to a little, as if making to shut me out. Had he closed it entirely, I do believe I would have turned my horse round and cantered away, but he did not.

I peered at the inscription beaten into the metal: "Behold, I have refined thee but not with silver; I have chosen thee in the furnace of affliction" *Isaiah 48.10*.

"Very well," I said. "I have read the words."

The gate moved again to admit me. I felt Danseuse's head push up against my restraining arm and she jangled her bit.

"Please follow me, Friend," said the red-haired man who, I now noticed, was wearing a leather tabard over his black coat and leggings. The tabard was very stained and blackened with use, like a worn saddle. I looked down at my own clothes. I was wearing brown velvet breeches and a brown coat edged only a little with carmine. The lace at my wrists and throat was limp. My own good sense told me that, for all their relative modesty, these garments were not sturdy enough for the days that were coming.

I stepped inside, tugging my horse, and the gate closed behind us. We stood in a kind of courtyard with a floor of cinders, very patchy with moss. A single tree, an oak, grew in the middle of it.

"This," said the man in the tabard, "is the Airing Court. We believe in the healing property of air."

"This is where they walk?"

"Yes. Round the tree and then round again, and so on, round and round, but the tree is not dull. It is a most restless and changeful tree. You see?"

"Yes. And now the spring is – "

"My name is Ambrose Dyer. I should have mentioned this at very first, for names are important with us."

"I am glad to meet you, Mr Dyer."

"And you?"

"I beg your pardon?"

"Your name?"

"Ah. Robert Merivel. Pearce and I were medical students together at Cambridge."

"John. We do not call him Pearce. He is John. And I am Ambrose."

"I believe, to me, he will always be Pearce. As he, in turn, addresses me as Merivel."

"Here, he is John."

"So I must be Robert?"

"And I am Ambrose. Now I shall name for you our buildings. The house itself we call Whittlesea House and this is where we, the founders and keepers, six in number have our rooms and where we eat together. And the three barns or *asiles*, meaning places of shelter, are called George Fox, and Margaret Fell, and William Harvey."

Despite the trepidation I was feeling, I smiled to myself. Even here, in this lonely place with its one oak tree, Pearce had remembered his mentor, for of course it was true that he carried the great WH with him everywhere in his circulating blood.

"Which barn is called William Harvey?" I enquired.

"The smallest," said Ambrose, "to the left of us, here. Where those very deep into their madness are put."

At that moment, as we walked towards the house, Pearce came out of it. When he looked up and saw me he appeared to gasp for air like a fish. And then, as I predicted he would, he broke into a stumbling run.

That night, I slept on Pearce's bed, with Pearce lying on a pallet on the floor not far from me. My mind seemed to inhabit a place much stranger than the room, so that I did not feel as if I slept but only fell in and out of odd, dreamlike trances. Each time I believed myself to be near to sleep I heard an echo of the King's voice, repeating the same words again and again: "I have refined thee, Merivel. Behold, I have refined thee. But not with silver. Not with silver . . ."

PART TWO

FIFTEEN

ROBERT

A month has passed. April has come. And it is as if, during this month, since my arrival at Whittlesea Hospital, I have been absent from myself. This morning, however, seeing my reflection in the parlour window I once again caught sight of him: the man you know all too well by this time; the person I asked you to picture wearing a scarlet suit; the Fool Merivel. And I could not prevent a sentimental tenderness towards Merivel from creeping over my skin, causing me to blush both with affection and with shame. It is this tenderness that has led me to continue the story, notwithstanding the dismaying fact that when I passed through the gates of the New Bedlam, I passed from one life into another and thus an ending of some kind has been reached. Under these things you may draw a line: my house at Bidnold, the colours of my park, Celia's face at my table. Neither you nor I will see them again. They have been consumed, not by actual flames, as were my dear parents, but by the fire of the King's displeasure. I must thus imagine them turned to ash, and so must you, for you will not be returned to them.

I have become Robert.

No one at Whittlesea (not even Pearce, whom I must address as John) calls me Merivel and many do not even know that this is my name. I am not even Sir Robert. I am Robert. And this is how you may picture me: I do not wear my wig except at Meetings (these are most strange yet moving things, which I will later describe), I go about my work wearing black woollen

breeches and a black woollen shirt which causes a vexatious
itching of my nipples. These garments are covered by a leather
apron, very heavy, that comes down to my knees. My boots
are low-heeled and of sturdy hide and ever soiled with the mud
of Whittlesea, which is like no other mud I have seen, being
blackish and slimy and drying – when it does dry – to a sulphurous
yellow crust. My belly, grown very fat upon Cattlebury's carbonados and syllabubs, is shrinking on the poor diet of herring,
frumenty, spoon-meat and water favoured by Pearce and
Ambrose and the other Quakers. Even as a child, I was a mighty
eater and the thinness of the food on which I am here forced to
live causes me a deal of misery. Two pigeons are roosting in the
poplar trees outside the Bedlam gate and I would dearly love to
see their plump breasts roasted and set before me on a plate. But
such thoughts I set aside, as I must also set aside a yearning
(almost perpetual) to saddle Danseuse and ride away from here.
For where should I ride to? All paths, outside this place, lead back
to the King. This, at least, I have been permitted to understand.
And so I remain, having no glimpse of any future.

I am allotted tasks, almost all of them of a menial and repellent
variety and having some foul smell to them. But I perform them.
The days I dread are those when I must work at William Harvey.
Open the door of William Harvey and you are opening the door
of hell. Yesterday, in William Harvey, a woman bit off the tip of
her tongue even as I lifted her to put fresh straw into her pen
and her blood spurted into my eyes and it was like a flame licking
me and I felt a contamination of madness. The house is well
named. There is an abundance of blood in it. There is blood in
puddles on the floor.

There are many rules we must all obey at Whittlesea. One of
these forbids any of the Keeping Friends (for so the small staff
of the Bedlam quaintly call themselves) to go alone for any
reason whether by day or by night into William Harvey. So it
was that when the tip of the bitten tongue fell at my feet and I
was splattered with blood, one Friend came quickly to my side.
It was Eleanor who came, the younger of two sisters – Eleanor
and Hannah – who are women of very sweet and sober disposition. She picked up the tongue tip and put it into her handker-

chief and with admirable fortitude Pearce presently sewed it on again. But I prefer not to dwell upon that. I will, instead, tell you a little about these sisters and about the other Friends who make up this small company and who have under their care one hundred mad souls.

The Whittlesea Hospital was founded two years ago by Ambrose and Edmund. Its first occupant was Ambrose's grandfather, an old seaman who lost an eye to Spanish pirates and who, when the King returned, believed himself to have died. He lives quite happily in George Fox. He has an eye of glass that he keeps in a wooden box. He daily remarks that he expected the grave to be darker and more silent and is most glad that there should be company within it.

Ambrose, as noted at my first meeting with him at the gate, is large, obstinate, gentle and very hardy, like a plant with a great growth of root and an indifference to frost or heat or hail or drought. If all the world were to die of some epidemic, I do believe Ambrose would die last of all. Without him there would be no Whittlesea Hospital. Without him, Pearce would still be at St Barts in London and the others, Hannah and Eleanor, Edmund and Daniel, would still be waiting for the revelation of what they call "the True Work shown to us through the Seed of Christ, which is in all people".

Edmund is a man of my age who has twice been imprisoned for entering Anglican churches and causing harm to the clergy by the throwing of cabbages to their heads. He has most bright and round eyes and a high voice and is very fond of order and cleanliness, and will, when it rains in great sweeps across the Fens, take off all his clothes except a ragged pair of drawers and run round and round the walls, the while soaping his face and his torso and even his private parts. If Hannah or Eleanor should glance up and see Edmund engaged in these ablutions, I have noticed that they smile at each other and then look away and continue with their work, but that the smiles stay upon their faces for some while. It is as if they find, in Edmund's ritual, some innocent pleasure.

Both are large women with wide hips planted on sturdy legs. They wear sabots. Hannah's eyes are grey, Eleanor's blue. I believe Hannah to be thirty and Eleanor three or four years younger. They love the Lord with a great abundant love and their charity towards His creatures is very bountiful. I do not believe I have ever met any women like them, for they seem to have no vanity at all, but neither do they pity themselves, nor will let anyone speak their minds for them. In the month that has passed, I have once or twice prayed to be ill, so that Hannah and Eleanor might nurse me. But most strangely, given the unhealthy Fenland air and the inadequacy of my meals, I have not been ill one day. I content myself by sitting near them at supper, for I find their stillness comforting.

The sixth member of the Whittlesea staff is Daniel. He is the youngest of them all and his face has that transparent quality of youth – as if only time will give it proper substance. He is no more than seventeen. Having seen nothing of the world, nothing that he sees causes him any fright or revulsion. He is accepting of all things. He does not flinch from what he sees and smells and hears inside William Harvey. And of the six Friends, he is the most accepting of me. There is no disapproval in him. While the others wish to convert me to Quakerism, Daniel does not. Rather, being told that I was once at Court, he asks me to tell him in secret what that world of the Court is and how men speak and how they dress and what things they devise as pastimes. So I find myself describing the game of croquet, and Daniel listens and repeats such explanations as "Red may now, having passed under the hoop, endeavour to roquet Black" with reverence, as if they were the Twenty-third Psalm. And the two of us are momentarily very happy until I remember that I no longer have any rightful place in the world where croquet is played and so would do best to forget its complicated rules. And so I break off and Daniel is, for a mere moment or two, cast down. "Why might we not," he asked me one day, "play a little croquet here, Robert?" I pretend to give this some thought before answering: "The sight of a croquet hoop would make John most unhappy, Daniel."

And so I come to "John", as I must now call my spindly friend, Pearce.

The joy and surprise with which he greeted me were soon

enough superceded by a return to the severity with which he always feels obliged to treat me. As I expected, he was neither surprised by my fall from Royal grace nor sympathetic towards my distress.

"When I saw what your life was, in that terrible luxurious house of yours," he said, "I prayed you would be taken out of it."

"Yet I, Pearce, was uncommonly fond of it," I felt obliged to remind him.

"John," he said.

"What, Pearce?"

"Call me John, if you will."

"I am bound, after all this time, to find that difficult."

"You find difficult *all* that is simple and good, Robert. That is the trouble with you."

This conversation took place in Pearce's room late on the night of my arrival at Whittlesea, I resting my wind-buffeted body on his narrow bed, he lying on a pallet (such as is used by the occupants of George Fox and Margaret Fell) on the floor. I looked at him – my friend and my refuge! He is thinner than ever he was, so that the bones of his wrists resemble ivory bobbins. He is suffering, here in this low-lying land, from a very thick catarrh which causes bubbles of spittle to keep bursting at the corners of his mouth and which has quite silted up his sinuses, so that his voice sounds as if it was issuing from his nose. For this catarrh, he is dosing himself with mithridate which, in turn, has inflamed his eyes. He is, all in all, a wretched sight.

Though Quakers are not fond of sermons, Pearce lying on a straw mattress and dribbling mithridate into his nostrils, earnestly delivered himself of a sermon upon the perfidy of the Stuart Kings. "None of them were," he said, "nor none will ever be worthy of the nation's trust. For the good of the nation is never first with them. What is first is their supposed Divinity that puts them outside or above the law, so that in all their actions they are accountable to no one, neither in their public nor their private life . . ."

While listening to this sermon, I found myself pondering not the truth or otherwise of Pearce's words, but my own absence of anger in the whole disastrous matter. Wounded, disappointed, afraid, melancholy: these I am. What I do not seem to be is angry. So, refraining from agreeing or disagreeing with Pearce's diatribe against the Stuarts, I simply burst out: "Why do I not feel angry, Pearce?"

"John."

"John. Why do I not feel angry, John?"

"Because you are a child."

"I beg your pardon?"

"A child, punished by selfish parents, does not feel anger. It goes to its little private corner to weep. Exactly as you have done. And if the parents should again hold out their arms, why then the child will come running into them, all glad to be returned and forgiven for something it did only in answer to their greed."

"But Pearce – "

"Just as, if the King were to call you back, you would go running!"

"He will not call me back. It is quite finished."

"No. But were he to do so, you would go. And this is how it is revealed to me that you are still a child, Robert. But, mercifully for you, your state of homelessness brought you to Whittlesea. Our task here is to cure you of childishness just as we are trying to cure the lunatics of their insanity. For the man in you could be most splendid, Robert. I saw the shaping of the man – before you reverted to being the child – and it is that man we shall restore to you."

I glanced down at Pearce. I noticed that by him on the floor, within reach of his cadaverous fingers, he had placed his precious soup ladle. And I smiled.

After that first night, I found that Pearce was not interested in discussing my past life or my loss of it. He wished me to put it out of my mind as speedily as possible and so from the following day (during which I was given the drab clothes I have described for you) I was expected to join in the work of the Keepers exactly as if I were one of them and a born Quaker. "Robert is well qualified to help us," Pearce announced to Ambrose,

Edmund, Hannah, Eleanor and Daniel over our dawn breakfast
of barley and water porridge. "He is not squeamish or frail. He
claims to have forgotten medicine, but I know that he has not.
So let us give thanks to Christ that He has sent Robert to us
and ask Him to sustain him in the work we shall find for him to
do."

There followed prayers of touching simplicity. "Lord, send a
light to show Robert the way," said Ambrose. "Dear Jesus, be
with Robert," said Eleanor. "God in Heaven, take Robert's
hand and be at his side," said Hannah. "And even when night
comes, still be at his side," said Daniel. "Amen," said Edmund.

I look round at the little company. Alas, I think, they do not
know me. I am John's friend, and he has vouched for me and so
they have taken me in. But they do not know how afraid I am.
They do not know that I have long been parted from God. They
do not know there is a madness in me which renders grass and
trees as lunatic lines and splodges. They have taken me in to
Bedlam, but they do not know that my spirit rejoices in chaos.
I am wrong for them and I will do them wrong, and they do not
know it. I opened my mouth to begin upon telling them what
kind of man I was, but no words came to me except mumbled
words of thanks for their prayers, "for which," I told them, "I
hope to make myself worthy." And I saw Pearce nod approvingly
at my sudden humility.

And so my first day at Whittlesea began. In the company of
Ambrose and Hannah I was taken on a tour of the Hospital. The
rain I had been spared on my journey was now drenching the
featureless plain, swept into squalls by the wind.

As Ambrose unbolted the door of George Fox and it swung
inwards, I, all unthinkingly, hurried in to be out of the wet and
so drew suddenly upon myself the nervous glance of some forty
men lying in two cluttered rows the length of the barn.

At once, a commotion began. Some of the men stood up. I
saw one clutch the hand of another, as if in fear. Some laughed.
Others moved forward and stared at me, as at a strange exhibit.
One rolled up his filthy nightshirt and giggled and bared his
buttocks that were covered in sores. The stench of the place
was very bad, the night pails being full and all the "Decayed

Friends" (as Ambrose termed the mad people) appearing lousy and unwashed. But none was shrieking or crying, as I has been told the mad of the London Bedlam did constantly. None was chained up, but could move freely about the big barn. And they were not in darkness. Four small, barred windows let sufficient light into the place for me to see that at the further end of it had been constructed a gallery, reached by two ladders and on this high gallery stood an enormous loom.

"I see there is a loom," I said to Ambrose. "Do these men weave things upon it?"

"Yes," said Ambrose, rubbing his large hands together. "The loom. Transported by cart from the workhouse shut down at Lynn."

My thoughts, which the man with the naked bottom still sought to preoccupy by jigging up and down in front of me, returned at once to Justice Hogg and my lost role as Overseer. Now, I would never succour the poor but serve the mad instead. But there appeared to be little difference between these two categories of people, many of the faces staring up at me having about them the same look of despair as I had perceived in the paupers gathering sticks near Bidnold.

"What is manufactured on the loom?" I enquired of Ambrose.

"Sail!" he said.

"Sailcloth? For Men-of-War?"

"No, Robert. For the fishing fleet at Lynn. They send us herrings in payment."

Ambrose then addressed the occupants of George Fox. He spoke to them kindly, as to a child, and they were mainly silent while he talked except for two at the further end who began to swear at each other in some of the foulest language I have ever heard. Ambrose instructed the men to roll up their pallets and take their slop pails to the cess pit and to put out the trestles for breakfast. I know now that this same routine is followed every morning, but Ambrose gave the instructions with great enthusiasm, as if he were announcing some happy new tiding. And indeed, when he had finished, one old man, around whose scrawny limbs were wound a great quantity of bandages, began to applaud. And Ambrose nodded at him and smiled. He then said: "And I will tell you now that great good fortune has come to Whittlesea. Behold Robert. He has come from Norfolk to help us all in our work for the Lord. Say his name to yourselves. Say Robert. And keep the name precious. Because he is your Friend."

The company then, to my embarrassment, started to mumble my name over and over again. Almost all were saying it, except one who began to utter a small piercing noise resembling very well the cry of the peewit. I did not know what was expected of me in the way of words, so I said nothing but performed a little obeisance such as I used to perfect before a looking glass in my Whitehall days. And I followed Ambrose out and we walked in the rain to Margaret Fell.

We found Hannah and Eleanor here. The pallets had been rolled away and the night pails emptied and bowls of cold water had been brought, in which the women of Margaret Fell were washing their faces and hands with a blackish soap. They were about thirty-five in number and of all ages, the youngest being no more than twenty or twenty-five.

"Tell me," I whispered to Ambrose, as I was shown the carding combs and spinning wheels with which the women worked to produce a grey lumpy yarn that was made into mops, "how have such young people been brought to madness?"

"By a hundred ways, Robert," he replied. "Madness is brother and sister to misfortune, not to age. Poverty is a prime cause. Abandonment another. We have one here, Katharine, who was deserted by her young husband in the middle of the night and now she will not, cannot, sleep and all her madness is from the exhaustion of her brain and body."

"Which one is Katharine?"

"There, washing her neck. With her clothes very torn. For this is what she does in the night: sits and tears to rags whatever we dress her in."

I looked towards this person. I saw a tall but thin young woman with black hair straggling to her waist and black eyes that reminded me of Farthingale's, except that they were larger and sadder and the skin under them bruised by her sleeplessness.

"There are cures for such an affliction," I said, remembering that at Cambridge Pearce used to chew mallow root and endive to still his moist brain into repose.

"Yes," said Ambrose, "and we try them for Katharine and sometimes she will sleep an hour or more, but a shortness of breath wakes her. She feels herself to be suffocating and speaks to us of weights on her head, pushing her down."

I was touched by the condition of this woman and, as Ambrose once again made the request that the inmates of Margaret Fell ponder my name and say it to themselves, I wondered at the power this word "sleep" has assumed in my mind. Days were coming, I was certain, when I would have to open my case of silver-handled surgical instruments and hold in my unpractised hand the scalpel with the words *"Do Not Sleep"* upon it. In allowing myself to become Robert I had surely ended what the King called my "dreaming time", and in my state of wakefulness much of what I longed to forget or ignore would now be grossly visible to me once more. And what must I come across on my very first day but a woman who slept not at all and whose wakeful stare – a perpetual, uncourted vigil over all the hours of light and dusk, darkness and dawn – had brought her to madness? Can there be, I thought bitterly, any more terrible exhortation on earth than that which the King had given me? When he gave the words to the engraver, what degree of suffering did he have in mind for me?

As if to answer this question, I soon found myself with Ambrose inside the third habitation of the Whittlesea Hospital, the place they call William Harvey.

I have already suggested to you that anyone entering here for the first time feels as if he has stumbled into hell. Except that it is not fiery. It is chill and dark and foetid, having only one small barred window in it and no rushlights or candles at all, for fear the inmates might wound themselves with an open flame or set on fire the straw pallets.

The people in William Harvey are kept chained up and harnessed to bolts in the wall and truly the existence of the King's lions in the Tower is more free than theirs. But these are people descended so far into madness that they would, if not clamped

into iron, commit obscenity or murder upon each other or
mutilate their own bodies which, from the great restlessness of
their limbs, appear as if truly possessed by some devilish power.

There are twenty-one of them: sixteen men and five women.
All have scars in their foreheads where blood has been let, this
and the trepanning of the skull (not practised by the Quakers)
being the most fearsome of the supposed cures for insanity. I
walked with Ambrose the length of the barn and I looked into
their eyes one by one and I remembered that it was of such
crazed and suffering people that Pearce had once said "they are
the only innocent of the age, which itself is a lunatic age, because
they are indifferent to glory". And a familiar shiver of irritation
with Pearce went through me, it being the case with him that he
believes too excessively in the truth of his own pronouncements,
some of which are most wise and profound, but yet others of
which are transparently foolish.

"Do you believe," I asked Ambrose (who had made no attempt
to persuade the inhabitants of William Harvey to learn my name),
"that Whittlesea can cure these people?"

He put his large hand on my shoulder.

"I believe, Robert," he said, "that if Jesus wishes it, they will
be cured. Already, we have seen cures in William Harvey." And
he then proceeded to tell me the story of the women who had
voided "two great worms", the very same tale Pearce had told
me on the way to Bidnold churchyard to dig for saltpetre, the
tale with which he had sought to convince me of the folly of
hope. It had affected me at the time, but now that I was standing
in the very place where it had happened, the story produced in
me a feeling of revulsion so profound that some bile came into
my throat and I believe I would have vomited had not Ambrose
spied my distress and opened the door of William Harvey so
that I could escape into the light of the damp morning.

That night (and all the month of nights since the first one), we,
the Keepers of Whittlesea, ate a supper of fish, vegetables and
bread cooked by Daniel in the kitchen and we spoke of our day
which, to me, had been worse than any day I had spent dissecting
cadavers at Padua or tending the poor sick of St Thomas's.

In the middle of this supper, I heard outside a wounding, familiar noise: it was the whinny of Danseuse. And of course I was once again tempted, then and there as I tried to swallow some greasy mackerel, to saddle my mare and ride away. But I did not. And Pearce had his eye upon me and seemed to know my thoughts. "Robert," he said kindly, "when you join us in our Meeting in our parlour, try to cast from your mind all old longings, so that you may be filled with the words of Christ and, through Him, speak to us."

"Yes, John," I said. "I will try."

Before the Meetings, the six Keepers (and now I, the seventh) take up lamps and go round the three madhouses being "tender". Our behaviour each night reminds me of King Harry's before Agincourt, except that we are not exhorting the lunatics to fight courageously on the morrow, but to still their souls in preparation for sleep. We inform them that Christ is in them ("as surely," I heard Pearce say, "as if He were the very blood that moves in a circle out from your heart and to it again") and is therefore keeping all safe during the night.

The straw beds are then laid out and the occupants of George Fox and Margaret Fell lie down upon them and cover their bodies, each with his grey blanket. And then we say a prayer over them and bid them goodnight and take the lamps away and they are left in their rows in the darkness. But the men and women of William Harvey are seldom quietened by our "tenderness", some not recognising night from day and seeming to have no knowledge of what sleep is until it overtakes them. And from my room, which is an exceedingly small place somewhat resembling my linen cupboard at Bidnold, I can often hear crying and howling coming from WH.

During the night, what is called a "Night Keeping" is made at two o'clock by two of the Friends together and we take it in turns to undertake this task, for which we must rise from our beds in the darkness and go in to each of the houses and make sure that none of the mad people is hurt or ill or trying some foul deed upon another. I dread the nights when I must take part in a Night Keeping. I dread most particularly the sight of

Katharine sitting up and making rags of her clothes. I have made up some ointment of saffron and orris and I smoothe this upon her temples, but as yet it has had no effect on her. It is always past three before I can return to my bed (there being always some malady to attend to or some comfort to give) and then I find myself so truly woken up by what I have had to do that I cannot return to sleep. And it is always at this hour that thoughts of Celia come into my mind. And I find myself wondering, does she still use my name and call herself Lady Merivel? Is Lady Merivel sleeping at this hour, or is she – as I imagine – singing to guests in her lighted rooms at Kew?

On my arrival here at Whittlesea, I made some attempt to justify my love for Celia to Pearce, describing it as a generous love, a love which was "useful", as the King would have it. He did not agree. He told me I was deluding myself. "It was an intemperate love," he said and, quoting Plato, informed me that "the intemperance of love is a disease of the soul," words which I have written down on a piece of parchment and wrapped around my oboe and put inside the sea chest I have been given in which I keep my wordly goods.

For reasons which are not yet clear to me, my mind seems to enjoy its greatest repose during the Friends' Meetings. I am quite silent within them. In the month that has passed, I have not been moved – by God or any other voice within me – to say anything at all. And sometimes very little is said by anyone and all we do is to sit in a semi-circle by the parlour fire.

It is most odd that I should even tolerate, let alone draw strength from such prolonged bouts of silence. At first, I was most restless at Meetings and impatient for them to be ended and felt my thoughts flying away from the room to lost places. One evening, Ambrose passed to me a piece of paper and asked me to read the words written on it and these were they: "Be quiet, that you may come to the summer, that your flight be not in the winter. For if you sit still in the patience which overcomes in the power of God, there will be no flying." And from that moment, I truly tried to be quiet and not to loathe but to love quietness, and so I began to fare better at the Meetings and at last to feel myself revived a little by the affectionate presence of John, Ambrose, Edmund, Hannah, Eleanor and Daniel.

And when they speak, prefacing even the most ordinary observations by "It has come to me from the Lord," I find myself very touched by what they have to say, so that I want to laugh. And this feeling of suppressed laughter is the nearest I have come for a long time to happiness.

I always wear my wig for Meetings so as to spare John and the others the sight of my hogs' bristles. There is a tidiness about the way they arrange the chairs that I don't wish to spoil. With the wig on, however, and with one of my coats (usually the black and gold, not the red) replacing the leather tabard, I resemble very nearly the Merivel of my former life and invisible under this old finery is the Robert of now. He is present, nevertheless. He is grateful for the warmth of the parlour fire and for the voices of Hannah and Eleanor which are so gentle and soothing that, when one of them is speaking, he sometimes finds himself asleep in his chair. But the one great trouble about Quakers is that they are bossy: they do not let you dream.

SIXTEEN

THE SCENT OF FLOWERS

The winds have gone and the air of April is still and quiet and warm. In the Airing Court, the big oak is putting out leaves of a green so succulent it brings saliva into my mouth. I do not precisely wish to eat these leaves but yet want to posses them in some way before the newness of them vanishes.

It has not rained here for some time and through the yellow crust on the mud of Whittlesea new grass is springing up and in the ditch outside the wall there are primroses and violets. Pearce seems most entranced by these flowers, as if he had never seen nor smelled any like them before. Not only does he pick them and examine them; I have observed him lie down on the edge of the ditch and stick his nose into a clump of primroses and not move for ten minutes at a time. I know from the vacant look in his blue eyes that his mind is at work on some experiment with regard to the flowers, but I have not asked him what it might be lest he infer from my interest in the thing a renewal of a more profound interest in biology.

Hannah and Eleanor are in the habit of thanking the Lord for giving us "kind weather", but I have come to the conclusion that to me such a springtime is cruel; in it I feel wanton and idle. I would prefer a return to hard skies and a clamped chill, these being a better accompaniment to the routine of my day, which is a most harsh one that affords me no leisure at all, but rather commits me to many hours of work of the most demanding kind I could imagine, namely work with my scalpel.

There is, adjacent to each of the main rooms of George Fox, Margaret Fell and William Harvey, a small ante-room, lit with oil lamps, in which patients are examined and cures and operations tried upon them. Before my arrival, Pearce and Ambrose were the only two physicians among the Keepers at Whittlesea and so to them fell the task of trying to alleviate madness with the knife. Now, I have been forced by Pearce to "render service to Whittlesea by placing such skill as you possess in the service of the common good", or in other words to join in the cutting and blood letting and to do it without complaint, for Pearce's eye is always upon me, watching and measuring. He knows very well how I recoil before this return to my former vocation. He knows also that were he and the other Friends to put me out from here, I would be at a loss to know in which direction to ride.

Mercifully, I have not yet been required to perform any large operations, but there is, by those who study insanity, a great faith put in phlebotomy, and this we undertake daily. The degree of suffering felt by a man who must have his head held over a bowl while a scalpel opens a vein in his temple I cannot calculate, but if I am the one who must make the incision I always feel obliged to apologise to him beforehand, and often feel tempted to add (yet do not): "Forgive me, for I know not what I do," for since coming to Whittlesea I have seen not one cure worked by a phlebotomy. As well as from the forehead, we let blood from the cephalic vein and many patients bear in their arms wounds that have been reopened so many times they will not close. Ambrose says of the cephalic phlebotomies: "In the bright blood let by this means, I can *smell* the choler!" His faith in medical science is no less complete than his faith in Christ and with regard to both practices I know him to be an honest and honourable man. But I can perceive no miracle cure in the opening of the cephalic vein. Invariably, the patients (even those who are violent) are quiet for some hours after the cutting, but soon enough return to their habitual state, the pain of their wounds surely adding to their other sufferings? In short, I am somewhat critical of the methods we employ here. We spill blood and with its flow believe we release poisonous humours, but do not know beyond all question whether we do or not. I remain silent, however. For it can avail me nought (do you note the biblical cadences into which my language has fallen?) to condemn a thing when I have nothing better to put in its place.

I have noticed, however, that there is one shortcoming in our modes of treatment, which are based upon the unspoken thesis that lunacy is a liquid thing, which may, drop by drop, or in a sudden heaving torment, be coaxed out of the body in streams of blood, vomit or faeces. I do not know whether or not lunacy is a liquid thing but, were it to be so, I would try natural as well as unnatural means of bringing about the body's excretions. And this we do not do. I would cause the lunatics to weep (either with laughter or with sadness, it would not matter) and I would cause them to sweat. For the first, I would tell stories; for the second, I would play music and let them dance. Yet neither tears nor perspiration are encouraged. With those who do cry we are stern, telling them to cease their wailing and remember Jesus who never wept for himself, only for the sufferings of others. And of course there is no dancing. The only exercise taken by the inmates of our Hospital is the passing of the shuttle through the warp of the loom, the turning of the spinning wheels and the slow shuffling round the Airing Court. And this overlooking of two beneficial evacuations of nature has begun to worry me, so that it keeps bobbing to the surface of my mind. It bobs up, in truth, so frequently and persistently that I may soon be forced to disturb Pearce's reverie with his primroses by revealing to him my thoughts upon the subject.

Word that I was once at Court has reached the inmates of William Harvey. How it has travelled there I do not know, unless the hand of the King may still be felt in the ice of the scalpel blade. As Pearce has stated, most of those in WH have no remembrance of the word "Court", nor could imagine what manner of thing a Court might be. But there is one, calling himself Piebald, a mutineer on the *Valiant Queen*, who now takes great delight in telling me that all men on earth with a rank above midshipman are bringers of pox and pestilence and suffering, and should be slain – as he single-handedly slew three officers – "to rid this England of the stink of privilege". Because I was once a "Court Prick", he includes me among those he wishes to kill, and each week he devises a new means of death for me, death and violence being all that occupy his mind, day and night.

And at night, alone in my linen cupboard, I can sometimes feel mortally afraid of this Piebald. Yet quite often during the day I find myself lingering in his pen, his ways of death being so ingenious that I find solace in them for my imagination. That I do this is, of course, most strange. Yet I find myself wondering, do many men of a cowardly disposition not secretly long to meet face to face that other who, without fuss or deliberation, will instantly take their lives from them? Is it uncommon to feel glad to have found him?

Piebald, My Redeemer

This evening, after the Meeting, I took up a piece of parchment to my room and wrote in a pretty script these blasphemous words.

On the morning of the twenty-first of April, finding myself once again staying awhile in WH to listen to Piebald, then noticing, on emerging from the place, that Pearce was walking across the Airing Court holding a bunch of kingcups to his nose, I came suddenly to the conclusion that we two might ourselves be going mad and that it would be possible to recognise in our behaviours – mine with Piebald, Pearce's with the flowers – the first footsteps of our madness. And no sooner had I addressed this possibility than I came stumbling upon a truth about the fate of the insane which had hitherto remained hidden not only from me but I believe from all the Keepers at Whittlesea. And it is this:

> The man who is merely ill will seek out, at the first sign or "footstep" of that illness, the services of a physician to help him to a cure; the insane man, on the contrary, is not taken

into any Bedlam or Hospital until his "disease" of madness is so far advanced that it may be beyond cure. In other words, though illness may be arrested early, madness never is – for the only reason that all men learn and know what the footsteps of illness may be, but who can say in each or any case what the footsteps of lunacy are?

Though it was almost dinnertime and the smell of broth in the kitchen brought on a little pain of hunger, I forced myself to go to my room and lie down upon my narrow bed and look very squarely at my supposed truth, following Fabricius's motto: "Let certainty be tempered with disbelief." And I imagined the great anatomist's gaze upon me.

At dinner, I was very quiet and pensive, so that Eleanor enquired: "Are you quite well today, Robert?" I replied that I was well enough but had discovered much, that morning, with which to occupy my mind. Ambrose looked at me benevolently and asked me to share my thoughts with the six Friends "if it may bring you help". I thanked him and said: "Alas, Ambrose, there is so little of the philosopher in me that it is very often the case that my mind is furiously at work upon some supposed great matter which, as soon as I try to put it into words, has the habit of flying out of the window." Edmund smiled. Daniel rose and ladelled a second helping of broth into our bowls. Pearce, dabbing at his thin lips with a coarse napkin, cast in my direction a look of disdain. (It has become a humiliating fact of my life at Whittlesea that, no matter what my mood is, Pearce behaves to me as if he were a mind reader, always knowing precisely what I am thinking.)

In the afternoon, it was the turn of the women of Margaret Fell to make their monotonous perambulation round the oak tree and I and Hannah were their overseers, walking round and round with them and conversing with them "on subjects that will gladden their hearts, such as the coming of spring and the sowing of the Whittlesea House vegetable plot with new lettuce and scarlet beans".

I fell into step beside Katharine and asked her how she regarded the oak, whether it was a thing of beauty or comfort to her, and she replied that she found it to be "quite full of a green death".

"What is this 'green death'?" I said.

"It is in nature," she answered, "sometimes in a part of a thing and sometimes in all."

"Do you see it in people? Do you see it, now, in me?"

"No," she said. "In you I see a waft of death. But it is not green."

"What colour might this waft be, then?"

She stopped and regarded me, thus causing the women behind us to knock into us. I gently took her elbow and led her on. I assumed that, after she had thought about it a while, she would reply to my question, but she did not. Her mind had moved away from the subject and onto the thing which torments her night and day, her desertion by her husband while she was sleeping. She began to recount to me – for the twelfth or thirteenth time – how, if he had been a small man he would not have got away without causing her to wake, but being very tall was able to step over her body with one giant stride. And so she began to imitate him, lifting up her skirts and taking great huge awkward steps, causing some of the women to stop walking and watch her and laugh at her and point, as at a lying mountebank. I let her stride on. She calls this imitation of the man who betrayed her a "Leaving Step". She says every man on earth has his own Leaving Step and I often try to calm her rage by agreeing with her and telling her that the King, being very plagued by fools from whom he wishes to walk away, has perfected his Leaving Step into a walk of unsurpassed elegance. Several times, she has asked me to "show the walk" to her. But to make a poor imitation of the King is something I cannot bring myself to do.

The day was very brilliant and warm and we kept the women walking around the tree for longer than the allotted hour. When Katharine had tired of doing her Leaving Step, she came beside me again and after a while put out her hand and touched my shoulder and told me that the colour of the waft of death she saw in me was white. Had she said scarlet, which is a colour that affects me very much, as you will already have noticed, I would have been perturbed by the revelation. But white was of no significance to me and so I immediately put the thing from my mind.

I did not know that on the evening of the twenty-first of April I was going to break my silence at the Meetings. Though very fascinated by the "truth" I had stumbled upon about the world's inability to try any cure upon the lunatic until he is – in all but a few cases – incurable, I had not planned to offer any discourse upon the subject until I had pondered what practical measures might be taken to remedy this situation. Still less had I plotted within myself to reveal to the Keepers my all-too-Merivelian ideas about the efficacy of weeping and sweating in the treatment of poisonous humours.

And yet, all these things came out of me. And the manner of their coming out was most memorable and strange.

I was seated at one edge of the little semi-circle we make at Meetings round the parlour fire. Near me, on an oak table, was a wooden bowl into which Pearce had put posies of primroses. There was utter silence in the room except for the crackling and spitting of the fire, and there is something about a Quaker silence which is absolute, as if Eternity were then and there beginning.

And in this quiet, I heard myself breathing in the smell of the flowers and after some minutes a certainty stole upon me that this perfume was slowly, with each breath of it that I took, being drawn up into my brain and there being alchemised into syllables and words. And it was not long before my brain seemed to be so full of words – as crammed with them as was the bowl with the primroses – that it began to hurt, and I put my head in my hands to try to get the hurt away. But it would not go. And so I opened my mouth and I began to speak, starting with the phrase, "It has come to me from the Lord," and in a perfectly logical fashion I set forth my argument, saying that madness may be born of many things but yet for all except those who are lunatic from their births there was a Time Before, a time when there was no madness in them and that this would be followed by a Growing Time or a Sickening Time, when the madness was coming upon them, precisely as all disease has a Growing Time. "And we," I said, "we the Keepers of those who are very far gone into a mad sickness, do we not all recognise that the men and women of William Harvey are much further from any help or cure than those in the other two houses? Likewise, is it not our daily fear to find an inhabitant of George Fox or Margaret Fell descended into an uncontrollable mad state, so that we would be forced to chain him up and put him in a pen in William Harvey? Thus we daily admit that madness is not a static thing but, just as all things in the world are changeful, so is madness and, like them, may change for the better or for the worse. But what we do not ask, dear Friends, is what were the Footsteps of each case of madness, in other words how it came there and when and in what manner it first showed itself, yet I, when I was a physician, was taught by the great medical minds of our age that few cures are likely to succeed unless each stage and symptom of a malady is understood. And this is what the Lord has revealed to me, that we should try with each one of those in our care to look back into past time and ask them to try to remember how it was to be in the Time Before and what thing or calamity came about to put them into the Sickening Time. And in this way we might discover the imprint of the steps to madness, there just under the surface, as the imprints of past ages lie under the surface of the earth . . ."

As I delivered myself of this long speech, I was not aware of how the others regarded it or me, but only of my need to get it out so that my brain would be free of it and no longer hurting in the press of words. I deliberately paused at this point and took in several great breaths and once more the scent of the primroses ascended to my brain and recommenced its alchemy and so I talked on, now making proposals, all of which, I said, had "come to me from Jesus Christ", for the questioning of all inmates of Whittlesea by the Keepers so that the Time Before might become visible to us. And I was entirely held now by my words, as if my words had become a liquid and I immersed in them, like a drowning man in a rushing river. So into the stream now poured all my outlandish things, my fantastical things, my cures by weeping and my cures by dancing, my suggestions for story-telling and the playing of music. As I spoke on these matters, I began to feel a merciful diminution of the pain in my head and so I lifted it up and talked on, staring at the fire, and in the flames of the fire I could see a most wondrous picture of Daniel, attired in the clothes of summer, playing a fiddle, and all the women of Margaret Fell skipping and dancing round him, seeming happy like children. And then the pain left me entirely and the picture vanished and I was silent.

I was very boiling hot. I took off my wig and wiped my face and my head with my handkerchief. I felt the eyes of the others upon me, but no one spoke. A full ten or fifteen minutes passed and the time allowed for the Meeting came to an end and Ambrose put his hands into his prayer steeple and mumbled: "Thank you, dear Lord, that in our presence Robert was moved to speak." And this is all that was said.

Mercifully, it was not my turn that night to take part in a Night Keeping, for as soon as we rose from our circle by the fire, I felt a shivering in my knees and a pain of exhaustion in my belly and I went to my bed and slept a deep, thick sleep from which I did not stir till morning.

When I woke, however, I felt in me a lightness of heart, such as I had not experienced since my casting out from Bidnold. I could not account for it, but was most grateful to find it there. (I have, since I arrived here, found myself pondering the thing we call happiness, for which, the King once told me I had a gift. I now recognise that my supposed "gift" was much less of a thing than, say, Hannah's and Eleanor's, they being two of the most contented women I have ever met.)

It was my task, that morning, to work in the vegetable garden with Pearce, together with some six or seven men from George Fox. (I report in passing that Pearce is so fond of this plot, so proud of its drainage ditches and of the infant pear trees he is trying to grow *en espalier* on its southerly wall, that he likes to oversee all work done there and becomes very vaporous with irritation if his seedlings are not planted in absolutely straight lines.) The sun was once again shining and I would have found my duty in the garden quite pleasant had it not been for Pearce's

behaviour towards me that morning, which was most irksome.
He acted as one who wished to have nothing to do with me
whatsoever, separating himself from any task in which I was
occupied and replying most curtly to all my attempts to speak
to him. Watching him from a distance planting beans, swooping
down on a freshly raked patch of soil like a long-necked bird,
using his long white fingers as a dibbling-stick, burying each
bean most lovingly and moving on, I remembered how on our
angling expeditions near Cambridge this mood of dislike for me
would sometimes come over him. Then and now, I find it most
hurtful and difficult to endure, particularly as I can seldom fathom
what it is I have done to offend him. On this morning, however,
I could only conclude that my outpouring of the previous evening
had not been to his liking. Some hours – or even days – would
probably pass; then Pearce would dissect my thesis with his
clever pecking mind and lay it in ruins before me.

Meanwhile, as I plucked weeds from the onion bed, I began
in a low voice, lest Pearce hear what I was doing, to talk to the
man called Jacob Lowe who was working alongside me and to
enquire of him what thing he most clearly remembered before
coming to Whittlesea and whether, in his past life, he had some
trade or calling. He told me he was a butcher and slaughterer.
He described to me the ease with which he could split a calf's
head and take out the tender brains. "But I was killed by a
whore," he whispered. "I died of her foul cunt. And this is my
second life on earth."

I requested him to describe his "death" to me. And he told
me that his testicles had swollen and burst "being full of the
pox" and out through these burst cods had poured his life.

I looked up at Jacob Lowe. His face was ruddy, his musculature
good, his nose prominent and not one whit decayed. From these
external signs, I felt it possible to conclude that, if he had once
suffered from the pox, he was now cured of it. Such cures are
rare but where they occur they have depended – in all cases I
have witnessed – on the giving of *mecurius sublimate*, of which
the chief element is mercury itself, that capricious metal to
which I once likened the King. And mercury is, if the dose is
not most carefully measured, a poison. I saw a man at St

Thomas's die of mercury poisoning and he died screaming and raving, as if a madness had suddenly come upon him. I smiled to myself and looked over to Pearce's stooping back. In the time it had taken me and Jacob Lowe to weed the onion patch, I had retraced the primary footsteps to this one man's lunacy.

Neither at dinnertime nor during the afternoon did any of the friends make reference to my speech of the evening before and Pearce's lack of charity towards me seemed to confirm that he at least had been most displeased by it. I thus kept quiet to myself my conversation with Jacob Lowe and waited for the Meeting to see if Ambrose might pass judgement upon my theory. But he did not mention it, and I confess I felt somewhat cast down to think that what had appeared to me as a revelation appeared to the Keepers of Whittlesea as a thing of no consequence at all. It was only some days later that I was to discover that their way with knowledge is a quiet way. They do not snatch at it or gobble it down; they take it into themselves slowly like a physic and let it course a long time in their blood before making any pronoucement upon it.

Meanwhile, Pearce emerged from his state of foulness towards me and bade me go with him one morning in search of yet more flowers. Not far from the Whittlesea gate we came upon some pale, sweet-scented narcissus, which Pearce instructed me to pick.

"You see," he said, as I gathered the flowers for him, "I am in a most troubling state of unknowing, Robert."

"Are you, John?" I said.

"Yes. For I vowed that in this springtime I would find an answer to a question that has vexed me for many years, namely, what is the scent of flowers? Why is it there? Do plants exhale? Is the scent no more than this exhaled breath? And if there is no exhalation, then in what part of a flower resides the scent?"

"Why do you wish to know this, John?" I enquired.

"*Why?* Because I do *not* know it. There is undoubtedly some Divine lesson hidden in the mystery, but until I have unravelled the mystery itself, I am shut out from knowing what it might be."

I held out my bunch of narcissus to Pearce and he took it

delicately from me, like a girl. I was tempted to say that the smell of the primroses had led me to knowledge I believed more useful than any he might derive from the study of flowers, but I did not.

SEVENTEEN

VISITORS TO BETHLEHEM

Last night I had a dream of Will Gates. I was in London, and walking to the Tower, and I came upon Will, in rags, begging at the Tower gate. I put some beans into his begging bowl and pretended I did not know him.

When I woke, very dismayed by this dream, I turned my attention to the struggle my mind was undergoing with regard to the word "oblivion". I do not need to remind you of all that I was endeavouring to forget when I was at Bidnold. Now, much of what I had consigned to darkness I am obliged to bring once more into the light. At the same time, back into oblivion must go my turquoise bed, my candlelit suppers, the Red Deer of my park, Celia's apricot ribbons, and of course the smell of the King's perfume which, according to Pearce, I only loved because it was the smell of power. Alas, all these things seem to have been carved into the very tissue of my mind, like graven images. Though many hours may pass during which I do not think of them, I do not believe I will ever succeed in forgetting them completely.

My bird, also, my Indian Nightingale, is very frequently in my thoughts. I know now that I was duped. The creature was a mere blackbird. But the strange thing is that I do not mind. For while it was alive, it gave me pleasure and the realisation that I was deluded only makes me smile. It is a fact about Merivel – and about many in this age – that they do not always wish to know the truth about a thing. And when the truth is at last revealed to them they cannot entirely dismantle all fiction from it. Thus, the blackbird, will for ever in my mind have about it the aura of an Indian Nightingale, which species itself does not exist in all the world, but is an imaginary thing. The King was right when he said that I was "dreaming".

To assist me in my task of forgetting, I have begun to pass some time each day with Katharine, it being my conviction that if I could help but one person at Whittlesea to a cure and see them walk out from here, I would start to feel useful and in this new-found usefulness confront my future, whatever it is to be, and not look so enviously at my past.

Though she is sometimes very confused, believing herself to be in Hell, Katharine will often share with me some secrets of her old life, describing to me how her husband was a stone mason and how, before he left her, he once took her with him to the dark, dusty space between the vaulted ceiling of a church and its roof and there committed with her acts of great profanity. She is able, also, to describe her symptoms to me, how, when she lies down to sleep, a pain comes in her abdomen and a great suffocating pressure on her head and how, if she falls into a state of almost-sleep, some spasm of her heart will put her body into a convulsion.

I have understood why Katharine tears her clothes: she is making what she calls "windows" for her limbs to see through, it being her belief that all of her mind and body must be watchful at all times, lest any come near her to do her harm or betray her. If her arms and trunk and legs are covered up, she has the notion that her body has become "blind".

Washing herself, I have observed, solaces her, particularly the washing of her feet, over which task I have seen her fall into a kind of trance. At one Night Keeping, I discussed this last phenomenon with Ambrose. The next day, he told me that he had spent the rest of the night awake, reading his medical books and had come upon something that he had half remembered – that the rubbing of the soles of the feet with black soap may succeed in drawing down from the brain the noisiness within it and so still it and let it rest.

This cure, then, I have begun to try upon Katharine. I sit by her and put her naked feet upon my lap, a cloth under them, and some warm water near me in a bowl. And I immerse the black soap in the water and hold her ankles with one hand and with the other chafe the soles of her feet with the soap. Always, she sits quietly while I perform this somewhat strange task and watches me intently, as if I were some work of ancient art recently excavated from a tomb.

My arm and wrist tire easily. I have not the stamina for this task of foot rubbing that I would like. But if I can continue with it beyond twenty minutes, I am rewarded by seeing Katharine's stare fade and her eyes blink and her head begin to fall onto her chest. Three times, she has truly fallen asleep for several minutes without any spasm or convulsion coming upon her, but the moment I cease my rubbing with the soap, she wakes. And now I feel most vexed that Ambrose and I have discovered a thing which is and yet is not a cure.

Still no opinions have been offered upon my outpouring at the Meeting. Pearce has informed me that the Friends are pondering my ideas, "somewhat forward and arrogant though your speech was, Robert", but this is all. But I am privately pursuing my search for the footsteps of Katharine's madness, in the expectation that these, when revealed to me, will help me to make her well. And it has been made plain to me through this search that Katharine is a woman of a most loving yet childish nature. So, together with Eleanor, who is gifted at sewing, I have made Katharine a doll out of rags (its face painted in oils by me with a small brush) imagining that if she were to grow to love it, it might comfort her at night, just as a doll or toy will comfort a child. It is a very crude thing, having no hands nor feet nor hair and dressed in a simple smock which, immediately the doll was given to her, Katharine removed and tore in pieces. She stared at the doll for a long time. After a while, she pulled some straw from her mattress and made a kind of nest of it on the stone floor and then laid the doll in the straw and called to the women near her to see what she had done. They pressed round her. One laughed a high squawking laugh, another tried to talk, but could only drool and dribble. Katharine looked from them to the straw and to them again. "Bethlehem," she said.

Now, at night, she says prayers to the doll, which she does not touch, but which has become the centre of her vigil. She believes it to be a little replica of the infant Jesus. The fact that its face – if it is like a human face at all – more nearly resembles the face of Rosie Pierpoint than that of a newborn Christ is of no consequence to her. It is the Jesus of her imagination that she sees.

With the coming in of the month of May, news came to us from Earls Bride that the plague, whispered about for so long, had taken hold in London, "so that there is a weekly tally of deaths now that is above seven hundred".

We were told "on the good authority of some upon the staging coach" that the King had removed himself and his Court to Hampton Court but might not be safe there for long. An outbreak of such virulence, said the people of Earls Bride, would creep outwards on the waterways and on the wind and the people themselves, fleeing the city, would bring it into all the shires upon their breath.

The Keepers of Whittlesea sat down by their fire and folded their hands and asked Jesus "not to sew the poisoned seed of the Black Death among us, that the suffering we daily witness here be not added to".

It was then proposed by Edmund (whose eyes and beard shine with such health that it is most difficult to imagine him laid low even by an ague) that the gates of Whittlesea Hospital be closed, allowing no one in except those from whom we buy straw and wood and flour and meat.

Since we are a forgotten place, few people ever make their way here and I remarked therefore that Edmund's proposed precaution was scarcely necessary. It was Ambrose who reminded me that from time to time the relatives of those incarcerated here make the journey from London or Lynn or Newmarket to visit them, bringing provisions, money and clothing. "And it is these," he said, "whom we must – for as long as the epidemic may last – turn away."

Eleanor, Hannah and Edmund nodded in agreement. Daniel rose and made an arch of his hands in front of his mouth and started blowing into it, like someone trying to teach himself to whistle. Pearce sniffed and took from his pocket his little phial of mithridate. He then delivered himself of his opinion that these visits of relatives "are all that defines time for certain of our Decayed Friends. If we prohibit them," he said, "we shall lose many of them to vacancy and so to despair."

I have noticed that the Keepers of Whittlesea are very cour- teous to each other in argument, Pearce alone among them being given to fits of sulking. And so it was that the closing of the gates to visitors was now discussed in a most amiable way, each one putting forward an opinion and listening politely to those that countered it. Only Daniel remained outside the argu- ment, now and then through his cupped hands making a very peculiar noise a little resembling the hoot of an owl I used to hear from my bedroom at Bidnold. No one paid this any attention at all.

I found myself on the side of Pearce. I knew, for instance, that Katharine's mother had promised to visit her in the summer- time and that she longed for this day and hoped her mother would put her arms around her. The notion that, because of our own fear, we would turn this woman away made me feel most uncomfortable. But Ambrose was very passionate in defence of Edmund's proposal. Better that some here should suffer deprivation and loneliness, he declared, than that we should perish and the Hospital fall to ruin. "For where," he asked, "would the survivors go then but to the London Bedlam, which is the saddest place on earth? And there, in all probability die from the very pestilence from which we are trying to protect them!"

Being a large man with mighty lungs, the voice of Ambrose is very big. To me, it appeared to fill up the small parlour so completely that when Pearce spoke again his voice sounded faint and reedy, as if there was no room for it.

And so it was decided: from that very night, the gates would be barred and under the inscription "I have refined thee in the furnace of affliction" would be posted a bill, giving notice that in time of plague no visitors whomsoever would be admitted to Whittlesea. Provisions or money could be left in a basket and would be given to the one for whom they were intended. The wellbeing or otherwise of any inmate could be ascertained by means of a letter to the Keepers.

Pearce was most unhappy with the decision, his disquiet causing a copious running of phlegm from his sore nostrils. And it made me feel afraid. I fell prey to the notion that all the world I had known and loved outside Whittlesea would sicken and die and that we and our hundred tormented souls would be the last beings left alive in England.

And so May came in, hot and still, and the light on the flat horizon danced.

So little rain had fallen since my arrival that we were forced to get water from our well to irrigate our vegetable plot and the nodules of fruit on Pearce's pear trees began to appear wizened, like the cods of an old man.

The primrose season was past and the grass in the ditches was brown and dry. Though Pearce talked of making us nosegays to sweeten our air and drive away the plague germ, he could find no flowers but a few late jonquils with which to make them.

Edmund who, as I have told you, loved a deluge for washing in, declared the heat to be "foul type of weather, ripening nothing but disease" and took to wearing his hat at all times.

I remembered the winter and the snow on my park and my thoughts about Russians, but these things seemed so very distant, it was almost impossible to believe that they had ever been.

The air of the nights seemed not much cooler than that of the days and in them I found sleep difficult, so it became my habit to get up many times in each night; sometimes only to stare out of my window in the direction of Earls Bride and then lie down again; sometimes to tuck my nightgown into a pair of breeches and put on my shoes and go quietly out to Margaret Fell and see whether or not Katharine was sleeping.

I had continued daily with the rubbing of her feet with black soap and I had begun to have some hope for this cure. I could now pause in the task or cease altogether and she would stay asleep for an hour. And whenever I looked at her sleeping thus, I would feel very moved by my own success.

So now, if I found her awake in the hot nights, talking to her doll Jesus, pulling her nightclothes or braiding and unbraiding her hair, I would sit down on the floor beside her pallet and bid her lie down, and then I would place her feet in my lap and begin rubbing them, not with any soap but only with the palm of my hand, and in not many minutes I would see her eyes close and a merciful wave of sleep come over her.

One night, being very tired out of this wakefulness of May, I too fell asleep on the floor of Margaret Fell while rubbing Katharine's feet and when I woke up I saw that Katharine had laid her blanket over me. I might have stayed some while at her side if there had not begun all around me an early morning clamour of the women to piss, so that everywhere I looked they were squatting down on their buckets and the smell of urine quite overpowered me and drove me out into the dawn.

I went to visit Danseuse, who is most plagued by flies in this hot weather, and I laid my head against her neck and thought about the early morning coming slowly to the Thames, unseen by Celia asleep with the King at Hampton Court. And I remembered Celia's longing for a child and began to wonder whether, in her, the King would create yet another bastard, while with his own Queen he could not produce an heir. These reveries are interrupted by the stamping of Danseuse who, since we rode inside the Whittlesea gates, has been restless and prone to fear. If she were not the only precious thing I own, I would open the gates and let her gallop away.

Some days after this, a great storm moved in over the Fens and the hard earth of Whittlesea was turned once more to mud. Pearce called all the Keepers together in the parlour after our mid-day broth to offer up thanks for the rain falling on his lettuces and his beans. These prayers done, Edmund took up his soap and undressed himself and went out into the deluge but returned, very agitated, a moment later to announce to us that two visitors were at the gates, an old woman and her daughter clamouring to be let in.

"Ambrose," said Pearce, "will you leave these people out in the storm?"

Ambrose went to the window: "The storm is moving east," he said. "It is passing."

"They must not come in!" said Edmund.

"No," said Ambrose, "they must not come in. And they will not. They will read the bill we have posted and they will leave."

"How if they cannot read?" asked Pearce.

Ambrose hesitated a moment before replying. "One of us will go to the gate and talk to them through the grille."

"I shall go," offered Hannah.

"No," said Ambrose calmly. "Edmund will go. He will go directly, for he does not mind the rain."

I watched from the door of Whittlesea House as Edmund, naked except for his frayed under-drawers, jogged out to the gate, soaping his chest as he went, and stuck his head into the small iron grille inset into the heavy portal. I could not hear what he said, for the drumming of the rain on the earth and on the buildings was very loud. Nor could I, from this vantage point, see the visitors, but it appeared they were very insistent for Edmund was so long at the gate he had succeeded in washing all of himself except his legs while he parleyed with them.

He at last came away and bent down to soap his knees and his calves. By this time, however, the storm had indeed moved off in an easterly direction and there was not enough rain falling to rinse off the lather he had made. Edmund threw his head back and glared angrily at the clearing sky before making his way to the pump, where he completed his ablutions. Only then did he return to us and tell us that the visitors had been the mother and sister of my would-be murderer, Piebald, and that they had come out from Puckeridge, some way north of London.

I went up to my room, which is indeed more of a room to me now and less of a linen cupboard, and looked out over the wall that surrounds us to the Earls Bride marshes. On the road to the village, I could see two figures walking, dressed in the clothes of very poor people. Every few steps, they turned and looked back towards us. Then the younger woman put her arm

round the shoulders of the older one and they walked on until I
could see them no more. Only after they had disappeared from
my sight did I "see" that the younger of the two, Piebald's
sister, carried a basket that appeared heavy. No doubt they had
come with provisions and, being turned away by Edmund, had
not thought to leave these at the gate.

It was this knowledge – no less, perhaps, than the knowledge
that these women were Piebald's kin – that made me swiftly
descend the stairs and inform Ambrose that I was going to ride
after the visitors to retrieve the gifts they had forgotten to
leave.

"Very well," said Ambrose, "but do not go so near them that
you breathe their breath."

"They do not have the plague, Ambrose. There is no plague
at Puckeridge."

"That we cannot know, Robert. The germ has come north to
us from Southern Europe and so may still be moving in a
northerly way."

"Very well. I will not go near them, but call out to them to
put down their offerings, which I will then retrieve. Are you
content that I should do that?"

"Yes."

"And say," intervened Pearce, "that we are sorry for their
wasted journey."

"I will, John."

And so I went out to put a saddle on Danseuse whom I had
not ridden for a long time. The storm had quite gone and, in the
bright sun once again shining on us, the inmates of Margaret
Fell were assembling for their airing, but I gave them no thought,
my mind being intent only upon overtaking the visitors.

At the sight of a saddle, Danseuse gave a whinny of joy and
her flanks shivered as I tightened the girth. And immediately I
had mounted her, she began to trot very fast towards the gate,
thus causing some fright to the women walking round the oak
tree. I tried to rein her in, but she pulled so hard with her head
that I was jerked forward and almost lost my balance. Then
Daniel opened the gate for us and we were out of Whittlesea
and at once my splendid mare began to gallop like a chariot horse

and in no time at all we had reached the straggle of poor houses
that is Earls Bride.

I had expected to overtake Piebald's visitors before reaching
the village, but there was no sign of them. Managing to slow
Danseuse to a quiet trot, I passed through Earls Bride and out
the other side of it, where the flat, muddy track led on towards
March. Because of its flatness, I could see some way down this
road and there was nothing and no one visible on it. I persuaded
my horse to stop. I dismounted and looked back at the village.
As I have informed you, it is a place without an inn or hostelry
of any kind, so I could not guess where the two women might
be. It was as if the bright air that still smelled of rain had made
them vanish.

Leading Danseuse by the reins, my hand close to the bit, I
endeavoured to turn her round so that I could return to the
village and knock on the door of one Thomas Buck (who is a
thatcher and the only jovial man in this sad community) and
enquire of him whether the two women had asked for shelter
or rest in any of the houses. But Danseuse would not let herself
be turned. She showed me a white, angry eye and reared up,
jerking the reins from my hands. I stepped back, involuntarily.
She is a large and powerful horse and, discomforting as my life
is, I did not wish to be crushed by her hooves and thus lose it
altogether on this lonely Fenland causeway.

But I see now that instead of stepping back, I should have
tried with all my might to catch hold of Danseuse's bridle. For
I was about to lose her. Once out of the Whittlesea gate, she
had smelled her freedom in the sunshine. Now, she saw the
straight, flat road before her and she took it. She kicked up her
heels in a final little dance of joy and then she bolted away, faster
it seemed to me than I had ever ridden her, faster even than on
our night journey to Newmarket, and I was left with one foot in
the ditch, staring stupidly after her.

Collecting myself, I did the only thing that came to my mind:
I ran after her, shouting her name, the while knowing this action
to be futile, as if a chicken tried to fly after an eagle. But then,
at my side, appeared two boys, very ragged and with no shoes
on their feet, aged about ten or eleven.

"We'll catch 'im, Sir!" they said and without waiting for permission from me, hurled their thin bodies down the track, calling: "Answers! Answers!" which they thought, from hearing my shouting, to be my horse's name.

I stopped and took a handkerchief from the pocket of my breeches and wiped the sweat from my face. Then I stood and watched. The speed of Danseuse had not slackened at all, but the boys did not seem to understand how easily she would outrun them, for they bolted gamely on, racing with each other to be the first to get to her and bring her back. I saw one of them stumble on the road made muddy by the storm, but he quickly recovered his balance and charged on. Seeing their determination it was tempting to hope, just for an instant, that if I waited patiently, I would, late in the afternoon, see them return, leading my mare between them. Yet I knew this would not happen. Danseuse would run until night fell. She would run until she was lame. She would never return to Whittlesea.

In less than five minutes, Danseuse and the boys passed out of sight. Feeling very stupid standing in the road, and remembering at length the errand on which I had come, I walked to the cottage of Thomas Buck. The thatcher was not at home. His scrawny wife, who is like a pullet with no flesh on her bones, informed me she had seen two women pass through the village but now they were gone along the road to March. I thanked her and she closed her door in my face. I had a great longing to sit down.

Recollected now, that day when I lost Danseuse, that day when Piebald's mother and sister and their basket of provisions seemed to vanish into the air, was one of the most momentous of recent time. For in it I passed from being a kind of visitor to Whittlesea (one who, whenever he heard the whinny of his horse always imagined some future hour in time when he would ride away, back into his old life) to a state of *belonging*. Since that day, with the stable once occupied by Danseuse empty, I have surrendered to Whittlesea. When I imagine my life passing, it is here that it passes. I shall change utterly. I will no longer be too "restless and dazzling" for fishing. I will be a quiet, brown

person. And my skills as a physician and Keeper I shall allow to
grow. And I am most moved by all this. For I see that all of it
will come about because of Pearce's love for me which allowed
me to come here and which – although I really do not know why
this should be – is the greatest love I have ever been shown by
anyone.

But I must tell you a little more about that day. Another event
of importance took place upon it.

The urchin boys did not return for an hour, during which I sat
on a pile of willow planks and counted the money that I had upon
me, which was fourpence exactly.

They were very disappointed that they had not been able to
catch the horse, both for my sake and for theirs, for they clearly
understood that there was reward in the thing and when I handed
them the two pennies apiece they looked long at the coins, as
if willing them to turn into silver.

I thanked them for their gallant chase and asked them, if
Danseuse should return to Earls Bride, to bring her to me at
Whittlesea. They nodded and one of them asked: "Why is he
called Answers, Sir?" to which question I could think of no reply
but the feeble pun, "Because he answers to that name and no
other." The boys appeared downcast by this, as well they might,
so I left them to go in to their suppers of corn porridge and
samphire and walked slowly back to Whittlesea, remembering
deliberately as I went along all the daring and brilliant rides I
had had on Danseuse since she was given to me from the King's
stable; and then, upon arriving at the Whittlesea gate, putting
them from me for ever and going in with a sprightly step, as if
the loss of my horse was nothing to me.

I went into the kitchen of the Keepers' house, it being my
turn to help Daniel prepare our supper, and there found Ambrose
seated at the scrubbed table looking most grave and troubled.
He asked me to sit down and I could sense that some news of
a terrible kind was going to be given to me. Daniel, scraping
potatoes in a bowl, looked from Ambrose to me and then to
Ambrose again and said softly to him, "Robert is not at fault in
this, Ambrose," and Ambrose nodded.

There was a long pause, during which Ambrose arranged his hands into their habitual steeple beneath his beard. He then told me, in a most sorrowful voice, that an incident had taken place that afternoon in Margaret Fell while I had been absent. The woman Katharine had bitten and torn her blanket into shreds and with these shreds knotted together a rope and with the rope endeavoured to hang herself from a crossbeam of the roof.

"Most fortunately," said Ambrose, "the screams of the other women brought us all running and we cut her down before she choked and died. But we cannot run any risk that she will try such a thing again and so, for the time being, we have had to put her in William Harvey."

The silence of the kitchen was broken only by the scraping of Daniel's knife on the potatoes grown by Pearce. I wished to speak, but felt a great choking in my throat. To hear these things about the one person I had believed I was helping caused such a shock to my mind that I was quite unable to speak. And the revelation that followed was the most terrible of all: when asked by Ambrose why she had tried to kill herself, Katharine had replied simply: "Because Robert has left me. He has ridden away."

That evening after supper, while the others assembled for their Meeting, I went into Margaret Fell and retrieved from Katharine's place the doll she called Jesus of Bethlehem. Then, breaking the rule that no Keeper must go alone into William Harvey, I went in there and found Katharine who was chained by one foot to the wall. She was sleeping. She had been dosed with laudanum and the smell of it was on her breath. I put the doll into the straw beside her and then came away.

EIGHTEEN

A TARANTELLA

I could not sleep that night. Near one o'clock, I rose and lit a lamp, being suddenly very tired of the darkness. And in the yellow lamplight I examined my hands, which is a thing I do sometimes when I am troubled, and in consequence I know the appearance of my hands extraordinarily well. My fingers are wide and red and the ends of them very flat, with flat nails. My palms are moist and hot. On the backs of my hands are a few hairs and some freckles. They are Merivel's hands, not Robert's, yet when they take up the scalpel they do not tremble and they do not err.

It was not my turn for a Night Keeping, but at two, I heard Ambrose and Edmund get up, so I pulled on my breeches and my boots and took my lamp and joined them. On our way to William Harvey (where, in truth, I hoped to find Katharine awake so that she could see me and know I had not abandoned her) Ambrose whispered to me: "The diseased mind, alas, is more prey to violent affections than that which is well."

I smiled. "I know that well, Ambrose," I said.

"Whereas," continued Ambrose, "the true saint loves all men and yet none in particular. And this is a vow that we, the Keepers, have taken at Whittlesea – to emulate the love of saints."

He said nothing more, only strode on very fast, but I knew that I had been reproached. I turned to Edmund, who still walked in step with me. "It was pity for Katharine, for her condition – which touches upon several unanswered questions in my own life – that moved me to help her, Edmund," I said. "I neither gave to her, nor sought from her, any promises of love."

"I believe you, Robert."

"But we cannot, each on our own, help all of them . . ."

"Although it is precisely this that we must try to do."

"And I believed that if I could just help *one* . . ."

"What did you believe?"

"That I would know at last that I was useful."

"Useful?"

"Yes."

"And why should you assume you were not already useful?"

"Because . . . it was once told to me."

"By whom?"

"By whom does not matter. That I believed him is what has counted with me."

"But it should not trouble you now, Robert. You are 'useful' to Whittlesea. All I would counsel is that, from now on, you stay away from Katharine."

"And yet . . ."

"Ambrose would say there can be no 'and yets'."

"I was so near to a cure for her!"

"Perhaps that is somewhat arrogant. Cures are not *performed* by us, Robert. Only Jesus cures. And we are his agents."

We were at William Harvey by this time and Ambrose had already gone in. Familiarity with this most wretched place has not lessened my loathing of it. Piebald knows how much I fear it and likes to play upon my fears. "Does it swallow you?" he asks. "Is it like the grave to your little soul?"

Mercifully, he was asleep that night with his snout in the straw, but as I passed him I noted, as if for the first time, how sinewy and fleshless are his neck and his limbs and I thought of his vanished provisions and then of the probability that if, one day, I unlocked Piebald from his chains and asked him to kill me with his hands, he would no longer have the strength.

Despite Edmund's advice, I went at once to the stall where Katharine was lying. I bent over her. She had woken from her laudanum sleep, but the opiate was still in her blood and she lay without moving. When she saw me, she attempted to sit up and in trying to move her leg found herself held down by the iron cuff on her ankle. She opened her mouth to cry out, but no sound came from her. I was about to reach out and put a hand on her forehead to calm her when Ambrose came into the stall. He knelt down and lifted Katharine a little and held a cup of water to her lips and she drank, but she did not look at Ambrose nor at the cup, but only at me and as she lapped the water her eyes filled with oily tears. "Speak to her," Ambrose said quietly. "Tell her you are not leaving Whittlesea, for your life is here now."

I endeavoured to do this. "My horse has ridden away," I said, "so there will be no more going out of the gate. And I shall be – "

I could not finish the sentence. Ambrose finished it for me: "With us all," he said. "Robert is with us all."

And I nodded. And Ambrose took away the water cup and lay Katharine down. And into my mind came the image of the husband, the stone mason laying his wife down on the bowed backs of the vaults and unbuttoning himself and asking of her acts of submission in the very roof of God's house.

Two days later, Katharine was returned to Margaret Fell. Ambrose instructed me in what he called "new ways" of caring for her. I could visit her only once each day and not at all during the night, except when it was my turn for a Night Keeping. The duration of my visits to her should not exceed half an hour. I was permitted to continue rubbing her feet with soap, "but only with the soap, Robert, and not with your naked palm", and told to show her no more attention that I would show to any in George Fox. "In this way," said Ambrose, "her affection for you will be held in check, but beware above all, Robert, that you do not let it flatter you and so seek it out."

I replied, as truthfully as I could, that I sought nothing from Katharine at all, only to find a cure for her sleeplessness.

"A cure!" said Ambrose. "I know of no other word that so beguiles us. Yet you, as a physician, know that certain states and conditions are not susceptible to cure – unless there be some intervention from God."

"I accept that," I said. "But with regard to sleep, I have recently begun to comprehend some of its mysteries . . ."

"I know you believe you do, Robert. Yet it may be that you are not yet as learned on the subject as you think yourself. Time will tell you, no doubt."

I sighed, being crestfallen by Ambrose's severity.

"Time!" I said moodily. "I was once told I was a man of my time, but at some moment – and I could not precisely say when – I think that my time and I parted company, and now I do not belong to it at all, indeed I do not really belong anywhere . . ."

"Beware your very vast self-pity, Robert," said Ambrose, "and bend your thoughts and your energies instead towards music."

"Towards music?"

"Yes. John and I and the others have now pondered long enough upon some words you spoke at a Meeting in spring. And we concede that to organise a little dancing – on midsummer's day perhaps? – might have some beneficial effect upon us all. So what do you say? Will you play for us?"

I looked up at Ambrose. His large face had a large grin upon it. I cleared my throat.

"I am not . . . as marvellous a player as I would like to be, Ambrose," I said. "Before I came here, I was getting some oboe lessons from a German teacher, but they were curtailed."

"Well, we are speaking of simple tunes, are we not: a polka, a tarantella?"

"Yes . . ."

"Will you do it?"

"If there was any among us who played a string . . . then the sound would be somewhat better and more rounded."

"Talk to Daniel. He has learned the fiddle and the two of you can rehearse your pieces in the parlour."

Ambrose left me then and I sat down in the kitchen, where this conversation had taken place, and began to imagine the women of Margaret Fell and the men of George Fox coming out into the sunshine and hearing music and looking about them stupidly, some of them being uncertain whether the sounds were there in the air or only there in their minds. The thought made me smile.

I took a radish from a bowl on the table and ate it and the harsh taste of it reminded me of my curing of Lou-Lou and, in the midst of my contentment about the forthcoming dancing at Whittlesea, I had a moment's longing for the sight of the old noisy river.

That evening, after spending my allotted half hour with Katharine (who, when I am with her is, in five minutes, soothed and calmed by my touching of her feet, so that she falls asleep with a strange smile on her face) I went to my room and unwrapped my oboe from the words of Plato, inserted a new reed into the mouthpiece and began to play a scale or two with the correct fingering taught to me by Herr Hümmel. To hold the instrument in my hands again gave me a feeling of peculiar happiness. I did not in the least mind the monotony of the scales, but rather delighted in them, endeavouring to play them faster and faster and finding my clumsy fingers almost adequate to the task.

I then paused, dried the reed, and embarked upon *Swans Do All A-Swimming Go* which, notwithstanding that my instrument was a little out of tune and my tuning skills very paltry, I declare I played more sweetly than I had ever done in the summer-house at Bidnold. As I finished the piece, there was a knock on my door. I opened it and found Eleanor there. "Robert," she said, "may I come in and listen to you? May I listen for a short while?"

"Well," I said, "you are welcome, but the while will be exceedingly short, for that little song is the only piece I know!"

As I have told you, Eleanor is a person of great good nature and, although I knew her to be disappointed at the severe limitations to my repertoire, she did not show her disappointment, but only said brightly, "Why then, play that one again." So she sat down on my bed (a cot it is rather, not a true real bed) which is the only place where one is able to sit in my linen cupboard, and I played the *Swans* for her a second time and when I had finished, she wiped her eyes with her apron and pronounced the music "most sweet".

Now, this week, with midsummer approaching and the stifling weather still with us and all of Whittlesea plagued by flies, I pass much of each day with Daniel who, just as I had imagined, is quite adept as a fiddle player and whose goal it now is to teach me to play on my oboe simple accompaniments to three or four sprightly tunes for which he possesses sheets of music so seemingly ancient and yellow and bedraggled it is as if they had once been dredged from the sea by Sir Walter Raleigh. One is called *Une Tarentelle de Lyon* and was composed by a person who signs himself Ch. de B. Fauconnier, and this piece is so fast that firstly, I cannot keep up with it on my instrument and, secondly, I wonder if Ch. de B. Fauconnier did not go mad in the writing of it and end his days in a Lyonnais *asile*. As I muse on this possibility, Daniel chides me gently for "having the habit of talking too much".

The anniversary of my wedding, the seventh of June, has come and gone. It is most strange to reflect that, when I put on my purple garb and my three-masted barque, I imagined that here was a new beginning that would bind my life ever more firmly to the life of the King; and to understand now that my wedding day began for me nothing at all but a year of great loneliness and striving and ridicule.

Though determined not to dwell upon any memory of my wedding, I did find myself waking very early on the morning of the seventh of June and recalling how I had gone out from the feast and flung myself on the lawn of Sir Joshua's house and cried, there to be found by Pearce, to whose life I do indeed seem to be bound and without whom I would truly feel myself to be very alone. And it came into my mind to thank Pearce, there and then, for his friendship, to tell him how, in my least action, I try to measure in my mind how he would see the thing and judge it. And how in this way – though I sometimes rail against it – he is present in all that I do, so that for as long as I live (whether here with him or elsewhere) he will always be with me, like Jesus Christ is with the true believers. But I did not stir, only lay on my little bed and watched the sunrise, and thought of my friend asleep, holding his ladle.

In my struggles with *Une Tarentelle de Lyon* and the other

dances, I soon pushed from my mind my wedding day thoughts. Daniel, being a far less condescending teacher than Musikmeister Hümmel, has succeeded in teaching me a great deal in a short while and I feel, in the making of this music, some of that uncontrollable excitement that afflicted me when I did my wild, splodged painting of my park. Hours pass and we play on, struggling always for a faster tempo, and these rehearsals of ours have brought great jollity to the house, the Friends clustering round us and clapping their hands and Edmund unable to restrain himself from skipping about.

"Music!" thunders Ambrose after grace one suppertime. "Why was music not always with us at Whittlesea?" And I look round the table at the faces which all nod in agreement and I marvel suddenly, that these Quakers, who love plainness in all things and loathe and detest the sung services of the High Church, should be so taken with the mad gallop of Ch. de B. Fauconnier that when at last we strike up our tarantella for the inmates of our Bedlam I am certain that Ambrose and Pearce and Edmund and Eleanor and Hannah will be the leaders of the mad revels.

Very seldom do letters arrive at Whittlesea, it being a deliberately forgotten place. The mail coach goes to Earls Bride and no further, so that any letters for Whittlesea are brought out to us by the village children and a penny given to them for each one delivered.

Since my coming here, I have written only one letter – to Will Gates whom I presume still to be at Bidnold. In some very inadequate sentences, I thanked him for all his pains on my behalf and apologised to him for the change in my fortunes. I asked him to keep for himself the painted cage of the Indian Nightingale and to be assured always of my affection for him.

I had received no reply, nor expected any. Writing words on paper is not one of Will's gifts. However, one day before the dance, as the Airing Court was being swept, an urchin arrived at the gate bearing a letter for me. It was from Will. It read thus:

Good Sir Robert,

*Your servant W. Gates is most thankful of your kindnesses
one and many, to him. He is well sorry for your departing. Yor
are in his memory in the cage, kindly given. And will be there fo
always.*

The tiding is your house has passed and land and all to
*French noble, Le Viscomte de Confolens, and a most forwardy
ticklish man preferring to regard his own wig and nose and Beaut
Spots in the glass than to note any good thing at Bidnold.*

*Merciful thanks Le V. is not much visiting here. But when h
comes, comes with a retenue of ladies, all French. Some ver
common seeming and shrieking out in their language and showin
their feet.*

*I am and M. Cattlebury to be kept hired here and so too th
grooms and maids, according to Sir J. Babbacombe.*

*But we are not paid our money. We have no wage from Le
Viscomte, Sir Robert, and I have writ to Sir J. Babbacombe to tel
him this.*

*My Lady Bathurst did arrive here in May and says to me C
Mister Gates what is to become of this place! And truly I did no
know what to answer. And she then weeping. And as I am c
Norfolk man and so backward in grace could not stop mysel
weeping also. But I am sorry for it. So keep you well, Sir and
Mister Pearce also. And if yo can write me any letter, I will be
happy.*

> *Your still remaining Servant,*
> *Wm. Gates*

I folded this letter after I had read it once and stowed it away
in the sea chest, thus hoping to put it out of my mind, for I do
not deny it made me feel sad. Pearce, as it chanced, came
seeking me on some errand just as I was putting the thing away
and saw at once (for nothing that I feel can I seem to conceal
from him) that some portion of my past was once again preoccu-
pying my mind, which should have dwelled only and entirely on
my great Cure by Dancing that was to be tried the next day.
He stood at the door and regarded me and without asking me
what my letter had contained, he said, in his sternest voice: "I

presume you are familiar with the Act of Praemunire, Robert?"

"No," I replied, "I am not, John."

"Let me enlighten you then. The Act of Praemunire permits the confiscation – immediate and without redress, upon the presentation of a warrant of Praemunire – of property, goods and chattels as a punishment for Non-Conformity. Hundreds of Quakers have lost their houses and their land under the terms of this loathsome edict. The suffering caused by it has been beyond what you could imagine. So do not believe you are singled out, Robert. You are merely one of many. The King has behaved towards you as towards a Quaker, and this is all."

Before I could make any answer to this, Pearce had turned and walked away leaving behind him in my room a faint smell of the mithridate with which he continues to dose himself, his cold and catarrh yielding to no cure at all, not even to the hot, dry weather.

When I woke the following morning, I was aware of a strange sound in the room, a sound with which I knew myself to be familiar, yet could not for a moment interpret.

I lay and listened. I knew it to be very early, for the light at the window was grey. And then it came upon me what I was hearing. I sprang out of my cot and drew back the hessian drapes at the window and I saw that I was not mistaken: a great sheeting rain was coming down upon us and upon all the preparations we had made for the dancing. The Airing Court, baked to a hard, yellow dryness by the sun, was to have been our dancing floor. Now it was already returning to slimy mud.

The Keepers (who are not usually cast down by any occurrence) seemed sad – every one of them including Pearce – at the cancellation of the dance. Into this sadness I cast a question that had been troubling me for some time: "When we at last begin the music and the occupants of George Fox and Margaret Fell come out, what is to happen to those in William Harvey?"

"They cannot dance, Robert," said Pearce.

"We cannot unchain them," said Edmund.

"But they will hear the music," said Ambrose. "We will open the doors of William Harvey so that the sounds reach them."

I was forced to be content with these answers, but was vexed to find a terrible pity for the men and women of WH coming over me, such as I had never felt before, not even upon my first sight of them in their rags and straw. And I remembered my journey to Kew with the tilt-man, how I had passed Whitehall and seen light at the windows and heard laughter and yet myself been outside on the flat, dark water; and I knew that what I detest about the world is that one man's happiness is so often another man's pain.

It rained for two days and in that small bit of time Daniel and I, to divert ourselves, invented some sweet harmonies and variations to my old tune, *Swans Do All*, so that it was transformed from a dull little song into music of great prettiness. And after supper on the second day, we got our instruments and played it in the parlour for the Keepers, and the thing which pleased me about our playing was that I could tell that Pearce was very moved by it, though he would say no more to me about it than, "Progress, Robert. You are making progress."

So it was on the last day of June, just past the summer solstice, that we opened the doors of Fox and Fell and led out the people. On a trestle table were three pails of water and some cups and ladles, and I watched how some of the men, before any dancing had begun, started to ladle water over their heads and laugh. And then others joined them and this playing with the water seemed to preoccupy them utterly, as if it was the thing on earth they most loved to do. But then Daniel and I began on a polka and slowly all the group clustered near to the wooden podium on which we stood and stared at us, their mouths gaping and some putting their hands over their ears. It was most difficult to play with this press of people on us. And then I saw Katharine push her way from the back of the group to the front, and she stood so close to me that I had to turn aside a little for fear of poking my oboe into her eye.

We finished the polka and I wiped my brow and some of the people applauded with their fingers splayed out like children and some laughed and some went back to the water buckets.

Ambrose then came and stood with us on the podium. Addressing the multitude of mad people, he said: "Today, instead of walking round the tree, we are going to dance. Robert and Daniel will play and we are going to skip or gallop. What steps we do, what patterns we make, do not matter. We can dance in a square or in a circle or each on his own like a dancing dot. Your Keepers, all of us, will dance with you. And now we are going to begin."

Ambrose stepped down and he and Hannah and Eleanor and the others each took one man or woman to be their partner and so we struck up another polka and the press of people turned away from us a little to watch those now skipping about, among whom was Pearce who had not the least idea how to dance a polka but was jumping up and down, holding the hands of an elderly woman, as thin as he, who began to cackle with a laughter so violent that she could scarcely breathe.

After the third or fourth time, perceiving that only a few joined in any kind of dance and many only stared about them in confusion and outrage, I saw that my experiment risked turning into a lamentable failure. Katharine had now sat down on the ground and was holding onto my boot, thus causing me to feel as if I was chained to the floor like those in WH, from which building we could now hear shouts and cries and a loud banging on the wall.

I felt very sick with embarrassment. "It is not working," I whispered to Daniel. "They do not understand what to do."

Daniel put down his fiddle and took off his waistcoat. His face was red and sweating. Then he picked up the violin again, twanged the A-string to tune it and said to me, "Try the tarantella."

I sighed. I thought of all the hours we had spent rehearsing the difficult *Tarentelle de Lyon*. They seemed utterly in vain. I blew some spittle from my reed, then I bent down and took Katharine's hand from my foot and lifted her up. And I spoke out to the so-called dancers:

"We shall play a tarantella for you," I announced. "This is a whirling dance. So why do you not whirl and turn and jump, or do anything you will? Pretend you are leaves flying, or children skipping."

There was some laughter at this. I smiled, trying to pretend I was very pleased and happy, then prepared myself to play. As I lifted up my instrument, Katharine reached out and caught hold of my arm and said to me, "Dance with *me*."

"I cannot . . . " I said.

"Robert cannot," said Daniel. "Robert *is* the music!"

"Dance with *me*," said Katharine again, and she began to pull at me, so that I was nearly toppled from the podium.

But Edmund was at Katharine's side now, having seen what was happening to me.

"Come," he said to her. "I shall show you a proper tarantella." And she let herself be led away.

"Save us from this, Daniel!" I whispered.

And he smiled that smile of his which is like the smile of a child.

So we began on the dance. The heat of the afternoon and fear of the failure of the venture made us play it as fast and urgently as we had ever done and, as we entered upon the second rondo of it, I began to have cause to give thanks to Ch. de B. Fauconnier, whoever he may have been, for he had indeed written a strange and stirring piece of music. As we neared the end of it, I whispered to Daniel that we should recommence and keep on because I saw that it held the attention of almost everyone assembled and that in their uncoordinated ways they were struggling to move about.

We played the tarantella five times without stopping and the sweat poured down my forehead and stung my eyes so that the scene in front of me became shimmery and lit with a strange bright winking light like the *étincellement* of a star. But I knew by the end of the fifth tarantella that everyone was moving, trying to spin and whirl and clapping their hands and some trying to sing and some wailing and some shrieking like the devil.

I have never seen nor heard nor been any part of any thing that was like this hour. And when it was over and we stopped playing and wiped our faces, I felt for the briefest moment of time that I was no longer merely myself, no longer Merivel, nor even Robert, but joined absolutely in spirit to every man and woman there, and I wanted to make a circle with my arms and take them in.

That night in William Harvey, Pearce and I, at the hour of the Night Keeping, found a dead woman.

The clamour and agitation in WH was terrible to witness and I knew that the music had caused it.

As we covered the dead body, on whom, Pearce informed me, we would perform an autopsy the following day, I said to him, "For two or three we have helped in George Fox and Margaret Fell we have sacrificed one here." He nodded. "None of us," he said, "gave this sufficient thought."

We administered a dose of belladonna to every inmate of WH who allowed himself to swallow it (Piebald spat his into my face) and left them to a misery that none of them had words to express.

It was a great relief to come out of WH and to go into Margaret Fell where, notwithstanding a very strong stench of sweat, there was a feeling of calm in the place and we saw at once that all the women were sleeping. Katharine, alone, was awake. She was sitting up and holding the doll to her breast – which was naked and out of her torn robe – as it might be to suckle an infant.

"Stay with her a few minutes," said Pearce, "and I will go on to George Fox. It's getting towards morning and your tarantella has made me tired, Robert."

It was my vow, these days, never to be left alone with Katharine. Ambrose and Edmund had helped me to see what harm I had – all unintentionally – done to her by causing her to feel for me an affection (a love even?) that I could not return. Since understanding this, I had stayed more aloof from her, sometimes getting Hannah or Eleanor to take over the task of rubbing her feet and once telling her that I was too busy to stay and listen to the stories of her past.

On this night of the tarantella, however, I did sit down beside her and took her feet in my lap and began rubbing them, being once again very moved by her condition of sleeplessness.

She sat quite still and watched me. After a few moments, she set her doll aside, then slowly, with a self-caressing hand pulled aside her nightgown and exposed her other breast to me. She licked her lips and regarded me, and in her exhausted eyes I could discern a slow, sleepy, all-enveloping lust. I let go of her feet and made as if to get up, but she reached out and held me, and moved the heel of her right foot up into my groin where, to my great shame and fear, I knew she would find me hard.

I prayed.

I prayed for Pearce to return.

I prayed to God to give Robert the strength to walk away and not let Merivel do as he wished, which was to lay the madwoman down beneath him.

And after a moment or two, in which I did not move, I heard a voice calling me softly from the door. "Here I am, John," I said. And I got up and followed my friend out into the cool air of four o'clock.

NINETEEN

IN GOD'S HOUSE

At the back of WH, enclosed by a low fence, is a graveyard. I was not shown this when I first came to Whittlesea, but discovered it for myself soon afterwards. There are at present six graves in it and I have been told that they were dug by the men of George Fox, "one of whom in his life before he came to madness was a grave-digger and can dig a very perfect and neat grave."

I asked Ambrose whether, when a man or woman died at Whittlesea, the body was not given back to relatives for burial in some place that might have once been their home. Ambrose replied that if the relatives came and asked for the dead person the corpse would be put in a coffin and given to them, "but few do ask, Robert, it being the case that very many of those here are deemed by their families to have died already." It was this remark of his, upon which my mind has often dwelled, that has helped me to believe in the death of Merivel and his replacement by Robert. Alas, however, Merivel now and again finds the grave an excruciatingly boring place and clamours to come out of it. I fear he may never be entirely quiet and obedient to death until he is actually buried (here at Whittlesea?) and the only sound to be heard near him is the sound of the Fenland wind in the grasses.

As Ambrose, Pearce and I began, then, on an autopsy of the woman found dead in William Harvey, a grave-digging party, under the care of Edmund, set out with picks and spades. The day was once again hot and I saw that as they assembled in the

Airing Court, a cloud of flies gathered round their heads. These flies made me feel depressed. In what had remained of the previous night, I had had a dream of Fabricius at work in his little anatomy theatre. He had been in an angry, difficult mood and had told us, his students, that we preyed on his knowledge – having so little of our own – like flies on a cadaver.

Towards ten o'clock, the body of the dead woman was laid on the table in the operating room in Margaret Fell. (There is, as I have told you, such a room in all three houses, but very few operations are performed to that of WH, the noise coming from the stalls of the inmates being too disturbing and distracting.) Ambrose, Pearce and I, wearing our leather aprons, slit open and tore away the ragged clothes that covered her and then we stood silently for a moment, each looking at the body and taking note of what we saw of external wounds and marks.

The woman was old, of more than sixty years, and the skin greyish and wrinkled and the muscles of the limbs and of the stomach seeming wasted and slack. The hair on her pubis was sparse and white and there was some of this same hair sprouting on her chin and on the aureoles of her nipples.

Ambrose began to record all abnormal things he found upon her, such as a red soreness of the naval and a bruising on the area of the sternum and Pearce wrote each thing down. I went to her head and took the jaw in my hands to open it and examine the teeth, which were very black and decayed and reeking of putrefaction, and so I reported out loud on my findings to Pearce. But I was so affected by the sight of the body that I could not refrain, at length, from saying: "Does it not strike you as a most terrible but true thing, that men in this world and age can come by fortune in many ways and have many currencies with which to barter, but that women have only one, and that is the currency of their bodies, and when this is spent they must all, high or low, depend upon the charity of some overseer or other?"

"In a Quaker house," said Ambrose, "all are equal before God."

"I know," I said, "but not in society. In society, all women who come to forty come to an impoverishment of a certain kind."

"For this and a thousand other reasons," said Pearce, "have

we turned our back on society. Neither Hannah nor Eleanor will ever be 'poor' in the sense that you mean."

"No," echoed Ambrose, "they will not."

"So be glad that you are here, Robert, and not where you once were."

In this way, adding a sniff that was like a neat full-stop to his sentence, Pearce declared the subject I had raised to be closed. Many of my utterances he believes to be a waste of my breath – "and we are allotted just so many breaths, Robert, and no more" – and indeed this one was a digression from the main purpose of the morning, which was to ascertain how the old woman had died.

None of us had been aware that she had been suffering from any illness, only a debility coming on her with old age and the ravages of her madness. Upon the opening up of her chest, however, we found the organ of the heart to have an encrusted and scabby appearance and the blood of her arteries and veins to be dark and sticky like treacle; and it did not take Pearce long to conclude that death had come with the cessation of the heart's pulse, the blood being too heavy to move. Ambrose and I nodded our agreement and I, for one, was relieved that we did not have to proceed to an examination of the liver or bowel. The autopsy concluded, Ambrose left Pearce and me to sew up the incision we had made and to clean and wrap the body for burial. I took a suturing needle from my box of instruments and Pearce was measuring for me a length of gut when he suddenly declared: "I am afraid of death, Robert."

I looked up at him, surprised. Towards the great subject of mortality Pearce had always shown an enviable indifference. When, on one of our angling trips near Cambridge, he had fallen from a little wooden bridge and almost drowned in the blanket-weed, he had shown neither fear of death nor gratitude towards me for saving his life by thrusting towards him a landing net with which I towed him into the bank. I had always believed that he thought of death as a kind of reward for his earthly goodness and abstemiousness and that in his hard-working life he sometimes found himself looking forward to it.

As I began to sew up the dead woman's chest, I now said as

much to him. "You of all people I did not think would be afraid of it, John," I said. And he nodded. "Until recently, I was not," he said, "but for a month now – and I am telling this to you, Robert, and to no one else, for I do not want to trouble the others – I have felt certain symptoms come upon me, certain symptoms . . ."

"What symptoms?"

"Well . . . this catarrh of mine . . ."

"It's no more than a catarrh."

"And a very cold sweating on the crown of my head . . ."

"Just part of the rheum or catarrh, John."

"And a violent coughing and choking at night, with much pain in my lung."

"Pain in your lung?"

"Yes."

"How great is the pain?"

"Sometimes so great that I want to cry out."

The flesh of the dead woman, pinched between my finger and thumb for the suturing, was icy cold and I now felt slide into my heart a cold worm of fear.

I stared at Pearce. "Are you telling me that it is pain in your lung that has given you thoughts about dying?" I asked him.

"Yes. For it does not seem to go away. Nor this cold sweating of my head, despite the hot weather."

I said nothing. I finished sewing up the wound and together Pearce and I washed the woman and inserted wads of flax into the damp orifices of the body and put the winding sheet round it. Then I said: "Let me come to your room after the Meeting this evening, and I will examine you."

"Thank you, Robert." said Pearce. "And you will tell no one?"

"No. I will tell no one."

"Thank you. For they are such good people, are they not? I would not have them lose any sleep on my account."

I had been troubled all morning by thoughts of Katharine, my lust for her being of that most loathsome kind, where the very feelings of loathing seem to excite rather than to repel.

Now, hearing that my friend was ill, everything went from

my mind, and I wished only for the day to pass so that I could make my examination of Pearce and allay his fears and mine by discovering in him some ague that would soon leave him – and nothing more.

The Meeting, however, was longer than usual that evening. After some moments of silence, Edmund stood up and said that he wished the Lord's forgiveness for what he was about to say, that he knew that the agitation he was in was unworthy and childlike, but something of great magnitude had begun to trouble him and that was the loneliness of Quakers.

He paused for a moment. No one asked him any question, but waited in silence for what he would say next. Then he took out of his pocket a crumpled piece of parchment and read some words as follows: "The Lord showed me, so that I did see clearly, that he did not dwell in temples which men had commanded and set up, but in people's hearts; for both Stephen and the Apostle Paul bore testimony that he did not dwell in temples made with hands, not even in that which he had once commanded to be built, since he put an end to it; but that his people were his temple, and he dwelt in them."

After this and in some distress, so that his rodent's eyes began to brim with tears, he said: "It has come to me, not from the Lord, but in some very fearful dreams I have had, that for every other kind and condition of worship there is some steeplehouse or temple or shrine or actual place where the faithful can go in, as if going to God's house like a visitor and where, outside of himself, he can feel the presence of God, his host. But for the Quaker there is no such place and if – as I have felt in these dreams of mine – he has some sudden perception that God is not there within him any more, where shall he go to find Him? He cannot go to God's house, for what he *is* is God's house! So what shall he do? Please tell me my good Friends, how shall he overcome his isolation and his loneliness?"

Edmund then sat down and blew his nose and as he fumbled for his handkerchief, his piece of parchment fell to the floor and for some reason this letting go of a thing that was precious to him, more than his anxiety or the words he had spoken, made me feel a great kinship with him and I would have stood up and tried to answer his question if I had had any notion of what the answer might be.

Some more silence lay on us then, but it was broken after a few minutes by Ambrose who reminded Edmund that Fox had warned us not to rely upon dreams and had said "except you can distinguish between dream and dream, you will mash or confound all together." And so a discussion of dreams began which lasted some while: how there are three sorts of dreams, one kind being caused by the business of the day and another being the whisperings of Satan and a third kind being true conversations between God and man.

Because I am still plagued with dreams of my past, with dreams of Celia in fact and of course of the King, I began privately to wonder in which category these dreams fell and so lost the thread of the meeting for a while. When I once more gave it my attention, I saw that it had become very passionate with, not only Edmund crying, but Hannah also, and Eleanor kneeling and taking up her Bible and declaring to us all that to enter the Book was like entering God's house and to begin to read from the Apostles was to feel a welcoming hand taking us in and guiding us and offering us nourishment "as we would offer cakes or broth to a visiting Friend".

This reminder to Edmund that if God mysteriously went missing from him, he could start to find him again in the Scriptures seemed to cheer and comfort him somewhat. I thought that the Meeting might end then, but it was Eleanor's request that we should spend five or ten minutes each seeking out some verse of the Gospels that was and always might be of particular comfort to us. And so we each went to fetch our own Bibles and then sat round in our semi-circle and made little readings from Matthew, Mark, Luke and John. All the Quakers, including Edmund, found passages most appropriate to what had happened during the Meeting about Jesus loving especially the poor and the childlike and saying, "Come unto me all ye that are heavy laden" and, "Suffer the little children" and so forth. But when it came to my turn, I chose the verse from Luke, Chapter Two, which describes the mortal fear of some common shepherds at the sight of God's messenger angel: "And lo, the Angel of the

Lord came upon them, and the glory of the Lord shone round about them, and they were sore afraid . . ."

I do not really know why I chose it, except that I seem to have known it by heart all my life and that I wanted to say to Edmund that God surely frightens us and makes us feel lonely just as often as he comforts us. Such fear, as in the case of the shepherds, may be a prelude to a revelation of great importance, but then again it may not be. In my own case, it is usually fear of suffering and death and a prelude to nothing at all.

I bade goodnight to all the Keepers. I went to my linen cupboard and lit my lamp and I took this with me to Pearce's room, so that we had two lamps by which to work. I also took with me my surgical instruments, cleaned meticulously these days, with their silver handles polished.

As Pearce sat down on his narrow bed, I said: "I'll wager you have caught a summer chill and this is all."

"No," said Pearce, "I have had chills before and this is not one."

"Well, let us see . . ."

I began by taking up a tongue depressor and looking down Pearce's throat, which did not appear inflamed though I noted that his tongue was a little swollen and coated and that his breath was foul. I then examined his neck for swellings and found none. Then, guided by his hand, I put my hand on that part of his head that felt cold to him and through his thinning hair felt it to be moist, as if there was a sweating there.

This done, I asked him to take off his coat and shirt and to lie down on his bed, so that I could listen to his heartbeat and his breathing.

While he undressed, I made notes about the strange moistness of his head, the cause of which I could not at first fathom. Then I looked up.

Pearce stood before me, folding his shirt into a bundle, wearing only his frayed black breeches and stockings. I thought back to the last time I had seen his arms and chest unclothed, which was during my vigil at his bedside in the Olive Room at

Bidnold. He had been as thin then as he always was as a young man, but now the change in his appearance was distressing beyond words to behold, for he was like a veritable skeleton, with his chest quite concave and every rib visible to me, seeming to have no covering of soft warm flesh on him at all, rather his bones appearing held together by his white skin.

"Pearce . . ." I stammered, forgetting in my shock at the sight of him, his constant entreaty to me to call him John.

"Yes," he said, "I know. I am grown a little thin."

"A little!" I blurted out. "What has happened to you? Have you been fasting?"

"No, I eat what is put before me. I do not know how this weight has been lost."

"Lie down!" I snapped.

Obediently, Pearce set aside his bundle and lay on his back on his bed. I brought the two lamps as near to him as I could and looked down at him and, truly, I wanted to cuff him about his head for allowing his body, invisible to us all inside his baggy clothes, to waste away to this degree.

I took up his wrist and felt his pulse and was relieved to find it quite strong. Then I bent over him and put my head on his chest and heard his heartbeat against my ear.

"It is the lung you should be listening to," said Pearce.

"I know," I said crossly. "Inhale deeply and exhale as slowly as you can."

The intake of breath was not smooth. It had a kind of spasm to it, as if there was a sobbing in the body.

"Inhale again and keep on with slow breaths until I tell you to stop," I instructed.

I listened for several minutes, moving my listening position a little after every second breath, then I told Pearce to turn over and I put my ear to his back, which is a most wretched part of the man, being very scabby with pimples, and all of what I heard made me afraid, for I was in no doubt that the lungs were in distress, having in them a quantity of mucus or phlegm which, if it is not got out, will in time fill all the lung tissue and bring the sufferer to a cruel death like a slow drowning.

"It is a poisonous congestion, is it not?" said Pearce, sitting up and rubbing his eyes, which I now saw were very heavy with tiredness.

"Yes," I said.

"And the sweating and coldness in my head?"

"Probably a beneficial evacuation. A means by which the matter is endeavouring to come out."

"And if it does not come out?"

"We will bring it out. But you must rest, Pearce."

"John."

"John, then! But you will be neither one nor the other and no name will matter one whit, if you allow yourself to die!"

"I cannot stay in my bed, Robert, when there is so much work to do here."

"You must stay in your bed, or the remedies I shall prescribe will have no help from you, only hindrance."

"No, I cannot. For we must reveal nothing of this to Ambrose or the others."

"Pearce," I said crossly, "please do not make me lose my patience! Have I not, a hundred times since we met at Caius, allowed you to command me and let you be wise and done this or that thing at your bidding? I *have*! So do not even consider contradicting me on this score. For I am determined you will do this one thing that I am ordering you to do, and that is to stay here in your bed and let us care for you and not to stir from this room till you are well. And if you do not do this, John, you will no longer be my friend or any true Friend to Whittlesea. You will be in your grave!"

Pearce then allowed his head to fall back on his pillow and he nodded. "Very well," he said, "but only for a little time. What will you prescribe?"

"Syrup of roses to warm your blood and soothe your coughing. A burdock poultice or a bread poultice for your head."

"And for the slime in the lung?"

"Sal Ammoniac."

"And a balsam?"

"Yes. We shall try several, dissolved in boiling water and inhaled."

"Good. It has all returned to you then, Robert?"

"What has returned?"

"The right knowledge for the right time."

"Perhaps."

"As of course it had to. For we can never truly unknow what we have known or unsee what we have seen, can we?"

"Probably not, John," I said. "Now please do me the favour of taking off your breeches and putting on your nightshirt."

Two weeks passed, during which I wished to turn all my thoughts and all my strength to the cures I was trying upon Pearce. But they were weeks in which I found myself subjected to a great clamouring from the people of George Fox and Margaret Fell who, whenever I went among them, begged me to let them come out and dance once again, informing me that dancing was the only cure for them and that all their madness was caused in the first place by the absence of music.

I laid the problem before the Keepers, but none had any solution. That the tarantella had had some beneficial effect on those allowed out that afternoon seemed certain; what was also certain was that, in those we had kept chained up, the music and clapping and shrieking had engendered feelings of rage and despair that took many days to subside.

Suggestions were made. Edmund declared it might be feasible to chain the inhabitants of WH one to another and lead them out across the Earls Bride causeway, out of earshot of the music. Hannah ventured that we could give them opiates to drug them to sleep. But we held back from approving either of these ideas, the reason being that both of them made us feel uneasy.

And so the clamour for the dancing went on and with it a clamour of another kind, which was from Katharine, who truly believed herself in love with me and whom I could not approach without she entreated me to touch her. The sight of her black hair, her strong legs and her full breasts began to occupy my mind to such a horrible degree that even as I sat at Pearce's bedside and covered his head, while he inhaled my balsam preparations, or I laid poultices on his crown, I would feel this clamour of Katharine in my body and I would grow hot and sometimes breathless and sick in my stomach. Then, silently, I would curse the day I had taken pity on her, and feel scorn for myself in the realisation that even in this action I had been moved by words once spoken to me by the King, so that even at Whittlesea – far, as I thought, beyond his reach – I was not yet entirely free of him.

Several visitors to Whittlesea were turned away by us during this time, our fear of bringing in the plague still being very great. One of these visitor's was Katharine's mother. She had brought her daughter a honeycomb and a pair of green slippers with some fine embroidery on them. When Ambrose informed her that she could not come in, she grew very angry and declared that all who care for the mad and the sick, though they pretend to be charitable people, are the greatest deceivers of the age, their only aim being to line their own pockets. She walked away still cursing Ambrose so violently that she, too, appeared to be touched with madness.

Eleanor gave the honeycomb and the green slippers to Katharine. When she knew that her mother had been turned away, Katharine began to cry. She told Eleanor that a cure for her condition existed in the world but that we were all too blind to see what it was.

July came in and, in this month, three things of importance took place.

The first of these things was the arrival of another letter from Will Gates, informing me that my horse, Danseuse, had walked in through the park gates at Bidnold "a little lame in her left hind leg and with no bridle on her, but only a saddle, twisted round". Will asked me to write to him, to tell him I was alive. "If you are alive, Sir," said the letter, "I will continue to keep and hide your horse from the V. de Confolens, so that you can get her for you again. But if, as I fear, you are dead, I will send W. Jossett, your groom, with her to the King, so that His Majesty can know of your sad end."

This letter, if I had not been so very preoccupied by the condition of Pearce and by the behaviour of Katharine, would have gladdened my spirits a great deal, not only because it made me laugh, but also because the news of Danseuse's return seemed to me miraculous and therefore to portend some good. As it was, there did not seem to be adequate space in my mind for the tidings that it contained.

Keeping an afternoon vigil by Pearce's bed, while he slept his snarling invalid's sleep, I wrote a short letter thanking Will and enclosing money to buy oats for my horse. "I do not know," I said in this letter, "how or if ever I shall come again to Bidnold, so if I have not come there in the space of one year from now, please return Danseuse to His Majesty the King and say that I am no longer in the world."

The second thing of importance was the beginning of a recovery in Pearce. I confess I felt not only relieved that my friend seemed to be retreating from a premature encounter with death, but also gratified that *my* syrups and balsams, *my* insistence upon rest and good nourishment (I had devised for Pearce a very good diet of coddled eggs, boiled meat, chicory and malted bread), were the means by which he seemed to be returning to health. When I listened to his breathing now, I could still hear a wheezing in the lungs, but the balsams and the Sal Ammoniac had helped him cough up a great quantity of phlegm from them and the burdock poultices had turned the moist patch on his crown to a dribbling sore, from which much foul matter was able to come out.

After three weeks, in which he slept every afternoon and was content to let us bring him his meals and to wash him and comb his sparse hair and generally care for him like an infant, he began to protest that he was cured and ready to resume what he called his "proper task, which is not the comforting of myself, but the comforting of others". So we let him get up and helped him to put on his clothes that were still very much too large for his thin body, despite the eggs and the malted loaves, and he came downstairs and went out into the sunshine and asked me to walk with him to the vegetable garden so that he could see his pear trees.

It is a feature of Pearce's character, as I think I may already have told you, that he believes himself to be the only person upon earth capable of carrying out certain tasks, one of which is the cultivation of fruit trees *en espalier*. It was thus that he expected, after three weeks' absence from them, to find his trees dead and shrivelled, and when he saw that they were not, despite the great heat of the last month, he assumed at once that it was God who had saved them and he knelt down in the vegetable garden and gave up thanks to his Maker when, in reality, he should have given up thanks to me and to Edmund who had spent many tedious hours watering the wretched trees, aware as we were of Pearce's wrath and sadness if we should let them die. I was tempted to inform him of this, but I did not. I stood and watched him praying and I knew that, as always, my irritation with him would not last, it being so diluted by my affection for him that it is like a single drop of aloes in a jug of mead. So, instead of reproaching Pearce, I, too, found myself conversing with God, who seems nearer to me here that He ever seemed at Bidnold. I asked Him to bring my old friend back to perfect health and I added: "I will remember to call him John, Lord, if you will remember to put some flesh on his bones."

And so to the third event of this month of July which, of all the things that have happened since I came to Whittlesea, is the worst thing, for now it haunts me continuously and I know that the shame it brings upon me is so great that were the Keepers to know of it, I would be sent out from here – my long friendship with Pearce notwithstanding – and ordered never to return.

It took place on a hot night which seems to have been so short, it was as if there was no darkness at all, but only a fading of the sky and then a lightening of it again.

I woke not long after midnight, having slept for only a few minutes. I felt full of trouble and fearful dreaming. Every part of me was sweating and filled with such an aching discomfort that I knew I could not lie another minute in my bed.

I stood up and looked out of my window and all that my eye would light upon in this particular pale midnight was the door of Margaret Fell and I knew that my struggle against my lust for Katharine was lost.

I put on a thin shirt and some breeches and then I let myself quietly out of my room and paused and listened in case any of the Keepers was stirring, but the house was silent except for the sound of Pearce's snoring.

Once out in the night air and feeling its sweetness upon my face, all fear of what I was about to do left me, so that I did not go to it with trepidation, as I should have done, but with a false joy, pretending to myself that it was an honourable thing and a thing that would bring peace and rest.

I opened the door of Margaret Fell and went in, closing it behind me. I did not move, but stood in the darkness until I could see the two rows of sleeping women. I looked over to where Katharine lay with her doll and her green embroidered slippers that she now also cradled to her and to which she sometimes spoke, as if to a child.

She was sitting up and looking over to where I stood. I did not go to her. I waited. She put down the slipper she had been holding and got up and came towards me. I saw the woman lying next to Katharine wake up and stare at her and then at me, but I paid this other person no heed at all.

As Katharine came close to me, I reached out for her with my left hand and with my right hand I opened the door to the operating room of Margaret Fell where only a short while ago I had helped perform an autopsy and wrapped a dead woman in her winding sheet.

The floor of this room is stone and on this stone I knelt down and pulled Katharine down by me and kissed her mouth and then her breasts. And both of us tore from the other our clothes, being very full of greed and readiness. And naked together we crawled into the dark space under the operating table. And there, it seemed, Katharine imagined herself once again above the vaults of a church, for she began to whisper to me that at last we were together in God's house. And though God may never forgive me for this, I confess I was excited by this blasphemy, and I did with Katharine in the space of an hour everything she asked of me and more that my own mind could devise. And this was no simple Act of Oblivion, but a love of the most Profane kind.

TWENTY

JOHN'S LADLE ALMOST TAKEN
FROM HIM

This night began what I now call my Time of Madness at Whittlesea.

There had been a Time Before. In the Time Before, as I have shown you, I believed that all my dealings with the Keepers and with the inmates were true and honest. I did not dissemble. I took out my lost skills from the darkness to which I had consigned them and laid them at the service of the community. I had been renamed and I strove to become worthy of that name. And if the old Merivel sometimes reappeared, sighing over his lost past, he also tried to make himself useful, as on the afternoon of the tarantella. As Pearce said of my oboe playing, it was evident to all that I was "making progress".

That "progress" could not continue after I entered the operating room of Margaret Fell with Katharine, for from that moment I became addicted to my own foulness so entirely that my mind, instead of contemplating the work of each day, was filled up with it and I entered willingly on the most terrible deceptions just to come to it again.

When I woke, on the morning after that first night, and remembered what I had done, I felt mortally afraid. I knelt down by my bed and confessed to God: "I have suffered a contamination of madness and now I am unclean and full of the Devil, but I will not do those things again, if you will help to drive the Devil from me!"

When I went down to breakfast in the kitchen, Hannah remarked that I looked pale, and I admitted to the Friends that I did not feel well that morning, it proving very difficult for me to swallow the porridge set before me, or even to hold my spoon because of a trembling in my hands.

I did not shun the work of the day, however, which included an airing for the inhabitants of William Harvey – always a most difficult and lengthy task, for before they can be brought out into the air all of them must be washed, some of their own excrement. And as the day progressed, the fear and shame by which I had been overcome upon waking gradually went from me and were replaced by a most acute longing to go into Margaret Fell and seize Katharine roughly by the hand and push her before me into the dark room and begin again on the shameless acts I had promised that morning to renounce.

And so began the pattern of each day during the Time of Madness: each morning, I vowed I would never, as long as I lived, touch Katharine again nor let her hand seek me out; each night, I lay and waited without sleeping for the moment when I could slip out into the darkness and go to find her.

It was soon known by the other inhabitants of Margaret Fell what kind of acts we performed in the operating room and the women would sometimes cluster by the door, listening, and when we came out some of them would claw at me, at my mouth and at my sex, and beg me to take them also. And this longing that they had and their knowledge of what I was doing made me feel very sick and afraid, for I knew that sooner or later some behaviour or word of theirs would betray me to the Keepers and I would be sent away. I was deceiving Pearce (perhaps for the first time in my life, for I had never before pretended to him that I was leading an honest life when I was not) and I was deceiving Ambrose and the others, who had taken me in and tried to make me one of them. But more terrible, perhaps, than either of these deceptions was my deceiving of Katharine who, finding herself in love with me, asked me to swear that I was in love with her and that, if the day came for me to leave Whittlesea, I would take her with me. And so I swore. But the truth was that I did not love her at all. Pity had drawn me to her, and my own lust, suddenly a most overpowering and demented thing, kept me there with her in the darkness. And when I asked myself whether, in time, I would grow to love her, I knew the answer: the possibility of my growing to love Katharine was as remote as the possibility of Celia growing to love me.

I had gone on, undiscovered in the Time of Madness, for about five weeks when, returning one night to my room near one o'clock, I heard a voice call out, "Merivel!"

I stood on the landing, shivering a little, certain that Robert had been found out at last and was being summoned as Merivel to be given his punishment. I waited and the voice called again, "Merivel!" And then I recognised it as Pearce's voice and I moved slowly towards his room.

I opened the door. He had lit a rushlight by his bed and was lying on his side with his face very near the taper and he held one of his thin hands out towards me, palm upwards, in the gesture of a beggar.

"John," I said, "what do you want?"

"Merivel . . ." he said again, and his voice sounded thick with his old catarrh, "I was waiting for you . . ."

"Waiting for me?"

"To come in. I heard you go out and I waited for you to return, so that I could call you and not wake the others."

"Yes," I said. "I go and walk in the air sometimes at night, if I cannot sleep . . ."

"I heard you."

I went nearer to Pearce. I know him so well that I can discern anger on his lips before he has uttered a word and I looked hard at him to see if it was there or not. It was not there, and the relief I felt was very great. What I could see, however, as I approached his bed, was that his face was running with sweat and that his cheeks (usually of such translucent whiteness it is difficult to believe that Pearce spends any of his time in the open air, let alone a great part of his day hoeing and pruning in his vegetable garden) had a hectic bright redness to them, the two things announcing to me at once that he had a high fever.

I went to him and laid my hand on his forehead. My hand burned.

"John . . ." I began.

"Yes. Very well. There is some fever. I was about to tell you that. I did not call you to repeat to me something I already know."

"Why did you call me, then?"

"I called you because . . ."

"What?"

"I cannot find my ladle. I think it has fallen and rolled under the bed."

I knelt down and felt about in the dust under his wooden bed, but could not discover it. I moved round and round the bed, searching under it as far as my arm would reach, but the thing was not there.

"I cannot see it, John."

"Please find it, Merivel."

"Why do you call me 'Merivel'?"

"Did I call you that?"

"Yes."

"When in truth you are . . . who? I cannot for just this one moment remember your other name."

"Robert."

"Robert?"

"Yes."

"And yet tonight, since this fever began . . . that name Robert seems to have slipped away from my mind and what I remember is Merivel and how we once together witnessed a very miraculous thing and that was a visible beating heart. Do you recall that?"

"Yes, I do, John."

"And you, because I could not, put your hand in and touched it."

"Yes."

"Yet the man felt nothing."

"He felt nothing."

"So pray for me, that I might become that person."

"Why?"

"To feel no pain in my heart or anywhere."

"Are you in pain?"

"Have you found the ladle?"

"No. It does not seem to be under the bed."

"Please try to find it."

"I do not know where else to look. Where shall I look?"

"Ssh. Don't raise your voice. You will wake the others."

"I shall wake the others unless you tell me about the pain. Is it the pain you had before, in the lung?"

"Could anyone have stolen my ladle?"

"No. And I will find it for you. Where is the pain, John? Show me or tell me. Where is it?"

Pearce looked up at me. His faded blue eyes, in this dim rushlight, looked a darker colour than they were. He withdrew his hand and placed it, in a hesitant way, against his chest.

I stood up. I told him I refused to continue my search for the ladle until I had listened to his breathing. Then I gently helped him to turn onto his back and folded back the bedclothes and laid my head (which a mere half hour ago Katharine had taken in her hands and forced to suckle her breast like a baby) first on his sternum and then lower on his diaphragm.

I found Pearce's ladle under his pillows and handed it to him. I told him I was going to boil water for a balsam inhalation, then I left him for a while and went to my room and washed myself, for the smell of Katharine seemed to cling to every part of me. I put on a clean nightshirt and combed my hair. Only then did I go down to the kitchen and begin to prepare the only remedies I and all the world of medical science could offer for my friend's condition, knowing as I worked that this time they would not be strong enough to make him well.

What I began that night and what we, the Keepers of Whittlesea, continued between us for ten days and nights was a constant vigil at Pearce's bedside.

On the fifth or sixth day, the pain of his breathing became so great for him that he whispered to me: "I would not have imagined longing, as ardently as I do, for my last breath."

We gave him opiates and as these entered his blood (there to

be circulated to every part of him, as proved by his beloved
mentor, WH) he seemed to fall, not into a sleep, but into a kind
of dream of the past, so that he babbled to us of his mother who
had been a widow for twenty years and who said prayers every
day of her life for the soul of her dead husband, a barber, who
had left her nothing but the tools of his trade with which, as
soon as her son had been accepted into Caius College, she cut
her own throat. She was buried not in the churchyard beside
her husband, but "at a crossroads, distant from the village; a
place where people on foot or on horseback or in carriages went
this way or that, but did not stop". He told us how, if we opened
his Bible at Matthew, Chapter Ten, we would find "the imprint
of a bird across the writing". He said he could not remember
what species of bird it was, only that it was small and that he
had found it "freshly dead when I was a child and my mother
still living". He seemed very anxious that we should see this
imprint, so I took up his Bible and searched for it and found
eventually – not in Matthew, but across two pages of Mark – a
brown greasy smudge, such as might have been made by the
accidental placing on the Holy Book of a hot cinnamon pancake.
I showed it to Pearce. "Is this it, John?" I asked. He stared at
it, his dilated pupils having difficulty focusing upon it. "Yes," he
said at last. "The viscera were removed, for I did not want to
pollute the words of Jesus. And then I laid the bird in and opened
out the wings and closed the book and put weights upon it and
pressed it like a flower."

I looked up at Hannah, who sat on the other side of Pearce's
bed, bathing his brow from time to time with lavender water.
She shook her head, showing me that she did not think this
story about the pressed bird could be true, both of us being
obliged to imagine the stench of the dead creature as it decayed
in its tomb of sacred words. Had Pearce been well, I would have
made the observation that the scent of death in a vertebrate
does not resemble at all the scent of death in a flower, but, very
far from being well, Pearce was by this time so weak that he
could barely raise his head from the pillow, onto which what
remained of his thin hair was gradually falling out.

The knowledge that Pearce was going to die was, during

those ten days, like something draped round me, something that I *wore* but refused to take into my mind. And I do not think that this refusal was based upon any false hope that Ambrose or I could save him. What I had understood, I believe, is that no amount of knowing in advance that I was going to lose my friend could adequately prepare me for the actual loss of him when it came.

On the seventh or eighth day of Pearce's sickness, both the pain in his lungs and his fever diminished for a while. He asked me to lift him up and prop him with cushions "but not any with tassels or jewels on them or any gaudy ones such as you had in your house". I smiled. I put my hands gently into his armpits (where there seems to be no flesh any more, only a webbing of skin) and pulled him towards me while Daniel set some pillows at his back. I asked him if he would try to eat a little broth. He said he would and Daniel went down to fetch it for him (there is broth always ready in this household, the boiling of bones with onions and greens being a very frequent sight in the kitchen), thus leaving me alone with Pearce.

I sat down beside him, just within reach of his breath, which smelled of sulphur. He began to talk, quite lucidly, just as he once did at Bidnold, about the theory of spontaneous generation, in which he has never truly believed but which seems proven by the appearance of the living maggot upon dead matter. "Is it possible, Merivel," he asked, "that the maggot is not spontaneously generated but – as has been hypothesised – emerges from an egg so small it cannot be seen by the human eye?"

"I think it is possible, John."

"And thus, it would follow, if the human eye cannot see these infinitely small things, there may be other pieces of matter of whose existence we have not yet the slightest perception, would it not?"

"It would."

He sighed. He was silent for a long while. Then he said: "It troubles me to take with me to my grave so much that I do not know."

"I would rather you did not talk about the grave, John," I said.

"Of course you would," he said acidly. "There are many matters, ever since I met you, on which you would have preferred me to remain silent. But that has not been my way. And now, there is one uncertainty I do not wish to carry with me. And that is what is going to happen to my things."

"What things?"

"Those few that are precious to me. You once called them my 'burning coals' in order to mock me."

Daniel arrived at this moment, thus sparing me the humiliation of having to compose yet another apology to Pearce, the syllables of which I find so difficult to pronounce, when what I longed for was for Pearce to beg my forgiveness for the thoughtless act he was about to commit: the act of leaving me.

Daniel set down a tray, on which had been placed a bowl of broth and a spoon and by the side of this a greenish fruit that Pearce immediately recognised as one of his own pears. He picked it up and felt it in his hand, then held it to his sore nose and sniffed it. "The perfume of pears," he said in the rapturous voice that always brought back to my mind our river excursions and Pearce's excess of joy at the sight of a mayfly, "I have loved for years."

Daniel grinned at me, then sat down beside him to help him sip the broth. Somewhat to my surprise, Pearce asked him gently to leave so that he could talk to me alone. The boy got up at once, passing me the spoon, and went out.

The broth was hot. I did not want Pearce to burn his mouth on it, so I took up a spoonful and blew upon it before guiding it to his lips. Silence descended upon us for a few moments as we both concentrated on the task of the spoon-feeding. But the effort of taking in sustenance seemed to weary Pearce very quickly and he told me to take the tray away and fetch pen and ink and paper instead.

What I wrote – although I do not have the paper before me, having been instructed to give it to Ambrose – I can remember very exactly, for it was perhaps one of the shortest wills ever made, Pearce's burning coals having diminished, as it were, to a mere few cinders. He bequeathed all his books, including his Bible to Whittlesea House. His clothes – those threadbare

garments that he wore without the least tremor of embarrassment or shame – he offered "to the inmates of our Hospital, so
that they may put on the garments of a true Quaker and be
tender towards each other", and the ladle he left to me, "this
fragile thing perchance being of comfort to him sometimes".
And this was all. The last line I was ordered to write stated that
"John Joseph Pearce, Quaker, possesses of his own no other
thing or things upon earth."

When I had written down everything (in the careful script I
am capable of if I take extreme care with the position of the quill
in my hand) I gave the paper to Pearce and helped him to sign
his name. I made no comment upon his gift to me of the ladle,
being so saddened and troubled by it that for a short while I
could not speak. When I found my voice again, it was to offer
Pearce a taste of the green pear, which he declined fearing, he
said, that it would give him a pain in his teeth.

Since the night when Pearce had called out to me on my return
from Margaret Fell, I had not visited Katharine. I had made a
bargain with God: I would not touch her nor let her come near
me again if He would give me Pearce's life.

I knew it to be a futile thing. I knew that Pearce was dying.
Yet I kept to it. And Katharine, finding herself abandoned by
me, came up to the house from the Airing Court and beat on
the door with her hands and screamed out for all the world to
hear that I was her lover. And that night, the ninth night of
Pearce's illness, I and the Keepers sat quietly at supper, they
looking at me sadly but saying nothing until the end of the meal
when Ambrose spoke. "When the time is right for Robert to
speak to us," he said, "then he will speak to us." And I nodded.
And we all rose and began to clear away the plates and dishes.

They knew that I could not leave Whittlesea until Pearce was
gone.

He died in the quiet time between the Night Keeping and the
dawn of the eleventh day.

I was with him, alone.

I closed his mouth. I took up his thin, white hands and folded them across his chest. And into his hands I put the ladle.

"Look," I whispered to him, "the ladle will not be taken from you."

Then I closed his eyes. And I sat down. And it was then that I was aware of the silence, and I knew it would be there for ever, and that whenever I thought of my friend or spoke to him in my mind, I would hear it again, and where before there had been answering words or messages of guidance or sniffs of disapproval, there would henceforward be only this: the Silence of Pearce.

I sat on the hard chair, leaning forward with my elbows on my knees, and cried. I did not try to stem my tears nor mop them up with any handkerchief or striped dinner napkin, but let them fall onto the floor and onto my thighs and run down my legs.

When I looked up again, there was a milky light at the window and Ambrose and Edmund and Hannah and Eleanor and Daniel were there with me in the room, standing by the bed with their palms pressed together in prayer.

A coffin was made for Pearce that day by two men from George Fox. It was too large for him, but we put him in it and packed his body round with branches of pear.

We held a wake in the parlour and this wake took the form of an all-night Meeting, during which, as and when we were moved to do so, we spoke of him or said prayers for his soul.

I tried, without saying any words, to gather into me what I could remember of his wisdom and what came to my mind was his despair at the greed and selfishness of our age which he believed was like a disease or plague, to which hardly any were immune, not even the poets or the playwrights, "because, Robert, even the creative spirit is whoring, and Piety, the mother, has given birth to Luxury, the wanton Daughter . . ." And these thoughts comforted me a little because through them it came to me that the things which Pearce had loved about the world had been so few – the tenderness of Quakers, the wisdom of William Harvey, the memory of his mother, the growing of trees *en espalier*, the light on a trout stream – that, though he declared himself to be afraid of death, he must also very often have longed for it.

I was trying very hard to imagine him in Paradise (I have frequently tried to envisage my parents here, but all my mind is able to conjure up is the Vauxhall Woods and I am inclined to doubt whether, if Paradise exists, it would resemble a place where Londoners go to have picnics), when Daniel suddenly said: "It has come to me from the Lord that John Pearce taught me many things by the example of his life and the greatest thing that he taught me was never to be blinded by affection, because it was his way to judge most harshly those he loved most, and so his loving of them never hurt them but only helped to strengthen them." I looked up and saw that Daniel was looking at me, and Ambrose, too, glanced at me, as if the two of them were waiting for me to speak.

I felt very hot, just as I had at the Meeting where I had suggested the story-telling and the dancing, and so I suspected that some words were going to come out of me, but did not know that when I spoke them they would reveal to me something that I had not, until I uttered it, understood. I wanted to stand up, but my legs felt very weak, so I continued sitting down and then I said: "In the silence which has fallen since John died this morning, I have listened and waited. It is as if I have been waiting for some word, not from John, nor from God, but from myself to myself and now it has come . . ."

Still, I did not know precisely what the supposed "word" was or what I was going to say next. I paused and took out a handkerchief and mopped my brow, and then I said: "In this quiet, I have understood one thing. And it is this: that all my love for women which, before I came here, was a very trumpeted and tempestuous thing, and even all the love I thought I had for my wife, Celia . . . all these loves were mere deceptions and not love at all, but only vanity and lust, for which I am ashamed. And in all my life I have truly loved only two people on earth, and these two are John Pearce and the King."

At the shock of hearing the King's name put beside Pearce's, all the Friends raised their eyes and cast upon me their sternest looks. I opened my hands in a gesture of helplessness, "You will

straightway say," I continued, "that my love for John Pearce is
worthy and my love for the King unworthy and that I should, as
indeed John often told me, cast it out from me. But it seems
that I cannot. For whatever I do and however far I travel from
my former life, I still find it there. But it is no longer a greedy
love. It asks nothing. It is like the love for a dead man; it is like
my love for John. For I will see neither man ever again. I will
never be with them. All I understand tonight is that these two
people I have truly loved – wisely in one particular, unwisely in
the other – and that no one else on earth has ever counted as
these two have counted with me. And for this knowledge, which
may have come to me from the Lord or from some other place,
I feel grateful."

The flush that had come into my face and body subsided after
some minutes, despite my awareness that the eyes of all the
Friends were still upon me. The air was very close with their
displeasure and I expected them to start speaking out against
me. But they did not. And I imagined each one of them wrestling
with his or her anger and conquering it for the sake of quietness
and for the sake of John.

And so the night went on and became morning and at six
o'clock, we drank some chocolate and ate some biscuits which
seemed to me to taste most strangely of charcoal.

Towards midday of the tenth of September, Pearce was put into
his grave and the yellow clay of Whittlesea packed tightly around
and above him. I had made certain that the ladle was put into
the coffin with him before the lid was nailed down. But at the
graveside I found myself remembering how, at Cambridge, some
cunning thieves calling themselves "Anglers" had tried to steal
it and all Pearce's possessions from him. They worked with a
long pole, on the end of which was a hook made of wire, and
such a pole had been thrust through Pearce's open window one
night while he slept. He had woken up to see a chair moving in
a glimmer of moonlight three feet off the floor and floating out
through the window. "It was only," he told me, "when the pole
came back into the room and I saw it move towards my ladle
that I understood there were villains at work and not ghosts.

And so I cried out angrily, and my shouting frightened them and they ran away." He laughed when he had told me this story and then he said: "Perhaps it is always easier to frighten away the living than it is to frighten away the dead? What do you think, Merivel?"

But I cannot remember what I answered.

TWENTY-ONE

KATHARINE ASLEEP

As you will have noticed by now, I have no great gift for solitude. After the death of Pearce, however, a longing to be alone began to possess me.

If I had still had my horse, I would have ridden out of the gates of Whittlesea and turned northwards and gone on until I came to the samphire fields and the dunes and the sea. What I would have done when I got there, I cannot say. Perhaps I would have sat down on a jetty smelling of tar and looked out towards Holland and turned my mind to the King's war for which my house and lands were helping to pay. Perhaps I would simply have sat down and remained sitting until I was mistaken for one of the Idle Poor and sent by an Overseer to a workhouse.

At all events, I could not get to the sea. I walked vainly out along the causeway to Earls Bride, but the sight of this sad place made me turn back. On my return, I had a waking dream of the empty, circular room in the West Tower at Bidnold. It was a dream of a place of light.

I returned to my linen cupboard and lay down on my cot and there was a silence in the house which soothed me for a little while. But then I began to hear all the accusations and lamentations to come, and I put my hands over my face. When I thought about Katharine, I felt cold and sad in all my limbs. She repelled me. No longer did I pity her, even, because it was for her sake that I was about to be driven away from Whittlesea and put back into a world where I had no place. And I had begun to believe that she – no less than those lost to a violent insanity, such as Piebald – was indeed corrupted by devils and that the evil in her had infected me and made me play the beast with her and that when I did these things I was not myself, but a man possessed by Satan. Pearce, by dying, had made me turn aside from my foulness. He had saved me. What I longed for now was to be quite alone with the memory of him; yet what awaited me was Katharine's pleading for one kind of love and the Friends' sadness at my betrayal of another.

I got up off my cot. I went out into the soft soundless rain. I walked to Pearce's grave and stood and looked at the letters of his name which have been burnt into a thin cross made of willow wood which, as the seasons pass, will surely warp and bend and become pale and so start to resemble his actual body. "John," I said, "I do not think that I shall ever find peace."

Some days after the burial of Pearce, I told the Friends, at the end of a Meeting, that I was ready to speak about the sins I had committed, but I requested that I should be allowed first of all to talk to Ambrose privately. There was some opposition to this, it being the Keepers' belief that secrets are very venomous things, "likely to bring illness and even death to any group or corporate body where they are permitted to breathe". But they had seen how greatly I had been affected by Pearce's abandonment of me and so granted me what I asked, out of sorrow at my weakness.

The parlour fire was lit, the autumn evenings now seeming chill. Ambrose seated himself before it and I knelt on the hearth rug like a penitent, warming my hands.

Though very filled with a nervous sickness, I began to speak with a strong voice. I told Ambrose that it was in my nature to be immodest and lecherous and how, as a young man, I had neglected my work at St Thomas's to go in search of women in the park and take them back with me to my rooms at Ludgate. "My fall from the King's favour, the very thing that made me take the road to Whittlesea," I said, "was caused by lust. Though I had promised never to lay hands on my wife, my desire for her became so great and importunate that I could not stop myself

from trying to touch her, thus making myself utterly ridiculous,
causing her a deal of distress, and bringing the King to a great
fury. So you see, Ambrose, that this greed I have to possess
women has been a bitter enemy to my prosperity and indeed to
my reason. There have been times when, recognising this, I
have found myself lamenting the fact that women had ever been
created!"

I paused. Ambrose nodded. This nod of his made me want to
ask him whether he had ever had a similar thought, but I did
not, it seeming very unlikely that this immovable crag of a man
ever suffered the torments of this kind of temptation.

"When I came to Whittlesea," I went on, "I believed that all
of what I had been in my former life I would no longer be. I
thought Whittlesea could re-make me."

"And has it re-made you, Robert?"

"It has re-made parts of me. John understood this when he
told me I had made 'some progress'. And perhaps – though he
never spoke of it – he knew that I would be tempted by Katharine
and that I would resist, but that eventually my resistance would
falter."

"And if he had seen it falter, he would have felt betrayed by
you Robert."

"Betrayed?"

"Yes. For it is understood by the Keepers of Whittlesea that
we stand towards those we protect as parents towards children.
And for the parent to lay any hand on his child for his own
pleasure and satisfaction is a betrayal of the most horrible kind."

I sighed. I was forced to admit to myself that this was indeed
how I had thought of Katharine and it was for a "child" that I
had made the doll, and thus the Time of Madness with her now
appeared to me more foul than ever and Ambrose's sternness
with me entirely justified.

I had not seen Katharine for several days, having been asked
by Ambrose to stay out of Margaret Fell. He now described to
me how – since my betrayal of my trust – Katharine could not
be induced by any means, save the giving of laudanum, to sleep
and how, day and night, she repeated my name and asked for
me and shrieked and sobbed and touched herself indecently and

how my very name had become synonymous with her madness so that the women of Margaret Fell told the Keepers she was suffering from a "lunacy of Robert, a most terrible derangement".

This description made me feel so afraid that all strength went out of my voice and I longed to curl up into a cowardly heap at Ambrose's feet (remembering for a fleeting moment that I had once lain thus before the Royal footstool) and be covered by absolute silence and darkness. Aware of my fear no doubt, Ambrose reached out and put his large hand on my shoulder.

"I know," he said, "that you are sorry for what has happened. We love you and we forgive you, Robert."

"Thank you, Ambrose."

"But I also know that you will want to make amends, and it has come to me from the Lord how you are to do this."

"It has come to you from the Lord?"

"Yes."

"What has He said? What am I to do?"

"You are to leave Whittlesea."

"I know. I knew that I would have to do this."

"But not alone. You are to take Katharine with you."

I looked up at Ambrose. I swallowed. I put my fists together and held them out in an attitude of supplication. "Ambrose," I began, "please do not ask me to do this . . ."

"I am not asking. The Lord is commanding."

"No! He would not . . ."

"Did He not hear you say that if you could cure one of them and see him walk out from here you would feel useful again?"

"Yes. I said that – "

"And He heard you. And now He has made it possible for you to achieve the thing you hoped for."

"But Katharine is not cured . . ."

"Not yet. But the *means* have been found. You have found them and only you hold them. The means are you."

"No, Ambrose!"

"Love is the means, Robert. If you love her, she will sleep and when she has learned to sleep she will no longer be mad.

And besides, she is yours entirely now, for she is expecting your child."

That night, I did not sleep.

What passed through my mind I cannot remember. All I know is that I was filled with a dread of the future so profound that all my life until that moment appeared to me to have been filled with a happiness I had never perceived. When George Fox first heard the word of God, coming directly to him, he declared that from that moment "all the creation was given another smell under me than before", and now I felt as he had felt, except that he had begun to smell the newness and freshness of things and what I had begun to smell was despair.

When Ambrose told Edmund and Eleanor and Hannah that "Robert is not shirking his responsibility towards Katharine," they were very tender in their behaviour, smiling sweetly at me and promising to pray for me. Only Daniel looked at me sadly. "It's a shame," he said, "that you were never able to teach us the game of croquet."

During the days that remained to me at Whittlesea, I tried to decide what road I would take when I went out from there, whether north to the sea or north-east to Norfolk or south to London, but I had no appetite for any journey nor for any arrival; I was filled with a loathing for my life. And so I chose the road to London, remembering the plague there and imagining that in the pestilence resided the ending of my story – an ending I had brought upon myself.

The Keepers fetched Katharine out from Margaret Fell. They bathed her and washed her and combed her hair and put a clean dress on her. And they gave her Pearce's room to sleep in, promising her that I would come to her and comfort her "with the tender love he feels for you and the child", and that, so comforted, she would indeed sleep.

And so I was forced to go in to the room where my friend had died and there was Katharine sitting quietly on the hard chair where Pearce used to sit and read, his knees neatly together, the book held up to his nose, like a fan, the words of

Harvey circulating so sweetly in his brain that it became oblivious to everything else.

When Katharine saw me, she rose from the chair and came to me and put her arms round my neck and began to sob and say Robert, Robert, Robert, twenty or thirty times. I held her. The dress she wore was made of clean linen and so the smell of Katharine was not the smell of her that I remembered. And for this change I was grateful.

I told her that we would be going away from Whittlesea. I told her that I loved her and that I would not abandon her.

That evening, she supped with us in the kitchen. She ate with a spoon in her right hand and with her left hand kept a hold on my arm. And that night, as Ambrose and the others had predicted, she went to sleep and did not wake till dawn.

The money that remained to me in the world was twenty-four pounds and three shillings.

With this, with my clothes and possessions put into two flour sacks, and with Katharine dressed in a woollen cloak waiting for me outside, I stood in the parlour of Whittlesea House, in the room of all the Meetings, and the Keepers came, one by one, and took my hand and bid me adieu.

The sorrow and disappointment that I beheld in their faces was a very terrible thing to endure and I wished for this leave-taking to be over quickly. But it could not be so, because there was a corner in each of their hearts that did not want me to leave and would rather have had me stay, my crime notwithstanding. And so they reminded themselves how the Lord had sent me to them "out of the windy sky", and how, in coming to Whittlesea, I had brought a great gift and that was the gift of my hands, which had helped them for so many months in their tasks of healing.

"How shall we manage?" asked Ambrose. "Now that mine are the only physician's skills? Pray for us, Robert, for life will be hard for us – without John and without you."

"Yes. Pray for us, dear Robert," said Hannah.

"And pray for me," said Daniel, "for if ever there is to be more dancing or skipping about, I will be the only musician."

"I will pray for you all," I said, "and remember you for ever, how you took me in and how it was never part of any plan that I had to betray you or make you ashamed . . ."

When Eleanor came forward to take my hand, as she spoke the words, "The Lord keep you, Robert," her eyes filled with tears and she looked down at my hands in hers, as if they were something precious to her.

"Do not cry for me, Eleanor," I said. "Please do not cry for me."

But she shook her head. "We will all weep for you sometimes, Robert," she said, "just as we will weep for John. For you are both lost to us."

So I walked out of the parlour for the last time and then out of the house and the Keepers came and stood in a cluster by their door and watched me go.

A cart had been hired for us. I threw my flour sacks onto it, then I took Katharine's hand and helped her up and got in beside her. I told the driver of the cart, a lumpish man with the fat buttocks of a woman, and his hair tied in a greasy bow, to make haste. I wanted to be gone now and not to look back. But the cart-horse was sluggish. We proceeded almost at a man's walking pace. And so, before we had gone very far out of the gate, I *did* look back. I turned and saw it all: the iron door with its inscription from Isaiah, where I had first gone in, the three great barns named by the Keepers after people who were sacred to them, the house that had contained my linen cupboard, outside of which the Friends still stood and watched me, and, beyond the walls, the cemetery where Pearce would lie for all eternity. On the day I had arrived there, I had believed myself the unhappiest man on earth. Now I knew that my unhappiness then was as nothing to my present sorrow, so that everything that I could remember about my time at Whittlesea seemed touched with a comforting light, as if it, no less than my time at Bidnold, was part of the day and what was falling upon me now was the night.

The actual night overtook us on our cart as we entered the town of March. I paid the man off. I knew I could not endure the sight of his fat rump for another day. He deposited us at an inn called

The Shin of Beef and we were given a room that smelled of apples, a quantity of them being stored in it on damp trestles.

I knew we were in a poor place, badly run and neglected, but Katharine, having been out of the world for so long, believed it to be grand. She thought the apples had been put out for us to eat (there being no supper available to us, not even the poor cut of beef after which the miserable inn was named) and so she ate them greedily, one after another, until she vomited up a mess of them into the bed. In the cold of one o'clock a maid no older than twelve or thirteen came and took away the foul sheets and put on some that were clean but damp and in this cold dampness Katharine clung to me and kissed me and some of the devils that were still in her came into my blood on her saliva and so I took her at last but with my eyes closed, so that I could not see myself or her, and with my hands covering her face. And with her breasts pressed against my back, she went to sleep. But I could not sleep, for the cold and smell of the place and for the great choking of misery that was in my heart.

We were forced to wait in the town of March for two days for a stage coach that would take us to Cambridge and so on to London.

On the first of these days, a Tuesday, a market began setting up at dawn outside our windows and so I took Katharine out and we walked among the stalls selling honey and fruit and candles and skeins of wool and beeswax and we found a man who, for threepence, would imitate the cry or growl or squawk of any animal or bird. And this person mystified and delighted Katharine so much that I was forced to keep paying him money for one imitation after another and soon felt very foolish standing in a gawping crowd and listening to a man pretending to be a chicken and a hog and a capercaillie and a new-born lamb. After almost a quarter of an hour, I said to Katharine: "We have heard enough now. Let us move on before he begins on all the beasts of Africa," but she begged me to let her hear one more thing and said: "You have not chosen any animal or bird yet, Robert, so now it is your turn." And so I took out another three pennies from my purse, and the man held out his leathery palm for them and said: "What is it to be, Sir? A screaming peacock? A howling wolf? Or – two for the price of one – an old sow and her suckling piglets?"

"The pigs," said Katharine, "tell him to be the pigs."

"No," I said, "not the pigs. A blackbird."

"A blackbird, Sir?"

"Yes."

"Well then we must have silence round about, we must have quiet among you good people. For the sound of the blackbird is a little thing and I cannot make it loud."

He persuaded the cluster of people round him to cease their chatter. He then cupped both his hands to his lips and through his fingers I could see his mouth making some ugly contortions. I closed my eyes and waited. And then the sound came, perfect and pure, and I knew at once that tears were coming into my eyes, so I quickly took out my handkerchief and blew my nose loudly, thus interrupting the blackbird imitation so rudely as to cause an outbreak of laughter in the little crowd. I then nodded to the man, who was scowling at me, and, taking Katharine firmly by the wrist, I led her away.

There being nothing whatever to do in March, I hired a rowing boat in the afternoon. The day was warm, like a day from summer suddenly come again, and I rowed downstream on the River Nene towards a place called Benwick. "It is too insignificant a village to attract to it any bird imitators," I said with a smile. But Katharine was not listening to me. She had put her hand into the water and seemed hypnotised by the sight of it and by the flotsam of leaves and waterweed that swam into her fingers. Her mouth hung open and she did not notice that her long hair had begun to trail in the river. Then suddenly she came out of her trance and laughed, and her laughter, which I had seldom heard at Whittlesea, sounded exactly like that of a child. But instead of feeling kindness or pity for her childishness, I felt only a great weariness with time which, with Katharine as my only companion, seemed to pass so slowly that it was difficult to believe that the day's sun would ever go down or the night's darkness ever break into morning. I tried to comfort myself by imagining that, if time had slowed down, I would not get to old age until long after I had passed it. But this little conceit brought me a mere moment of solace, for I knew that I no longer minded about growing old or indeed cared much about whether I lived or died.

That night in the apple room, when I lay down on the bed, my shoulders and my back aching from my afternoon of rowing, Katharine came and stood by me and lifted up her skirt and told me to put my hand on her belly and complained peevishly that I had never done this nor wanted to do it and that therefore I did not love the child inside her.

I turned my head and looked at her belly and I said that I found it most difficult to love anything in advance of its being. But she did not understand what I meant by this and I had no will to explain it, so I soothed her by stroking her belly and she began to tell me everything she would do for the child when he was born and how she would let no one but me ever take him from her, for what she feared now was the jealousy of barren women who would come when she was asleep and steal her baby "and leave me with the nothing that I had". And so, to comfort her, I said – as if telling one of my Tales of the Land of Mar to Meg Storey – we would build a fortress round the child, we would put him in a high tower and let no one near him except ourselves, "so that not only will he be safe, he will neither see nor feel any of the unkindnesses of the world, nor its scheming, nor its ugliness, for everything he will see from the window of the tower will be beautiful . . ." And Katharine was so entranced by all this nonsense that she fell asleep standing up and so I got off the bed and lifted her up and laid her on it. And then I did not know where to put myself, not wanting to lie down beside her, so I sat down on the hard chair that had been placed near the window and thought I would look out at the stars and see whether I could find Jupiter and its little girdle of moons, but the window was grimy and all I could see was my own reflection in it and I saw, suddenly, how I had aged a great deal in a short time and how my face, which I still thought of as wide and smiling, had become gaunt and worried.

And my thoughts turned to Celia. I do not know if it was my search for Jupiter that brought her to mind or the changes I

observed in an appearance that had always been so distasteful
to her. I thought of my famous Letter of Apology to her which
I had spent so many hours trying to compose, but which had
never been written, a pathetic short note being sent in its place.
So now, I wrote it in my mind. I told her I had understood that
love puts reason to sleep. I told her that it was my misfortune
now to be the object of a love I could not return and that the
furies of guilt and the furies of loathing hounded me day and
night and that the pain of these was as cruel as the pain of love
itself. "And so I can measure now," I concluded in my imaginary
letter, "how much I made you suffer, Celia, and for this suffering
caused by me, I ask you to forgive me."

For reasons which I do not completely understand, this Apology to Celia took away from me sufficient of my anxiety for me
to be able to fall asleep in the chair. But it was not a contented
sleep, for during the night I had a sad dream of my mother, in
which I went to speak to her in Amos Treefeller's old room but
found that she could neither see me nor hear me and so, believing
that I was not there, put on her bonnet and went out, leaving
me alone.

The warm weather that had returned the previous day accompanied us on our journey to London and I noticed, as we
came near to the city, that the grass beside the road was brown
and parched and all the fallen leaves dry and brittle, as if no rain
had come for a great while. I could see a little cloud of flies and
insects outside the window of the coach, moving with us, so I
enquired of our fellow passengers, "What has the weather been
in London since the summer?" And they told me that you could
not say what it had been "since the summer" for the summer
had never truly gone, but stayed on "most sultry and horrid"
and that no cooling breeze nor fresh shower had come to the
capital for months, "so that the smell of the place is getting very
foul and all who are wise are journeying out of it and not into·
it".

Once begun, then, on the subject of the weather, the people
in the coach now became very talkative on the subject of the
plague – as if they had longed for days and nights to describe it

and dwell upon its horrors but had lacked any audience to listen
to them. (I have often noticed how it is in the nature of many
men and women to revel in tales of horror and misery, but I find
it to be a very odious thing, and I know that one of the traits I
admired in the King was the way he made light of his past
sufferings and did not bore anyone with them.) It was told to us
how, when plague came into a house, every person in it but the
sufferer ran out of it, mothers abandoning their children, servants their masters, wives their husbands, "so that hundreds
die alone each day and then they are not found and so their flesh
rots and is preyed upon by rats who carry the germ back to the
streets, and the stench of the dead in some parts of the city is
beyond what you could imagine . . ."

I was tempted to say that, being a physician, I was quite
familiar with the smell of corpses, but then I was glad that I had
not made this reply, for our fellow travellers began to reveal to
us the hatred that was felt for everyone in the world of medicine
– from the surgeon to the apothecary – for their inability to find
any means of prevention or any cure. "Doctors," announced a
loud-voiced woman seated opposite me, "are become the people
most despised in England." And she sucked on her teeth, loving
the taste of the venom in her mouth.

We came at dusk into Cheapside, where Katharine's mother
lived. We got out of the coach and the two sacks containing my
worldly goods were handed down to me.

I stood still and took my first breath of the city. The scent of
the air did not seem to have been altered by the presence of
the plague. What I did notice at once, however, was a strange
quietness in the street and beyond it, which was like the quietness of snow. It was as if the city had fallen into a trance, or
else become a place that I was not really standing in, but only
saw and heard from a long away off. I looked all around me. I
could see a group of children running after the coach. I could
see two women standing on a doorstep, one holding a baby. A
cart, loaded with barrels, passed and I could hear the hooves of
the cart-horse, but very quickly this sound and the sound of the
children shouting faded and died and there was silence. I bent

down to pick up one of the flour sacks. As I did so, I saw
Katharine lift her skirts and squat down to piss into the gutter.
"When you begin to carry a child," she said, "you do your
business wherever you can and you cannot wait." At that
moment, her mother came out of the house. She put her hands
to her mouth and stared at the daughter she had given to the
Keepers of Whittlesea, then crossed herself, as if in fear.
Katharine, red in the face from the exertion of emptying her
bladder, looked up at her mother and began to laugh. And I do
not think I have ever witnessed – between two people long
parted from each other – a more awkward meeting.

The mother is a tall, fleshy widow of forty or forty-five. She
likes to be called by her two Christian names, Frances Elizabeth,
as if they were joined together to make one name. She makes
a living by writing letters for those who cannot read or write,
but I have seen her writing and it is an ugly hand and her spelling
is poor. A little sign by her front door reads: *Frances Elizabeth
Wythens. Letters Written. One penny per line.* She learned to
write, not from any school or teacher, but from her dead
husband, who was a clerk in the Office of Patents. "He was,"
says Frances Elizabeth to me on our first night in her house, "a
most conscientious scribe."

The house is narrow and dark and over-heated by the fires
she keeps burning, one upstairs and one down, as a prevention
against the pestilence, which has already visited two families in
Cheapside. The place smells of smoke and of old varnish and
camphor, and the windows are narrow and grimy. The room we
have been given reminds me a little of the room I had long ago
at Ludgate, which is only a short walk from here. In my bed
there I knew oblivion of the very sweetest kind, but in this one
I cannot seem to come to any unconsciousness or any forgetting.
I lie awake and listen to the silence that has fallen upon London.
It is Katharine who sleeps. Her tangled hair falls onto my
shoulder and her arm is laid across my breast.

PART THREE

TWENTY-TWO

A PROPHYLACTIC

Not long after our arrival in London, while on an errand to buy ink for Frances Elizabeth, I met a group of men attired in rags and scourging themselves with cruel little whips, like the Flagellants of the Black Death in 1348. We were in Change Street and I presumed they were going up to St Paul's church to pray for an end to the pestilence. And so, finding myself very curious to know what solace this hurting of their flesh afforded them, I followed them.

I noticed that whatever people we met coming in the opposite direction looked on these Flagellants with great fear, as if they themselves could be the source of the plague germ, and they crossed the street so that they would not come near them. And I thought how a great fear of one particular thing may often create in people the *habit of fear*, so that everything which is not familiar and comfortable to them makes them afraid. And this thought was followed by the realisation that, because I no longer hold my life to be a lovely and precious thing, I am no longer afraid of anything at all, not even of death. And I smiled to myself for, unannounced, the King walked into my mind. And he looked at this new fearlessness of mine and sniffed and said: "Good." And then, as is his way, he turned and walked away, not deigning to comment any further.

We were nearing St Paul's. I did not know how long the praying of these Flagellant people might last once they went inside the church, and so, mindful of my errand of the ink, I

decided to approach them straight away and ask them to spare
me a few minutes before they began their prayers.

Coming up to the group from behind, I noticed how, on the
shoulders of two of them, there was a rash of small wounds, as
if the skin had been pricked and burst, and that some of these
were infected and running with pus. And so I began my conversation with them by saying (quite loudly, so that they would hear
me over their wailing): "Let me tell you good people that I am
a physician and if ever the pain of your wounds becomes greater
than you intend . . . I could give you a balm for it, to make it
less . . ."

They turned and all stared at me and I saw that their faces
were smeared with a white paste they had put on to make
themselves resemble skeletons. I understood then that it was
their intention to frighten people away and, indeed, they appeared somewhat affronted that I had had the temerity to
approach them.

"Our pain," said one of them curtly, "is never greater than
we intend, nor is it less, and as for you, the physicians, why do
you not punish yourselves?"

I replied that, in my own case, fate had punished me so well
that I felt relieved of all necessity to do so and I laughed at my
own flippancy, hoping perhaps to elicit some answering smile
from the Flagellants, but getting none. So I moved quickly to
my question. "Look about you," one of them said in answer,
"and you will see, not London, not a city with which you were
once familiar; you will see a place come to chaos. The man who
must live within chaos will go mad very soon. But we shall not.
For we do not see it nor hear it nor smell it. All that we feel,
all that we know is our own pain."

I thanked them and left them to go on their way. I walked
very slowly towards Cloak Lane, where I hoped to purchase the
ink for Frances Elizabeth, provided my ink-man had not died of
the plague while I had been away. As I walked, I pondered the
words and actions of the Flagellants and asked myself how best
I should live in this "place come to chaos" in order to keep such
sanity as remained to me. And I decided not to turn my face
away from the sufferings of the city but to try to measure them

and define them. I would walk about. I would try to paint a picture of the plague (no, not on canvas!), a picture in my mind of where it was and how it travelled and all the things men and women had devised to make it leave them. And so I formulated a kind of plan with which to confront the slowness and sadness of time. And this making of a plan cheered me.

As Katharine grew heavier with her child, she became very heavy with sleep. And the mother, too, as if in sympathy with her daughter, would nod and doze over her letters in the room kept hot by the fire, and so I would creep out of the house, leaving the two of them to their dreaming, Katharine's white arm trailing down towards the floor, the mother's head fallen onto the table.

They did not ask or seem to care where I was going. They knew I would return, for Katharine had made me swear upon the green slippers never to practise or perfect any Leaving Step. And so I embarked on my "picture" of London, going sometimes north from Cheapside, but most often south towards the river and my old haunts, knowing that in these places every change would be visible to me and all of what I saw I would understand.

I did not visit Rosie. In her very street were two houses marked with the words "God Have Mercy On Us" and nesting near to the water at Southwark I saw a great quantity of rats. Yet you could not say that Rosie Pierpoint was in greater danger of the plague than any in Lambeth or Spitalfields or Shoreditch, because the disease did not seem to follow a traceable path along the ground, but rather to come out of the air, like seeds carried on the wind and falling here and there at random.

There was some noise, still, upon the river, but less than there once was, many of the fops and gallants and their women having fled into the countryside taking all their shrieking with them. I was told that some of the bargemen were starving, for lack of trade, and so made it my habit to have myself rowed some way on the water every afternoon. And for this act of charity, I was rewarded with the gossip of the river and heard how, to add to the melancholy of London, hundreds of poor seamen, sent away from their ships unpaid, had come in to the capital to beg money from the Navy office, and how these, because they had no shelter and no fire, were easy victims of the pestilence "but have no place to die in, Sir, but the street and so do make some disgusting deaths in the gutter".

"Why are they not paid?" I asked the bargemen and all of them gave me the same answer, which was that there was no money, the King "being very wasteful of what the Parliament gives him, as if he believes he has only to feed them false promises and they will shit gold on and on". And so I thought of what the King had said about his "honey-moon" being over. I had not believed him, but I saw now that he was right: he was loved less than before. Except by me.

It was only after several weeks of my wanderings about London that something of great importance became clear to me: I was not merely trying to understand the calamity of the city, I was trying to find for myself some role within it. So I began to ask the bargemen and the vendors of eel pies and the ink-man in Cloak Lane and everybody who would talk to me, "What can I, a trained physician, best do at this time?" But I got no satisfactory answers. Some people spat at me, as if the word "physician" had rendered me utterly repellent to them. Others advised me to go home and close my door and burn cleansing herbs over my fire and wait for time to pass. Others again began taking off their clothes and exhorting me to examine their bodies for spots and swellings. No one told me how I could become useful. And I think I would have continued aimlessly walking, noting, talking and watching if I had not one night woken up beside Katharine and heard in the room and in my mind a silence so profound that it is beyond words to describe because I cannot liken it to anything on the earth. I lay in it and looked at the dark and waited to understand what it was. And after a few minutes (minutes I could not *hear* passing but only sensed them pass) I knew that what had returned to me was the Silence of Pearce.

It is a thing that I find very difficult to endure, so lonely does it make me feel. I could not continue to lie motionless within it, so I rose and went down to the parlour and sat by the embers of the fire and waited for morning. But it was winter by this time, and I knew that this wait would be long, so to occupy the time I went upstairs again and fetched from under the bed (where I kept my few books and letters in one of the Whittlesea floursacks) the copy of William Harvey's *De Generatione Animalium* that had been given to me on my day of departure by Ambrose. It was Pearce's copy. It had been read so many times by him that the pages had become as thin and fragile as the petals of flowers, so frail in fact that one hardly dared to turn them. The black leather in which the book was bound was stained and torn, but it had been held for so long against Pearce's heart that it smelled faintly of him and, on putting it into my hands, Ambrose had said, "This was a part of John and is a replacement for the ladle."

I laid the book on my knee and opened it, turning the pages carefully, one by one. Certain of Harvey's Latin sentences had been underlined by Pearce and on almost every page there were annotations in Pearce's minuscule writing. In the heart of the book, seemingly put there long ago and forgotten, I discovered two pressed primroses and laid into the pages with them was a piece of waxed paper upon which the Greek word προφυλακτικός, meaning "prophylactic" had been written. Beneath this was a list – in English as far as I could decipher it – of ingredients, followed by short instructions as to how they should be mixed.

I took up this paper and brought it nearer to the light and I was able to see that underneath the list and the instructions Pearce had penned several of the ornate question marks with which all his medical books are peppered, the symbol having an absolutely precise meaning to him, denoting always "Absence of Proof". I was about to lay the thing back in the book, when I noted that one of the ingredients Pearce had written down was buttercup-root and my memory told me that, although this fleshy bulb is seldom used these days in any medical preparation, it is and always has been included in every preventative men have ever devised against the plague germ, *Pastuerella Pestis*. And so I concluded – rightly, as I was about to see – that what I held in my hands was Pearce's own prophylactic against the pestilence.

That Pearce should have written the thing on waxed paper
was perverse of him, for ink cannot properly adhere to it and
so the writing will soon enough become invisible. Luckily, he
had employed a very sharp quill (he was always extremely fussy
about his pens and liked them to be thin) and so, when I
held the paper *in front* of the light, the words were magically
illuminated, having been scratched into the wax.

And so my little role in London's great tragedy was revealed
to me: I would become a pedlar of Pearce's prophylactic. I would
merchandise hope.

The money remaining to me at the time of my arrival with
Katharine in London was almost gone. We ate food bought by
Frances Elizabeth and kept ourselves warm with coal paid for
by her. In return, I helped her with her letters, correcting her
spelling mistakes and teaching her some elegant phrasing. She
seemed content with this arrangement, but I was not. The
notion that all that stood between me and destitution were
letters of complaint and supplication (written for poor people
who could not truly afford the price of the words) made me
uneasy and afraid. And so I vowed to myself I would make a
living by selling Pearce's remedy even if, to do so, I would have
to have as my customers the relatives of the dead or dying and
so find myself entering those houses marked with red crosses
and with the words "God Have Mercy".

I paid five guineas to an old apothecary I had known during
my time at Ludgate. For this sum, he made up a large quantity
of the medicine (it tasted quite pleasant, being infused in Malaga
Wine) and sold me a gross of bottles. Hanging on the door of
his shop, I noticed one of the strange, bird-like headdresses
worn by doctors going into plague houses and I asked him
whether I might borrow this from him. "You may keep it,
Sir," he said, "for that doctor comes here no more, nor goes
anywhere, nor has breath."

I took it down and put it on. It is made of leather and covers
the head and face and shoulders entirely. In it are set two
eye-pieces made of glass and a long beak through which one is
able to breathe with difficulty, it being stuffed with sachets of

pot pourri, put there to protect the wearer from the corrupted air. With the headdress goes a leather mantle (not unlike the tabards we used to wear at Whittlesea) and thick leather gloves that reach to the elbows. Once inside these garments, I knew that whoever I have now become – whether Robert or Merivel or neither of these or a composite of the two – I had rendered myself completely unrecognisable, even to those who knew me well. I did not even look like a man, but like a duck, and I thought how fitting this was, for in peddling Pearce's prophylactic, the efficacy of which had never been proven, I was about to become no better than a quacksalver.

This realisation, though it dismayed me for a while, did not prevent me, as I walked back to Cheapside wearing my duck garb, from feeling an attack of laughter coming on when I caught sight of myself in the glass of a low window. Not even in my fur tabard nor in my three-masted barque had I ever looked so completely and utterly ridiculous. I laughed for so long and so uncontrollably that all who passed me, I could see from my little eye-holes, shunned me as one gone suddenly mad in the street.

I will describe to you how the winter passed.

In December, I went into a plague house and found a man newly dead from the disease and kneeling by him his wife, holding his dead hand and weeping. I asked her what could I do for her and she told me that no one on earth could help her, for the sneezing and shivering that are the first signs of plague she knew would come upon her within a short time. I was about to turn and leave when I heard myself say (in a voice I did not recognise as mine, muffled as it was by the duck snout): "If no one on earth can help you, why not let one John Pearce, who is under the earth, save you from death?" I then held out to her a bottle of medicine. She looked at it for a moment, but then shook her head and returned to her weeping. Despite my very dire need for money, it was beyond me to ask this brave, grief-stricken woman for the one shilling and threepence I usually charge for the remedy, so I nodded to her and went out, leaving the bottle on her table. Four or five weeks later, this person, who had been seeking me for several days, found me and put her arms round my neck and kissed my beak. She had taken the medicine and the symptoms of plague had never come and so she believed that I had saved her.

From this time, when word of this success began to spread, my business prospered. People arrived at Frances Elizabeth's house asking for the medicine, thus relieving me of the need to go into plague houses in search of customers. Frances Elizabeth banked up her fires and burnt herbs on them and would not go near the strangers at her door. And more and more she and Katharine stayed upstairs in the bedroom, Katharine in the bed (where from time to time I made love to her without telling her that it was a love born of loneliness and need, and not of desire) and Frances Elizabeth in a rocking chair. And the two of them dreamed of the child to come and sewed bonnets for him and knitted blankets for his little crib. Katharine would hitch up her skirts and put her hands round her belly that was grown so large and heavy, by the coming of the new year, she looked like a woman come to full term. And the mother would lay her head gently in the middle of the abdomen, where the navel protruded like a rosebud, and feel the kicking of the baby's limbs. They seemed to long so ardently for the birth that this longing took all their time, so that the letter-writing was neglected and even I, downstairs in the parlour with my bottles, was forgotten so that I had the illusion sometimes that I was free once more, as I had been as a student, and not tied to Katharine or to anyone in the world and that I could walk out into Cheapside and start my life all over again.

I did not give the unborn baby a great deal of attention. I thought of him as belonging only to Katharine and to her mother and not to me, as if I had made them a present of him. They wanted their present to be male. They wanted the son who could rise to prosperity in the Office of Patents and they named him Anthony, after the dead father. And one evening, an astrologer was summoned. This astrologer frowned when he learned that I was born under the sign of Aquarius and whispered some words to himself that I did not catch. He predicted that the child would be large and healthy and that, in its infancy, it would learn "a very pretty way with laughter". He set the probable date of

birth as the twenty-fifth of February and went away richer by
ten shillings, leaving Katharine and Frances Elizabeth disappointed that he had not told them more.

"Of what use is laughter?" sighed Frances Elizabeth. "It has
never brought anyone to riches."

My birthday came again. I made no mention of it and there was
no rejoicing. I was sullen all day, remembering the foolish
Dégeulasse and the false hopes of his wife and daughters. And
towards nightfall I thought of Celia, of her grace and sweetness
and of her singing.

In the same week, I met, in the apothecary's shop, a man
who had been alive for ninety-nine years. He told me that the
plague was caused by the tiredness of the earth and that this
was but the first stage in the ending of the world. I nevertheless
persuaded him to buy a bottle of Pearce's preventative, it being
his ardent wish not to die until he had reached the age of one
hundred. Before paying for his bottle, however, he asked me
what was in the mixture. I told him that it contained crushed
rue, sage, and saffron with boiled buttercup-root, snake-root
and salt and that these ingredients were infused with Malaga.
He smiled and nodded and pronounced the medicine "clever" and
left, and as he went out I saw the apothecary bow obsequiously to
him.

"Who is that old man?" I asked.

"Do you not know?" said the apothecary. "Do you not recognise the fleshy nose and something in the set of the mouth?"

"No."

"Ah. Well, to me, there is a family likeness. He is the only
surviving brother of William Harvey."

For reasons which I do not completely comprehend, I was so
affected by this revelation that, instead of returning to Cheapside
as I had intended, I walked to a nearby tavern, The Faithful
Dray, and ordered myself a small flagon of wine.

I had not drunk any wine for such a great while that a very
little of it rendered me categorically drunk and I sat in my corner,
foolishly sipping, glad that I was not known in The Faithful Dray
and so forced to enter into any conversation. I was about to

order a second flagon (having now remembered that solitary
drinking can be an oddly enjoyable pastime) when I heard
someone say, very meekly and politely: "Good morning, Sir
Robert."

I looked up. A man stood before me, so cadaverously thin
that his face resembled a skeleton more nearly than the painted
faces of the Flagellants. On top of this gaunt visage, he wore a
blond wig, once fine but now matted and greasy and clogged
with old powder. He had on his back a torn green coat and the
hand he held out to me was encased in a green glove. I stared
and blinked. And then the knowledge of who he was seeped into
me. It was Finn.

If he had not had the courage to apologise to me for spying on
me for the King, I would have got up and left him, without any
regard for his sorrowful condition. But the first words he spoke
were words of apology, and following on these came the story
of what had happened to him. And both the apology and the tale
were pitiful, the first being very stammering and clumsy and the
second being full of suffering and humiliation.

You will remember that, while I was delirious with the
measles, Celia left me and returned to the King, taking Finn and
the finished portrait with her.

During this journey, Finn began to dream. He dreamed of the
King's hand slapping him on the back and pressing a purse full
of gold into his palm. He dreamed of all the commissions to
come (ah, the beauty of that word "commission" for all the
unknown artists and poets!) and all the imaginary arcadian
landscapes in which he would place his famous sitters.

After the dreams came the arrival. The portrait of Celia was
unloaded from the coach and Finn carried it himself down the
length of the Stone Gallery, believing that on this occasion the
doors to the King's apartments would be straight away opened
to admit him. But they were not. He waited in the Stone Gallery
for two days, his mind so enchanted by his imminent preferment
that he left his spot only once to eat a little meal of bread and
sausage and to relieve himself. He slept with his head on the
stone.

On the third day, he was summoned. The King looked down at the portrait (behind which Finn was humbly kneeling). His Majesty ordered lamps to be brought near to it. Then he leaned down from his great height and scratched at the pigment with his nail. A flake of burnt umber came off and adhered to his finger. He examined it and called for a silk handkerchief in which to deposit the flake. The handkerchief was brought to him. He flapped it at the picture. "Gaudy," he said, "and shallow. The antithesis of Lady Merivel. Take it away."

Finn saw the folly of protesting. He saw that to argue with the King would avail him nothing and lose for him the little money he would be given for the portrait, if he remained silent. And yet he protested. He came out from behind the picture and began to describe the pains he had taken with the thing, his care with the background and the fondness Celia had shown both for him and for the portrait. The King turned his back on him and walked away towards his bedchamber. Finn shouted after him that he owed him at least the seven livres promised in the contract and that no man would trust a King of England who did not keep his word. The King stopped in his tracks and called for his guards. Finn was arrested and sent to the Tower.

He languished in the Tower for seven months. He was not charged, he was forgotten. Celia's intercession eventually secured his release. He was ordered never to come to Whitehall again or to any place where the Monarch resided. He made his way to Norfolk, believing that Violet Bathurst would help him, but he found the Bathurst household in dereliction. Old Bathurst had died and been put into his mausoleum and Violet – whether in sadness for the loss of him or for the loss of me one cannot say – courted a daily oblivion in the fine Alicantes her late husband had hoarded in his cellar. She gave Finn fourteen shillings and the stuffed head of a marten cat and sent him away. Going out from her house, he was bitten by one of Bathurst's hounds desperate for the taste of blood.

And so he returned to London, where he expected to die. He earned a poor living painting scenery at the Dukes Playhouse, but his anger against the King and against a world that would

not value him was so great that it gnawed at his body as well as
at his mind. It was, literally, wasting him.

All of this he told me at The Faithful Dray. We got so drunk
together, we fell unconscious onto the floor and when we woke it
was dark and the landlord was throwing a bucket of water over us.
We went out into the street and vomited into the gutter. Then I
took Finn home with me to Cheapside, and Katharine and Frances
Elizabeth looked up from their sewing and stared at his hollowed,
suffering face. I invited him to sit down at the table and after a
while some knuckle stew with barley was served to us. As Finn
spooned his to his mouth, I noticed tears coursing down his
cheeks. They dribbled into his bowl of stew, making it more salty
and watery than it already was.

Finn slept on a cot in the small dark room where Frances
Elizabeth wrote her letters. He liked its smell of ink and paper
and sealing wax and, after his first night in it, he asked me if he
might stay a month or two ("only until the spring comes, Sir
Robert . . .") at the low rent he could afford as a scenery
painter.

Frances Elizabeth agreed. Gradually, her house was filling up
with people, but she did not seem to mind. From being a very
anxious-seeming and complaining person, she had become calm
and enduring, and I surmise that she had found her years of
solitude very difficult to bear. She never talked to me about
Katharine's madness or about the day she had taken her to
Whittlesea, or what had driven her to abandon her daughter.
She never said that she believed Katharine was cured. It was
as if she did not wish to remember the past – the death of her
husband on the very steps of the Patents Office, the desertion
of Katharine by the stone mason, the coming of sleeplessness
and lunacy – but to savour the present and plan for the future,
when her grandson would come into the world and grow to
manhood and responsibility and let the women rest.

After the coming of Finn, however, when she heard me
addressed as "Sir Robert", she began to write a letter to the
Ecclesiastical Courts requesting that her daughter be allowed
to divorce the stone mason "who has disappeared into the very

aire" so that she could marry the father of her child. I sat down by Frances Elizabeth and gently took the quill from her hand. I intended to inform her that I, too, had a wife to whom the King himself had married me, but then I found I could not say these things to Katharine's mother, so I informed her instead that I did not believe there was any "e" on the end of "air" and that her writing was not as elegant in these letters as it sometimes was and that churchmen "being very fond of show and outward appearance" would be influenced in their decision by the beauty of the hand. So she tore up the letter and started it again, but I did not stay to watch her.

Two things brought me a little solace at this time: the first was the knowledge that Finn had suffered after his betrayal of me; the second was the discovery that, after all we had endured and done, we liked each other. I felt protective towards him. He believed there was some Divine purpose in our meeting in The Faithful Dray and that if he stayed with me his future would be revealed to him, as if he were the sitter in the portrait who one day comes sufficiently alive to turn and see the sylvan glade at his back and so discovers he can step from the dull foreground of the picture into a place of enchantment.

We did not talk very much about the Court, nor about the precarious nature of our two lives. We talked about Norfolk and our mutual fondness for its wide skies and its wet wind and the order and peace of its great parks. We talked about the Indian Nightingale: how, each in our own fashion, we remembered it as a significant thing. And we talked about Katharine and the peculiar ways in which, without meaning to, we sometimes bind ourselves to another person for all eternity.

With Finn in the house, I found that, when I could not sleep at night, I had only to imagine him downstairs on his cot for my loneliness to recede a little and I began to hope that, even after the child was born, he would still be there, lying a few feet from the ink-wells.

As the astrologer had predicted, the breaking of the waters of Katharine's womb occurred in the early morning of the twenty-fifth of February.

I dressed myself quickly and lit rushlights and positioned them round the bed. Frances Elizabeth put coal on the fires and went out to fetch the midwife, who lived in St Swithins Lane. Finn woke up and wandered about the house in his night-clothes, staring.

The midwife was a shy person, small, even dainty. She looked like a flower-seller. I said to Frances Elizabeth, "Perhaps you have fetched the wrong woman?" But I was shooed away. Women are the sole overseers of birth, as if the process of it must be kept forever secret from men.

Before I left the room, I asked Katharine whether she was afraid. She replied that the pain of the body had no terrors for her, only the pain of the mind. "Your leaving of me I fear," she said. "Nothing else."

I breakfasted with Finn upon some chocolate cake and then walked with him to the playhouse where, he admitted to me, he was at work upon some Venetian columns made of thin wood. "Well," I could not resist saying, "your day will be pleasant and easy, Finn, for you have had much practice with columns." I waited for his smile, but it did not come. Indeed, he seemed crestfallen.

I idled my way home, stopping to buy some opium grains from my apothecary, in case Katharine should need to be stilled to sleep after the baby was born and then calling in, as had become my morning habit, at The Faithful Dray for a glass or two of wine. By the time I returned to Cheapside it was past mid-day and as I walked in I expected to be informed that my son, Anthony, had come crying into the world.

But he had not come. The house was noisy with women, neighbours of Frances Elizabeth who had come to help and gossip and wait. They built up the fires to an even greater intensity, dousing the coals with acrid-smelling potions. One of them made a batch of twenty-eight jam tarts. Another, who was a laundress like Rosie, washed all the crib blankets and dried them on a clothes-horse in the parlour. Another sang Scottish songs, one for each of her seven children and one for the eighth child who had died.

From time to time I was given news of Katharine. The labour

was slow. Her body, for all that it was large, was weak. It could not seem to help the child to be born. And slowly the afternoon came on and then the dusk and still Katharine laboured, submitting every ten minutes or thereabouts to pain so severe that I could hear her cries even in the parlour where I sat and waited, passing the time by playing arpeggios upon my oboe.

Finn returned and we and the women had a poor supper of the jam tarts eaten with a boiled custard. After this, I felt very sleepy, having been woken so early in the morning, and would have gone to bed except that I had no bed to go to. So I played a little Rummy with Finn, dozing over the cards, so that he won five games one after the other. He went off to his cot in the ink-room and I lay down on a settle and one of the women covered me with a woollen cloak and I slept that fiendish kind of half sleep that is filled with dreams and daydreams flowing in and out of each other.

It was morning, however, when I did wake at last. I pulled my limbs into a sitting position and listened. After a moment I heard Katharine's cry come, but it was a weak, piteous cry, as if she really did not have the strength to make any sound at all.

I crept up the stairs and knocked on the door of the bedroom. It was opened by the midwife and she let me come in. I went to the bed, beside which Frances Elizabeth was sitting, holding Katharine's hand in hers. At that moment, the pain came again to Katharine's body and I saw her arch her back and open her mouth to scream, but, as I had guessed, her exhaustion was so great that no scream came. I looked at her face, and then touched it gently. It was waxy and cold and her lips were white and cracked. "Katharine . . ." I whispered, but she could not speak or even smile.

"What is to be done?" I said to the midwife.

"The baby is large, Sir, and she cannot push it out of her."

"What is to be done, then?"

"We can do nothing. Only wait and pray."

"And then?"

"If she begins to slip away . . ."

"What?"

"I have seen the mother begin to slip away, and then there is only one way to save her."

"To cut into the womb?"

"Yes. To send for a surgeon."

I nodded. I looked at Frances Elizabeth, but she did not look at me. She knew perhaps as well as I that to save Katharine the surgeon would sacrifice the child, even cut it out from her body, limb by limb.

I left the room and went downstairs to the parlour. The fire was low, so I put a little coal on it. I knelt before it and did not move.

At half past ten, I heard two of the women go out and I knew that they were going to try to find a surgeon.

Then I got up and went into the kitchen and heated water and washed my hands. I knew precisely what I would have to do.

An hour later, the women returned. They did not bring a surgeon because at this time of plague no surgeon could be found.

Finn, who had no columns to paint that day, came and looked at me. His face was green.

"Merivel," he said (for this is how he addresses me now). "What are you going to do?"

"Finn," I said, "I am going to prevent a death."

He swallowed. Then he took up the woollen cloak under which I had slept and wrapped it round himself, and stood huddled inside it, as if it were old Bathurst's cowshed – a place of retreat.

Then I began to give my orders. I told the midwife to wash Katharine's abdomen and to put clean linen under her. I sent two of the women to fetch pledgets and bandages; to another I gave the opium grains and told her to pound them and mix them with water.

Meanwhile, I fetched my scalpel and my suturing needle and cleaned them. In my heart, I felt not fear, as I should have done, but a welling of excitement that seemed no less intense than that which I had felt in the coal hole of my parents' house when I dissected the body of a starling.

I went up to the room. Katharine's eyes were glazed and

staring, her breathing shallow like the breathing of the little dogs I had once tended.

There were six women in the room. When a little of the opium mixture had been dribbled into Katharine's mouth, I positioned them like sentinels – two to hold down her upper body, two to hold her legs and two (including the midwife, for whose small careful fingers I was about to be grateful) to help me.

The day was bright. Light shone into the room and glimmered on my hands on the scalpel blade.

I said a prayer, not to God, but to my mother and to Pearce. *Help me now*, I asked.

Then I cut.

I cut into the skin. Beads of blood appeared, like the strand of a necklace laid on the belly from the navel to the pubic hair.

I cut into the tissue and the bright blood flowed over the belly. Hands holding the pledgets reached out and the lint began to soak it up.

I cut into the peritoneum and so into the abdomen. In a calm voice, I instructed the midwife and my other helper to put their hands into the two sides of the wound and hold it open. This they did and I laid down the scalpel and took more lint from them to staunch the bleeding. And as the bleeding lessened, I saw revealed to me the coil of Katharine's bowel and the sack of her bladder and the wall of the womb itself.

I wiped my hand on some linen. I did not look at Katharine's face nor allow myself to imagine her suffering. All of my attention was concentrated in my hands.

I cleaned the scalpel, wiping blood off the exhortation "*Do Not Sleep*". I positioned the blade above the lower third of the womb and I cut transversely across it.

Again, blood flowed. Onto my hands. Onto the folds of the bowel. I laid the scalpel aside. I put pledgets on and saw them fill with blood. I removed them and pressed clean ones on. I felt a single droplet of sweat slide down my forehead and sting my eye. I could hear my own heart beating and, for one tiny vessel of time, no longer than a single second perhaps, I lost all consciousness of where I was.

But I did not faint or falter. I parted the lips of the incision I had made in the stretched wall of the womb and felt pressing against my fingers the head of the baby.

"Help me now," I said to the midwife, "for my hands are too large to go in. I will hold open the abdominal incision. Put your right hand under the head like a shoe-horn and, not wrenchingly but gently, lever it out."

So I came to Katharine's side and the young midwife I had likened to a flower-seller reached into Katharine's womb and took out the child, first easing out the head, as I had instructed, then putting her small hands under its armpits, and pulling forth the little slippery body.

It was alive.

But it was not Anthony. It was a girl.

TWENTY-THREE

A LIGHT ON THE RIVER

In Genesis, we are told that before Adam's flesh was opened and the rib taken out to be made in Eve, "the Lord God caused a deep sleep to fall upon Adam". I have always considered that this was most thoughtful of Him, for it spared Adam a great amount of pain and, as a physician, I have many times wished that I could bring such oblivion upon my patients before hurting them. Fabricius once talked about a certain Arnold of Villanova, living in the fourteenth century, who had discovered the secret of a sleep that would not be broken by pain, but no record was ever made of the ingredients of the secret and so it has never been whispered to us down the ages. My wish, then, has not been granted, and when I took up my scalpel to make the incision in Katharine's belly, I did not pray for any oblivion for her, knowing it to be an impossible thing; I prayed only for myself – for my own skill.

When I cut into the abdomen, however, she passed into a sudden and profound unconsciousness. It was not caused by the little dribble of opium we had put into her mouth, for opium works slowly and stealthily. I decided at first that the great agony given to her by the wound had made her faint. But several hours passed and she did not come out of her coma. Her breathing became stertorous, like the breathing of Pearce in his last illness. And so I did not know what this sleep could be, unless it was the sleep of coming death.

I could not sew up the slit in the womb, the wall of it being

stretched so thin that the sutures would tear it, so I left it to
heal and close of itself in its own time. The abdominal incision I
stitched together and sprinkled with a little *Pulv. Galeni* and
had the women put lint on it and bandages that encircled the
buttocks to bind it. All this I did without Katharine being aware
of what was done to her body or even that her child had been
brought out of it living like Julius Caesar and like the good
Macduff of Shakespeare's play, *Macbeth*, the story of which had
been told to me by Amos Treefeller in his back room smelling
of polished wooden hat-stands.

The baby was taken away by the midwife and the other women
to be washed and examined and then bound in swaddling. They
told me that the infant's head was covered with a soft down "of
a reddish colour" and that it was a well-formed child "with a
good and lusty cry". And they held it up for me to see its face
and I saw that it had a little flat nose like my own. Then they
asked me: "What shall we call the baby? What name had you in
mind?" And I replied that I had no name in mind, having been
told that my child would be a boy and christened Anthony.

The women looked at me reproachfully and snatched the child
from my sight. And when they had gone, I sat down and rubbed
my eyes and for the first time told myself that I was the father
of a little girl, breathing and alive. I put my hands together in
the kind of prayer steeple Ambrose used to make and asked for
kindness from God and the world towards my girl. "Let her
have playthings, as many as I can afford," I added, "but let her
not *be* a plaything for any man." And as soon as I had whispered
these thoughts, I decided upon the name Margaret, which was
my mother's name and thus to me a serious and precious word.
So I got up and went to the women and told them that the
baby would be christened Margaret after my mother and after
Margaret Fell. They nodded their approval and from that moment, when the child cried and they comforted it, I heard them
saying, "Hush, Margaret, all is well."

Yet it was not true. After some hours, during which Katharine
did not stir nor move any of her limbs, the midwife uncovered
one of her breasts and pinched the nipple, trying to make the
milk come, but despite the great heaviness of her breasts there

did not seem to be any proper milk, only a little weeping from the teat, which, when the midwife touched it and then licked her finger, had a bitter taste like bile.

"Put the baby to the nipple nevertheless," said Frances Elizabeth, who stood by her daughter and combed her black hair over the soft pillow, "and it will make the milk come."

So Margaret was laid on Katharine's stomach, above the bandaged wound, and her little mouth tickled until it opened and the teat put into it. She began to suck but quickly spat out the teat and screamed and would not, no matter how the midwife tried to persuade her, stay on the breast and suckle. She was put back into the crib and covered with the blankets and quilts made for Anthony. I ordered that a wet-nurse be found.

I sat by Katharine. I picked up her hand, which felt hot with a fever, and held it in mine. I looked at her face – not as the face of a poor woman towards whom I felt utter indifference but as the face of the mother of my child. I wanted to love the face and feel tenderness towards it, but I could not, so I got up and went downstairs, being afraid that Frances Elizabeth would look at me and read my thoughts and my feelings.

I found Finn sitting by the fire in his undergarments, sewing patches onto his Lincoln green. His raggedness has become very dire and, had I the money, I would buy him a new suit of clothes. Nevertheless, the sight of him mending his things made me smile and I could not resist saying to him: "Ah Finn, a new profession, I see: tailor."

He had the wit to laugh. Then he said: "I do not know what to do, Merivel, about how poor I am."

"Well," I said, "why do you not paint my portrait?"

"What?"

"You heard me, Finn. But do not paint me as a rich man, dressed up in satin or with a sea battle going on behind my head; paint me as I am, in my old wig and in my shirtsleeves and in this simple room."

"And how is that to gain me any money?"

"I will pay you what I can. But then, if the picture is good, you will take it and show it round in the coffee houses and in this way get more commissions, not from the fops but from ordinary citizens – clerks at the Navy Office, silversmiths, lawyers, haberdashers and so forth. They will not pay seven livres for a picture, but they will pay something because there is no man alive who does not feel his status improved by a portrait of himself upon the wall."

I presented this suggestion to Finn as if I had been giving the idea very close thought for some time, when, in reality, it had only that second entered my mind. Having offered it, however, I saw that there might be something in it and so did Finn, for he put down his sewing and looked at me and his look was bright and full of hope.

On the evening of that day, Margaret was lifted out of her crib by the midwife and wrapped in shawls and blankets and taken to the house of the wet-nurse. I accompanied them, because I wanted to see the woman, to make sure she was not diseased nor her house dirty.

It was the house of a money-lender. It was tall and narrow and overhung the river. In one room of it the broker did his transactions and wrote out his accounts; the rest of it seemed filled with children – eight or nine of them – from all the ages of two to twelve, and when the wet-nurse greeted us she held in her arms a tenth child, a fat baby of six months or so.

She showed us into a parlour. I saw a good fire burning and smelt the familiar smell of herbs being burnt upon it to keep away the plague germs. She laid her own baby on a little rug before the fire and took Margaret into her arms. She was a woman of perhaps thirty-five with a gentle smile that reminded me of Eleanor and Hannah. She put a finger to Margaret's mouth and she began at once to suck on it. Then one of her children, a little boy dressed poorly but with a healthy colour in his cheeks, came into the room and stood by his mother and peered at Margaret's round face.

"She look like a flat little button," he said.

"Hush," said the wet-nurse. "See her eyes? Colour of corn-flowers."

We did not stay long, for the impression I formed of the woman was good. She told me that her milk was plentiful "and

not sour, for I shall never eat any soft fruit nor drink cider" and
that she was "a very wakeful person, attentive to all my little
ones". When I gave her some money, I wondered if she would
be allowed to keep it for herself or whether she would have to
surrender it to her husband, who would lend it out at interest.

We walked back along the wharves. "It is strange," I said to
the midwife as I looked at the water, "we did not really have
any winter and now here is the spring already."

That night, I lay on the floor beside Katharine's bed. The midwife
had been called away and the other women had gone back to
their families, so the household returned to what it had been
before the birth, except that Katharine's voice was no longer
heard within it; only her snoring and her sighs.

When I dressed her wound in the early hours of the morning,
I saw that blood was seeping constantly from it and that blood
flowed very freely out of her vagina into the linen under her,
and I did not know how this haemorrhaging could be stopped or
why the wound was not beginning to clot and knit together.
Then I remembered that at St Thomas's we once performed a
cephalic phlebotomy on a man bleeding from his anus and that
this making of an external cut staunched the flow of blood inside
the bowel.

So I took up her arm. It was cold, with a damp sheen to the
skin. I found the vein and cut and let a little blood drip into a
basin. And at this moment, Katharine opened her eyes. She
stared at me, into my face and into my mind. The stare did not
falter. It remained. It saw all that I had done and all that I had
tried to feel and could not. I turned away from it, looking round
at the empty crib. I thought that when I looked again the stare
would have softened and become forgiving. But it had not.

So I put my hand out. That is all I did. I did not whisper any
last blessing or say any prayer or utter any words at all. I only
put out my hand and closed the staring eyes.

Frances Elizabeth wept for the death of her only child and Finn,
who has the heart of a gazelle, wept for Frances Elizabeth,
remembering her kindness in saving him from destitution with

a knuckle stew and a canvas cot in the letter-room. But I did not weep at all.

I walked out of the house and went and sat in a coffee house and drank bowl after bowl of sweet coffee. And the talk and smoke and laughter of the place, though I was not a part of them, I loved exceedingly for they had the smell of life returning.

Then I had a great mind to shit and found a place and did it, and even this I found pleasurable and after it felt very cleansed, as if I had been given a new body.

I passed all the day walking about the city considering what I might do with the next bit of my life and by the time the dusk started to gather around me, I had decided what it was.

Then I returned to Cheapside. On my way I bought some white violets from a flower-seller. I bought them for Katharine – to put into her hands or to lay upon her wound – but then both the flowers and the gesture of putting them on the body seemed to me to be dishonest things, and so I threw them into the gutter.

Katharine was put into the ground in the churchyard of St Alphage.

I wrote to the Keepers of Whittlesea and in this letter I said: "She is at rest now, in the sleep of eternity," but I repented afterwards for putting down so sentimental a thing.

I made a vow. I vowed I would never again be moved by pity. For I see now that in my "helping" of Katharine I was not acting unselfishly (as I believed) but only trying to do some good to my own little soul.

The night of the burial, two seamen from the *Royal James* knocked at the door. They asked Frances Elizabeth to write on their behalf to the Duke of York, to beg that the wages owed to them be paid. I told them she could not do it "having today buried her daughter", but that I would write it for them. They thanked me and asked me to tell the Duke all their miseries and hunger, but to "set them down in no more than six lines, Sir, for this is all we can pay for".

I went to the letter-room to begin on the thing and there I

found Finn stretching onto some wooden slats a piece of canvas
he had stolen from the Playhouse. It had been painted upon
already. It appeared to be a small part of a building – a castle or
a tower.

"What is this, Robin?" I said. "The foundation stone of your
new mansion?"

"Yes, it is," he replied. "For I am going to paint your portrait
over it and your portrait – as you have suggested – is going to
begin for me a new life."

When he had finished stretching the canvas, he propped it up
against some books on the very table where I worked on my
letter for the seamen, thus casting an irritating square shadow
onto my paper. I said nothing. I watched him take up a brush
and palette and put onto it some white pigment. He then began
to cover the entire canvas with this white, obliterating the piece
of castle. And seeing all this white go on as a prelude to the
painting of my face, I remembered a thing to which I had given
no thought for a long while and that was the white "waft of
death" that Katharine had seen in me in the time of her madness.
It sent into my belly a little worm of unease, so I put it at once
from my mind and concentrated upon my letter. I wrote it in
the stylish, neat hand with which I used to write my epistles to
the King. I said, "If England does not cherish and care for those
who have fought in her wars, what is to become of them and
what is to become of England? Surely, Sir, they will both
sicken?"

Then, being in the mood for letter-writing, I took up the quill
again and wrote to Will Gates, telling him all that had happened to
me and requesting that one of the grooms ride my horse to London. And when I thought about Danseuse, I marvelled at the
notion that so swift and fine a creature could still belong to me.

Some weeks passed, during which Finn's portrait of me began
to emerge (like a face coming out of a Norfolk mist) from the
white canvas. In it, I appear somewhat grave – as if I were a
reeve or a librarian – yet my eyes are filled with light. Finn
wishes to title the picture *A Physician*, thus rendering me
anonymous, but I do not mind. The only nuisance was that I had

to sit still for several hours at a time with my hand uncomfortably poised in the act of taking up the scalpel from my box of surgical instruments.

I watched the picture carefully for any signs of fiction and untruth. But I am glad to say there were none. Behind my head is no imagined Utopia, but some plain, dark panelling. I congratulated Finn. I told him this was the best work he had ever done and saw a very foolish grin break out over his face.

In these weeks of the portrait we offered to leave the house in Cheapside, and indeed I was anxious to leave it for I did not like sleeping in the bed where Katharine had died. But Frances Elizabeth wept and begged us to remain, so I replied that I would stay until summer. Finn, I suspected, would remain longer than that, so fond did he seem to be of the room where he slept and where he now worked upon the picture, thus forcing Frances Elizabeth to do her letter-writing in the parlour. But she never complained about this dispossession. She was ready to make any sacrifice to keep at bay her widow's loneliness.

In late spring the portrait was finished and in the same week Danseuse was returned to me.

I was much moved by both things.

I was not flattering Poor Robin when I told him the picture was very fine. It was no gaudy piece of work: it was sober and dark. Yet the face of *A Physician*, lit by a cold watery light, reveals the warring complexities within him – his love of his vocation and his fear of what it reveals to him.

I gave Finn seven shillings for it, one tenth of what he might have got from a rich man, but almost all the money that remained to me after I had paid the groom for his journey with Danseuse and found stabling and oats for her.

She was in excellent condition. Her rump gleamed. Her saddle and bridle had been soaped and polished and in the saddle bag was a letter from Will, which ran as follows:

Good Sir Robert,
It was a mighty joy to me to get a word from you and know you are in London, where God keep you safe from the Plague.

I am sending a Boy with your mare, she has been galloped a little every day and fed good hay so do not fear we have put her out of our mind.

I can report this same bad Pestilence is come to Norwich where most terrible for all. Except, on getting a smell of this news, the Viscomte de Confolens has gone back to France and is no more seen here, which is not terrible but mighty excellent, for I and M. Cattlebury we did Detest and Loathe him. Pray he will not return.

We are glad your life goeth on and we send you our blessings for your little girl Margaret which is a name well loved in my family and in all Norfolk I do think as well.

> *Your servant,*
> *Wm. Gates*

Having read Will's letter which – as his letters always do – made me remember him very fondly and brought to my mind my easeful life at Bidnold of which he had been a part, I was impatient, suddenly, to get up on my horse and be reminded of what it was to ride about the streets, instead of tramping through the mud and dirt of them on foot.

I rode first to Shoe Lane, to the little dark shop of an engraver that I used to pass when I had my rooms in Ludgate. I went in there and ordered to be made a small brass plaque with the words *R. Merivel. Physician. Chirurgeon.* chased into it.

I then remounted and turned Danseuse round and put her to a pleasant trot. And, trotting all the way, we went along Blackfriars and crossed the river at Southwark Bridge and so came in a very short time to the house of Rosie Pierpoint.

I will not deny that what followed was very pleasant. If I had once believed that my desire for Rosie had been snuffed out by the loss of other, more precious, things, I now saw that, after all that had passed, its vital flame still had a little breath.

While I have become thin on Quaker porridge and widow's stews, Rosie has prospered and grown fat and the sweet dimples above her bottom are deep and when she smiles there is a fold of flesh under her chin. And these things delight me.

She told me that, since the plague came to London, there has been "a craze for washing and for the boiling of pillowcases in lavender water" and that she could not remember a time when her business had "blossomed out more".

No longer did she eat meals of fish and bread: now, she was able to buy chickens and pies from the cookhouses and cream from the dairies. She worked hard but, as a reward, she spoiled herself. She believed that her fires and her cauldrons of perfumed water and the good food she ate kept her safe from the plague "for it is the poor and the cold who die from it, Sir Robert, and not the likes of me".

We lay in her bed all afternoon and I told her the decision I had come to, which was to set up in London as a doctor and surgeon once again and to make my living in this way and no other. And she sat up, leaning on her elbow, stroking the moths on my stomach with her fat little hand and said, "Everything, then, will be just as it once was, before you went to Whitehall," and I was in no mood to contradict her, so I nodded and replied, "Yes. As if the time between had not existed."

I left her towards evening. As she put a wet farewell kiss upon my mouth, she told me that the King had returned to London. "But take care," she said smiling, "that you do not go near him, for you do not want your life to go round in a circle!"

I did not go near him. Of course I did not.

I borrowed two shillings and ninepence from Frances Elizabeth to pay for my brass plaque and I nailed it to her door, under her own sign, *Letters Written*.

As the summer came on, the plague appeared to be dying down and, because people believed that it was leaving them, they had no cause any more to despise the physicians. And so the sick and the hurt of Cheapside and its neighbourhood began to come to me – some sent by my old apothecary friend, some because they had seen my sign, and some cast upon my doorstep by the tide of rumour and gossip that washes through the coffee houses and the taverns.

Most often, I would be fetched by some relative or neighbour of the sufferers and so would treat them in their homes; sometimes, they brought their wounds or their pain to me and there was no other place to receive them and tend them than the parlour, so that in time it became an operating room like those we had had at Whittlesea and Frances Elizabeth, chased out of her letter-room by Finn, was now deprived of her parlour by me. Even now, she did not complain. She bought a little escritoire and put it in her bedroom and wrote her letters there, her hand and her phrasing becoming more and more elegant and assured as time passed and her fear of solitude diminished.

On Tuesday afternoons – as was my old habit – I would visit Rosie and we both grew very comfortable with this arrangement, neither of us wanting more from the other than these few hours could give. I no longer gave her money, but I would take her gifts of food: a dressed capon, a jar of mincemeat, a pat of butter. And sometimes we would eat a little supper together, sitting at her table by an open window and listening to the sounds of the water.

"You can hear the noisiness of it," she said one evening, "coming back."

It was coming back everywhere. It was as if London had decided to chase away death with laughter. In the coffee houses, Finn found a great clamouring of people ready to pay twenty or thirty shillings for a portrait, because they believed in the future again and could even foresee a time when these same portraits would hang in the houses of their grandchildren on grander walls than any they would ever live to own. And so they came, one after the other – merchants, barristers, schoolmasters, drapers, cabinet-makers, clerks – and sat where I had sat, near the empty ink-wells of the letter-room, and Finn gave them their immortality on stolen canvas. I watched them go out with the finished pictures and no matter how coarse were their features I saw them softened and made glad by this image of themselves that they held in their hands. The next stage was that they would send their wives, to have a twin portrait hanging the other side of the fire. And when Finn saw that this was happening, he fell into his old ways of wanting more than he had and so the price of the pictures went up to thirty-five shillings and then to forty and then to forty-five.

One Tuesday evening, I returned home to find a third plaque

on the door. *Elias Finn*, it read, *Portrait Painter to the Rising Man*. When I went in, I found him drinking Alicante with Frances Elizabeth and he was dressed from neck to foot in new clothes. Apart from the shirt and the shoes, they were all green, even the stockings. "Ah," I said, "I see you have been back to Sherwood Forest." But he only smiled thinly. The thin smile said: "The day for those old jokes has long gone, Merivel."

I can report to you that during this summer of 1666 I began to feel comfortable with my life, for the first time in a very great while, as if it and I were once again in step. When I am old, I shall remember it: The Time of the Three Plaques Upon the Door.

Then there was a June morning that came and after that morning almost all of this comfort that I felt went away.

It was a Sunday. I woke very early. I looked out of my window and saw that the sun was not yet up and I had (I really cannot say why) a sudden desire to *see* it come up over the river – something I had not witnessed for a great while.

I dressed and crept down the stairs and went out. The streets were silent. I heard the bell of St Alphage toll four o'clock. The air was cool, almost cold, and I began to think that, after all, there would be no visible sunrise. Yet I walked on. And when I came to the water, I sat on some little steps where tilt-boats and barges land their passengers and waited. Lying on the river was a white mist, so thick that I could not see the further bank.

The sky began to lighten and now I could see that there were no clouds in it at all and that, but for the mist, the sunrise would be as perfect as those I used to see from my Whitehall chamber.

I stared at the mist, or *thought* that I was staring at it and then I suddenly found that it was all around me and that I and the steps and the few boats moored by them were all become invisible within it. I looked up. I could no longer see the sky. Yet I did not walk back up the steps nor move any of my limbs. I knew that something was about to happen. It was as if time had stopped or held its breath.

I waited. I could feel my heartbeat very heavy in me. Once again, I sensed a lightening of the sky. I felt cold and put my arms around myself. Then, coming near to me, I could hear the splash of a pair of oars and heard the water at my feet begin to slap against the river wall and the steps.

The mist rose. As the sun came up over the housetops, it began to lift off the water and disperse.

And then I knew what I was about to see . . .

His back was towards me. He was skulling upriver and the sun, as it fell onto the river, caught at his jewelled sleeve and glinted there.

His skiff drew level with the steps. He was so close to me now that I could hear his breathing. I put a spread hand in front of my face so that he would not recognise me, but I need not have done so, for he did not look in my direction but only at his pathway on the water and at the sunlight making it gleam.

He went past me, but I did not take my eyes from him. Through my fingers I watched him until he went round the curve of the river and was out of sight.

TWENTY-FOUR

THE HABERDASHER'S WIFE

As I have told you, my life just prior to this June morning had become an ordinary, industrious and quiet thing and I found myself at peace within it. I believe that if, during this time, I had been able to go fishing with Pearce instead of being visited by his Silence, I would have conducted myself like a true angler and not frightened away the trout.

From the moment, however, when I glimpsed the King on the river, my old foolish desire to see him and be returned to his favour began to possess me so completely that I could no longer feel at peace with anything at all. I became curt with my patients. At mealtimes, I was silent and morose. The joys of Tuesdays seemed less than they had been. And instead of going to the coffee house or the tavern to drink and talk, I would embark on solitary walks to the river and sit where I had sat that morning and scan the water for the sight of the little skull-boat, and write, in my mind, innumerable drafts of the letter telling the King of my usefulness.

As the summer progressed, the contents of this letter changed for I had thought up a new ploy (beyond the simple mentioning of my own diligence) to get the King's attention: I would write to suggest that because I was now a mere physician, with little money and no estate, His Majesty might come to feel that it was no longer fitting for me to continue to hold the titular role of Celia's husband. In which case, should he so decide, I would offer no obstacle to an annulment of the marriage, believing as

I did that it was Celia's right to be married to a man more honourable than I could ever be . . .

I did not send this letter. I recomposed it fourteen or fifteen times in my head and one evening, while Finn played cards with Frances Elizabeth by the parlour fire, I sat down in the letter-room and wrote out a very elegantly phrased version of it, putting particular emphasis upon my return to medicine, my daily usage of the King's gift of the surgical instruments and my great repentance for my foul behaviour towards Celia, "a sweet, innocent woman who deserved much better of me than I gave and for whose happiness I say a daily prayer".

I folded the thing (after reading it so many times, I soon knew it all by heart) but did not seal it or put the King's name upon it. I went up to my room and took down Pearce's battered copy of *De Generatione Animalium*, put the letter inside it and returned it to the bookshelf.

I said to myself: You have written it now, Merivel, so let the writing of it quieten your mind, so that you can return to where you were and be happy, once again, with what you had. And after the writing of the letter, I tried to bring this about. But I did not really succeed. And the yearning that I had to see the King was as deep and immovable as the yearning of a lover.

Sometime towards the end of July, I went one evening into Finn's studio (for so the letter-room was now designated) and saw on his makeshift easel the portrait that he had painted of me.

"I suppose you are going to obliterate me by painting over me, is that it?" I asked Finn. "You put me over the top of a piece of pretend masonry and now you are about to white me out – the seven shillings notwithstanding."

"No," he said calmly. "Not at all. I am very fond of my portrait of you."

"What is my face doing on the easel, then?"

Finn came over to the easel and took down my portrait and lifted onto it a newly-finished picture of a woman, aged about fifty-five, dressed in a little lace bonnet and a black dress of puritan simplicity.

"See?" he said. "An identical pose to yours. The same attitude, the same concentration upon the hands, the same cold light on the face. The moment I saw her come in, I decided I would position her exactly as I positioned you. I had your portrait on the easel because I was trying to compare the two."

I looked at the woman, whose face had been finely rendered by Finn. It was a face of great gentleness, which reminded me very forcefully of my mother. And when I looked down at the hands, I saw that Finn had placed between finger and thumb a small feather, dyed red.

"Who is she?" I asked.

"I forget her name," he answered. "She is a haberdasher's wife."

I looked up sharply at Finn. He shrugged his green shoulders, as if to say "this is all I know". I then looked back at the portrait. The resemblance of this person to my mother seemed now so remarkable that I found my thoughts wandering away to a place where they had never before been: Supposing it *was* my mother? Supposing she had not died in the fire? Supposing the woman Latimer had tried to rescue had not been my mother, but the maid?

I knew that I was in a Place of Impossibilities. I left it as quickly as I could, but still fell to wondering in a more general yet fanciful way why the likeness was so profound and whether – in a world so tormented by fashion – there was some unlikely connection between haberdashery and gentleness of spirit, between the measuring of buckram and a soft heart.

That night, because she was in my mind all evening, I had a dream of my mother. She came and looked at *my* portrait. She put her hand up to the canvas and scratched away at it until she had obliterated a bit of my forehead and revealed the white pigment underneath. Then she said: "On the surface, he is whole, but beneath the surface, he is filled with a most peculiar broken light." And then I woke and remembered the words of Wise Nell, the so-called witch in Bidnold village, how she had said that I would suffer "a long fall", but had not said what would come after it, whether there would be any end to it or any "after", or whether I would go on and on falling deeper and further into confusion.

Some moments passed. Then I rose and lit a taper. And, stealthily and secretly – as if I imagined faces beyond the window looking in and observing me and sneering at my weakness – I took down Pearce's book, lifted out my letter to the King and read it through. Then I wrote the King's name upon it, melted some sealing wax with the taper flame and sealed it. "It cannot be helped," I whispered to the anonymous faces outside in the dark, "for I shall have no peace nor be cured of my yearning till I have some word from him . . ."

The next day, I delivered the letter to Whitehall and hurriedly came away.

While waiting for the King's reply – to take my mind out of the waiting – I went to the money-lender's house to visit Margaret.

She was asleep in her crib. Only her sleeping eyes and her flat nose were visible to me, but I could tell from her pink colour and her regular breaths that she was not ailing or sickly and the wet-nurse informed me that she sucked well and cried with great strength "and seems altogether very likely to live, Sir". And so I felt a sudden piercing joy in the realisation that this baby, whom I had brought into the world with my own hands, would grow to childhood and beyond childhood and that I would watch her growing and come to love her and take her on Sundays to the Vauxhall woods to look for badgers. And these thoughts were quite new and strange to me, so that it was difficult to believe that it was I who was thinking them.

I gave the wet-nurse some money.

"How long until she can be weaned?" I asked as I left the room.

"A good year, Sir," she said. "I do not let any of them go until then." She smiled and lightly tapped her breasts, as if showing me riches of which she was modestly proud. Behind her, two of her girls, both with pretty ringlets, smiled and giggled at me and then dropped each a little cheeky curtsey. I bowed to them, feeling my face flush.

As I trotted back to Cheapside on Danseuse, I thought what

an unlooked-for pleasure it would be for me to have a pretty daughter. I imagined hiring for her a maid, who would wash her petticoats and curl her red hair into ringlets. But then I remembered that Margaret appeared to have my features (not the straight, thin nose and dark eyes of her mother) and so she would never be pretty. Indeed, she would probably be categorically ugly and so come to the only future that these times allow to ugly women – unless they be famously rich – which is a future of loneliness and low estate. So I began to consider how I might prevent this, by getting for her teachers of music and teachers of *petit point* and scholars who would guide her not only through the poetry of Dryden but through the work of all the great poets from the beginning of time, so that her accomplishments and her wisdom would get her a kind husband if her face did not.

For some while, as I rode, my thoughts turned upon Margaret's future and upon the great unfairness in society (once noted by me at an autopsy at Whittlesea) which allows men to prosper by many means and women by one means only. Until I turned into Cheapside, I felt most vexed, on behalf of my daughter, at the great unkindness and stupidity of this, but then the sight of my plaque upon the door drove everything from my mind but the expectation that, during my absence, an answer to my letter to the King had arrived. I dismounted and hurried in. There was nothing for me.

"Why do you ask?" said Frances Elizabeth. "Are you waiting for some news?"

"No," I replied, "it is only that my apothecary said he would send word when a curative I asked him to prepare for me was ready. He lacked some of the essential ingredients . . ."

I do not remember how many days passed before a letter arrived. What I remember is that time began to move very slowly once more and that I spent a great deal of it imagining myself grown old and the King grown old, and in all the years that passed no answer ever came, yet my expectation that it would did not diminish and so all that filled my life was a waiting that never ended.

I became very prone to error. A patient came to me with a pain in his gut that I diagnosed as a bleeding. I performed a "sympathetic phlebotomy" to stop the haemorrhage, but a day later he returned and showed me an iron nail brought up out of his stomach by means of a vomit, prescribed by a rival physician. My diagnosis had been so faulty as to put the man's life in danger. He made me take the nail in my hand and advised: "Put it where you can see it each day, so you are reminded of your error – that this mistake will drive out others."

I did as he advised, being very chastened by this incident of the nail (though how a man could come to swallow such a thing I could not fathom, unless his wife or his cook had wished him harm and concealed the object in a pie). But this did not prevent me from making other, smaller errors and from becoming very forgetful and absent-minded, so that, during this time, I won not a single game of Rummy, lost my purse in a tavern, stuck my eye with a quill pen, fell off Danseuse when she shied at a pigeon in the street, missed a Tuesday afternoon (thus incurring a fierce slap to my face from Rosie Pierpoint) and began to fall behind with this, my story – as if I understood at last that I was not truly the author of it, but that every twist and turn in it had been set down by the King.

And indeed, the next episode in it had his controlling hand upon it: he invited me to supper! He did not acknowledge my letter so many times perfected, nor make any reference to its contents. His note was short and curt. It read thus:

Merivel,
  Why do you not sup with us upon Sunday Next?
  We shall expect you here at our chambers at nine o'clock.
                    Charles R.

I received it on the morning of Monday, the twenty-seventh of August, towards ten o'clock. I was in the middle of cauterising a thigh wound when it was brought in to me and I burned my hand with the cauterising iron in my haste to break the familiar seal. And then, when I had read it, my next thought was the thought of a vain man: that I had no outfit fine enough to wear.

*   *   *

The tailor I went to was an old friend of my father's. He made the suit in five days out of affection for him, not for me. The material I chose was silk and the colour navy blue, braided with cream. It was neither fussy nor gaudy and I was most pleased with my choice.

I then went to a shoemaker and ordered a pair of shoes with heels modestly high and buckles of pewter, burnished to resemble silver. Thence to a milliner's in Crofter Lane. The hat I commanded was black with two soft blue plumes upon it.

And so to my wigmaker. He looked at me long. He had not seen me for many months. "Sir Robert," he said, "if I had not known it was you, I would not have known it was you," which puzzling sentence made me laugh and it was in my laughter that he recognised me, for then he said, "But *now* I see you. Now I see that the change in you is not entire."

He is very fond of sack. He likes to pour himself and his clients a good few thimblefuls of it while he measures their heads and displays his different styles and quality of wig for them to see. So we sat down together in his shop and he talked about the world ("for the world, though seeming big to some, is of course very little, is it not, Sir Robert, being really no larger than the shadow cast by the Palace of Whitehall?"), and who had found favour and who was out and what were the fashions of the summer, and I learned from him that the King had a new mistress called Mrs Stewart who outweighed all the others in beauty. "And they say," said the wigmaker, "that his old loves are gone from his mind to make room for this new one, even Lady Castlemaine herself."

"And my wife?"

"Ah, your wife, Sir Robert. *There* is a mystery! For she has not been seen anywhere for some time and the gossip goes 'either she is a-bed with child or else she is a-bed with Sir Fancy Newlove or else she is a-bed weeping', but I can tell you that no one seems to know for certain which kind or condition of bed she is in!"

It was almost suppertime when I left the wigmaker's shop, with the hot sun beginning to go down. I walked home slowly, leading Danseuse by the bridle, and what came to my mind were some words of Sir Joshua Clemence, that to get the King's love he believed his daughter would sacrifice everything and everyone in the world, including her mother and father. I sighed as I remembered them and the voice of quiet resignation in which he had uttered them.

These moments I will not forget until I die:

I am not left to wait in the Stone Gallery. I am shown into the Royal apartments as soon as I announce myself to the guards.

I enter the familiar rooms. Though it is a stifling evening, a fire is burning in the grate of the first chamber.

William Chiffinch, the King's most trusted servant, bows to me and tells me that His Majesty, being very hungry on a whim, has begun his supper which he has ordered to be served in the small room where all the clocks are kept.

I follow Chiffinch and, as we near the room, which is no bigger than a closet, I hear once again the riotous ticking and jangling of time, by which the King is so fascinated and moved.

I go in. The King is wearing a cream-coloured coat, but tied around his neck is a scarlet dinner napkin.

Though I am sweating and my heartbeat is as noisy as any of the clocks, when I see the dinner napkin I smile. And so it is my smile that the King first sees when he lifts his eyes from the chicken leg he is devouring. And it is as if this smile of mine has some magical property to it, for the King lays down the chicken leg and stares at me and it is the stare of someone spellbound. He brings the napkin to his mouth and wipes his lips, but does not take his eyes from me.

I bow very low, sweeping my new hat before me and when I come up from this obeisance, I see that the King has risen and moved out from the little table on which his supper has been set and is now walking towards me. At my back, I hear Chiffinch close the door.

His Majesty stops, two feet from me. He reaches out a gloveless hand and puts it under my chin and tilts my face up, examining, it seems, every crease of it and every pore and even the shape of the skull beneath, so intently does he look at it.

Then he shakes his head, as if in great sorrow at something, and yet over his face spreads a smile of such infinite kindness that I know on the instant that not one vestige of his anger with me remains and that, even if on the very morrow his mood will again turn against me, on this particular evening, the second of September 1666, he feels for me nothing but affection.

I begin to speak. "Sir . . ." I stammer, "I am so glad to find you well . . ."

"Hush, Merivel," he commands, "say nothing. For as you know, I see it all and understand it all. *N'est-ce pas?*"

"Yes, Sir."

"Exactly!"

And then he laughs and brings my face to his and smacks a kiss upon my lips and orders me to sit down and eat.

"It's a picnic," he says. "This is what I thought we would have: a picnic. We may eat as messily as we please, so go on, Robert, put a chicken on your plate and some eggs and there is a little cold salmon here and Chiffinch will return in a moment, as I have instructed, to pour you some white wine."

I have no appetite. I tell the King I have been living very frugally and do not think that I can consume an entire hen.

"Well," he says, "they are Surrey hens – very noisy while they lived, we are told, and very succulent in their flesh, so why do you not take up a little thigh and taste it and then, as you eat, your appetite will come back to you."

I do as instructed and, indeed, I do find the taste of the chicken thigh as delicious as any meat I have ever eaten. Chiffinch returns and some cold, fruity wine is poured for me and I sip it slowly and feel its sweetness entering my blood and moving round me, making me feel calm and serene. The noise of the clamouring clocks, of which there are above two hundred, seems to diminish after a little while and it is as if the King, too, has noticed this diminution when he looks up from his food and says: "Time has waited for you, then, Merivel. As I believed it would."

I only nod, not knowing what comment I am expected to make upon this statement. The King puts his jewelled hands into a finger bowl and rinses them and wipes them on his napkin and continues: "So that now you can teach *me* something instead of being my pupil: you can teach me about madness."

I hear myself sigh. "Sir," I say, "there are so many kinds of madness and folly – of which love, perhaps, is both the sweetest and the most fearful – that I hardly know where to begin. However, one evening when I was in this Fenland place, which is a place quite outside the world that we inhabit here, I did find myself moved – by the scent of some flowers, it seemed to me! – to speak my thoughts about the Footsteps of Madness. These I could relate to you, if you wished, for it was a most strange thing to me that they were never heeded or commented upon, it appearing to me quite as if my listeners did not hear them, or could not hear them. And what I now wonder is whether no one in my life *can* ever hear them or understand them, except you."

"Most probable. Relate them, then."

And so I begin. I do not merely set out for the King my thesis upon the tangled pathways to madness and the great reluctance of the world to explore the reasons why each one is taken, but lay before him everything I have learnt about my own foolishness and everything I have done to cure myself of it. In short, I anatomise my heart. I reach inside myself and take hold of it and lay it before him. And all the while, he listens, sometimes grave, sometimes smiling, as if – even though he "knows it all and understands it all" – the story that I tell him is new and full of extraordinary things that have never before been told to him, neither in the Clock Room nor in any other place in his Kingdom.

Presently, it grows dark and Chiffinch brings lighted lamps and positions them round us.

We eat grapes, spitting the pips into a silver spitoon.

And the King comes at last to the subject of Celia, intertwined with which is the subject of his new love, Mrs Stewart, for whom, he whispers to me, "I have a most maddening folly, Merivel, so that were I with her upon a certain parapet, and supposed to be showing her the planet Jupiter, I would turn my back upon the entire starry universe just to cup her breasts in my hands."

We burst out laughing and this laughter turns into the kind of giggling we used to indulge in on spring afternoons on the

Whitehall croquet lawns. And so the whole question of Celia is accorded no seriousness at all, as if she were a toy we had once thrown about from one to the other and had long grown tired of.

"I do declare," says the King at last, "that your idea of an annulment may be very useful, for then I shall be able to compensate Celia for the loss of my person at Kew by giving her a new husband: a young, handsome one this time! What do you think? Will this console her? What about Lord Greville d'Arblay's son, who is a very beautiful boy?"

I reply that I cannot – knowing Celia the little that I do – make any guess about who or what may compensate her, but the King, suddenly serious, shakes his head and says quietly: "That is not so. For we both know that nothing in the world will make up for what she has lost."

"Yes, we know it," I reply, "but it is Uncomfortable Knowledge."

"Precisely. So where shall we consign it?"

"I do not know, Sir."

"Yes, you do."

"Where, then?"

"To oblivion, of course."

And so we change the subject, and the great matter of my wife, the King's mistress, seems to pass out of my life entirely, so that my memory of Celia's face and of her singing voice fades and floats away into silence. And I feel a profound peace coming upon me, a peace such I cannot remember since I was a child and sat in the quiet of Amos Treefeller's room while my mother stroked my hair and told me it was the colour of sand.

In this state of quiet and content, I decide that I will tell the King about my child. And I discover that the story of Margaret moves him very much and he, in turn, tells me what a great love he feels for the first of his bastard children, the Duke of Monmouth, and advises me not to neglect my child "but let her into your life, Merivel, and give generously of your self to her".

I nod and promise that I will and then, because I am thinking about Margaret, I turn my head and look out of the open window eastwards along the river. And this is what I see. I see a great patch of orange light in the sky. I turn back to the King. "Sir," I say, "look there! If I am not mistaken a great part of the city is burning."

No sooner had I said this than we heard voices in the chamber beyond us and then there was a knocking at the door. The King rose at once, his mood of kindness leaving him on the instant, so that his countenance appeared suddenly dark.

Men began to crowd into the chamber. One I recognised as the clerk from the Navy Office, with whom I had once learned about the patience of a marble cutter. And it was he who now related to the King how an easterly wind had sprung up within the hour and was now blowing the fire "along a great pathway half a mile in width".

Forgetting me entirely, the King went with this man and the others into his Drawing Room and I heard him command them to fetch out the Lord Mayor and give him orders that all the wooden houses in the path of the fire be demolished, "this being the only way we can employ to halt it and put it out". The men went away in great haste and I heard the King shout to Chiffinch to go tell his brother, the Duke of York, what was happening and to send for a groom to saddle a fast horse.

And then he went rushing out of the great doors to the Stone Gallery without any word to me or any backward look and I was left alone in his apartments and the only sounds were the chiming and pinging of two hundred clocks, each in their own time beginning to strike the hour.

I remained where I was for several minutes, with my thoughts in a most tangled condition. Then I saw all at once what I had to do: I had to reach Margaret. I went down into the courtyard and asked for my horse. While waiting for her to be brought to me, a gust of wind blew off my hat and sent it spinning away into a flower bed. I retrieved it and held it in my hand. Then I mounted Danseuse and rode out of the gates and turned eastwards in the direction of the money-lender's house, which, as far as I had been able to determine from my sighting of the flames, lay in the very heart of the fire.

The wind was indeed fierce and blew into my face and ruffled

Danseuse's mane. As we got near to the City, I saw countless pieces of charred matter, lighter than air, being carried on the wind and falling softly like snow all around me. And then I could smell the burning and with every breath seemed to breathe the smell more deeply into me, so that it made me choke and gag and I spat on the cobblestones.

The streets, now, were very packed with people, some moving with me into the stench and the smoke, carrying ladders or hauling handcarts, some in their nightgowns, just standing about in the street and staring, others giving way to fear and calling on God and the King to put out the flames.

I turned northwards up St Anne's Alley. I gauged that westward of London Bridge everything along the river was burning, so that to get to the money-lender's house I would have to skirt right round the fire. But the smoke now began to creep down into the streets like a fog and having turned north, then east, then north again and then east again I found myself in a street I did not recognise and with all sense of direction gone from me.

"Where am I? What street is this?" I asked about me, but no one seemed to hear me or pay me any attention, so all I could do was to press on, turning north, then east, then north again, trying to judge from the smell of the fire whether I was moving round it or still towards it and searching every narrow street for some name or landmark that would tell me where I was.

I was about to make another northward turn when I heard straight ahead of me a great commotion of people and then I saw through the smoke that a single tongue of flame had swept down upon the roof of one of the houses causing a sudden mighty panic with people rushing from doorways into the street and looking up at the flame that was beginning to spread out along the eaves, then running back inside to try to save their children and their possessions before the fire came to them. For they had not expected it so soon. The great front of fire was still many streets away. But some burning thing – a sheet of music, a plumed hat, or I know not what – had come out of the sky and fallen on this one house, and all around me I imagined the fire travelling thus, carried on the wind, on pieces of silk, on love letters, on lace collars, swirling and leaping and floating down at random and immediately catching hold.

The calamity come upon this street was such that I did not feel able to turn my back upon the people's plight. Had I been close to the money-lender's house, I might have done so, but I was still far, far from it and I now understood that my effort to reach Margaret was a futile thing. I had begun it too late. By now, my daughter would either have been saved or have perished in her wooden crib. I could not alter what had already happened. So I decided to dismount. I tied Danseuse to a post and took off my coat and went to give what help I could towards the saving of worldly goods and piling them onto carts and barrows, going into the rooms of strangers and taking up whatever I could carry: chairs and candlesticks and pictures and cushions and piles of bedding and chamber pots and ink-stands and toys.

I was aware, for the first time, of the approaching heat of the fire and stood still for a moment in the street, wiping my brow and watching the roof of the house that was beginning to catch alight. My eye moved downwards, to try to see how and where and how fast the flames travelled, and it was then that I saw, above the door, a sign painted on iron and rattling backwards and forth in the wind: *Arthur Goffe Esquire. Milliner and Haberdasher.* But this was not all that I noticed. I saw, too, that the door of this house was closed and that it was the only one in the street from which people were not coming and going, hauling clothes and furniture.

And so I threw down whatever I had been holding (and I do not know what it was or whether I broke it when I hurled it away) and ran towards the haberdasher's and beat upon the door and shouted, but heard no answering shout. One other man, then, left the saving of his own goods and saw with me what was happening, that in the very house where the fire had come in people were still sleeping. From his piled-up cart he fetched an axe and gave some blows to the door so mighty that it fell off its hinges. We stepped over it and went in, but found ourselves at once surrounded by pitch smoky blackness, so that, before we had reached the stairs, a foul choking and sickness, caused to us by the smoke, forced us to turn round and come out again into the street.

"Who is in there?" I asked the man, who was spitting into the gutter, "how many people?"

"Only her, Sir."

"Who?"

"Goffe's wife."

"Just her?"

"Yes. The haberdasher's gone to France to buy some special Frenchy thread, or some poxy thing."

"We cannot let her die. We must go in again."

"We can't get to her through that smoke. We shall die ourselves."

"No. We must try again. If someone could bring cloths soaked in water to put round our faces . . ."

"No, Sir. We cannot do it."

"Bring cloths! Someone find water and a cloth!"

"You'll die, Sir. You'll veritably perish."

"And let us call and shout to her."

"Will do no good. Stone deaf she is."

"Deaf?"

"Stone. As my prick to a Sunday sermon."

So I saw her in my mind, then, lying in her silence, lying neat and straight in her bed as my mother had lain and downstairs in the workroom all the boxes of buttons and cards of lace and drawerfuls of braid waiting to burn . . .

"Please!" I shouted. "Someone fetch me a wet rag or napkin!"

I do not know who heeded my shout. But, in the next minute, a soaked cloth was put into my hands and without hesitating at all, I tied it round my face and went back into the house at a run and hurled myself at the stairs and then a muffled voice behind me said: "All right, Sir. I'm with you. Try not to breathe."

We groped our way up the staircase. On the landing, a flickering light from the flames now beginning to touch the window revealed us to an open door and lying wedged between it and its frame with her arms outstretched was the body of the haberdasher's wife. We both saw it at the same moment. Without wasting precious breath upon speech, we crawled to it and each

took hold of one of the woman's hands and tugged her towards
the stairs. Then, my large companion nodded to me to let go
the hand that I held, and he stood up and lifted up the haberdasher's wife and put her over his shoulder like a sack and I
passed in front of him and guided him down the stairs and out
into the street and he carried her thirty paces away from the
burning house before he laid her down.

Coughing and retching so violently that a gobful of chicken
returned itself from my stomach to this London street, I knelt
down by the woman and turned her over on her side until she
began to splutter and to draw air into her lungs.

"Alive, Sir, is she?" asked the man.

I nodded. Then I looked down at the face of Mrs Goffe, wife
of the milliner and haberdasher, and I saw that the features of
it were very pinched and thin with the mouth turned downwards
and mean and that she did not resemble in any way either my
mother or the woman in Finn's portrait. But it did not matter,
for those were the faces that had driven me on.

Two women came out to us. They wrapped Mrs Goffe in a
blanket and laid her on a cart piled up with sacks and bedding.
One of them brought water in a bowl and held a ladleful of it to
my lips and I drank. The haberdasher's wife did not speak or
even cry out as the flames engulfed her house; she only stared
and began to chew upon the lace ribbons at her throat. I
wondered if this terrible night would send her mad, so that her
life had been saved only to be squandered away in a Bedlam.

A great weariness now began to come upon me and I knew
that I could not continue with my attempted circumnavigation of
the fire. I would return to Cheapside and then begin it again the
following day. I put on my coat and untied Danseuse from her
post, where she was prancing and sweating with fear, and was
about to mount and join the push of carts and people going
westwards when one of the women came to me and thanked
me for helping them and asked me for my name, "So that
tomorrow I can include it in my list of them I pray for, Sir."

"Well," I said, "my name is Merivel. I am a physician. If Mrs
Goffe does not quickly get well, bring her to me." Then I handed

the woman one of the little calling cards with *R. Merivel. Physician. Chirurgeon.* engraved upon it that I keep in a pouch on Danseuse's saddle. She took it and put it into the pocket of her apron. "I cannot read, Sir," she said, "but I will give the card to Mrs Goffe and she will remember you."

TWENTY-FIVE

MARGARET RETURNED TO MY MIND

Neither Frances Elizabeth nor Finn believed that the fire would travel as far as Cheapside. Between it and the main body of the flames a gap had been made, thirty or forty feet wide, by the hasty pulling down of houses, as instructed by the King, and it was thus that almost everyone living west of this gap imagined themselves to be safe.

On the morning of Monday, I went and looked at the gap. And then I looked up into the air above the fire and saw the blazing debris that was still being hurled upwards and whipped onwards by the wind and I knew then that the flames would cross the gap and come to us.

I returned to the house and told Finn to start packing up his canvases and Frances Elizabeth to bring down her escritoire and beg some room for these things and anything else they wished to save on a neighbour's cart. But they paid me no heed.

"Why has the gap been made if it is not going to protect us?" Finn asked stupidly. I gave him no answer. I went into the parlour, where Frances Elizabeth was calmly stoking her coals as she did every morning, and took up all my surgical instruments and cleaned them and laid them neatly in their case. Into a large box I put all the powders and remedies and lint and bandages that I kept in the house. I took them to Danseuse's stable and strapped them onto her back. Then I returned and dragged from under my bed the sack containing my oboe, my letters from the

King and other remains of my "burning coals". Into this sack I put my new clothes and wig – all now blackened with smoke and stained with sweat – and fastened this also to my horse's saddle.

And then I came to Finn and Frances Elizabeth and said: "I am going now to find Margaret, so I shall say goodbye to you."

They both stared at me. "Are you telling us," said Finn, "that you are not coming back?"

"Yes, Finn, I am," I replied, "for there will be no house to come back to."

Moments after I had uttered these words the first sliver of flame fell upon the first house in Cheapside and so the word was carried from house to house, "Cheapside is lost! Save what you can and then go. Go west and go fast, for the speed of the fire is very great."

So then the panic in our house had no equal anywhere in London, Finn and Frances Elizabeth suddenly intent upon saving every last thing in every room. And though I wished to walk away from them, I could not do it, so I fetched my horse and allowed her to be loaded up like a mule with canvases and brushes and cooking pots and sacks of provisions and dresses and I know not what else. Finn would have put his truckle bed onto her if I had not stopped him and Frances Elizabeth her escritoire, because no cart could be found to take them, and even as the fire came closer and closer the two of them held onto these things and refused to be parted from them and when we set off at last, with Danseuse staggering under her heavy load, they attempted to lift them up and carry them and for a long time I heard them behind me, puffing and groaning and saying to each other, "We can do it, we can do it."

We were in a great herd of people and had to keep moving on or have them fall on us and trample us, but for a brief moment I did pause and look back and it was then that I saw that the fire had gone from the top of our house to the bottom and all that still stood was the front door in its frame with the three plaques upon it. The sight of this affected me more than I had anticipated. I had thought myself to be more or less indifferent to the place, but I was not. And I remembered on the same instant that one precious possession of mine had been forgotten and was now burnt to ashes with the house and that was Pearce's copy of *De Generatione Animalium*, the only remnant of him that I had.

When we came to Lincoln's Inn Fields, we stopped and sat down there on the dry grass, as did everyone else going out of Cheapside and its lanes and alleys. And by late afternoon a vast multitude of people had come there and for every one of them crying and lamenting there were four or five beginning to laugh and gossip and sing songs and share food around, as if they were on a picnic outing with no cares in the world. From Frances Elizabeth's kitchen seven jars of plums had been saved and some bottles of ginger wine and a white cheese in a bag of muslin, so we supped on these and on other provisions given to us in exchange for them and began to make instantaneous friendships with everyone around us.

The talking and the eating went on far into the night, when the fire once again lit up the whole sky and it was all, in the strangest of ways, an enjoyable thing. Near two or three in the morning, I heard Finn begin to tell everybody round us that he was a portrait painter and to offer to paint portraits then and there for twenty-five shillings, notwithstanding the fact that not one person there had any wall on which to hang them. The knowledge that, even in adversity, his commercial heart could now beat so strongly made me smile and I think it was with this smile still upon my face that I fell asleep.

I parted from him and Frances Elizabeth the following morning. Neither the escritoire nor the truckle bed had got as far as Lincoln's Inn Fields, so I was now forced to set down on the grass beside them all the things they had loaded onto Danseuse, and the sight of them surrounded by half-finished portraits and copper saucepans and pairs of shoes would have been somewhat sad had it not been for their great cheerfulness. I had anticipated that the loss of the house in Cheapside would put them into despair, but it did not. For what they seemed to have discovered was that it had not only housed them and their little fledgling businesses; it had also harboured their mutual liking and affection. And I was certain, as I left them, that when I found them again it would be in some place together and I imagined them in a low room smelling of oils, lying side by side in bed and doing their sums.

It took me all of the day to skirt round the fire, going as far north as I could to avoid the smoke, but by evening I had reached the Tower and could see from there that the cluster of tall houses among which was the money-lender's house still stood and had not been touched by the fire, so I whispered into the hot air a prayer of gratitude.

When I arrived at the house, it was the money-lender who greeted me and I went with him into his Accounting Room and he showed me some new scales and weights of which he was very proud, "precision", he said, "being my great passion, for everything in the world can be weighed and measured in some form, can it not?"

I was about to open my mouth to say that I did not believe that it could be when his wife came into the room carrying Margaret, who was wide awake and not bound all in swaddling as she had been when I had seen her last, but dressed in a pretty bonnet and wrapped in a shawl.

The wet-nurse began to talk about the fire and how she and her husband and all the children had knelt down in a long line and prayed that the direction of the wind would not change. As she recounted this to me, she put Margaret into my arms. This was the first time that I had held her or indeed held any baby at all and I did not know if I should lay her in the crook of my arm or put her little face over my shoulder, or what. So I sat down on the hard chair where the clients of the money-lender sat and laid Margaret on my lap and looked down at her. She had grown very much and her face was as round as the moon. Her eyes, I now realised, were very large and clear and she looked up at me gravely for a while, then began to kick her legs inside the shawl and to blow little frothy bubbles out of her mouth.

"See her hair, Sir?" said the wet-nurse after a while. "Colour of fire, it is." And she bent down and eased back the rim of the bonnet and I saw some soft red curls there. I touched them gently and felt, under my hand, the living warmth of her head.

*   *   *

That night I spent with Rosie Pierpoint.

This being Tuesday and I not coming to her in the afternoon, I flattered myself that she would have become anxious for me, imagining me burnt alive or crushed beneath falling timber. But when she saw me, she seemed neither relieved that I was still living nor even particularly pleased to find me there, but preoccupied only with the film of soot and ash which, having been thrown up into the air, was now falling and settling on everything and turning grey every piece of linen that she washed and ironed.

Her house was stifling. She had closed all her windows and sealed every crack and draught in her efforts to keep out "the poxy grime". "But it still comes there," she said. "No sooner do I hang up a sheet to dry it or spread out a kerchief to press it than it comes there, see?" She held up some items to show me the dirty streaks upon them, then threw them back into the soiled pile and screeched: "How am I to get any work done or make one penny while this goes on? I shall starve, that's what I shall do! I will die a slow death by starving and I would have preferred a quick one in the flames!"

I took her into my arms and tried to quieten and soothe her with kissing and after a while her crossness did begin to wane sufficiently for me to tell her that I had no home or place to sleep any more and that I would pay her a good rent if she would let me stay with her for a time, until I could find some rooms and make yet another new start upon my life.

She pulled away from my embrace and looked at me squarely. She put her hands on her hips.

"For how long?" she asked.

"What?"

"How long will you stay? A week? A month?"

"Well," I said, "I cannot say. It may be difficult to find rooms, for I will not be the only one seeking them."

"Then I must have compensation, Sir Robert."

"Compensation for what?"

She sighed and turned away from me, busying herself with the lighting of a lamp.

"Can you not guess?" she said.

So then I understood. It was not merely the "craze for washing" or the perfuming of pillow cases with lavender that had caused Rosie to prosper. With Pierpoint gone, she had resumed her whore's antics with a ready will and it was the money got in this way that had enabled her to buy capons and cream and all the rich foods she could no longer live without. And I thought how strangely my mind had worked, over the years, with regard to Rosie Pierpoint. I had known from the start that she was a drab and a jade but, whenever I had needed her, I had put this knowledge from me, liking to imagine her on her own, doing her work and eating her meals and rising at dawn to perform her little ablutions that I had once witnessed, and never ever picturing her with other men. It is the same thing, I said to myself, as the story of the Indian Nightingale: I have believed what it pleased me to believe.

I crossed to Rosie and put my hand out and stroked her hair. "Of course," I said, "there will be compensation. But now let us go to bed and love each other and drive from our minds everything but this – even the smut and the soot."

I found two cold, airy rooms above a lute-maker's shop on the south side of the river. The sounds of the lutes came up through the cracks in the floor, stretched and fragile and thin.

Autumn rain fell onto the blackened city and turned the ash to paste and bloated the river so that all the half-burnt wharves fell away and floated on the water to the sea. I looked out of my high windows and tried to rebuild London in my mind as it had been. But I found that I could not remember how it had been, so that it was lost to me entirely and this realisation made me so moody and sad that I fell into the habit once again of staring for very long periods of time at the backs of my hands as if I vainly believed that I, Merivel, could remake the city.

I was not alone in feeling this sadness. For every person that I treated for burns in the months following the fire, another came to me with an ailment he could not name except to call it "a melancholy of all the body and mind". I laid red balsam and barley water on the burns, but I did not know what to lay upon the melancholy. More than once my thoughts returned to Wise

Nell and her blood of swallows. In short, I began to wonder whether all cures of sadness do not have within them some element of magic that is beyond my understanding.

Listening to the lute maker and the skittering of rain on my windows I, one evening, turned my hands round and began to trace the lines on my palms, to see whether I could read a future there, but I could not, for no one had taught me how to interpret the creases. I noticed, however, that the love-line – particularly that of my left hand – divides very soon after starting and becomes two. This discovery not only made me smile, it also encouraged me to believe that other accurate knowledge was indeed written on my hand if only I could read it correctly and so began, in an indolent sort of way, a search for a chiromancer which I soon abandoned, it seeming to be the case that full half of everyone left in London professes and calls himself a chiromancer and for small sums of money will snatch up any hand and claim to see in it some glorious destiny. One told me that I would discover a cure for old age, another that I would be saved from drowning by the eating of a quail pie "because that you inadvertently ate the feathers too, Sir, and so it is they will buoy you up above the waves", and another that I would be remembered for ever for a deed I had not yet done or a journey I had not yet made. I was at first very adept at pretending to believe such predictions, but then this pretence suddenly wearied me and I became indifferent to all versions of my future and able, as the autumn passed and the winter came on, to live each day for itself and not to waste too much time dreaming.

I had no word from the King. I did not expect any, for after the burning of the house in Cheapside he had no immediate means of finding me, no way of knowing, even, that I had not perished in the fire. I could have written to him, but I did not. For it seemed to me, as my fortieth birthday approached, as if I had spent so much of my swiftly passing existence composing letters to the King in my mind that I had run out of words.

And this is what I believed: I believed that if, one day, the King *wanted* to find me, he would find me. I did not know how. I could not even imagine how. I only knew that he would. And that it would not prove to be very difficult for him, for such is

his power that surely no corner of his Kingdom is invisible to
him and no person within it beyond his reach?

One day in early spring, being invited to a little supper party by
a lawyer I had cured of an ulcer, I took down my navy blue
and cream coat (cleaned and restored by Rosie to its former
smartness) and the matching silk breeches to put them on.
Having no looking glass in my rooms above the lute-maker, I
had become somewhat neglectful of my appearance, only now
and then catching sight of myself reflected in a window pane.
Thus I had not seen what I now saw in putting on my suit: I had
grown most peculiarly thin. The waist of the breeches was too
large for me by more than two inches, so that the wretched
things would not stay up, and, when I put the coat on my back,
it hung out from my body like a cape. I pulled up my shirt and
regarded my stomach. It appeared shrunken and a little wrinkled
and all the moths on it, having lost so much of their territory,
were crowded up together in a dense mass.

   I sat down upon one of the four chairs with which these rooms
are furnished (a chair so delicate and spindly I often wonder
whether the lute-maker did not manufacture it himself as a
diversion from hollow things) and tried to *read* my altered
appearance, like the reading of a palm, for what it signalled and
what it portended. For in the whole of my life I have never been
thin. I was a podgy baby, so my mother used to tell me, and
the moiré suit I wore as a boy was always stretched so tight
across my chest that I remember minute buttons exploding from
it sometimes when I laughed. Even as a student I was fleshy
and by the time of the fifth beginning to this story I was, as you
will recall, very comfortingly fat. Now, all the flesh was falling
away and every bone in me being slowly unsheathed and made
visible. It was impossible not to think of Pearce wasting to stick
and sinew inside his clothes, and so as I sat there – a thin man
on a thin chair – I began to consider the possibility that I was
dying.

   I examined my memory for aches and hurts. I listened to my
own heartbeat and to the noise of my breathing. I got up and
pissed a little into a pot and stared at my urine, looking for

cloudiness and beads of blood, then smelled it, like a connoisseur of wine, sniffing for acid and putrefaction. Then, forgetting entirely about the lawyer's supper party, I took off the too-large clothes and lit a quantity of candles and placed them near to the window and so was able to see myself mirrored in it. Anyone on the river looking up would have chanced upon a most hilarious sight: Merivel, as nude as Adam, peering at parts of his anatomy – his tongue, his armpits, his nipples, his nose, his groin and his knees – for signs of swelling or discoloration, shivering a little in the cold March evening and appearing altogether as scrawny and fanatical as the original naked Quaker of the burning coals.

I could find nothing wrong with me. My heart sounded strong, my body was unmarked, except by its loss of fat and by time itself. I put on my nightshirt and lay down on my narrow bed and thought of everything that had happened to me since the fire and I saw that my life had become a somewhat solitary thing and that within it there was one abnormal phenomenon which was that now and again I would see and hear things that were not there. One of the things I heard was a dog yapping on the stairway. Once, I had been so certain that the creature was there that I had opened my door and expected it to come in wagging its tail, but there was no sign of any dog whatsoever. And the things I saw were no less troubling and inexplicable: I saw, growing on the slimy steps by Southwark Bridge, a clump of primroses which appeared so real to me that I bent down to pick one, but there were no flowers growing there, only a pale yellow handkerchief carelessly dropped by a fop pirouetting into a boat. Another time, I saw in the hand of one of my women patients a lump of black soap, but when I uncurled her fingers her palm was empty.

I lay and considered what this hallucinatory tendency might portend – whether a weakening of my brain or the unlikely arrival in me of visionary powers. But I could come to no conclusion about it and after a while, with my eyes half open on the flickering candlelight, I fell into a dream of Bidnold, believing myself to be there, lying on the carpet from Chengchow and smelling woodsmoke and sunlight and the perfume of wealthy women. And the whole of this dream was filled with such magic that when I woke from it, to see all the candles dripping grease onto the floor, I did not move one muscle of my body, but only closed my eyes and tried to dream it again.

And after this night, what took hold of me was not any illness or sliding towards death, but a colossal epidemic of dreaming, so that night after night I floated into Bidnold and landed light as a plume and brushed the surfaces of things – the polished tops of tables, the stretched brocade of scarlet sofas, the milky satin of cushions, the tooled leather spines of books, the dented pewter handle of the coal scuttle – and then was carried by the wind out into the sky and hung like a ghost above the park, filling myself with colour so that I became fat with it, with the purple of the beeches and the lush green of the grass. There were no people in these dreams, yet they were dreams of the most sensual kind from which, when the morning came, I did not want to be parted. So I began to prolong them into the day, rising later and later, long after the lute-maker had begun work and the noise on the river had reached to its morning crescendo. I was addicted to them, as to an opiate, and went about my physician's round drugged by the memory of them and by the great quantity of sleep I was inflicting upon myself. I knew that I should be trying to shake off this sickness of dreaming, but I did not seem to have the will to do it.

One evening in April, the lute-maker came up to my rooms to show me an instrument he had made, the sound of which, he said, was the sound he had heard in his mind all his life but had never achieved until then.

To celebrate this new perfection, he brought with him a flagon of sack and, without noticing what we did, we consumed it all, little by little, so that the hour grew very late and our minds utterly addled and foolish. And in my drunkenness, I told this lute-maker about my dreams of a place that had once been mine and how every night, now, I returned there like a spirit and how I did not believe this dreaming would ever end. He looked at me with his eyes that are nervous and bright like the eyes of a buzzard and said to me: "Why do you not go there, Doctor

Merivel? Why do you not see it again and then this seeing of it in your dreams will cease."

The next day, I wrote to Will Gates.

I told him that I had been possessed by a great longing to return to Bidnold, just for a brief time, no more than a day and a night, so that I could remind myself what it looked like and see with my own eyes "certain combinations of colour and light, Will, that I do not think exist anywhere in the world but there". I said I would be content to sleep in one of the servants' rooms, or even in the stables with Danseuse, because all that I wished to do was to visit the place "like someone invisible and not in any way to pretend it is mine or try to possess it again except in my mind".

While I waited for Will's reply, my dreaming of Norfolk was interrupted one night by a dream of Whittlesea and when I woke from it I decided that if indeed I was going to make the journey to Bidnold, I would not return directly to London, but go on to the Fens and tell the Keepers about the death of Katharine and the survival of Margaret and beg of them some other small relic of Pearce to replace the book consumed by the fire. And once I had decided upon this second visit, I no longer thought of this pilgrimage into the past as a foolish and self-indulgent thing. It seemed, on the contrary, to be a journey of the utmost importance: until I had made it, I would not be able to begin upon the future set down in my palm or indeed upon any version of the future whatsoever or come at last to any ending of this story.

I did not have to wait very long for a letter from Will and when it came it woke in me the same mirthful delight I had once felt in a stage coach at Will's first sighting of London.

O, Sir Robert, said the letter, *You cannot know how much we are all here every one of us who remember you filled with joy at this Great Coming Event which is your Arrival at Bidnold.*

Please, Sir, be assured we will make all very fit and nice for this fortunate Returning, viz. M. Cattlebury will bake a lardy cake and one of his Carbonados and all the Dust Sheets which do cover things since the V. de Confolens comes no more here will be taken off. And do not think you must have any poor bed in a

stable. You can sleep in a Comfortable Room, viz. The Olive,
where once we tended on Mister Pearce.

Send us merely some word of the day of your Arrival – for
reasons of M. Cattlebury's purchasing the beef and seasoning it
for the Carbonado. Which word he awaits with great Eagerness,
as do I,

your servant
Wm. Gates.

The date I decided upon was the twenty-ninth day of April in
this year of cold spring rains and fitful sunlight, 1667. Because
I wanted to ride to Bidnold on Danseuse, the journey would
take me several days, but I knew that I would savour each stage
of it, no matter what weather I chanced upon, and that when I
found myself at last under the enormous Norfolk sky, I would
lift up my head and shout.

It rained on the day that Danseuse and I left London, but after
that, as we went north-east, we came upon cloudless days.

As we travelled, I asked myself what changes I expected to
find at Bidnold and I knew that what would be most visible to
me would be the emptiness of the place, its lack of belonging.
The Viscomte, as far as I could determine from Will's letters,
had only ever used it as a place of entertainment and seduction.
He had never inhabited it fully or bothered to grow fond of it
and now he never visited it at all or paid the staff their wages.
Will and Cattlebury had remained, paid by Babbacombe I assumed, but I imagined the gardeners and the grooms and the
chambermaids and the scullery boys all drifting away, so that
little by little the house and the garden and even the park would
be falling to neglect and decay. I thought of Will's sadness at
this. I saw his brown, creased face. I saw him plead with me to
do something to halt the decline of a place that he loved as much
as I, and heard myself inform him that I could do nothing at all,
it being out of my hands now and quite outside my life.

I did not let these thoughts cast me down. In the whole
journey I had hardly a moment of sadness and whenever we
stopped for the night I lay long asleep, dreaming myself already
there.

So we trot down into Bidnold village, past the Jovial Rushcutters and past the church, and then we make the left turn into the park through the great iron gates and Danseuse flicks her tail and gives a snort and the speed of her trot increases.

There is a fresh breeze and the shadows of fast-moving clouds sail across the grass. The chestnuts are in full candleburst. A cluster of deer grazes under them and, as we come on, the animals raise their heads and look at us.

We round the curve in the drive and there it is: Bidnold Manor in the County of Norfolk, the house snatched from the Anti-Royalist, John Loseley, and given to me in return for my role as cuckold, the house where all my foolishness was contained, Merivel's house.

I rein Danseuse in and slow her to a walk. We are now at the very spot where, one freezing morning, I began to run after Celia's coach and fell down on some ice and tore a pair of peach-coloured stockings. The parkland is moated here and beyond the moat is the south lawn with its great cedar trees and as we walk sedately forward I notice that the lawn is neatly clipped and edged and that round the cedars have been put carved stone benches.

My eye is on the front door now. I remember the heaviness of it and the gladness I always felt when it opened for me and I went in and heard it close at my back – as if I had known all along that the house would belong to me for only the briefest time.

The door opens now. Will Gates comes out and is followed by Cattlebury and the two of them stand side by side and look towards me with dazed expressions on their faces, as if they had been brought forth to witness the passage of Halley's Comet or some such peculiar wonder. This sight of them makes me smile and I call out: "Will! Cattlebury! Here I am!" but my voice does not carry to them for, although I think I am smiling, I am in fact crying like a child and cannot seem to get any hold upon myself to stop my tears which fall so fast and so abundantly that the whole scene before me trembles and moves and it is difficult to keep my balance on my horse.

She halts and I climb down and I see Will and Cattlebury hold out their hands, so I take them in mine, one in each, and hold very tightly to them and force out from my choked heart a burst of my old laughter.

"Sir," says Will, "you are got very thin."

I nod. I am endeavouring to speak.

"We will remedy it, Sir Robert," says Cattlebury, "with carbonados."

"Yes," I say. "We will. With carbonados."

I was mistaken when I imagined neglect and disrepair.

Though empty of any owner, each room at Bidnold appears clean and dusted and perfumed, as if in readiness to receive one.

Little remains of my vulgar decoration. The carpet from Chengchow is still in place upon the Withdrawing Room floor, all its colours cleaned and bright, but the walls are no longer red and gold; they are hung with a dove-grey damask and the scarlet sofas are gone. Yet the room is grander than before. Above the fireplace is a gilded Italian mirror. Every chair and footstool is upholstered in peach silks and Prussian blue velvets. Equestrian portraits (from which Doric columns and Sylvan glades are not entirely absent) grace the walls. There is a card table of maplewood, a chequer table of ebony and ivory, a spinette made by the Frenchman, Florent-Pasquier. At the windows the brocade drapes are heavy and rich.

"I did not imagine," I say to Will, as I look round this beautiful room, "that the Viscomte was a person of such exquisite taste."

Will looks embarrassed. "Me," he says, "I liked all your scarlet and pink, Sir Robert."

I laugh. We go on into the Dining Room, scene of my candlelit suppers with Celia. My oak dining table is still in place, but the walls have been panelled and the ceiling carved and embossed and painted yellow and blue. It reminds me of a state room, forbidding almost in its formality, and again I remark to Will that the picture of the Viscomte I put together from his letters does not match that which I am forming of him now.

"Well," mumbles Will, "it probably would not, Sir, because in a letter you cannot tell all there is. You have to leave out a great deal, owing to briefness or lack of words."

"True, Will," I reply, "but you led me to believe he did not really care about the house, and in this I see that you were mistaken, for he has furnished it very finely."

Will shrugs his shoulders, upon which hangs a new rust-coloured coat. "He does not come here any more," he says, "and I hope he will not."

"Then what is to become of all these furnishings?"

"I do not know, Sir Robert."

"They are to lie shrouded in dust sheets for all time?"

"I cannot say."

"What, Will?"

"I cannot say whether they will be shrouded for all time."

"What were the orders given?"

"Beg pardon, Sir?"

"What orders did the Viscomte give regarding the furniture?"

"He gave none."

"None? He just left without any word?"

"Without so much as a word, Sir."

"Then he surely intends to return. He might return today, tonight, at any time."

Again, Will shrugs. His squirrel's eyes do not look at me. "He might, Sir. But I do not think that he will."

I abandon this conversation and I go with Will to the Olive Room, which is absolutely unchanged in every detail from the day when I sat in it for thirty-seven hours and watched over Pearce's sleep. The thought that I will sleep one night in it between cold linen sheets under the green canopy with its scarlet tassels is a very affecting one and I sit down upon the little window seat and thank Will for making this room ready for me. I feel tired suddenly and I know that in my tiredness I have, once again, begun to see and hear things that are not here. On the stairway, when my glance fell onto the hall, I fancied I saw a footman wearing livery glide silently from the door of the Morning Room to the kitchen passageway, and now, as I turn and look out at the sighing trees and flying shadows of the park, I seem to hear, very far off, the same whimpering of a dog that had once caused me to open the door of my rooms above the lute-maker and peer down into the dark.

It is the middle of the afternoon. I tell Will that I will rest for a little while. So he leaves me and closes the door. I do not sleep, or even shut my eyes, but lie and listen to the wind and marvel at where I am.

Though I feel somewhat solitary and foolish, Will and Cattlebury insist that supper is served in the Dining Room.

I have put on my blue and cream suit. I am not placed at the head of the table, where I used to sit, but at my right hand, as it were, as if I were my own favoured guest.

The room is lit by numberless candles.

"Blow some of them out, Will," I say. "I do not need a hundred pieces of light to eat a carbonado." But he refuses. "You were fond of light, Sir Robert," he says. "You used to tell me that."

The meal that Cattlebury has prepared for me is very rich and I disappoint him and Will by being unable to eat more than a few mouthfuls of it. I see these two men look at me and think, He is not like his former self, and it touches me to know that the old Merivel – so despised by Pearce and by Celia and causing such irritation to the King – was to them a person of substance.

The Burgundy wine I am offered smells of summer fruit, yet has so strong an effect upon my blood that when my meal is ended, I can hardly rise from the table, so heavy do my limbs feel.

"Lord," I say to Will, who helps me up, "it is as if old age had come upon me in the space of half an hour."

"You are tired, Sir, after your journey, that's all."

"Either that, Will," I reply, "or I'm dying."

"Well, Sir Robert, you cannot die in the Dining Room. It would be most horrid. So let us get you to your bed."

I tell Will that what I wish to do is to go out into the park, above which the clouds have sped away and uncovered a round white moon, and walk all round the house and take some breaths of the spring night. He looks at me and shakes his head, as if he believes the air will pierce my lungs like a knife, but I stumble out into the hall towards the door pulling him with me. "Come on, Will," I say, "for this is all I have, this one night."

I see the door open and then I stare out and I see a cold light falling across the lawn and I smell the earth. And then I do not remember anything more at all.

I wake under the green canopy. In the scarlet tassels hangs a sweet memory of Pearce.

The room is warm. I am wearing my nightshirt and my nightcap. I do not know what time it is, or what day, but seem to understand that I have slept for a long while.

I touch my face and find it very rough with stubble. I am a sight, I think, a terrible sight lately . . .

I draw back the bed curtains. On a little oak table is a china plate with a lardy cake upon it, and this discovery of the cake wakes in me a colossal hunger, as if I had not eaten for an entire week. So I cut myself a slice and cram it into my mouth with disgusting haste. Then I eat a second piece, dropping crumbs down my chin and onto my lap.

What I decide next is that the day upon which I have woken, whatever day it may be, is full of sunshine. I cannot see it yet, because this Olive Room faces north, but I know that, if I go to the front of the house, I will find it: a dazzling light.

So I leave the room, just as I am in my nightshirt with cake crumbs at the corner of my mouth, and go out onto the landing and, as I predicted, I see the sunlight falling upon the stairs. I stand and look down. And there, after a moment or two of blinking and rubbing my eyes and taking off my nightcap, I begin to see and hear a most peculiar commotion: the hall is full of dogs. There are seven or eight of them – little Spaniels like my poor Minette – and they are running in excited circles and yapping.

I try very hard to decide whether the dogs are truly there or not there at all except in my dilapidated mind, but I am quite unable to judge. I must go down, I tell myself, and try to touch one of them and, if it does not disappear or turn into a yellow scarf like the clump of primroses, then I will know that it is a living thing and not any hallucination.

I am barefoot, but the wood of the stairs, burnished by the sun, feels warm. And then I notice, as I go down, that the front door is open and I can see shadows on the gravel, as of people moving about, and somewhere in my brain, that has been so crammed with sleep, I know what this must signify and yet the meaning of it refuses to come to me except very slowly . . . so slowly . . . like an old memory that lies rusted and neglected and half hidden . . . and then I have reached the hall to call one of the dogs to me, but they all come, they all flock around me and jump up onto my legs and to my outstretched hand and wag their tails. I am surrounded by them. They are certainly real, Merivel, I inform myself, for two of them are biting the hem of your nightshirt and already you can hear it tearing. But I do not try to push the dogs away. I like their excitement. I think how sweet and pretty they are. So I start to play with them, dangling my nightcap towards them so that they jump high to try to bite it, then snatching it away and, as their yapping and frenzy increases with my teasing of them, I hear myself begin to laugh like a child.

And then a very long shadow falls across the golden floor and across me and across my laughter. At the same moment, one of the dogs starts to unwind the entire hem of my nightshirt. And then I look up. And I see the King.

Affecting not to notice that I was without my wig and unshaven and barefoot and wearing a torn nightshirt covered in cake crumbs, the King invited me, in a soft and gentle voice, to take a turn with him in the park.

While a cluster of liveried grooms and footmen – directed by Will, also strangely garbed in livery – unloaded a great many trunks and boxes from two magnificent coaches, we walked down the drive for a little way, then turned left into the grass towards a line of deer grazing in some shade. The dogs ran ahead of us, chasing each other and barking.

We had gone this far in silence. Then the King suddenly stopped and turned and looked back at the house.

"It is mine now," he said.

I looked at it. Bidnold Manor in the County of Norfolk . . .

"What, Sire?" I said.

"You heard me, Merivel. Now it belongs to me."

"To you . . . ?"

"Yes."

"And the sale to the Vi – ?"

"It was never paid for. Money was promised. Money I wished to use to fit out a ship. But it was never given. So Bidnold is to *be* a ship now."

"Be a ship?"

"Yes. Do you understand?"

"Not entirely . . ."

"It is to be *my* ship: in other words, the place in which, from time to time, I can sail away from care. Now you see it, *n'est-ce pas?* You, of all people, now you comprehend it, don't you Merivel? It is the place where I shall come to dream."

I nodded. The King watched me. I wanted to tell him that he could have chosen no better place, but under his gaze it was difficult to bring out the words.

"You need not comment," he said after a moment, "for I know everything you feel. But look at this. Do you remember to whom you gave it?"

"Look at what, Sir?"

"At this."

The King held out his hand (encased in an emerald coloured glove) and I saw in his palm a small piece of card, very soiled and curled and thinned by time. I took it up and peered at it and, after looking at it blankly for a second or two, recognised my name upon it, *R. Merivel. Physician. Chirurgeon.* and my old address in Cheapside.

I looked up. Across the features of the King now spread the smile, the effect of which upon my heart it is impossible to describe.

"Yes," he said, "your card. Shown to me not long after the fire by one of my hatmakers, Arthur Goffe. He told me that it was you who had saved his wife."

"Well, I and another man, much larger and stronger than me. But I did not know this was one of your people."

"No. Of course you did not. And even if you had known, it

would not have been me who drove you to bravery. It was others, was it not? A certain glovemaker and his dear wife?"

"Yes."

"How fortunate, Merivel. For it is one of my beliefs that we cannot truly live until the debts we owe our parents have been paid. For they and their deaths can never be forgotten. Is that not so?"

"Yes."

"Even in an age in which we wisely practise the excellent art of oblivion, certain things remain."

"Yes."

"And another thing, if I am not mistaken, is your love for this place."

"Yes. I love it. From the day when I first saw it – "

"So I knew you would come back here. Gates and I were entirely agreed. We knew that one day you would come and that this is how I would find you."

"You knew?"

"Naturally. But I remember also that there was always one room that entranced you, a round room in the West Tower, and yet I heard that you had never found any use for it."

"No. I think that when I lived here what I used to believe was that this room was . . . beyond me . . . too high, or some such thing . . . as if I could not understand what I should put in it . . . as if, almost, it was a part of my mind that I could not see."

"Why do you not, then, go and look at it now?"

"Now?"

"Yes."

"Well, Sir, I will, if you wish, yet I would prefer to continue our walk."

The King gave a hoot of laughter, which disturbed the deer and sent them bounding away.

"'Continue our walk'! 'Continue our walk'! Look at me, Merivel."

I tried to look up into the King's face, but the sun was in my eyes, so I shaded them with my hand.

"Go back to the house," instructed the King, "and go up the

stairs and into this empty room. And see whether you can make sense of it now."

"Very well, Sir."

"Then we may continue our walk if you wish."

"As you will, Sire."

"Off you go, then."

I paused and stared up at the West Tower. It was many, many months since my thoughts had returned to this room, which had never, in truth, been a proper room at all, but only a vacant space. Now I noticed that on the three window ledges were clustered some white birds.

"Fantails," said the King. "Very pretty, I think. It might be that, from time to time, you may decide to open a window and let them in."

"I beg your pardon, Sir?"

"Into your room."

"Let the birds into the room?"

"Into *your* room."

"My room?"

"Yes. I am giving you the room. It is yours. Until my reign is over and another age comes. Until then it is restored to you – in return for the life you saved and in return for the man you have become. It is your room and you can come and go from it as you please, and I will never take it from you."

Do you see me now?

I am in the room.

I am standing in the white room in my torn white nightshirt.

Merivel. Just as he was. Do you see him? He has no wig on his head. His hogs' bristles itch. He puts a hand to his cheek and discovers a cake crumb.

But I am not thinking of him. What has returned to my mind, in this high white space, is Margaret. I hold her in my arms and take off her bonnet and put a soft kiss on her fiery curls and she squeaks and kicks and blows bubbles into my face and then reaches out a fat little hand and takes hold of my nose.

I laugh and remove her hand and carry her to one of the windows, where we can hear the pigeons murmuring. I hold her up and show her the great expanse of the park that I once saw as wild, undisciplined lines of yellow and green, and dark splodges of brown and purple, and above it the sun which, in the absence of any device by which to measure time, tells me that it is mid-day on the fairest April morning of my life.

I do not know how long I remain in the room. Perhaps, when you glimpse me for the last time, the dusk is already falling. I wrap Margaret more tightly in her shawl, for it is getting cold now, and together we move towards the door. "Tomorrow," I tell her, "I must go on to Whittlesea. But one day soon – before you have learned to walk, before I have grown too frail to climb the stairs – I shall bring you back."

Sacred Country

Winner of the James Tait Black Memorial Prize

ROSE TREMAIN

At the age of six, in 1952, Mary Ward, the child of a poor farming family in Suffolk, has a revelation. She isn't Mary. She's a boy. An inexplicable mistake has been made and, somehow, it will have to be rectified ... So begins Mary's heroic struggle to change gender, while all around her others too fight to discover a place of meaning in a savage and confusing world.

'Hypnotic . . . curiously beautiful and strikingly original'
The Spectator

'Brilliant . . . a strong, complex, unsentimental novel, luscious in some passages, wonderfully restrained in others'
Times Literary Supplement

'Rose Tremain writes comedy that can break your heart . . . Her book is one to admire and enjoy. It is funny, absorbing and quite original. I've read nothing to touch it this year'
Literary Review

'A remarkable novel . . . The product of a truly original mind, whose inventions are magically unforeseeable'
The Times

'A strange and magical book . . . wholly captivating'
The Daily Mail

'Meticulous storytelling, period re-creation utterly convincing. A considerable work'
Melvyn Bragg in The Sunday Times Books of the Year

SCEPTRE